# MEET THE AUTHOR

## TEASERS, TRAILERS & MORE...

# EXPOSURE

PRAISE FOR
# EXPOSURE

"Dellaira has done the impossible; she has captured our era's messy murky unknowing heart and done so with immense compassion and uncompromising verve and vaulted herself in the process into the top ranks of our literary culture."

—JUNOT DÍAZ, author of
*This Is How You Lose Her*

"*Exposure* gracefully probes the ways the past can reach into the present and test everything we thought we knew about ourselves and those we hold close. A captivating and beautifully crafted story."

—CAITLIN MULLEN, author of *Please See Us*

"*Exposure* is a must-read. In a time when so many cultural conversations turn black and white, this brilliant book provides a way to truly see two sides of a story. Dellaira delivers a novel so gripping and breathtaking, you'll be compelled to continue discussing it long after you've finished."

—STEPHEN CHBOSKY, author of
*The Perks of Being a Wallflower*

"A compelling story of ambition, becoming, grief, and desire. Mysterious, haunting, and seductive."

—SANJENA SATHIAN, author of *Gold Diggers*

# EXPOSURE

## AVA DELLAIRA

ZIBBY BOOKS
NEW YORK

Library of Congress Control Number: 2024933051
Hardcover ISBN: 978-1-958506-67-7
eBook ISBN: 978-1-958506-68-4

Book design by Neuwirth & Associates, Inc.
Cover design by Mumtaz Mustafa

www.zibbymedia.com

Printed in the United States of America
10 9 8 7 6 5 4 3 2 1

To Gloria Jean and Tommy D, in loving memory

And to all the grievers, the survivors, and the strivers,
with the dream that we may see each other

# PART
# ONE

# 1

2004

The college kids meandering down Fifty-Seventh Street in the thin sun never see Noah. He is a neighborhood kid of little consequence to them, part of the landscape, a Black face beside the new blossoms, the old Gothic buildings, the Hyde Park restaurants. Noah works at one after school, bussing tables, cleaning up after those college kids just like his mom did.

They don't know that he's hoping to be one of them—a U of C student—soon enough. He's waiting to hear from the admissions office, checking the mailbox daily, his stomach tied in knots. His mom wanted him to go, back when she worked in the cafeteria. He'd understood, even then, that ambition is an act of rebellion against what the world believes about him.

Noah stuffs his hands into his worn puffer jacket, fiddling with a hole in the pocket, and sits down to wait. The bus is late.

Juliette gets off the 6 at Michigan and Monroe and walks up to the Art Institute. She is wearing her brown suede "Chicago coat" that her mother bought on sale at Bloomingdale's last spring in celebration of her acceptance to the university. She has worn it every day since she arrived in the city, starting when it was still too warm, sticky summer heat hanging on to September afternoons, and long after it grew much too cold, when other kids were in parkas down to their knees. How could she and her mom have known, when they admired Juliette's image in front of the department store mirror, that this coat would never stand up to the meaning of winter here?

But now it is springtime, and finally her Chicago coat is right for the weather.

She enters the museum, tucks the coat under her arm like a child's blankie, and goes straight to her favorite section—the impressionists and postimpressionists. Monet, Degas's ballerinas, the Toulouse-Lautrec painting she and her best friend Annie loved in French class. And then, her favorite of all, van Gogh: *Weeping Woman, The Poet's Garden*. She sits on a bench in front of *The Bedroom* and then she is crying. Grief is like this: omnipresent. The room clears, as people wander in and notice her and turn to wander away.

Noah has come to the Art Institute to visit his mother—or his mother's favorite paintings, rather. When his mom used to take him here as a kid, they always started at *The Bedroom*. The first time Noah came alone, looking for his mother's ghost, he was eight. She had been dead a year. While his uncle Dev was at work, Noah took the bus downtown. He came on the free museum day, like he and his mom used to. He circled the paintings they used to see on the map and tried to remember their usual path. He didn't let himself cry, because then someone would notice that he didn't have a mom with him like he was supposed to.

———

Juliette is alone in the gallery when she feels someone come up and stop a few feet behind her. As she and her unseen companion take in the painting, she has an urge to reach through the silence.

"The room's so empty," Juliette says after a moment, without turning around. It is not, technically, empty—there are lots of things in it—but perhaps whoever stands there knows what she means.

She swivels around and sees Noah from the creative writing class she's been teaching at Hyde Park High School, his arms wrapped around himself.

"Hey," he says, and then he moves away.

She gets to her feet. "Wait—"

He turns. She is desperate, suddenly, not to let him leave her with her loneliness.

"What are you doing here?" she asks.

"Looking at art." His voice is soft, devoid of the sarcasm his statement might imply.

"Me, too," Juliette says, with a little laugh. "Do you wanna walk together?"

"I'm just here to see a few things," he says uncertainly.

"I'll let you lead the way?"

After a split second, he nods. "Okay."

There is a mystery to Noah's trail through the museum, journeys through long corridors, between floors, passing by exhibits without a glance and then purposeful stops at a series of scattered paintings. They make halting conversation. Although she felt she knew Noah through his writing when he was her student, Juliette realizes now that they've hardly

5

spoken to each other. He was talented, a quiet type who always sat in the back. He tells her he misses her class. He hasn't been able to attend this semester because he has basketball practice—he's too small to make anything real of it, but he figures he ought to play with his team for his last year.

Given a chance, sadness will always change shapes; sadness does not want to be itself, would prefer to be anything else, and as Juliette follows Noah between paintings, the river of grief inside of her branches off. A stream of yearning moves through her chest, and then, desire. He's standing so close to her that she begins to want him to touch her. He's in high school, Jesus, her former student, but does it really matter? She's only a year or two older than him, and he wasn't exactly her student, since it wasn't a real class . . . just an after-school, volunteer thing.

The accompaniment of Noah's former poetry teacher on his private, sacred ritual is strange, to say the least. When they stop in front of a painting, Juliette gazes at it with fierce intensity, as if she were reading a crystal ball, and Noah wonders what she sees. It stops him from wishing she'd go away.

Her beauty is neglected, but therefore more potent—outfit oddly matched, hair tangled, as it always was in class. Skirt askew on her hip, lips chapped red against her pale skin. He sees the way she looks at him, how she glances at his mouth, his biceps.

She smokes while they wait for the bus, offers him one. He doesn't usually smoke, but he takes it anyway, lets her lean in to light it for him, cupping her hands against the wind. He inhales, pulling the flame into his chest, and their eyes catch. Juliette averts her gaze first, pours smoke from her mouth. A gust of wind further tangles her hair. It's half-cloud, half-sky weather.

Does Noah sense, somewhere in his body, that years from now he will struggle to remember this—the afternoon spent at the museum with Juliette, their chance meeting? Probably not. The sensation he feels—as if he is somewhere else, watching himself—is not uncommon for him.

He thinks of Juliette's comments on his poems, written in her perfect cursive: *Beautiful!! Wow, Noah. Gorgeous turn!* Or sometimes, especially for his darkest writing, simply: *!!!* The papers would often come back to him stained with coffee or wine, but he didn't mind—those tiny traces of her messy humanity offset his vulnerability. Noah had never thought of himself as a writer before he signed up for Juliette's class, but in it, he discovered the hint of a new kind of power. The power of an artist.

"I've never read one of your poems," he tells her. "And you've read all five of mine."

She smiles, drags a long drag from her cigarette.

"I want to read some of your work."

"Okay," she says as she exhales.

"I used one of the poems you gave us in my application essay for U of C."

"You did?" She looks pleased.

"Yep."

"You applied to U of C?"

"Yeah." That is one of the reasons he signed up for the creative writing class last fall in the first place—he thought it would look good on his application.

"You seem different," he says, "than a lot of the kids there."

She smiles, understands it's a compliment.

By the time their bus arrives, he knows he'll get off at her stop.

# 2

Juliette is still removing her gloves—pulling the dirty black fabric from her fingertips, which smells vaguely like cigarettes—when Noah puts his hands around her waist, bends over, and kisses her. It is a serious kiss that wastes no time, and it catches her off guard. His hands, still cold, run up under her sweater. She lets out a little yelp. He sits down on her bed, where her rumpled rose quilt is tangled, much too big for the narrow dorm mattress. The springs let out a small squeak under his weight. He pulls her toward him. Warmth spreads through her, and Juliette can feel the numb in her fingers tingling back to life. The furnace clicks and hisses. She kisses his neck, and he groans. His lips find hers again. She likes how he kisses with abandon, she realizes. She likes his full lips. She nibbles the bottom one, puts her hand on his chest. He stops abruptly, smiles at her.

"You wanna put on some music?" he asks.

"Oh, yeah. Sure."

She feels self-conscious flipping through her CDs, trying to select the right thing. Finally, she picks *Songs of Leonard Cohen*, and instantly regrets it. Too sad. A few seconds in, she stops it and swaps it out for a mix from Annie. As Nico sings "I'll Keep It with Mine," she leans over Noah. Runs her nails down his back. "I must be a pretty bad teacher, hooking up with my student."

He smiles. "Should I call you Miss Juliette?" he asks. In class she'd gone only by her first name. His hands are running up her sweater again.

"You can call me Miss Marker," she says.

"How about I'll teach you a thing or two, Miss Marker."

Her body gets hot all over. "How old are you, anyway?" she asks.

He pauses for a split second. "I'll be eighteen next week."

"So are you, like, illegal, then?"

He raises his eyebrows and gives her a little smirk. "Nah," he says, before he unzips his pants and pulls it out. She's a bit shocked. Even more so that she complies, bending to her knees. But most of all, she's surprised by how much she likes the feeling of him in her mouth—it's different than other times she's done this. He does not close his eyes or look up at the ceiling. He stares at her.

"You're good at this, Miss Marker," he says, his voice low, and her heart quickens.

When it's over she feels cheated; she wants more, wants to feel him touching her. Noah lies back on her rose quilt. She doesn't want to walk down the hallway to the bathroom, so she steps into her closet and spits into a T-shirt, throws it in the hamper.

When she comes out, she's almost surprised to find Noah still on her bed, his eyes closed. She watches him, his mass of twisted curls, his long lashes, his hands with their long fingers resting on his chest, as if he were holding himself. He looks so pretty lying there, but the sadness in Juliette's stomach has already returned. Eventually, his eyes blink open.

"You got any water?" he asks. She finds a half-drunk bottle of Dasani that rolled under her bed, offers it to him. He stands and pulls his pants on, throws his head back, downs it. He studies the photographs on her wall: she and Annie entwined in the big oak bed at Goldstone, wrapped in this same rose quilt. A self-portrait of Juliette's mother in the garden, with Juliette, a half-naked toddler, at her breast. Blossoms rain around them.

"That's you?"

"Yeah. And my mom."

"She's beautiful," Noah says.

"Yeah." Juliette goes to the window. Cloud cover renders the sunset invisible.

"So are you," he adds.

She turns back, smiles at him.

"You wanna get a drink soon?" he asks.

"Sure. Yeah."

"Friday?"

"Okay."

"You have a fake ID?"

She shakes her head no.

"Let's go to Jimmy's, then. I'm cool with the bouncer. We played basketball my freshman year before he graduated."

Before he leaves, Noah gives her a kiss on the forehead, a gesture that surprises her with its tenderness.

As the door shuts, a cavernous emptiness opens inside Juliette, as if the physical contact between them put into relief just how lonely she is. She sits by the window, staring out at the kids passing by, huddled into their coats. Her sociology paper remains untouched on her computer. In her drawer, she finds a bag of raw almonds, eats them one by one for dinner. She heats water on her hot plate for a cup of mint tea, makes her bed, tucking the three-hundred-thread-count sheets her mom bought her around the flabby plastic-covered mattress. She tries calling Annie, hangs up without leaving a message. She's already left too many. She stuffs a towel under the door and opens her window, leans halfway into the cold air to smoke a cigarette.

When she's finished, Juliette tosses it, watching the still-lit embers splatter over the concrete. Without going to brush her teeth, she pulls off her pants and slips under the sheets.

She misses making love to Annie, misses the person she was the night that they were first together, misses the distant laughter of her mother with her friends, the sense of a future about to unfold before her, the warmth, the closeness, the feeling of being at home.

# 3

Noah cannot calm the flutter in his stomach. Unless you count high school dances or the handful of times that his uncle Dev chaperoned him and a middle school girlfriend to the mall, he has not been on a real date before, although he's been sleeping with U of C girls for over a year now, since the winter of junior year when he tore his ACL, had to sit out the basketball season, and needed some kind of salve for his depression.

Dev works nights, so Noah's mostly alone in this small apartment, his bedroom a curtained-off portion of the living room, his uncle's hairs from shaving littering the bathroom sink, the fridge empty save for milk and beer, the freezer stocked with microwave dinners. He normally puts on the TV, eats at the little table, does his homework, tries to sleep. But when Noah struggles to breathe, he knows he needs to leave. Sometimes he'll only go to the lake and smoke a joint, staring out at the waves, catching snatches of laughter on the wind. Sometimes he'll wander from Woodlawn back into Hyde Park, following the college kids into house parties he can see glowing through apartment windows, their rap music flooding onto the street. Inside, he'll find them packed into a living room, passing joints and dancing badly to Jay-Z on an old wood floor sticky with spilled alcohol.

He'll find a bottle of vodka on a stained counter beside possible mixers, down a drink as he makes his way onto the porch flooded with more kids smoking and talking about Plato and Naomi Klein and Foucault's "bodies and pleasures," and introduce himself as Noah, a first-year. He's a film buff and will impresses them with references to obscure foreign films. The same girls who ignore him in the daytime, who cross the street to avoid him at night, will find him attractive, charming—he's one of them after all, they'll think, but different enough to be novel. He'll ask her—whoever she is, tonight—where she's from and listen to her unravel stories of escapades on golf courses, ocean water, and ice-cream shops. Most likely she will invite him back to her dorm room or apartment.

The college girls, with their long hair scented of strawberries and bergamot, their tangled pixie cuts, their dangling earrings, their glasses, the simple warmth of their bodies, the way they take him in is a comfort. He likes the feeling that he's made them see him. In the time they spend together, he has power, and for as long as the spell lasts, that power eclipses his fear—the fear that comes from knowing he's alone in the world, from knowing how easily he could be brushed aside, ground down to nothing and no one.

But when it's over, normally, Noah forgets them.

Juliette is different. Juliette lingers. The smell of her: earthy, strange, flowery. A sharp kind of sweet. The image of her mother and her child self, looking on from the wall in their sprawling California garden. They were foreign, golden; theirs was a life of privilege.

Maybe it's just that the lights were on, that he and Juliette were sober, that it was six o'clock, sun only starting to drain out of the sky. Maybe it's just that they haven't slept together yet, that there's something left to chase. But there have been other girls who give blow jobs and don't want sex. Normally, Noah takes the offering, thanks the girl, and moves on. This is different. There is something about Juliette he can't shake: her strange combination of fragility and authority, the way her hands flit nervously like birds, the way she licks her chapped lips. The way that she knows he is looking at her, wants to be seen, almost begs for it. He can remember her in front of the classroom so clearly, lecturing: *Poetry is like music, where the lyrics and melody are one . . .*

It bothers Noah the way images of her cling to him, stoking desire. There is a reason he has one-night stands and moves on. Grief is like this: persistent hunger. He lost his mom when he was a child, and now he's addicted to women, takes comfort in them, but won't let himself get close. Because no matter how much you love someone, no matter if you love her with the entirety of your being, she can leave. Can die. If you don't get attached, obviously, you can't get hurt.

It's the most basic shit in the book, yes, but Noah has not really thought about it like this until now, now that he's standing in front of his mirror getting ready to meet Juliette at the bar, now that he's put on enough cologne that it makes him dizzy, now that he's gone through three hoodies.

The low sunlight travels between buildings, through the bare oak branches and into the window, just enough to cut a small gash across his chest. He rinses with Scope, pockets a

AVA DELLAIRA

fistful of one-dollar bills from Salonica, the diner where he buses. He locks the door behind him, anxious to get to Jimmy's, to see Juliette. He imagines that if he can gulp her in, maybe he can regain control of his longing, dampen the flame of his desire.

# 4

It's already nine o'clock. Juliette will be late. She takes a tiny bottle of airplane-sized whiskey from her drawer, downs it for courage, and pulls her coat over her outfit: a pair of black tights and an old, oversized white T-shirt belted with a red scarf. A little edgy, a little Edie Sedgwick, it was all she could come up with when she remembered she left most of her wardrobe damp in the washer, smelling of mold.

A pink supermoon makes eyes at Juliette the whole way down Woodlawn. The wind has gone quiet, and the air is nearly warm on her cheeks, or at least it is a softer kind of cold. Paired with the pleasant burn of whiskey in her belly, she feels almost alive. She throws her cigarette into the gutter as she arrives at Jimmy's and sees Noah standing outside, hands in his pockets, hoodie up under his leather jacket. Though he's still in high school, Noah looks no different from the college kids—handsome, dark-skinned, only slightly taller than she is, but muscular. She smiles at him. He smiles back; it's a pretty smile. Has she seen him smile before?

"Sorry I'm late," she says.

"No worries. You good?"

"Yeah."

The bouncer at the door daps Noah and allows them to slip in. Juliette likes the dive-bar smell soaked into the wood floors—years of bodies and cigarettes and booze. Noah and Juliette navigate their way through the haze of smoke to a table in the back. As Noah disappears to get them drinks, Juliette slips off her coat and sits, letting herself drown in the noise, "P.I.M.P." on the jukebox mixing with the voices of college kids deep into alcohol-fueled debates. Noah returns with a Jameson and ginger ale for Juliette, a beer for him, and three cheeseburgers in paper trays.

"You want one?" he asks as he slides a tray across the table.

"No, thanks. I don't eat meat." Juliette's been a pescatarian since she visited the Southern California Farm Sanctuary with her sixth-grade class.

Noah shrugs, takes it back.

She sips her drink, trying to think of something to say.

"A rat died in my wall. In the closet." That's what caused her to throw most of her clothing into the washer. Even after facilities maintenance cut out the body yesterday, the decay had seemed to permeate everything.

In the wake of her loss, the smallest traumas blur into the life-shattering ones, the smell of the dead rat bleeding into the texture of ash.

"Happens a lot in old buildings," Noah says.

"It does?"

He nods. "Yup." Noah's still eating his burgers. The smell of the meat is suddenly making Juliette feel sick.

"I need to get quarters for laundry before I forget. You

want anything?" she asks, quickly slurping up the rest of her drink.

"I'm good."

Juliette orders a new drink, pays with cash she takes out of the ATM, and asks the bartender for her change in quarters. As she returns to the table, she sees Noah watching her from across the room. The T-shirt she's wearing feels shorter now than it did in her dorm. She tugs it down, but it comes back up as she walks. As the hemline grazes her thighs, she can feel her body responding to Noah's eyes.

"I like your outfit, Miss Marker," he says, as she sits.

Her cheeks flush. "Thanks. Most of my clothes were dirty. Cause, you know, the rat."

He laughs. It makes her laugh.

Luckily his burgers are gone. She sips her new drink; she's drinking fast, her body turning noodly, her nerves disappearing. She's glad she mentioned the rat dying in her wall; having told Noah takes away some of its ominous power, makes her feel less lonely, maybe. She decides, then and there, that she'll be herself with this boy. She might as well be; she could use an actual friend.

"So, what's LA like?" he asks.

"It depends what part."

"What's your part of LA like?"

As she finishes her third drink, Juliette finds herself telling Noah about her mom, about Annie, about Goldstone, her Topanga Canyon home named for the dirt road where it is tucked all alone into the end of the cul-de-sac, on the edge of a cliff. She tells him about the fruit trees, the photographs, the chickens, the deer, the ocean, her girlhood bliss. She doesn't talk much about her mother's death but instead tells stories from childhood, from high school, painting a glorious picture of her former life. Grief is like this: a conjurer. He listens intently, allowing her to revive her forsaken world inside the crowded bar.

Juliette's now drunk enough she wants to keep drinking. Noah gets them another round. Is it her fourth, or fifth? She's lost track. Depends if you count the whiskey shot before she left.

She learns less about Noah than he does about her, but he tells her U of C is his top choice of school because his mom wanted him to go. She is dead, too.

Juliette's grief is fresh, still warm like blood just out of the body, whereas Noah's is old, childhood grief, ossified into the bone around which all new emotional tissue has grown. But they recognize something in each other, she thinks—the existential wound of motherless kids, maybe.

She bites her lips often, tucks her hair behind her ears. As the conversation lulls, their eyes rest on each other's and Juliette feels something grab hold of her deep in her belly.

When she gets up to pee, the room spins. Maybe she should have eaten something for dinner. The sea of bodies seems to hold her aloft as she drifts in the direction of the bathroom. Prince is singing. Juliette mouths along as he reminds her we're all gonna die. Better live in the moment then, let yourself go crazy. Another whiskey, maybe. She shakes her hair out a little. Stares at her face in the mirror. The pieces don't make sense to her. She tries to see the girl in the car with Annie, the girl in her mother's arms, the girl in front of her mother's camera, but she can't find her. The person she sees here looks tired, too old, a sad stranger. She wishes she hadn't had so much to drink, yet she wants more. She splashes water on her face, takes out a tube of red lipstick once stolen from Annie and reapplies it.

She wants him to see her.

"Let's take a picture," she tells Noah when she returns,

pulling out the Nokia phone that used to belong to her mom and holding it at arm's length. "Come on." He leans in close to her. She sticks out her tongue and licks his cheek—a trick she used to play with Annie—and snaps the photo. He laughs and wipes off her slobber. She sends the picture to Annie, types a message: *this is noah. if u think im trying to make u jealous i am.*

"I brought a poem," she tells Noah, intending to make good on her promise to share one with him. She took her time selecting it, and now, however many drinks in, she has the courage to offer it up. She wants him to know her; she wants to be known.

Later, she won't remember this part of the conversation—the alcohol is seeping in, sending dark clouds over sections of her mind.

She reaches into her mini backpack, pulls out her journal, the one that Annie gave her for her birthday. The paper is hand-pressed, with rose petals. She flips it open and stops on a page near the end. She reaches it out to him.

"Here," she says. "You wanna read it?"

"I want you to read it to me."

"Right now? It's loud in here."

"In your room, then."

Juliette feels her cheeks getting warmer. "Okay."

They walk out together.

Noah does not know that Juliette is dead two days later.

20

# PART
# TWO

# 5

2008

Noah parks his Impala and walks into the air-conditioned Arrivals Level, searching for Jesse. She finds him first, comes up behind him, and puts a hand on his shoulder. Her shiny brown hair is pulled into a smooth bun, and she is wearing the black-and-white striped dress he remembers from Chicago, just starting to fray at the seams—the one that she'd left in a crumpled pile in the corner of his dorm room after the second night they made love, when she went with him to breakfast at the Medici in leggings and one of his hoodies.

"Hi," she says, her voice soft.

"Hi. You made it."

She carries her green leather purse, wears a mashup of elegant silver and gold jewelry that he's never seen on her before, gracing her narrow wrists and delicate collarbones.

And there is something else, something he can't put his finger on. It's as if a layer of her, the top layer, has been peeled off. She's brighter, shakier, shinier, sexier, sadder, lovelier than she'd been—as if her grief were an exfoliant to her surface-level

protections, and he now sees at least one layer deeper into her
true self.

The scent of her, though, is the same, he discovers, as he
wraps her in a hug. It makes him want her.

"How was your flight?"

"Okay."

They've been on the phone nearly every night for the past
six weeks since her dad's death, Jesse sitting outside under her
father's grapevine, sobbing, Noah listening. But now that she's
right here next to him, it seems somehow difficult to speak to
her, hard to find their way back to the ease of three months
ago; their "college years" have evaporated. He doesn't know
what to say, and the effort of trying to come up with conversation distresses him. Which makes it even harder to find any
kind of flow.

Jesse looks as if she's floating on the pavement as she follows
him to the car, only half there. He settles her suitcases into the
trunk and turns on the engine, switches *Back to the Trap House*
for *Kind of Blue* on the CD deck. A mix of smog and seawater
drifts through the window as Noah navigates the mess of airport traffic. He regrets not having brought flowers or
something.

"Are you hungry?" he asks eventually.

"Kind of. I ate like three bags of those blue chips on the
plane."

"I have some fruit at home. And I got you some potstickers.
They've been waiting in the freezer all week."

She smiles at him. "Sounds great."

In Chicago, when they made the trek to the North Side together to shop for groceries at Trader Joe's, Jesse always
bought bags of frozen potstickers, which she cooked for dinner

when they returned, browning each side perfectly with hot sesame oil while Noah put away the food and lit candles at Jesse's little table. They shared a proclivity for domesticity that they'd identified in each other right away.

They are halfway through the forty-minute drive by the time Jesse speaks again: "I was sitting next to this woman on the plane who got mad drunk and started telling me about her dad. He died when she was my age."

Noah nods, uncertain how to respond. Several minutes later, Jesse picks up the thread she'd seemed to drop and continues: "He flew small airplanes, and she said when she was a kid, he'd take her out. He used to tilt them straight up and then dive. Like a roller coaster but in the sky."

"Sounds terrifying."

"She was saying how there's something about being in the hands of your father that makes you feel invincible. I guess that was the point of her story. How after he died, she lost that."

Noah nods again. "I'm sorry, Jess." Noah never had a father, doesn't know that feeling. He merges onto the 105 and the traffic eases up. He floors the gas, which is slow to pick up.

Noah has been lonely here. He is used to lonely; in the long stretch between losing his mom and falling for Jesse—most of his life, really—he's felt that way. But he has a harder time hiding his vulnerability from himself now, knowing he has no lifeboat, the University of Chicago BA with honors he fought so hard for buried in a box in the back of a tiny closet in his barely furnished apartment, every Audi and G-Wagen and Porsche cutting him off. He turns up the music in his busted Impala to drown them out.

25

"You're going to build your own ark one day," Noah's mom used to say. "You're going to build an ark, and we'll sail away." She'd ask Noah where he wanted to go, and he'd make up different answers every time—Hawaii, Africa, the moon.

What Noah had wanted most was to buy his mom a big house, all to herself—in his child's mind, he would live with her there, forever. She wouldn't have to work in the cafeteria anymore. Instead, she'd stay with him, reading books, making pirate ships, barbecuing by the lake with Uncle Dev and popping popcorn for movie nights. Taking the train to the Art Institute. After they saw all the paintings she always liked to see, he would buy her a strawberry ice cream from the fancy shop downtown; he wouldn't have to count out dimes and nickels and quarters to see if he could pay. He would be somebody.

Since he got to Los Angeles four months ago, Noah's been nearly choking on desire. The amorphous ambition that has driven him for most of his life has taken shape: the shape of Hollywood, the city that creates culture. He longs to be part of it.

Because Jesse's dad was dying and then dead, Noah hasn't let her know he's been struggling to get a foot in the door. He hasn't mentioned scouring Craigslist for anything related to the movie business before settling on his job waiting tables.

Mostly he'd found veiled ads for any number of roles in porn shoots—in front of or behind the camera—or barely disguised schemes for taking advantage of the legions of Hollywood newcomers, blinded by hope. But he was persistent in his search, and alone in the apartment he was paying for with leftover work-study money he'd saved in Chicago—the apartment he'd be able to afford for only one more month—he sent out hundreds of emails, résumés attached. They resulted in two interviews.

The first, which had seemed promising—*if you're young, talented, and looking to break into the movie business, this is the role for you*—turned out to be casting for a prospective reality show about being young and broke in Tinseltown. Noah declined.

The second was for an internship with an independent film producer, who went unnamed in the ad. Noah drove his Impala down Sunset, past the 99 Cents store and the bodegas, the trendy coffee shops and ice-cream parlors and body shops, past the Walk of Fame and the Sunset Strip, into the luxe green of Beverly Hills. The speed at which worlds changed here—by the block—made Noah dizzy. He turned up into the hills of Bel Air, pulled over to consult his map, and finally parked on a narrow street outside a house too big for its yard. It looked like a bully of a house, bloated and pushing its way toward the next lot. He double-checked the parking brake, not wanting the old Impala, gifted by his uncle for graduation, to meet its death rolling down the hill.

When he got out, Noah re-tucked his white button-up shirt—despite slathering on deodorant before he left, he was sweating through it—into the black slacks that kept riding up. He'd bought new clothes for the interview at the T.J.Maxx in the tangle of midcity Los Angeles; he even bought a briefcase. When he rang the bell, a girl a few years older than him answered, barefoot, wearing a floaty skirt and a midriff T-shirt. He'd gone too formal.

The girl was Katie, the producer's assistant. She stepped outside and walked Noah around to the guesthouse, where she climbed up to a deck and sat on a blanket on the ground. He awkwardly followed suit, crossing his legs as if he were in kindergarten. She extended hers so that her unmanicured toes nearly touched Noah.

"It's an internship," she said, right off the bat. "So there's no money."

"Oh."

"Everyone's gotta intern at first. That's how it works here."

"Okay. What do people live on?"

"Either your parents pay or, you know, you find a way."

"Word."

There was an awkward pause, as if Noah was supposed to be asking the questions instead of Katie.

"So, what kind of movies do you guys work on?"

She pulled out a joint and lit it. "Different stuff. We have a thriller we think will do really well in the Chinese market that he's trying to find funding for."

Noah declined the joint she tried to pass. As they continued the conversation, he gathered that the producer had only ever made one movie, and that was in the '80s. Noah had seen it; it had garnered an Academy Award nomination for Best Foreign Film (it had been shot in Argentina), and for Best Picture. In the two months he'd been alone in LA, he'd made a project of watching every Best Picture nominee since the inception of the Academy Awards. He thought of it as a course of study, an effort to use his evenings productively whenever he wasn't on the phone with Jesse. He was on 1991. Katie was impressed by this. Her toe began to brush against the side of Noah's stiff dress pants. She looked like a lot of the college girls he used to have sex with, but he wasn't into it. He felt as if he were choking. It was hot as fuck. LA was so much different than he'd imagined it.

"I, um, gotta bounce," Noah said eventually, standing up, tugging at the tight neck of his shirt. A job with no money working for a waifish white girl, to try to get the chance to be noticed by a producer who had not made anything in over twenty years. He would have done it, maybe, or tried to—he was that desperate—if her toe did not keep brushing against his pants, if she weren't staring at him as if she wanted something.

Noah's third interview, which had been his most promising, came through Cal, a friend from the University of Chicago, where the two of them had gravitated toward each other as the only two Black kids in their first-year dorm, although they are different kinds of Black. Cal is half-Black, grew up in LA with a white mother who is a facialist to the stars and a Black father who works at a record label. He wants to be an actor. Cal went to a hippie, private K–12 school where the kids apparently never wore shoes, and Noah had been vaguely scandalized when Cal used to walk into Noah's room with his toes out. Before Jesse's arrival, Cal was the only person that Noah knew in Los Angeles, so even though they were not super-close at school, Noah asked him to get a drink, and they began going to happy hour together, joking about whether their credit cards would bounce when they tried to pay for their three-dollar beers. Cal, of course, had a net of family money that Noah did not, but they found some camaraderie over trying to break in. Cal forwarded Noah a mass email from a high school friend of his older sister's, saying that she was looking for someone to replace her as a director's assistant.

Noah wrote and rewrote the note he sent along with his résumé, carefully worded in an attempt to express his enthusiasm without sounding thirsty. He would have been excited no matter who the director was, but he really liked this guy's movies. When he woke up on his mattress on the floor, logged in to his laptop, and found an email inviting him to interview, his heart felt like the flutter of bird shadow passing over the wall.

Having learned his lesson, Noah ditched the black slacks and shiny shoes and wore fresh jeans and Air Force 1s. The assistant was, again, a white girl, who introduced herself as Olivia. She looked more professional than Katie—long, straight blond hair, big white teeth, and an outfit that swished around her narrow frame in an expensive-clothes kind of way. She walked Noah through an office to a vacant conference room, where she sat down across from him in the sea of empty chairs.

"So, what scripts have you read lately?"

"I just reread *Pulp Fiction*. For inspiration—just, the way he uses imagery is— "

"I mean, like, scripts floating around town. Unproduced stuff."

"Oh. I don't know. I haven't really—"

"Okay, no worries." She tossed her hair with her hand. "Tell me about yourself. Where are you from?"

Noah gave her his standard answer: "I grew up outside of Hyde Park. My uncle raised me after my mom passed. Before she died, she worked in the cafeteria at the University of Chicago, and she always wanted me to go there. I graduated with honors, with a dual major in film and sociology."

"Aww. That's amazing," Olivia said in a voice that was too high.

They were living in a "postracial" America, hypothetically, now that the first Black man in history had secured the Democratic nomination for president, but this white girl and everyone else were looking for someone like Cal, it seemed. Not someone like him. No matter how glossy Noah tried to sound, no matter the college degree he busted his ass for, beneath it all Noah was still the haunted kid looking for a way in. It's almost as if this girl could smell it on him: the desperation to become more than he'd been slated for.

Noah felt himself sinking as he rode the elevator back to the parking garage, knowing he didn't get the job. He'd been fighting this feeling that landed like dead weight in his chest—of being nothing, of being nobody—for as long as he could remember. He promised himself that soon enough he'd be the writer of one of the "unproduced" scripts they were trying to get their hands on.

A few weeks later, he found a job waiting tables (even that required persistent effort), and threw himself into studying, reading screenwriting books, outlining movies; if he wanted to break in, the best way would be to write something great. When Jesse told him she was coming to LA, he moved off the help-wanted ads and started using Craigslist to find deals on house stuff instead, picking up every possible extra shift at the Hard Rock and using his tip money to spruce up the still-half-furnished apartment in preparation for her arrival. He was spending every last penny, but it didn't matter—soon enough he'd make some real cash, he told himself. He bought string lights to drape over the doorframes, colorful hand soap dispensers. His mother used to have a set printed with fish.

Noah had already been taking pride in making himself espressos with a stovetop Bialetti, and now he walked to the hipster coffee shop down the block and sprung for fancy beans. He bid on a Navajo rug from eBay—a little southwestern style to make Jesse feel at home. He was still sleeping on a mattress on the floor, but he bought white linen curtains from IKEA, and they looked romantic against the French windows in the bedroom. He got two yellow vintage desk chairs for a steal at a secondhand shop and put them in the kitchen, where he imagined he and Jesse sitting together working. Three months after graduation, she felt like a person who existed in another dimension. He imagined feeling the heat of her body next to his on the mattress, the curtains fluttering.

"I like it here," she says now, as they step out of the car in front of Noah's building. "The air smells good."

There is a plump moon in the sky, just shy of full, at four thirty. She turns back to look at Noah, and as her eyes seem to focus, her form solidifies. The invisible strings of tension in Noah's body begin to let go. LA feels suddenly softer with her in it, the ripe sun spreading itself over Jesse. It feels like it could be their city.

He studies her face carefully when she walks into the apartment, but he can't tell what she's thinking. She's always been hard to read. He carries her oversized suitcase into the bedroom.

She says nothing, walks over and kisses him deeply. The distance between them dissolves.

# 6

1999

As Annie's dad parks in the informal driveway next to a grove of oaks, Annie tugs down at her jean cutoffs, made too small by her recent growth spurt. She feels dizzy from the winding drive.

They are in another world, one Annie hadn't known is right here, twenty-five minutes from her and her father's San Fernando Valley neighborhood of strip malls and palm trees.

"I'll walk you in," Annie's dad says, sipping from his metal water bottle, adjusting the old corduroy cap atop his head.

"That's okay, Daddy. I'll be fine." He wants her to have a friend at her new school. After Annie told him about Juliette, her father made a point of introducing himself to Juliette's mother during parents' night at Ventura Academy, where Annie has just started ninth grade.

"Okay, then," her dad says reluctantly. "I love you, Annie-Bo-Banny."

"Love you, too." Annie kisses her father's cheek and gets out of the car, into birdsong.

———

"Yay, you're here!" Juliette exclaims as she opens the front door. Annie waves goodbye to her father, already feeling herself shape-shift as they step inside the home. A record player scratches out the last notes of *Blood on the Tracks*, side A. In the large, open kitchen/living/dining room, a long wood table holds various vases of flowers and herbs. Ocean birds fly across wallpaper behind a blue velvet couch. There's an island for cooking, copper pots hanging above an ivory oven and matching range. But what Annie notices first, as everyone must, are the fine art photographs covering the walls, the most striking of which is a huge print of a child with pale skin and dark, tumbling hair, wearing nothing but a green tutu, standing under a pomegranate tree, reaching up on tiptoes to grab the fruit. It is Juliette, of course. Annie stares, transfixed.

"That's one of her most famous," Juliette says.

"Whose?"

"My mom," Juliette answers, as if it were obvious. "She's a photographer. I thought I told you."

The photographer mom's sole subject seems to be her daughter; Juliette is everywhere, at all ages. On the walls of her home, Annie's new friend appears legendary, mythical, outside of time.

Annie follows Juliette down the hallway, past the bathroom, and into an expansive bedroom with a king-size bed, hand-carved from oak. Plants press against the panes of the tall French windows, as if the room had sprouted up in the middle of a forest. Two dream catchers hang over the bed. Annie's a financial aid kid at Ventura Academy. She guesses that Juliette is not—the house isn't large, but it has the kind of elegance that requires money.

"Put your stuff wherever," Juliette tells Annie. "My mom will take the couch."

"You share a room with your mom?"

Juliette shrugs. "The other room is tiny. She uses it for her studio. She has a darkroom in the closet."

Juliette wanders back toward the kitchen and pushes open the double French doors. The yard is epic. Annie's eyes dart over a garden, a handmade chicken coop, a grove of fruit trees, a long stretch of grass that drops into dense oak forest. On the expansive redwood deck, Annie gets her first glimpse of Juliette's mother: black bikini, large straw hat, sunlight spread over skin tanned to golden. A thick novel splayed open across her hips.

"Mama. This is Annie. Annie, this is my mom, Margot."

Margot sits up, moves her book, sips from a tall glass of ice water stuffed with mint leaves. Her face is olive where Juliette's is pale, but the shock of beauty is the same.

"Hi, Annie." When Margot shines her bright smile on Annie, it makes her feel overly exposed, as if its light would reveal her to be unworthy of her new friend. She tugs at her too-short shorts and takes a step backward, half-obscuring her body behind Juliette's like a nervous toddler.

"Hi," Annie answers, and jumps as a lizard darts by inches from her foot.

Margot laughs and breaks into song. "Welcome to Goldstone, where the birds sing and the lizards roam . . ."

"Where the fruit ripens and the flowers blossom . . ." Juliette chimes in. "Welcome to Goldstone, where two princesses have their home . . ." She turns to Annie, explaining, "We made it up when I was a kid." Juliette exhibits none of the embarrassment of her mother that Annie has witnessed in other girls.

Since she was small, Annie has always felt a streak of jealous resentment toward her friends who had moms and took them for granted—the girls who sprawled over just-cleaned carpet or neatly made canopy beds and rolled their eyes when their well-meaning mothers came in carrying plates of apple slices and cheddar cheese. The girls who would hardly look up when their mothers flipped on a lamp as the winter sun grew dim, who didn't avert their eyes from the television when their mothers came in the door and kissed them, stroked their fine hair.

Annie coveted these mothers for her own. The mothers who stayed to watch their ballet lessons, made perfect lunches, tucked them in, braided their hair, volunteered in their classrooms, doled out endless supplies from their purses—lip gloss, sun-screen, Fruit Roll-Ups. But in her corner of the valley, Annie has never encountered a mother like Margot, who seems to be an exclusive brand of California Woman. At once bohemian and elegant, in tune with the natural world and the art world. Maternal but free. The kind of woman who will throw on a sheer shift and wear her bikini to the market in the canyon to buy expensive olive oil to make dinner for her daughter, which she does shortly after Annie's arrival.

Pizza night at Goldstone-where-the-princesses-have-their-home does not mean Domino's—it's an all-out, from-scratch affair. Margot kneads dough, Annie and Juliette forage ingredients from the garden, and then the three of them make a disaster of the kitchen crafting their "Roman"-style pizzas. One has peaches, sage, and burrata. Another, fresh basil, fresh tomatoes, tiny clams. When dinner is served, Margot pours the girls tiny glasses of Riesling to match her larger one, to Annie's surprise. In the golden-hour sunlight, it's enough to make her head swimmy.

Annie normally answers questions about her parents suc-
cinctly: my dad's an English teacher at Reseda High, and my
mom died. But tonight, the wine has loosened Annie's grip on
herself, and she responds to Margot's queries with candor.
Because her life feels so regular, it's hard for even her to imagine that she was born on a commune in The Middle of
Nowhere, Northern California. Another commune member
delivered her. When she was a year old, her dad fled with her.
When she tells the story at dinner, Margot's fascination makes
Annie feel that perhaps the buried wounds in her history hold
some secret value.

After dinner, Margot, Juliette, and Annie stay out on the deck
to watch the sunset. Once the pulse of cricket song begins to
take over the night, Margot pops popcorn and they change
into pajamas to watch an old movie on the small TV in the
living room. Juliette debates between two of her favorites—*La
Dolce Vita* and *Breakfast at Tiffany's*—neither of which Annie
has seen. Margot and Juliette both wear silk nightgowns.
Annie has brought boxer shorts and a giant T-shirt, the usual
sleepover uniform at her old middle school, but Juliette offers
to lend her a gown to match theirs. Its luxuriousness makes
Annie self-conscious. She keeps running her hands over the
silky fabric as she sits tucked into the corner of the couch,
while Juliette drapes herself over her mother's lap, Margot sipping gamay now and playing with Juliette's hair, as Sylvia
splashes through Trevi fountain.
    None of Annie's old jealousy, none of that desire, compares
to the spark of electrical longing ignited in Margot's
presence.
    When the movie is nearly over, Annie lies down, placing her

head only inches from Margot's available leg, and a moment later, she feels the woman's fingers in her hair. The pleasure of Margot's tenderness makes Annie feel a little bit high, almost.

When she closes her eyes, Annie sees her own mother's image arising out of nowhere: the clear, freckled skin, the ice-blond pigtail braids, the blue eyes—an almost unnatural blue, like the ocean on acid. Annie remembers the vertigo of looking back at herself in a stranger's face, the desire to please her mother, to connect to her, and to run from her, the unsettledness in her stomach that made it hard to eat, that made her want to hold tightly to her father's hand under the dark wood table.

The final time Annie saw Indigo, a year and a half ago, blurs into all the times before. She had no idea those hours would be the last she spent in her mother's presence. Annie and her dad arrived in the tiny mountain town of Willow Creek, as they always did, and saw Indigo's "borrowed" tractor in the parking lot of the Big Foot Steakhouse. Indigo didn't have a vehicle of her own; no one on the commune had anything of their own. She broke the rules by leaving Six Rivers Ranch, which is why she could never stay longer, why she could never travel farther.

Annie's mother was already seated in one of the big leather booths that seemed to swallow her up. She appeared an unsettling mix of child and adult, nearly ageless: she had breasts (though never a bra); she was fully grown, but seemed overwhelmed by the sights and sounds of the world, like a baby might be. When Annie arrived, she stood and wrapped her awkwardly in her arms, smelled her head.

Annie's father did most of the talking throughout the dinner, as he always did, reporting to Indigo about Annie's achievements in school, swim team, soccer. Indigo appeared to be listening closely, but rarely said much of anything as she ate her baked potato—she and Annie both always ordered baked potatoes with sour cream, butter, cheese. When they finished their dinner and sat waiting for the glass dishes of strawberry mousse they always ordered for dessert, Indigo reached across the table to press a small treasure into Annie's palm. Over the years Annie had gotten several beaded bracelets, a hand-sewn pouch, a pair of earrings with dangling stones, a crocheted hat Annie never wore, a crystal that Indigo said was for protection. That night, she gave Annie a tiny heart and said, "So you'll remember I love you." Annie and her mother did not normally tell each other "I love you." Annie sat for the rest of the dinner staring at that heart— hand-carved from wood, stained red—rolling it around and around in her palm, until she looked up an found that Indigo was staring at her.

In the big oak bed Juliette normally shares with her mother, she strokes Annie's hair in much the same manner as Margot did, shadows of jacaranda leaves wavering in moonlight. It should be weird, maybe, but it doesn't feel weird. It feels perfect, and Annie melts into the touch. "You're lucky," she says softly, "that you have a mom."

"I know," Juliette answers. "You can share her, if you want to."

Annie thinks no one has ever said anything kinder to her.

"Wanna go outside and smoke a cigarette?" Juliette asks.

"Okay."

They sneak past a sleeping Margot and out to the garden. Juliette opens a pack of Nat Sherman Fantasias and lights a pink one, hands it to Annie. The stars are a whole different creature out here in the dark night of the canyon.

"My mom named me," Annie says. "On the commune. Even though the kids were supposed to belong to everyone."

"Annie?"

"Anais Dawn. At least it's not Moon Berry or something."

"How did I not even know your name?" Juliette sounds hurt.

"I don't know. My dad put it on my birth certificate, but he started calling me Annie as soon as we left."

"Anais Dawn is a beautiful name," Juliette says. "It suits you."

"No, it doesn't."

"Can I call you Anais?"

"No."

"Dawn?"

"No."

"Why do you hate it?"

"I don't. It's just not mine." Annie wants to cry.

Juliette leans over and kisses her on the lips.

Annie wants Juliette to kiss her again. She wants to be back in the red vinyl booth with her mother, studying her face.

But she will not grow up and know her mother more deeply. Her mother will never appear at the doorway to her and her father's home, having renounced the commune, as Annie occasionally allowed herself to fantasize she might. Annie will never learn what Indigo felt while Annie was growing inside of her, will never learn what made Indigo stay when Annie's father left with her, why her mother let them go.

Annie could count the number of hours she spent in Indigo's presence after the age of one, all of them during the thrice-yearly dinners for which Annie and her father drove all day. They are all Annie has left of her mom; they are almost nothing. Grief is like this: the foreclosure of a future.

"My mom was a hippie, too," Juliette says. "A different kind, I guess. But I think the idea was the same. They believed in love. And freedom, and just because it didn't always turn out to be what they thought—just because they grew up—the idea of believing is still beautiful."

Annie nods.

"Hold on," Juliette says. "I wanna play you this song."

Juliette goes inside and returns with a small boombox. She skips forward on the CD until Joni Mitchell is singing "Woodstock," and Juliette begins to sing too, in a sweet soprano, promising they are stardust, golden. That somewhere, there's an Eden to which they might return.

Annie is enraptured.

"Let's not ever get old, okay?" Juliette says when the song ends. "Let's be dreamers forever."

"Okay."

And like that, Juliette sweeps a paintbrush over Annie's origins, changes the story: her parents were young people who believed in something. Whatever tragedy befell her mother, her journey had been noble. She'd been looking for a way back to the garden that we all came from.

Deep down, Annie senses the devil that began hunting Indigo before Annie was even born. The one that scared Annie's father enough to run. She can feel it sitting between them in that booth in the Big Foot Steakhouse, stopping Annie's mother from ever truly becoming a mom.

But Annie lets Indigo's image dissolve—as it always had

41

when she and her father retreated down the 5 freeway—and trains her gaze on Juliette, drinking her in, birthing a loyalty that will shape the rest of Annie's life. The dark ocean spreads out on the horizon. Tonight, Annie knows, is the beginning of everything.

# 1

## 2000–2001

Once a month, Juliette's father takes her to the Westfield Village Mall and lets her pick out a present before bringing her back to his house in Thousand Oaks. She tells Annie that she's come to think of the new purses, the CDs, the dresses as something between a form of bribery and an apology for enduring an evening with his wife, Jana, and their twin eight-year-old boys. Juliette has described it in detail: at every dinner, her father laughs at the boys' attempt to snort chocolate milk through their noses, Jana serves a tuna or green bean or three-cheese casserole, and then they retire to the overstuffed couches in the living room, where Juliette studies the fireplace mantel, packed with framed family photos of the four of them in various matching outfits. Juliette appears in a single school portrait buried on the edge.

After dad-dinner nights, she always wants to get drunk.

It is on such a night that Annie and Juliette are introduced to Lucas at a concert at the Hammer Museum. He is an art student on exchange from Sweden, hosted by a friend of

Margot's. Afterward, Lucas drives the girls to the beach, blasting Finnish hip-hop, letting the wind blow his shoulder-length white-blond hair. Juliette plays with a gold necklace purchased by her dad that afternoon, the thin chain laying over her collarbone. She fawns over Annie, applying lipstick to her in the backseat. "Isn't my friend pretty?" she asks, a rhetorical question. Lucas is pretty, too, with his green eyes and high cheekbones—Annie can tell that Juliette thinks so.

At the beach, they drink warm prosecco from a bottle Lucas retrieves from his trunk and pass a joint. Juliette throws off her clothes to skinny-dip in the ocean, howls at the moon. She kisses Annie on the lips in front of Lucas, who stares with interest. Undoubtedly, he is hoping to sleep with Juliette, or hook up, at least, but parked outside of Goldstone, Juliette tells him good night. He protests, then asks to be invited in. When he gets nowhere, he makes a final request, asking Juliette to touch Annie's breasts. Annie laughs.

"Can I?" Juliette asks.

Annie laughs again. "Sure, I guess."

Juliette does it. Annie's cheeks flush; she can feel Lucas's hungry gaze. Juliette tries to exit with a kiss, but Lucas grabs hold of her wrist, pleading, "Come on, you can't leave me like this," as he puts her hand on his dick. Juliette takes it away, but he puts it back.

Finally, she lets him follow the girls out of the car, but she won't allow him to come inside. Instead, she gives him a blow job—her first—at the edge of the driveway in the dark shadows of the oak trees, while Annie waits for her on the back deck, smoking and watching the waxing moon.

As Lucas's car starts, Juliette comes to join Annie, silently reaching for her cigarette.

"Is it weird," she says after a moment, "that I was thinking about you while I was blowing him?"

Annie laughs a little bit. "Maybe."

"I mean, thinking about what I'd tell you about it—like even while it was happening, I was already telling you in my head."

"What were you going to tell me?"

"I don't know. I guess it had less to do with the actual thing and more to do with the little things. The oranges in the moonlight. They looked like little planets."

"Did you like it?"

Annie can see Juliette searching for her response.

"His penis was smoother than I thought it would be." Juliette drags from the cigarette, letting the smoke spill out of her mouth. "It lasted a long time. I wanted it to be done." She lies down on Annie's lap, stares into her eyes. "Never leave me, okay?"

"I won't." Annie recognizes the look on her face—that confused, swirling feeling of power and helplessness, of being both the blade that could slice and the bread.

Annie was thirteen when her dad told her that her mother had died. Annie didn't cry; instead, she felt a sickening hollow feeling settle deep in her body, as if something had been carved out of her: a cantaloupe scooped clean with the melon baller she loved to use. She held her eyes open, forbidding herself from blinking, until they burned and watered with tears and her father rubbed circles into her back. Grief is like this: a permanent vacancy.

Annie and her dad had been planning to meet Indigo in Willow Creek as they did every early summer, but after they got the news, he took Annie to Six Flags instead. They drove to Santa Clarita and rented a room at the Marriott. Annie ordered a baked potato for dinner at the hotel restaurant, and chocolate mousse for dessert—they didn't have strawberry. The next day they went to the amusement park, and though she'd never been one for scary rides before, Annie went on all the roller coasters, even the upside-down ones, while her dad stood on the sidelines, giving her his biggest smile when she emerged dizzy.

When she and her father returned from their trip, Annie packed up an old trunk with T-shirts and Teva sandals, bug spray and cans of Pringles. The YMCA summer camp where she'd gotten a job as a CIT was in the mountains somewhere in the middle of California, halfway to Six Rivers.

Trevor worked in the kitchen. Annie didn't know how old he was, only that he was not fully adult but not a kid; maybe he was eighteen, maybe twenty-two. He performed simple magic tricks for the younger children, making them laugh. The camp food was notoriously terrible, but Trevor gave Annie special treatment—if she wandered into the dining hall in the middle of the day, he'd let her trail him into the kitchen and make her a grilled cheese sandwich, or sometimes he'd sneak her boxes of strawberries that she devoured sitting on the cool metal prep table in the back of the kitchen. One afternoon, he asked her if she wanted to come with him to smoke a cigarette. She said yes, despite the nervous flutter in her stomach. She had never smoked before. They hiked behind cabin 8 to sneak across the river. Trevor held out his hand for Annie as they stepped over the rocks peeking out from the rushing water and pulled her to sit beneath a pine tree on the other side. The smell of the forest here reminded Annie of Willow Creek. When she and her dad would step out of the car to check into the Big Foot Motel, the roar of motorcycles in the thin, still mountain air had made Annie uneasy, but she'd loved how it smelled: clean. Trevor held his cigarette between his fingers for Annie to drag from and laughed when she pulled the smoke into her mouth and spit it out. When he reached out and put his hands on her upper inner thigh where her jean shorts ended, Annie froze. A buzz of adrenaline traveled from her stomach up to her chest and back in an instant—the strange shock of a finger in an outlet—and then his mouth was on her mouth. Why didn't she run away, cross back over the river, and return to camp? Why didn't she tell him to stop? Her body recognized the feeling, like the roller coaster she'd just ridden at Six Flags: woozy, thrilling, totalizing. Her hands gripped the edges of his shirt as he put it on the ground for her to lay her head on, while Trevor with the dirty blond hair and the yellow stained teeth and the crooked grin and the small blocks of muscle on his shoulders went down on her. It was tingly at first. She focused on the pine tree overhead, the two black crows circling the sky, and soon she couldn't feel her legs. She went numb from the waist down. When it was done, he jerked himself off under a tree. Annie pulled up her shorts and looked away, watching the river. As they crossed back to camp, she still had no legs. Back in her cabin, rest hour was ending. She climbed up to her top bunk and stared at the wood ceiling and saw those two black crows circling.

When her father came to pick her up two days later, everyone hugged goodbye. Trevor tugged at her arm and asked for her address. In the rush of the moment, to avoid awkwardness, she gave it to him. When she arrived home, she got letter after letter. She was alarmed at the scrawl of handwriting that looked as if it belonged to someone so much younger than he was, the misspellings, the backward grammar. The notes were not overly sexual in nature. He told her again and again how beautiful she was, how special, said he dreamed of her. Wondered if she'd be coming back to camp next summer, and when he could see her.

Annie didn't write back. She stuffed the notes into her bottom drawer, the same drawer where she kept her mother's trinkets. She started dating a boy in her seventh-grade class who could play Beatles songs on his guitar. They would go for long walks in her neighborhood at dusk, make out in the park. When he pushed his leg between hers, she let him; when he reached his hand up her shirt, she stared up at the stratocumulus clouds (she'd learned to identify cloud types in science class) spreading out in waves across the sky, low and nearly touchable. Her stomach turned; her body buzzed. It asked for more.

Annie had thought she was alone with the knowledge of that uncomfortable ambivalence—dread turning to desire and back again. But after Lucas, Annie recognizes it in Juliette.

When they dress up and go out to a senior party, to the Beverly Hills Hotel, where they catch the attention of rich older guys, to the beach, where they lie out in their bikinis, it's a game they are playing together. They do not participate in hookups with boys so much because it feels good, though sometimes it does. They do it because they are drawn to the thrill of the illicit. They do it because they want to be seen. They do it because sometimes a blow job seems like the easiest way out of the back of a car. They do it because there is something terrifying about the sexual hunger of boys, its urgency, the total way it takes over the boys' bodies and minds. They do it because the boys beg, because they are afraid that if they refuse, they might unearth an awful rage beneath the boys' desire. They do it because they have wounds buried beneath their own skin, wounds they do not understand and cannot name.

When Annie and Juliette don't feel like going out in search of more novel adventures, Saturday night begins with speeding up the 101 to Matt Brody's, a senior boy who lives in the foothills of Calabasas in a prefab mansion perched on roaming land, complete with two horses and a stable. If Annie's father knew she was sleeping over at a senior boy's house, of course he would not let Annie go. But by the time sophomore year is under way, she often spends the whole weekend at Margot and Juliette's, coming home just in time for her and her father's sacred Sunday suppers. The girls are able to rely on Margot's permission. Juliette, who turned sixteen in August, has her driver's license and an old Land Cruiser Margot bought her.

Matt looks like a Ken doll, with tanned, plastic-smooth skin. He takes too much Ecstasy, swallowing a candy-colored pill almost nightly. It makes him slow, and stupid, and also sweet. A beautiful boy with a broken brain. He hooks up with everyone, but there's something about him that makes it feel less predatory than it might. He smiles from across the room—aloof, gentle, quietly in need, and the girls come to him.

His father is a fancy movie producer who's always on set, and his mother, rumor has it, is having an affair. When she returns from wherever she's been in the mornings, she finds her living room strewn with high school children draped over couches, asleep on the floor, entwined, bodies over bodies, mouths open like babies.

Annie and Juliette love getting high and walking out to the stables to visit the horses in the moonlight, the way Dancer and Boogie trot over to greet them, the smooth sides of their necks, the tickle of their lips. Getting ready for Matt's parties includes packing their purses with carrot sticks and apple slices.

Annie cannot reconcile Juliette's childlike relationship with her mom—still sleeping in her bed!—with the freedom that Margot permits, even encourages in Juliette. But for Juliette, and now for Annie, too, there is always somewhere safe to come home to—every drunk night at Matt's is followed by a sun-drenched morning, waking on the floor in each other's arms and driving back to Goldstone to make Sunday pancakes. Juliette and her mom move in synchronicity in their twin ponytails, drifting together and apart in an effortless ballet, beating eggs, sifting flour, cutting fruit, singing along absently to *Blonde on Blonde*.

Christmas lights blink on in the early dusk as Juliette's Land Cruiser pulls up Candy Cane Lane, Annie's street in Tarzana named for the holiday displays that draw traffic all through the season. Though Annie and her father's house is one of the more modest on the block, it is one of the most brightly lit. He goes all out: glowing Santa Clauses, rooftop reindeer, twinkling icicles dripping everywhere. The day after Thanksgiving, Annie always makes hot cocoa and turkey sandwiches and carries them up to the rooftop to help him work.

Her father comes to greet the girls at the door now in his apron and wraps Annie into a hug. She can smell the garlic and sauce drifting out of the house.

"How was your weekend, Tulip? I missed you."

"I missed you, too, Daddy." Annie always feels a twinge of guilt in her stomach, knowing she's left him alone.

Juliette often stays for dinner, as she does tonight, and her dad cooks up a proper Italian feast while the girls compose poems with the magnetic poetry set Annie got her dad for Father's Day—a good gift, she'd thought, for a high school English teacher who once wanted to be a writer. The suburban home is devoid of the sophistication of Goldstone, but her dad is a true chef in his own right. "I guess we both have one good parent, at least," Juliette jokes.

Annie's dad and Juliette's mom are too different to be real friends, but Margot often compliments him on raising a "spectacular" daughter. He must assume that Annie's becoming a woman and needs other women, a mother figure; it's the only reason he'd let her stay away for so long. He must think that he is no longer enough for her. It breaks Annie's heart to admit it, but he's right.

Spring arrives early in Los Angeles; come March, Margot serves freshly baked strawberry tarts alongside dry prosecco for dessert. The nights are growing warmer, the smell of jasmine is everywhere, and the dinner guests are lingering outdoors, bubbling over. Juliette and Annie lie on their bellies in the grass, buzzed off their own small glasses of prosecco, refilled a few times over.

"Will you braid my hair?" Annie asks Juliette. They're planning on going out later, if they can draw themselves away from the pleasures of Goldstone. Juliette straddles Annie, sitting on her butt, and begins pulling Annie's hair back to weave it into a crown.

"I think Mom maybe sleeps with Lina," Juliette says.

"Lina?" The reporter for *Vanity Fair* with wild curls, a father from Turkey, and a mother from the Midwest is always at Margot's dinner parties; she has been close with Juliette and Margot for years.

Annie follows Juliette's gaze into the tangle of adults and picks out Margot and Lina dancing together on the deck, holding their glasses of bubbly—Lina moves her body sensually. Margot floats, effortless and airy. There is a silent laughter, a nearly tangible light passing between them.

Margot has a boisterous social life, but never a boyfriend. Juliette said she dated a French painter for a while when Juliette was little, and then not again, not that she can remember. But Margot and Lina? Margot with a woman? Annie wouldn't have imagined it; she's intrigued by the thought, a slight heat crawling into her cheeks.

"She used to sleep on the couch and have breakfast in the morning, sometimes. I assumed it was 'cause they were getting drunk, but I think they were probably having sex. I feel like Mom sometimes goes over there now when we're spending the night out."

"Why wouldn't they just be together?" Annie asks.

Juliette shrugs. "She doesn't want anyone to get in the way of our lives. We like it the way it is."

As if on cue, Margot descends the stairs and makes her way to Juliette and Annie, picking up plates of tarts and ice cream that she delivers to them in the grass.

"Thanks, Mama," Juliette says.

Margot never really appears drunk, but there is a slight sheen on her, dewy sweat, and her smile is just a bit broader than usual.

"How are my girls?" she asks. And then, before they can answer—"Wait. Stay right there." She hurries off, calling back, "Julie, don't finish the braid!"

When she returns, she is carrying her camera. She reads the light on Annie's face with her meter, on Juliette's, and begins silently shooting, squatting in the grass with the ease of a child. An electric thrill runs through Annie's body, her heart skipping, her palms clammy. Juliette resumes braiding, placing another bobby pin between her teeth, accustomed to the dance of the photographs. Annie looks at Margot for a moment, then looks away. When she looks back again, Margot lowers the camera and smiles at her.

"You girls," she says, her voice warm with affection, admiration. She raises the camera back to her face and continues to shoot.

That evening begins Margot's new series based on Annie and Juliette's friendship. Making pictures together becomes part of the vocabulary of Annie's days and nights at Goldstone. Margot believes the art is its own engine; their job—the three of them—is simply to be present and allow the magic to happen. She might show up at any moment with her camera, as the girls put on makeup, change outfits, read to each other in the tub, sit on the deck in their swimsuits, bleeding strawberry juice onto their bellies. Sometimes, Juliette summons her: "Mommy!" she calls, as she and Annie sprawl in the garden, still in their silk nightgowns, drinking tea. "Bring the camera, Annie looks too pretty." Annie beams, quietly.

The same images of Juliette that hang on the walls of Goldstone are displayed in galleries, museums, rich people's homes. There have been think pieces written about the ethics of Margot's art, right-wing religious groups, even, who labeled it pornography. But all of it has only served to make the photographs themselves more popular.

Annie wonders if she, too, will have her image displayed in prominent places one day. Most important, being in front of Margot's lens feels like being adopted into the family.

One month after her sixteenth birthday, on the final night of her sophomore year, Annie loses her virginity to Matt Brody in his bedroom, while outside Usher plays and kids drink cough syrup. It's hard for Annie to say exactly why she does it. Is it that she imagines she might be the girl who changes Matt, saves him? Is it just that the adrenaline hit she got from blow jobs has begun to wear off and she needs a new ride, a faster roller coaster? It's that body high she's seeking—the way, after the death of her mother, upside down on the Viper at Six Flags, it was impossible to feel sadness or anger, eclipsed as they were by the seismic thrill, the rush of danger. Or perhaps Margot's photographs have given her a fresh confidence, and she's eager to make use of it.

Annie's the one who climbs atop Matt in the bed, sheets smelling slightly of Old Spice and Tide, still vaguely damp with sleep sweat; she's the one who takes off his clothes and then her own, until she's no longer certain what to do next. He takes over, puts on a condom, pulls her on top of him. It hurts but it is a good hurt, and Matt's blue-green eyes suddenly seem as if she could swim in them forever.

When they're done, he rolls over to sleep. Annie tiptoes out of the bedroom, in search of Juliette. The house is dark, and she has to step over kids asleep on the living room floor. Outside, Annie finds Juliette jumping on the trampoline, two boys watching her. She holds an oversized plastic sippy cup; she seems very drunk.

"Where were you?" Juliette asks, slurring, when her eyes land on Annie.

Annie doesn't want to say, because of the boys. "I was looking for you."

"I was looking for you!" Juliette shoots back. "Ask them!" She sips from her cup as Annie climbs onto the trampoline.

"Yo, can you get out of here, please?" Annie asks the boys. "We want to be alone."

They protest, lingering, but when it's clear that they won't get past Juliette's cock-blocking friend, they wander off. Annie brings a blanket from the house to cover them, and she and Juliette lie on their backs on the trampoline, watching the stars.

"This was my aunt's favorite color," Juliette says, pulling the crocheted blanket around her chin. "She called it damask rose."

"I didn't know you had an aunt."

"My mom's sister. She moved to Mexico and then she died when I was eight. She was one of those California crystal people. Her hair was super-long, down to her butt, which when I was little I thought was cool, but in retrospect was kinda weird—that's how she was. But Mom loved her—of course she loved her, she was her sister. So I loved her, too. Jeanie watched me when Mom had gallery stuff or whatever. She was learning to be a masseuse. She'd practice stuff on me. I guess it was kinda fucked up." Juliette laughs abruptly.

"What do you mean 'practiced' on you?" Annie asks.

"I don't know. She was, like, really lonely, I think. Fuck—" Juliette interrupts herself. "I'm spinning." She crawls to the edge of the trampoline. "Annie, I don't feel good." She curls into herself in a fetal position, won't move, won't get up. Annie makes her sip water, though Juliette doesn't want it.

Annie curls her body around Juliette's and pulls the damask-rose blanket over them. It's a new moon tonight. The stars are absurd.

Annie hums their song, "Woodstock," and before long Juliette begins to sing along. They belt out the words to the night sky, Juliette's voice high and sweet and choral, Annie's off tune and low, incanting the promise of stardust in each of us.

Before she leaves with Juliette the next morning, Annie finds Matt in bed and whispers in his ear, "I was a virgin."

He half-opens one eye and looks at her.

"I want you to teach me," she says, and gives him kitten eyes, rubs her head against his hand. She can tell it works when he asks her what she's doing later.

In Juliette's Land Rover on the way home to Goldstone, mascara ringing her tired eyes, Juliette asks, "How was it?"

"What?"

"Sex. With Matt."

"How did you know?"

"I'm your best friend."

"It was different than I thought. But I liked it."

"Did you bleed?"

"I don't know. It was so dark." Then Annie adds, "I think I like him. I want to do it again."

"Uh-oh," Juliette says.

"Yeah."

Juliette squeezes her hand tightly. "You're still mine, though."

"I know." And it's true—she belongs to Juliette.

Annie's father, to her surprise, has found his own love interest. "What do you think?" her dad asks Annie after their first

Sunday dinner with Sandra. The librarian with the cable-knit sweater has nothing in common with the effervescent types Annie tried to set her dad up with over the years—a waitress who gave her extra cherries in her Shirley Temple; her friend Kelly's divorced mother in middle school—but she suspected her father was smitten when she watched him form a scrap of a poem on the fridge, while waiting for the onions to caramelize: *you are elaborate like shadow wine in a deep summer dream.*

"She's okay," Annie replies. She watches her father's face, handsome, with lines starting to crack his forehead. She thinks of him alone, all those Saturday nights until he started eating out with Sandra at the Chinese restaurant in Encino that he and Annie had been going to since she was little (a detail Sandra had revealed at dinner).

"I mean, she's nice," Annie amends. "I'm glad you're seeing someone."

"Thanks, Annie-bo-banny. I'm out of practice, if I ever had any. That's for sure." He ruffles her hair. "You know you'll always be my number-one gal."

She crawls into his arms, smells his same aftershave he's always had. "I love you, Dad."

Her father does not know anything about her own romance. Annie goes to Margot for advice about birth control.

She starts visiting Matt outside of the party nights, driving down the 101 on summer afternoons, perfume dabbed on the insides of her thighs, her clean, shiny hair whipping itself into a froth. There is something arrogant about Matt: he already knows he'll get what he wants. But there is something vulnerable, too, slow and muted, that makes Annie feel just safe enough: her orgasm is a controlled free fall, the roller coaster that will drop and ride back to the top. She feels a new kind of power, making him moan. Showing him her beauty, letting him worship it. Juliette often comes with her for the drive and feeds the horses while Annie and Matt disappear into the bedroom.

Back at Goldstone, Annie and Juliette lie in the sun, taking turns reading novels aloud to each other, letting themselves burn again and again until they turn shades of gold. They make lavender lemonade with the herbs and lemons from the garden. They swim in the Pacific. They pick peaches to sear on the grill for Margot's dinner parties. Margot takes their pictures. Even when Margot is not there, Annie feels as if she's watching them.

It does not startle Annie when she wakes in the big oak bed one morning to Margot's camera hovering over her. Juliette is still asleep. Margot smiles at Annie, a warm, secret smile, and smooths Annie's hair with the back of her hand.

Bashful, Annie looks away. *Ignore me,* Margot often instructs Annie and Juliette when she appears with her camera as if out of nowhere. But this morning Margot reaches out, gently turning Annie's face back toward her.

Margot takes the photo. And another. A tear runs down Annie's cheek; she does not know why. Margot photographs it, then brushes it gently away.

Juliette stirs, half-waking, and nestles into Annie. Annie reaches her hand up to play with Juliette's hair, still holding the camera with her gaze, wanting to keep it captive. The shutter clicks, and there is the cover of Margot's *Young Adults* book.

In medium-format film, Annie and Juliette are destined to become icons of young womanhood in its complications, vulnerabilities, glories. People will say what they will about the photographs, but for Annie's part, she's never felt as seen as she does in front of Margot's lens. She is part of an exclusive world of girlhood, of womanhood, she feels, and the glow she gets from Goldstone she carries to Matt; it is what makes him captive to her.

Juliette and Margot make Annie more than a Valley girl, more than a motherless daughter having teen sex with a teen drug addict, more than a plain, freckle-faced sixteen-year-old waiting for another thrill ride. They make Annie worthy of poetry. Margot's photographs are proof.

# 8

2008

Growing up, before the cancer, her parents' love colored Jesse's childhood, the texture of it almost palpable. Now each tender moment with Noah—their jazz on Sunday morning, watching the sunlight catch his lashes as he lays his head on her belly—triggers a longing for what is gone: sweet corn tamales for breakfast or Eggos with too much syrup, her father's laughter as he spun her mother around the kitchen. Grief is like this: a romantic. In the afterglow of lovemaking, when they lay tangled together, fall air wafting in through the window and breaking over their bodies, Jesse often looks at Noah and thinks of her mom and dad, wondering if this is how it felt for them, back then. She learns to love in the shadow of loss.

In the worn, Spanish duplex in Silver Lake, there is breakfast on the yellow chairs in the little nook with their laptops touching across the table, espresso Noah makes on the stovetop, buttered French bread and strawberries. They sit together for hours, typing away, Jesse quietly wandering through the world of her book—the novel she's determined to write.

Noah, on occasion, pulls Jesse out to share a line he's just composed in an excited burst, to ask her opinion about a character's turn, the structure of a scene. He is writing his first screenplay, a movie he's determined to direct one day. They will share a cigarette, maybe, in the afternoon, take a walk. Noah uses his iPhone to frame shots, describes the way the camera will sweep over his old Chicago block. Then it's back to their laptops.

Noah, who wants to write and direct movies, dreams of leaving his mark. The image haunts him: fingerprints of enslaved people still etched into the bricks of streets they laid in the South, the plantation homes they built, the only traces they left. He has vowed that one day, people will know the name his mother gave him. "You can be anything you wanna be," she'd told him. "Just make sure they know your name. Noah King. You come from royalty, baby."

For Jesse, it's different: writing is about taking shape inside of herself, running her hands over the messy mass of feelings again and again until they become legible. It is a private world where she keeps her grief, wades through it, plunges into it, tries again and again to open her eyes underwater and find treasure.

The first diagnosis arrived three days after her fourteenth birthday, dissolving life as she'd always known it. Her mom, a white woman whose family owned a dry-cleaning business in Albuquerque, is tender, wistful, a dedicated mother, but it was her dad, a third-generation Mexican American who worked at Sandia Labs in quantum optics, who was the family's center: warm, booming, commanding, with a monumental smile. Her father, who cooked feasts for them—his own mother's Mexican food, mostly, because he wanted his daughters to grow up with it—would soon have to be fed through a port in his chest. Her daddy, who had thrown them high into the air and caught them, who had held them up in so many ways, would be chained to his bed by IVs, the muscle dissolved off his body.

There would be periods of remission, periods of hope. Each time the cancer came back it felt like walking off a cliff that they hadn't known was always right there.

The cancer returned for the fourth and final time at the end of Jesse's junior year in Chicago. Her dad pursued each available avenue to each eventual dead end—the immunotherapy trial, the trip to Ohio to meet with a renowned surgeon—and lost his last battle five weeks after Jesse's college graduation.

Watching her father waste away in the middle of the summer was cruel, when the world was so resplendent, spilling over with life, the cottonwoods shaking their green leaves by the riverbed, the sun waking early to announce itself, searing through the impossible pain of the day, her father asleep, mouth open, cheeks hollow, in his recliner. He sipped water and then threw it up. Chewed on ice. Smoked weed. Told Jesse in a voice that was the faded color of her father's voice, like his overwashed red shirt, that he still considered himself a lucky man. That he won the lottery with her and Lucy as his daughters, to have married their mother.

Then he went to sleep one night and didn't wake up. They were fortunate—it happened peacefully—but it didn't feel fortunate, their father's body in his bed in the dawn light, breathless. The house filled with emptiness that was thick enough to drown them.

"Do you want me to come and visit?" Noah asked, again and again, during their hours on the phone.

"No," Jesse said. "I'll come to you." She needed him to be the lifeboat, her escape. She could not stay in her childhood home where her father died. She didn't have the strength to figure out what life she might build on her own. So she packed a suitcase and got on a plane to Los Angeles.

Three months after her arrival, Jesse is still looking for a job, spending her days walking through every corner of Silver Lake with her résumé, driving down Sunset Boulevard into Hollywood, West Hollywood, through Beverly Hills, where she instantly felt ill-equipped for even a position behind the counter at Starbucks. In the evenings, if Noah is at work, she spends hours on the phone with her sister, who is both Jesse's best friend and her opposite.

Growing up, Lucy was the happy-go-lucky baby of the family. After their father got sick, she tried to cure him through comedy and could always make him laugh, even during the worst points in his treatment, with goofy songs and dances.

Jesse, on the other hand, was always "mature," more so after the cancer arrived, as if her virtue might make a difference in her father's chances of survival. She made sure she had only perfect grades to report, helped Lucy with her homework, her mother with the cooking and the laundry and her dad's intravenous feeding.

Jesse arrived at college with a leg up on the lessons of being an adult: she folded her clothes neatly instead of leaving them piled in the hamper, stocked her mini-fridge with fruits and veggies instead of subsisting on packaged ramen like her roommate. She never had any interest in making herself throw up after having heard her father puke into the toilet all night, didn't party with abandon like other kids did. Her biggest vice was cigarettes, a habit she'd brought back from a study-abroad trip in Paris. When she went to the neighborhood bar, Jimmy's, after she finished at the library, she never had more than two drinks. Like a housewife who pours a glass of wine at five o'clock on the dot or an unfulfilled husband who sips a couple of Scotches before bed, Jesse learned to self-medicate in a controlled manner, making escapism sustainable.

But now that college is over and her father is dead, she feels as if she's failing at becoming an adult. Everyday tasks in a new city feel more difficult than they should be—circling for parking in grocery store lots, only to have a spot swiped; waiting in line for an hour at the bank only to be turned away when she learns she's forgotten the necessary piece of mail. Worst of all, she has no choice but to dip into her dad's life insurance money. Noah has covered the first months of rent, but she can't ask him again when he's working double shifts to pay his half and she has a whole 100,000 dollars just sitting there.

She cries as she logs in to her bank account and transfers 1,000 dollars out of the savings where she's stored the 100k. That money, the last thing her father left her, has become a symbol, a tie to all that he worked throughout his life to provide, and she promised herself that she'd honor him by doing something of true value with it one day. In the meantime, sitting in the account in its round, perfectly lump sum, it's a testament to her father's undiminished bounty. To start to see it go—to realize how quickly it could be lost into rent checks and bags of food from Trader Joe's (or, as her younger sister Lucy's money is quickly going, into an all-consuming whirlwind of grief: dresses that will one day no longer fit, cocktails at fancy restaurants, bottles of expensive wine that sit half-drunk in the fridge)—is to understand that he's really gone.

When Noah comes home from his Sunday brunch shift in his Hard Rock T-shirt smelling of grilled meat, his old apron tossed over his shoulder and a wad of one-dollar bills sticking out of his back pocket, he finds Jesse crying over the chili (her dad's recipe) she is stirring on the stove. When he asks what's wrong, she tells him she's run out of savings and had to dip into the life insurance.

"How much?"

"A thousand," she says. "For now."

Noah frowns, confused. "So you've still got ninety-nine thousand."

"But—" Jesse says, unsure how to explain her irrational sorrow. Grief is like this: self-absorbed, a tornado. "I wasn't supposed to touch it."

"I'll get you the thousand dollars," Noah says, the mildest touch of helpless frustration in his voice. "I can pick up extra shifts. You can put it back."

"No," Jesse says, almost snapping. "That's not the point." She knows she's being impossible, but she can't help it. Her cheeks are hot. She feels worthless, feverish, lost.

"This is what your dad meant you to have it for, to help you after he was gone. I'll get you the cash or you'll find work soon. You'll sell your book. We'll put the money back."

"Okay," she says, stirring her chili unnecessarily, pushing the floating meat round and round the pot.

Noah kisses her head, draws her away from the stove, turning down the fire, and she lets him. She lets him pull her into the living room and onto his lap. Her body feels suddenly soft and tired and liquid. She collapses onto the couch as he lies on

top of her, and the weight of him is a comfort, an anchor. She
lets him pull off her panties under her red flowered dress, lets
his warmth fill her, and then she comes alive. Fucking Noah
feels like an affirmation of life, an insistence on it.

When they are finished Jesse serves her chili with corn bread
and they curl up on the couch. She'd just as soon turn on *The
Bachelorette*, but she tolerates Noah's Best Picture project. By
now he's made it all the way to *The Pianist*.

In the end, finding work in Hollywood—or adjacent to it—
comes easier to Jesse than it did to Noah. Jesse receives a forwarded email from Elenore, a friend from the U of C who grew
up in Venice Beach. Elenore's sister needs someone to fill her
role as a personal assistant for Dexter Lilly, a "big producer"
responsible for a string of Oscar-nominated movies.

When Jesse arrives at Dexter's house in Laurel Canyon, she
immediately recognizes that he and Elenore share a particular
brand of West Coast affluence. Despite being generations
apart, they have ratty Birkenstocks, expensive haircuts with
beach-kissed highlights, perfectly white smiles and an easygoing confidence in common.

Dexter also has a stack of gold bracelets he wears on his
wrist, a handsome face wrinkled in the appropriate places,
and four daughters. His dedication to them makes Jesse feel
at ease during her interview on his picturesque deck. Even if
Dexter is very "Hollywood," he is also a father. He seems
pleased that Jesse wants to be a novelist; he says it's better
that she's outside the industry and won't be hounding him to
read her scripts. He doesn't seem overly concerned about
Jesse's prior work experience or lack thereof. Mostly he asks
about her education, her aspirations. She blurts out, suddenly,

that her dad died recently; she isn't sure why she says it, except that it is difficult for her to tolerate having any extended interaction without making this essential fact known.

Tears spring to her eyes; she wipes them quickly away. She'll never get the job.

"Sorry," Jesse says.

"Don't be," Dexter replies. Sari, the smallest, blondest daughter, maybe seven, is jump-roping distractedly in the yard while she watches them. He calls out to her to get Jesse some water.

When Sari returns with a large plastic cup and a swirly straw, Dexter asks if they ought to show Jesse around the house.

"Come on," the little girl tells her, taking Jesse by the hand. The home is at once rambling and luxurious, one room unfolding into another, wood ceilings and Spanish-tile and various girl paraphernalia strewn about—lipsticks and fluffy sweaters, Barbie dolls, crumpled bikinis. They find Maya, the next eldest girl at nine, reading *The Amber Spyglass* on the window seat in the living room. Lexi, who is, as Sari announces, a "preteen," is at a friend's pool party. Their oldest sister, Kat, a sophomore in high school, is at the beach.

"Think I should hire her?" Dexter asks Sari playfully, as they wander out onto another deck at the back of the house and find a pool strewn with fallen purple flowers.

Sari frowns with seriousness. "Yes."

Noah takes Jesse out to lunch to celebrate. He never mentions how hard he'd tried to get a job like the one she walked into—it doesn't matter that as a white-looking girl from a good family she has a better chance at all this. What matters is that she's happy, that she'll stay.

———

Many of Jesse's duties with Dexter involve his daughters—they already have a nanny, hired by their mother (an Italian actress who divorced Dexter six years ago), but they are always needing one thing or another, and Dexter believes they should have someone they can relate to, someone like Jesse, he says.

Sari is the easiest to win over, but the older girls warm to Jesse soon enough, plopping into her old Volkswagen and dialing the radio to rap, putting their feet up on the dash, asking for her help with makeup or homework or fixing a snack. Occasionally Jesse feels the whispers of resentment, as she walks into the beautiful Laurel Canyon house that does not belong to her, as she performs some combination of duties representing a fusion of wife, mother, and maid: sorting through Dexter's mail and paying his bills, booking his travel, calling the pool guy, hunting down Sari's lost jacket, rubbing the stains out of Lexi's skirt, being jostled out of the way in Erewhon as she searches the cold-pressed juice case for Dexter's favorite green detox drink, trying not to cringe as the grocery bill that she charges on Dexter's Amex rings up to almost as much as she'll make all week. She stuffs the grocery bags into the back seat of her Volkswagen and cleans out the Lilly family fridge before she unloads the food—throwing away bags of wilted kale, uneaten leftovers in glass Tupperware. Washing and cleaning the new produce, chopping and bagging Pink Lady apple slices and sticks of celery ready for peanut butter, strawberries with their tops cut off, just as her own mother had always done for her and her sister, Lucy.

Dexter's family life only occasionally reminds Jesse of her own lost childhood, but there are the ice-cream sundaes Dexter makes that call back her dad's malts, and seeing Dexter and his daughters eating popcorn with Parmesan on the couch, watching old movies—*Charlie and the Chocolate Factory, E.T., The Princess Bride*—on TV, she can almost smell her father's cologne, can almost feel her cheek against his shoulder. In these moments, the pang in Jesse's chest is enough to make her need to escape, and she will invent a reason to run an errand or feign a phone call.

Still, the job is good for Jesse. She's making more money than she ever has, more than Noah does in his double shifts at the Hard Rock. Most important, working as Dexter's assistant shows Jesse that she can live in the world again. She spent the earliest days of her mourning in a helpless wave of lost keys, lost credit cards, forgotten appointments, grocery bags left in the store. Now, caring for Dexter and the girls reminds Jesse that she can care for herself, returns her to the capable woman she was. Yes, sometimes she breaks down and cries in her car on the way home, but when she looks back at these days, she will think of the years she was an assistant for Dexter as the years she became a writer. As hard as she works for him, she works harder for her dream. Living someone else's life gives her the fire she needs to fight for her own, the fire she needs to burn through the grief and become the woman her father raised.

# 9

2009

Noah and Jesse wake early and make love. Noah loves to make love to her like this, when she's half-awake, still supple with sleep, smelling of herself. Heat radiates off her body; she shakes and moans under his weight.

Noah does not have to work today—his first day off in ten days. He could close his eyes and drift off again, but she's up making coffee, the thick, warm smell wafting into the bedroom, and he wants to be close to her. He knows if he rolls over and closes his eyes she'll be gone, off to yoga and the farmers' market and he'll wake again alone. He pulls himself out of bed, follows her into the kitchen. She smiles and hands him the coffee she was about to sip, starts another.

Though they spent plenty of time at each other's apartments in college, Noah has not lived with a woman since his mom died when he was seven, and now that Noah and Jesse have moved in together, have begun to move into each other, there is an opulence to it that rivals the California winter sun, spilling itself everywhere: her smells, her cooking, her nails running along his back, her lacy underwear mixed in with his in the pile of clean clothes on the couch.

He is somewhat unique among early-twenties males, in that Noah already knows he wants to be a father. He saw how it transformed his uncle, saw Dev fall in love with this son. The summer before Noah started college, Dev came home and told him, "Erica's pregnant." Erica, his on-again, off-again girl-friend of years. Dev looked stunned.

"Shit," Noah said. "What are you gonna do?"

"What do you mean what am I gonna do? I'm gonna raise a baby," his uncle said.

When he first saw Dev holding the tiny boy, Noah recognized a joy taking shape in his uncle that had never been there before. He saw how all those nights spent working security for the university, posted out in the freezing cold on the Midway, took on new meaning for Dev. He was no longer just a security guard; he was someone's dad. He was providing for his child.

If it was complicated for Noah to see his father figure love a son in a way he had never quite loved Noah, Noah didn't allow himself to become aware of it. Though Noah had lived with Dev since Gracey died, he never really thought of him as a dad, and Dev didn't act like one. He took care of Noah—he'd promised Gracey he would—and he cared about him, of course. But there was never the wild, deep, madly-in-love feeling that is there between a parent and a child. Noah was his mother's; Noah and Dev both knew that. They'd been placed together because of a tragedy.

Noah preferred staying with Dev to his grandparents, because Dev left him alone, mostly. After the Acme Steel plants started shutting down for good and Noah's grandfather lost his job, his grandparents moved to St. Louis, where most of his grandma's family was. The rest of their extended family in Chicago fretted and fussed, heaped food on Noah's plate, tried to make him play sports, tried to get him to dance like he had with his mother, tried to turn him back into the boy he'd been with Gracey. But Noah couldn't become that kid again, and he felt that Dev understood that. Dev made sure Noah ate, that his fades were clean, that his clothes fit, that he showed up with what he needed for school. Beyond that, he let Noah be.

Noah was already at the university by the time Eric was born (naming him for his mom had been Dev's idea—"You made him, girl!" he'd said to her, grinning with pride), but Noah would go by to see Eric on the weekends and watch him sometimes while Dev was working so Erica could get something done. Eric's tiny hands, his locked-in gaze, his big smiles cracked the armor that had become second nature to Noah. Holding his cousin, Noah felt a soft place inside of him that he'd almost forgotten.

When Noah and Jesse started dating, Eric was a year old, and they began taking him out for ice cream or for walks in the park. Jesse bought him her own favorite childhood books for Christmas every year.

Noah doesn't say it out loud, but he thinks about it all the time now; how Jesse will look when she's got a big round belly. He'd barely even associated desire and pregnancy before, but now sometimes they'll be having sex and suddenly he'll be thinking about how he wants to put a baby inside her.

Because both Noah and Jesse work full-time and then some, they spend nearly all their other hours writing. Today they have decided to take a rare day off and drive to the beach. It is not yet nine o'clock, and there is hardly any traffic as they sail down the 10 freeway with the windows down, playing *In Search Of . . .* by N.E.R.D, nostalgic college music. When Noah came to pick Jesse up from her dorm for their first date, he'd arrived in this same Impala, smelling like too much cologne, blasting "Brain," and Jesse was smitten. (She'd been listening to TV on The Radio and Beach House, along with everyone else she knew.)

In Santa Monica, they buy second coffees and walk on the quiet shore beside the long winter tides. Last night, the first Black president of the United States was inaugurated. Noah and Jesse watched at Cal's house along with his parents and his new girlfriend, Suraya, toasting with cava in the middle of the day. Noah doesn't talk on the phone all that often, but he called Dev and Erica in Chicago, could hear the party in the background. He asked them to put four-year-old Eric on the phone and couldn't help saying what Dev had surely already told him: "See, look at that. You can be anything you want to, even president!"

Hope is not a feeling that Noah is accustomed to. The bubble swell it builds in his chest is almost uncomfortable. But holding Jesse's hand now, the waves lapping at their toes, Noah hears the line from the poem again in his head: *In today's sharp sparkle, this winter air, / any thing can be made, any sentence begun . . .*

Six months later, summer is peaking in LA, beaches packed body to body, heat rising from the blacktop even after dark. It's sweltering in the apartment, which has no AC. Jesse takes her laptop to the porch, a glass of iced coffee sweating in her hand, a hint of worry in her belly as she sits down to read Noah's just-finished screenplay. Noah has described the story of *The Red Balloon* to her again and again—a reimagined, feature-length version of the classic, in which he uses elements of magical realism to make social commentary. It stars a boy in South Side Chicago. Moments after his mother dies, the balloon floats in through the window. Jesse knows it is Noah's story, knows he's been playing it in his head over and over, already seeing it on a big screen. He has grand dreams that he'll sell the script and break in, buy her a house with a pool like Dexter's one day, that he'll be the hero of his family, sending money for Eric to go to a fancy school, helping his granddad live out his last years in comfort.

*What if it's no good?* she worries. How will she be able to tell him?

But it is wonderful.

When Noah comes home that evening, sweaty and smelling of spilled mimosas, she tells him she loves the script, and the look that crosses his face reminds her of the sky in the moment when the sun first makes its way through the morning haze. A supernatural glow.

Jesse spends the next days editing, crossing out lines, writing ideas in the margins. They go back and forth like this: Noah writes draft after draft and sends them back to her, until every line has been polished and polished again and they decide it is finished. And then comes the question: *What next?*

Noah's and Jesse's collective pool of Hollywood contacts is small, but they know a few people from Chicago who are in the "business": a friend of Cal's sister, a guy who dated Jesse's roommate in college and is now a manager, a girl Jesse knows through Elenore who just got promoted to be a junior executive at Paramount. They all have a version of the same question:

"Who is the audience for this?" Elenore's friend says she's happy to get coverage on the script if it will help and sends Noah back a document grading the story he's poured his heart into with a C−.

At Hard Rock, every so often someone Noah works with— an actor or a writer—will report having gotten an agent, or will even give their final notice because they've done the impossible and broken in. An aspiring writer asking for help reeks of desperation; Noah knows that. But the truth is, he is desperate. He sucks it up and asks a couple former waiters to send his script to their representatives. They forward him the replies: "Good looks, but I don't think this is something I can sell." "So sorry, but my reading pile is too high, don't think I can get to this till next year."

What had made Noah think that someone like him could break into Hollywood with a knockoff indie social critique/ grief story about a boy from South Side Chicago? Why would anyone want to make his little movie? The realization happens in slow motion: He is still just a nobody. Of course.

Jesse feels his disappointment in her stomach, her sternum, her lungs. When they've exhausted all other avenues, she resorts to asking Dexter to read.

She tries to bring it up casually. After she's reported on the hotel she booked him for his upcoming trip, as she's walking out, she gathers her courage and turns back. "Oh, Dex?"

"What?"

"My boyfriend just finished his first screenplay. I was wondering if I could bug you to read it. It's called *The Red Balloon*. Inspired by that movie, obviously." She smiles nervously.

"*The Red Balloon*?" Dexter raises a skeptical eyebrow.

"Yeah. It's, like, a brilliant use of magical realism . . . It stars this orphan kid. After his mom dies, the balloon helps him survive, find beauty again, escape danger. When the boy steals a candy bar from a corner store 'cause he's hungry, the balloon leads him down an ally to escape the security guard, and then into this abandoned building, and when he gets there, he finds this old man . . ." She's rambling. "Anyway, the action sequences get a lot more intense . . . It's, like, really gripping," Jesse says, her voice off-kilter. She'd practiced her pitch, but somehow it comes out garbled.

Dexter examines her for a moment. "I hired you 'cause you were never gonna ask me to do shit like this, remember?" Dexter smiles, but she knows he means it.

"I know, but—"

"You get this favor once," he says. "Are you sure this is the one? Is this the best thing he's ever going to write? Is this the best version of it?"

"I don't know," she answers. "I mean, it's his first script. But it's really good."

"Well, think about it," Dexter says. "If you still want me to read, I'll send it to Kasey, and if she likes it, I'll take a look." Kasey, his other assistant, the one who works in his office, schedules meetings, writes coverage for him like the kid who gave *The Red Balloon* a C− grade.

"Okay," she says, and walks away.

When she gets in her car, Jesse rolls up the windows to scream, bites her steering wheel. She picks up Dexter's dry cleaning every day. She answers homework calls from Maya at 10:00 p.m. She runs their rich-ass lives. And Dexter makes that big a deal about her asking him to read one script? Fuck him.

Noah is the only one who matters.

When Jesse arrives home with Chinese takeout, she finds Noah watching basketball in bed.

"I asked Dexter to read *The Red Balloon*," she says.

"You did?"

"Yeah. He said he thinks you're really talented, and that you should keep writing."

"He did?"

"Yeah."

"That's it?" Noah asks.

But Jesse can see in his face that it will be just enough. That even a morsel of encouragement, of recognition, from the outside world will spur him on.

Jesse shrugs, gives him a rueful smile.

"Does he know any agents he could give it to?"

"He said he thinks that for an agent, you need to start with something more commercial. But he said once you've done some other stuff, he thinks you could make that movie one day. I think he meant it, about you being talented."

"All right." Noah gives a slight nod, keeping his face neutral.

"It's gonna happen," Jesse says. "I promise. It might take a while. But you always hear people at the Oscars or whatever talking about movies that took years to get made."

"Yeah." He reaches out to pull her close to him.

Noah doesn't tell her that he knows now that she's lying. It doesn't matter—her belief in him is enough. He will cling to it like a life raft, as he once had his mother's.

# 10

2009–2012

Noah outlines movies endlessly, rereads his screenwriting books. In an effort to produce something more "commercial," he writes a romantic comedy and then a thriller, both starring people of nondescript race.

No dice.

He takes his Impala to the car wash, waits in line behind the Lexuses and Mercedes and Porsches, trying not to notice how pretty the new Panamera is. He tries not to notice when women make eyes at him. He tries not to care—why should he care—when the attendant comes over with his keys and whoever is sitting outside in the plastic chairs watches him walk over to his now-gleaming but still-busted old ride. He always overtips.

He takes Jesse's Jetta to the car wash, too, because she never does it herself.

He eats extra helpings of the cheesy enchiladas or carne asada Jesse makes for dinner in memory of her father, and then spends two hours at LA Fitness the next day trying to burn it off—in Hollywood, looks matter. He takes protein, and creatine, and avoids eye contact with the women who look him up and down with interest, avoids eye contact especially with the men who are there every day like he is, the middle-of-the-day shift for the aspiring-somethings trying to muscle up, trying to steel themselves against disappointment.

Noah and Jesse drive out to visit Jesse's mother, Sara, making their way through Death Valley, drunk off desert stars. Sara, who had been so strong throughout Jesse's father's illness, has simply wilted after his death. It seems no shower of love, even from her girls, can raise her back up, but Noah is able to bolster her in a way her own daughters cannot. Noah does many of the things Sara's husband once did, taking out the trash, complimenting her dress, asking for second helpings of her attempt at her husband's enchiladas, spinning her around the living room, even.

On the two-year anniversary of her dad's death, Jesse and Noah make love in her childhood bed. She is ravenous, biting his thumbs as he puts his hand over her mouth to keep her from screaming.

Jesse cries when they are done, pulls her thin pink sheets up to her chin, and Noah holds her, her cheek pressed to his naked chest.

"I miss him so much," she whispers.

"I know." Noah passes his hand over her hair. "We'll have babies one day, and he'll come back to you. You'll see him in their faces. You'll pass on all that love he put in you."

"Promise?" Jesse whispers.

"I promise," Noah answers.

Noah and Jesse sneak out to the backyard with Lucy, and the three of them sit under the grapevines to share a joint.

Noah picks grape after grape, surprised and seduced by the musky flavor, rendered more potent by his high. He remembers their nights on the phone after Jesse lost her father, her sobbing as she ate the fruit. He'd never seen grapes on a vine before, and when Noah pictured her in his mind's eye, he imagined big green supermarket grapes instead of the small globes with powdery, thin skins.

Back in LA, Noah goes to the Sunset nursery after his brunch shift and picks out a potted mandarin tree for their porch, which he begins to tend fastidiously.

Noah and Jesse go to their favorite French cafe for four-dollar glasses of wine at happy hour, filling up on the free baguette, and then wander through The Grove, the adjacent outdoor mall, to the Barnes & Noble, where they imagine Jesse's book on the new-releases table. They get up early to go to the first morning shows of movies at the ArcLight in their hoodies—cappuccino and popcorn for breakfast—and dream of the day when they will be here, in the quiet theater, watching Noah's first film. They are in it together, touching knees beneath the table while they type. They are twins, they say.

The few friends they have must coerce them into outings, but Elenore succeeds in talking them into a drive to Antelope Valley to see the fields of poppies in bloom. They eat the sandwiches Jesse has made and the mushrooms Elenore has brought and stay for hours, minds blown by the orange waves. On the way back, Jesse has a panic attack. She says something about what happened in Paris that Noah can't quite interpret. The only thing that calms her is being pressed against Noah's chest, so Elenore drives while they cuddle in the back.

Noah and Jesse's "couple friends," Cal and his girlfriend,

Suraya, bring them to a party at the home of a moderately successful actor—a good opportunity to network, Cal tells Noah. The house has mirrors everywhere. Suraya, who is tall and always wears heels, towers several inches above Cal, who remains committed to bare feet, ditching his shoes at the door. It is a phenomenon, in Los Angeles: when people meet each other, rather than striking up conversation about a movie, the weather, or politics, the first question is, almost always, "What do you do?" Suraya raises her thick, dark eyebrows and replies, "I dance. I cook. I act. I meditate. I party. I read. I teach yoga. And you?"

Cal, who has an equal flair but an easier smile, grins at his girlfriend. Though Suraya did not grow up rich, she has an air of privilege about her that stems not only from her perfectly manicured fingers and hair, but her lack of need to please anyone, a trait of which Jesse is a bit jealous. When asked the same question, Jesse always says simply that she is an assistant for a producer. She never mentions her novel, which she keeps tucked away like a private love affair.

Grief is like this: an adventure, Jesse's book begins.

Her protagonist is a teenage girl whose father is dying of cancer. The two of them are on the run together, dodging charges for petty theft and bounced checks and eventually a bank robbery they commit in order to pay for his treatment. When he dies, he leaves her behind as an orphaned outlaw, days after her eighteenth birthday. It is by turns a coming-of-age story, a thriller, a fairy tale. The closer Jesse comes to finishing the book, the more it pokes holes in her heart, makes her feel queasy, fluttery, anxious.

She dreams of quitting her job, tired of the late-night texts asking her to come over and fix the internet or pick up high-lighters for a science project and allergy medicine, tired of end-lessly collecting the girls' stream of discarded jackets, socks, shoes from all over the house as Dexter reminds her to call the home security company, to make sure Sari has an aisle seat on their first-class flight to London because she gets claustropho-bic. But of course, Jesse cannot quit—not unless she wants to burn through her dad's life insurance money, which she would never allow herself. It is the prospect of a life as a novelist that sustains her; it is her life with Noah.

Noah writes an action comedy, then a romantic drama. With each new script he finishes, he asks Jesse to read and edit and read again. They go back and forth until the draft is as close to perfect as they can get it. Each time, when Jesse reacts with enthusiasm, Noah's longing swells up. As he takes orders at the Hard Rock in his freshly bought skinny jeans, stained with splashes of soda and splotches of mysterious grease, he feels it like a physical pang—the need to be more. It isn't about just the car, or the clothes, or the house, of course. It is the ache to be known. To be seen.

The pain of burst hope is a certain kind of pain, a pain with teeth, with lingering marks. But it is a pain Noah learns to accept.

Each time he starts again, he lets himself believe that this next one will be the one.

Noah buys a plane ticket for Eric's seventh birthday, and he flies out on his first trip alone. Noah and Jesse stock the fridge with "kid food"; they buy sidewalk chalk and race cars; they make a bed for Eric in the guest room with a new stuffy. But Eric knocks on the door before 11:00 p.m. to get into bed between Jesse and Noah. Noah makes him chocolate milk, Jesse rubs his back, and when he falls to sleep, snoring softly, they make eyes at each other over his curly head and don't need to say what they're both feeling: *we could do this, become parents; this could be our own child between us.*

They are both impatient to get there, or to get closer, at least. The years are racing by.

Noah writes a black comedy, another thriller; they join the graveyard of scripts sitting on his laptop. He has to try something different.

He goes to industry mixers with Cal, who is good at these kinds of events, weaving through the crowds effortlessly with his slender frame, his mess of lose curls, his big laugh. Noah, meanwhile, spends too much time choosing an outfit and then ends up hovering at the edge of the sea of designer purses and tailored suits, wiping sweaty palms on his pants. He buys Xanax off one of the bartenders at work to quell his anxiety and tries again at the mixers.

He finds Katie's email address, the pot-smoking girl he met in his first months in Los Angeles, who assisted the aging producer. He writes her a note, wondering if she can let him know if there's another opportunity to work with them.

She writes back forty-one minutes later—*You must have a sixth sense 'cause we just fired this intern. He was a bummer. Come by on Tuesday if you want.*

Noah is hired on the spot.

Between shifts at the Hard Rock, he drives to Bel Air to run errands for free. Lenny, the producer, is usually on the phone when Noah arrives, talking with exaggerated passion. There is a rotating cast of younger men around, most of them close to Noah's age, often emerging from the bedroom in the mornings.

Katie, the only woman in the house, spends most of the day working in Lenny's office, coming out occasionally to smoke a joint or give Noah his tasks. Noah buys macrobiotic sandwiches for lunch whenever someone whom Lenny deems important comes over. He takes Butch III, the third bulldog in a succession of Butches who sleep at the foot of Lenny's bed, to the vet. He buys parrot food for Tyga, the bird named by one of Lenny's past boyfriends, whose lasting legacy in the house is having taught Tyga to say "Rack city, bitch" on repeat. Noah does all of it on the off chance that eventually Lenny will take an interest and read some of Noah's work, fall in love with it, and make his first movie in twenty years using Noah's script. Or that at least Lenny will somehow connect Noah to a new set of contacts who haven't already rejected him.

When Katie rests her hand on his biceps, Noah tells her he has a girlfriend. She tells him that she does, too.

When Jesse finally finishes her novel, Noah gets his shifts covered and stays in bed all weekend with the book as she circles him with anxious expectation. And then, as she is getting out of the shower on the third day, he comes in. "It's so beautiful, Jess," he says. He launches into his thoughts right there, as she stands naked in the bathroom. He has already emailed his notes. When she reads them later, still in her towel, she feels a surge of gratitude. He pushes her harder than any of her other readers could, and she gets back to work.

She writes painstaking query letters to agents that she edits and edits again. She sends them out, mostly over email, but some older, more established agents still prefer submissions by mail. She goes to the post office to select her stamps—she buys Cactus Flowers, First Moon Landing, Voices of the Harlem Renaissance, Bengal Tigers, and selects one for each letter based on what she imagines of the agent she's querying. She buys new pens from a stationery store on Larchmont Boulevard and addresses the envelopes in smooth black ink and drives back to the post office to put them in the mail, superstitiously wanting to deposit them into the big blue box herself.

It is not until now that Jesse can fully taste her own hunger. Like many women, she had learned to dampen her ambition, even in the privacy of her own room. She'd dreamt of getting published, yes, of living the life of a writer instead of an assistant. But the part of her that wants what Noah wants, not just to be published, but to become significant, legendary, even, had hardly made itself known. Now, as she officially sends her book into the world, she is surprised by the ferocity of her own desire.

She waits, and reads, and folds laundry and drives to the sea and goes for walks and picks up Sari from ballet class and Maya from soccer practice, drives Lexi to the Westfield mall during rush hour, and buys groceries for Noah and herself and counts out Dexter's pills into his pill case and tries not to count the days.

The rejections trickle in slowly. She doesn't say anything about it to Noah. She stitches up the wounds swiftly and moves on, has an extra glass of wine that evening, maybe.

Jesse mails new letters to new agents, juices the few fruits harvested from Noah's mandarin tree on the porch, celebrates her birthday with a visit from Lucy and her new girlfriend, Mei, who come on their way to travel in Central America.

Lucy insists they all go to Disneyland. She and Jesse visited once as children on vacation with their parents, and they repeat the childhood joys they remember, filling up on Dole Whip and cotton candy. Jesse is just as terrified on Splash Mountain as she was as a girl, gripping on to Noah as she once had on to her dad.

On Lucy and Mei's last night, they go to the Beverly Hills Hotel and order sidecars, their father's drink. Jesse gets drunk and cries in Lucy's arms.

"Don't leave," Jesse says. "Stay with me."

Lucy hugs her older sister, promises they'll visit again soon. Jesse wants to keep her, but she knows she cannot; Lucy's way of surviving her grief is to stay in motion.

Before work Jesse makes yogurt and berries for herself and for Noah, brings it to him in bed. He's under the covers with his laptop, writing before he has to go to his internship.

"Bye, Strawberry," he says, pulling at Jesse's arm so she won't go. She has her purse over her shoulder; she's almost late.

"Bye, Blueberry," she answers.

He kisses her nose. She laughs.

"No, wait, you're not a blueberry, 'cause you're bigger than I am," she says.

"Watermelon?" he offers.

"Bye, Watermelon," she says, as he pulls her on top of him.

"Careful, that's racist, though." He smiles.

"Okay, Pineapple," she says.

"But you're more like a pineapple," he says.

"Why? 'Cause I'm sweet and sour?"

"And you take a lot of work to get into," he says.

"Who says you don't?!" she retorts.

He laughs.

"Just 'cause it's all the good fruit now," she says, "doesn't mean I didn't have to work for it!"

He grins. "Touché." He lifts her fingers to his lips, then shakes her hand. "Nice to love you, Jesse."

"Nice to love you, Noah."

He pulls her back once more for a kiss before releasing her. "Come back soon."

"Promise."

As Jesse walks out, down the eucalyptus-lined path, past the tangles of jasmine, she tells herself that she will remember what it is like to love Noah on September 6, 2012, how it fills her on a regular day.

Maybe some part of Jesse senses that she will miss this feeling of being on the brink. The time in which everything is still possible. She is miserable at her assistant job. Noah confronts failure after failure in his quest to get noticed. Still, they have told each other that their dreams will come true, that one day they will be writers, moviemakers, and the strength of their love bolsters that claim, makes it sturdy enough that they can believe in it.

# 11

2003

On Goldstone Road, string lights twinkle, trays of oyster shells float in the melting ice on the long wood table under the oak, voices scatter into the warm night. Juliette is nineteen today, the fourth of August, and everything is possible. She tosses her head back to slurp one of the last oysters, sips on the small glass of Riesling her mother poured for her. She is lit by the string lights, by the soft glow of a fading sunset, by her laughter.

Juliette has the same texture as these last days of summer, Annie thinks: the ripe fruit hanging heavy on its branches, sweetest of the season, the sunlight turning richer, softer. That feeling she gets in her stomach before the thermostat can register it: the ache of nostalgia that says the end is near. The air will chill, the leaves will fall, the darkness of night will inch its way into the afternoon. But—not yet! For now, these are the golden days. The peaches and plums burst with juice, the ocean water is warm, and they can lay out in their swimsuits, in their girlhood, forever.

———

Annie, sitting beside Juliette, wears her hair in the same crown braid Juliette first gave her four years ago. She sips her wine and runs her finger over the red print of her lips left behind on the glass. A mild, salty air brushes against her hot cheeks.

Margot arrives from the kitchen in a black silk dress, rumpled just enough to match her just-rumpled-enough hair, carrying homemade pizzas that Annie and Juliette helped assemble before the party. Juliette slips a little bit more Riesling into Annie's glass. Leonard Cohen's voice drifts out of the house, mingling with the conversation of photographers and reporters and authors and gallery owners and producers of independent films who have all watched Juliette grow from a tiny, precocious, wide-eyed child into a "remarkable young woman."

A couple years ago, Annie and Juliette would have been figuring out where to party later, whom they'd hook up with, but by now they're bored with it all and prefer Margot's dinner parties. They know how to talk to these grown-ups. They like impressing them, they like feeling adult themselves, and they like the way the adults look at them as if they possess an invaluable treasure: their youth. They like knowing that later they'll surreptitiously pick the unfinished bottles of wine off the table and pour them into a canteen, shout out that they are going on a walk, and stumble together through the dark, letting their long shadows lead the way, passing clove cigarettes back and forth, talking about the future: if you fell in love with the best trombone player in Paris and he wanted you to live with him in his apartment in the Marais and go to jazz clubs and drink fancy French wine every night, would you choose him, or would you stay with me? If you went on a Safari in

Africa and the guide was the most beautiful man you'd ever met, and he asked you to marry him and you could spend the rest of your life making love and watching the lions and leopards, would you choose him or me? If you met the most brilliant poet and he wrote you love poems he read aloud to you under the stars, would you choose him or me? If the future president proposed and promised to go down on you in the Oval Office every night, would you choose him or me? It's a game they play. The answer is always the same: *You. I would choose you.*

For now, as the sky darkens, Margot carries out a peach pie lit with candles, and the grown-ups erupt into an enthusiastic chorus of "Happy Birthday." Annie watches as Juliette leans in, taking her time with a wish as wax begins to drip onto the perfect golden crust. They have graduated high school. They are about to start the rest of their lives. The August of their girlhood, ready to drop from the branch.

Annie unconsciously brushes her fingers over her lips. She feels as if there is a soft animal inside her, turning over, waking up. It is ravenous. It knows, Annie thinks, that the season is changing soon—knows that it must satiate its hunger while there is still fruit on the trees. Margot brings out the good Scotch, and the adults linger outside around the firepit, passing a joint. Juliette takes a half-finished bottle of wine from the kitchen. She fills the bathtub with bubbles and puts on Nico, and Annie sits beside her on the floor, drinking from the bottle and reading to Juliette from the Audre Lorde book she bought for Juliette's birthday—along with Eavan Boland, James Galvin, and a pretty journal bound in blue and gold, where Annie has written her own poem to Juliette and left the rest of the book blank for her to use next year.

Juliette dips her head underwater for a long moment before she comes up with her dark hair slicked back.

She looks at Annie. "How will I live without you next year?"

"I don't know." The smell of the gardenia bubble bath is intoxicating.

"We were stupid for not going to the same school."

"I'd never have gotten into U of C."

Juliette turns off the tap, and the absence of running water leaves a sudden silence.

"If in New York you meet a modern dancer from Alvin Ailey who takes you on walks in Central Park when the leaves are changing, and holds your hand and buys you chestnuts and goes down on you every night and makes you coffee and toast with jam every morning, and he wants you to marry him and never come home to me, who will you choose?"

"You," Annie says. But for the first time she worries. She worries about choosing Juliette as much as she worries about Juliette choosing her. Their lives are splitting. They will no longer spend their days together. They will no longer share the nuances of the way the sun falls through a room; they will no longer share the fruit they collected from the trees or the details of the book for their English class; they will no longer share clothes mashed together in a giant pile, or the same shade of lipstick pulled from each other's purses, or their reflection in Margot's photographs. If they each grow into their new lives, if they build lives in their new cities, maybe they won't know how to come home to each other, maybe the canyon between them will grow too deep, maybe they won't know how to tell each other what if feels like to walk through the streets of Chicago or New York. Maybe they will fall in love with other people.

———

Annie lies in her underwear under the rose-printed quilt, reading the poems to herself now. She is tired but alert. Every sensation registers in her body: the cool sheets on her skin, the sight of Juliette moving through the candlelit room as she dries and dresses after the bath, the murmuring laughter of Margot and her last lingering friends drifting in through the window.

As Juliette gets into bed, her leg brushes over Annie's leg under the sheets and the feeling blows through Annie's whole body with a gale force. When she feels Juliette's leg a second time, Annie knows that what has woken inside of her has woken in Juliette, too; she knows that it is the defenseless animal of desire, who has been here all along, between them, sleeping. As Annie lets her hand creep tentatively forward and rest along Juliette's hip, her heart lands each beat with an ungraceful thud.

Juliette rolls over and smiles at her, and without a word, without a hesitation, kisses Annie. As she climbs on top of Annie, the thick, damp curtain of Juliette's hair falls around them, hiding their two faces from the world. Annie is still, she is on fire, as Juliette starts to move her body over Annie's, and then Juliette giggles.

"I love you," she says, and sounds like a child. It is enough to remind Annie that it isn't a sudden stranger she is about to make love to, but her best friend, her chosen one, her Juliette. She squeezes Juliette's leg between her own, she runs her hands over her breasts, she flips her around so that her dark hair falls over the pillow and moves her mouth down Juliette's body. Juliette stuffs the rose quilt into her face, bites down on the fabric to keep quiet while outside the adults continue their chatter, getting a little drunker, a little louder.

When they are done making love Juliette says she wants to go to the sea, and then she wraps her arms around Annie and drifts off with her head on Annie's chest while Annie lets her hand fall asleep under Juliette's weight, dreaming half-awake dreams of fairy-tale forests, galleries of photographs, her mother, lost in a crowd.

The next morning, Annie wakes up to Juliette's hand brushing over her underwear, Juliette's mouth on the back of her neck, and they make love again, Margot asleep in the next room on the couch.

They do not tell Margot about their newborn romance, but Annie feels as if she must know, must smell the electricity between them, no less distinct than ozone. Or maybe she'd already seen it, sensed their desire even before Annie and Juliette became aware.

Annie and Juliette make love constantly for the next ten days, until Juliette calls Annie, choking on her own cries.

The only words she can say are "No. No. No."

And finally, "No. Annie. She's dead. She died."

Annie knows who Juliette means, of course. Her body drops out of itself.

# 12

The car hit Margot while she was crossing the Pacific Coast Highway, on her way back from a swim. She was dead in seconds. Juliette is nineteen now, so there will be no state apparatus to swoop in and make sure that she is cared for, that she has a guardian, that she is guarded.

Annie arrives with her dad, comes rushing into the house and finds Juliette curled, unmoving, on the bed. The next days are a blur: a cascade of disbelief, raw despair. Juliette's father helps with the arrangements; Annie's does too. Juliette plays hostess to the stream of mourners, just as her mom would have, ordering bagels and lox, cheese plates and charcuterie spreads. She goes through Margot's hidden stash of dry Riesling at an alarming rate, as people move in and out of the house—the same adults who populated Margot's parties, who have seen Juliette grow up over the years, who, just weeks ago, were sitting outside, getting drunk in the garden. They grip Juliette's arms too tightly. "You look so much like her," they say, tearing up. Juliette nods vaguely, sips her wine. "She loved you so much," they say. "You were her whole world." And "Honey, tell me if you need anything, anything at all. I'm always here."

And then they are gone.

For the next days, grief is like this: when she isn't sobbing, or sleeping, Juliette sits out in the garden under the peach tree, spooning Annie's mashed potatoes—the only thing she can eat—into her mouth slowly in the heat, rubbing the mint leaves between her fingers. It seems Juliette could stay there forever, rooting into the ground of Goldstone.

Lina comes to offer whatever form of maternal comfort she can muster, but Juliette has no room for anyone else's grief, and she shuts up like a clamshell, refusing to witness Lina's tears.

Annie's dad brings dinner, pasta dishes, biscotti. In the moments he is there, he is the grown-up, the caretaker; Annie feels palpable relief at his presence, which is quickly eclipsed by guilt: her friend will never again have the solace of her parent. Annie wants him to carry her to the car like he did when she was a girl, to take her home, but instead she kisses him good night and stays with Juliette, while he goes home to Sandra.

Juliette's own father offers his guest room to his daughter, but Juliette, of course, declines. At first he, too, comes around a couple times a week to bring dinner and sits at Margot's long table, making sporadic attempts at conversation—the weather, the Dodgers, the twins—while Juliette silently picks at her food. But soon he starts calling instead to invite Juliette to eat at his house with him and Jana and the boys, now twelve, almost intolerable. Juliette accepts the invitation once, but the twins' rude humor and Jana's doting over her sons—*More milk, sweetie? Here, honey, let me get you another napkin—* fill Juliette with rage. Grief is like this: fire. She sits there, tears running down her cheeks, waiting for someone to notice. Her father does, she thinks, but decides to ignore it.

Finally, Juliette texts Annie in the middle of the meal: *please come get me.* She stands wordlessly and pushes her chair in, goes to wait outside her father's home sweet home, with the sunflowers and the bikes. Moments before Annie pulls up, Jack comes out to sit beside her, pats her back in silence. When Annie's Toyota arrives, hovering along the curb, Juliette gets up and doesn't look back.

There is Annie, and only Annie.

In the confines of Goldstone Road, Juliette spends the final weeks of the summer of 2003 piling dishes in the sink, padding around the house in the same sweats. Annie washes the dishes, runs baths for Juliette. She washes the dirty sweats while Juliette is in the tub.

Eventually, Annie persuades Juliette to get out of the house and drive down to the beach for a walk. The sky is gray, wearing the marine layer like a mourning cloak. They are quiet, watching the pelicans dive. People say grief comes in waves, but Annie has not yet seen Juliette's recede. She cannot think of what to say; she cannot remember ever having been at a loss for words beside her best friend. Suddenly, without warning, Juliette turns and runs straight into the sea, wearing her same sweatpants, and dives under. Annie's heart stops. She runs toward the water, ready to go in after her, when Juliette finally surfaces.

That night Annie walks into the bedroom to find Juliette dressed for the first time in weeks, wearing her mom's flowy skirt, her eyes painted dark, her hair down and wild. They use their fake IDs to get into an out-of-the-way bar in the valley, where Juliette drinks too much, makes eyes at anyone who glances her way. She goes to the bathroom and takes too long to return; Annie finds her in a dark corner, making out with a man too old for her by at least twenty years. She interrupts, pulls Juliette into a cab with her. She is angry—angry at her for being reckless, angry at her for making out with someone else—but Annie won't say it, not now. Juliette senses the anger anyway. She reaches out, touches Annie's wrist. Her voice drops into a childlike whisper.

"Sorry," she says to Annie. "Don't be mad."

"You have to be careful," Annie answers. Whatever sexuality had blossomed between them so briefly is over for now. Juliette is untouchable.

Or, rather, she wants Annie to touch her only as a mother would touch a child—her back tickled, her head stroked or laid in a lap, her body spooned gently. Annie sings to her: over and over, she sings "All the Tired Horses," which Margot used to sing for a lullaby when Juliette was a little girl. Juliette clutches Annie in her sleep, the grief coming off her body like heat.

The dread in Annie's stomach is constant, a dizzying sense that the world has spun out of control, that it will never be righted. There is no room for Annie's grief beside Juliette's, which demands all the space in every room.

Part of Annie feels that Margot should be recording this, that if her camera could capture her daughter curled into herself in the garden, sobbing in the tub, drinking the weeks-old cooking wine when she runs out of Riesling, then she could somehow weave beauty into the pulverizing loss, could transform this grief into art.

After Juliette has gone to sleep one evening, Annie picks up the Bronica and looks through the lens, but she finds no trace of Margot's magic. There is no one to behold them now, no one to rescue their girlhood from time.

"I had a dream I was in a desert," Juliette murmurs, half waking when Annie gets into bed. "All I could see were hills of white sand. I kept walking and walking and nothing changed. I screamed, but then I realized there was no one to hear me, no one to see me, so I must not be there. Like I didn't really exist. It was just this feeling of nothingness."

Annie brushes the dark hair away from Juliette's forehead. "I see you," she says quietly. "I'm here. You're here."

Juliette looks at her.

"We're here," Annie says, confirming it. "We're still here."

Juliette nods.

"What do you want to do?" Annie asks. August is nearly over. Annie's father has been asking Annie about leaving for school. Annie's desperate to get out of Goldstone, to stop their free fall.

"We can take the year off, go spend it in France," Annie suggests. "You have the life insurance and the money from the photographs. Maybe I can get a job teaching English."

Juliette shrugs. "My mom already bought my ticket to Chicago."

"Are you sure you still want to go?"

"She already bought the ticket," Juliette says, again. "And we got my Chicago coat. And all the dorm stuff."

Annie feels her guts twist up: it was the last plan that Juliette made with her mother, Margot's last contribution to the direction of her life, and so Juliette will follow it.

Annie is meant to go off to school in a week, Juliette in three. Annie asks Juliette if she wants her to change plans, but Juliette says no. Annie can't miss the beginning of the year. Annie is scared to leave—Juliette doesn't seem ready to survive on her own—but she also feels a guilt-ridden sense of relief.

Their last night together, Annie insists they throw a dinner party, just for them. They make Margot's Roman pizzas and a tart with the last of the summer peaches. They both get properly dressed up—lipstick and Margot's jewelry. They light candles and eat in the garden and get drunk on the last of the good Riesling (the two bottles Annie had hidden from Juliette while she was binging). They cry because everything is lost, but they promise to call every day, to visit, to write, to love each other forever.

# 13

2013

By the time Noah gets off his shift and finishes his side work—refilling the ketchup bottles from a giant jug, wiping down sticky menus, slicing lemons—and cashes out past seven, he exits to an absurdly lovely spring evening, purple-skied, warm-aired, soft from distant ocean water. A nearly full moon rising. If you can't find some hope on a night like tonight, you're done for.

He takes a hit of a spliff on the drive down Hollywood Boulevard, past the throngs of tourists, the out-of-work actors in character suits, and calls Jesse, leaves a message: *I'm on my way, just wanted to tell you to go outside if you aren't already, the sky is crazy beautiful. Love you.* He turns into the canyon in his dented Impala, dog hair from Butch III ground into the passenger seat, and turns up Kanye singing about working at the Gap and waiting on his spaceship. Noah remembers wandering the streets of Hyde Park as a high school kid with this album in his headphones, promising himself to fly away.

He pulls up to Dexter Lilly's house, where they're staying for the next five months while Dexter's away on set (the girls are with their mother). Jesse decided they needed a change of pace, and some air-conditioning, so they packed up their old apartment into boxes, planning to save on rent and get a new spot when Dexter returns. Noah got rid of bags of belongings but carted his impossibly heavy potted mandarin tree all the way here. It has become a symbol—one of the only things in his life to come to fruition.

The tree now sits in the garden, where he finds Jesse with her laptop and her wine, framed by plum blossoms, her skin luminous in the low light. She is in the final stages of rewrites on her book, working with a fancy agent. After months of blind queries, one of the first women who Jesse wrote to replied, asked to read her manuscript, and then to sign her. She is in front of her computer at all hours, and Noah has seen how she picks up her phone constantly to check her inbox after sending in a draft, waiting for Ellen's reply, while she pretends there is nothing happening.

Meanwhile, five years into his move to LA, and Noah has nothing to show for it but a bank account that gets drained every month, a closet full of black T-shirts with grease stains, and a newfound knowledge of the gourmet food preferences of pets—venison and squash for Butch III; bean sprouts, zucchini, blackberries, and apricots when they are in season for Tyga the parrot.

Noah's two closest boys from college went to New York after graduation and are both making six-figure salaries already. John is working his way up in the restaurant world, and Afreem, who's in finance, got married last fall. *That artist life takes time*, John tells Noah over text, trying to be kind. But these dreams Noah's been reaching for feel further away by the day.

He's begun to feel that only his relationship to Jesse—her elegance, her intelligence, her success—differentiates him from the wayward Hollywood boys rotating through Lenny's house. Boys who came here to become someone but couldn't find the right ladder to climb. Boys who came with nothing and so are likely to have next to nothing, forever.

When Jesse sees Noah arriving, she shuts her laptop. She looks at home here, as if she were made for a house like this, and Noah feels a flare of shame that he cannot give it to her, the life she deserves.

"Hey, boo," she says.

"Hi," he says, and kisses her.

"How was work?"

"Fine. The usual bullshit. How's writing?"

"Okay."

"You heard from Ellen?"

"Yeah," Jesse says, without inflection. "She sent a few last notes." She gets up.

Jesse doesn't talk about how Ellen is about to send her book out to publishers. She keeps her joy, her eagerness, her anxiousness from him. He knows that she doesn't want to draw attention to her own success, but it makes him lonely.

"You don't have to stop."

"I was gonna go in anyway. You wanna watch something?"

That night Noah undresses her and pulls her on top of him, slaps her naked ass. "I love how you fuck me," she says. When they are done, he pulls her in to his body, wraps himself around her, and holds her, and, for a moment, doesn't feel so useless, so small.

He creeps out of bed once she is asleep and goes into the kitchen, where he sits at the table, eating peanut butter out of the jar with a spoon next to his old, heavy-ass laptop.

The simple darkness would almost be easier to take than the slim chance, the sliver of golden light through the door that has been left open, just a crack—maybe this time, maybe the next one.

He starts to type.

Two months later, the summer is beginning to peek out from under the "June gloom." Jesse is lying next to the pool, basking in the sunlight, when her phone rings. It's Ellen; she's sold the book. The advance is far more than Jesse could have hoped for as a first-time novelist, and Ellen's turned it into a contract for a second book (though Jesse has no idea what she'll write).

Jesse hangs up and dives into the still-cold water of Dexter's pool. She is about to become an author. She's about to become an author! She swims back and forth, trying to wear herself out, to quiet the thrill and the fear pulsing through her body, but no matter how hard she swims, she can't feel the exhaustion in her muscles.

Noah is inside writing. Finally (How long has it been, an hour? More?) Jesse wraps herself in a towel, her hair still dripping, and goes in through the French doors, stands in front of the long wooden table where Noah types, deep in focus. Her heart beats rapidly from the exercise or the adrenaline or both.

He looks up at her, raises his eyebrows.

"What's up?"

"Ellen sold it."

He stands, grinning. "Jess. I knew it! I'm so proud of you."

He wraps his arms around her, pulls her against the muscles

of his chest. She presses her wet head to his T-shirt, feels her body finally release.

He lets her go.

"How much?" he asks.

"Two hundred and twenty . . . thousand . . . But that includes a second book."

"Damn," he says, taken aback. "Wow."

"Yeah. I mean, I don't get it all at once. It comes in pieces. For the different stages. It'll be over a few years, by the time I finish the second book and it comes out and all," she explains, trying to lighten the weight of the number that hovers between them.

Noah nods. Jesse is dripping water on the floor.

"I'll buy you dinner tonight." She laughs.

He smiles back, but it doesn't reach his eyes. "I was gonna try and get a little more work in," he says.

"Okay. Maybe we could go in an hour or two?"

"Of course. Whatever you want."

"Okay. I'm gonna go shower," she says.

She does, and when she comes out, she finds him still typing in the kitchen. She pours a glass of wine and goes out to the porch to call her mom.

Sara bubbles over with happiness, wants to hear every detail, tells Jesse she is going to make a sidecar to celebrate, in honor of her father. They add Jesse's sister, Lucy, to the call. Lucy screams in delight, calls out to Mei in the background. "Oh my god, my sister sold her book! She's gonna be a real author!"

Jesse smiles.

"I have a famous sister," Lucy says to her, and Jesse laughs.

Jesse wishes they were back in Albuquerque, going to the Slate Street Cafe, the fancy restaurant where the three of them had often eaten after leaving the hospital, ordering truffle fries to make themselves feel better. She aches for them in that moment, her mother and sister. She aches for her dad. This, the achievement she has been striving for, and she cannot share it with him. She watches the purple flowers floating into the pool, the flat blue sky, and wonders if it will always be this way: will every moment of happiness give way to grief?

Jesse finishes her wine and goes inside, puts on a dress and mascara, ties her hair back the way that Noah likes it. She wanders into the kitchen, where he is still typing, and feels a twinge of impatience.

"Are we going to dinner?" she asks.

"Yeah." He is still looking at his computer. "Where do you wanna go?"

"I don't know. I was thinking we could just go down the hill to that little place we always pass by, next to the market."

"Okay. I need to change." He squints at his screen, types something.

"We don't have to if you don't want to," Jesse says, holding in her mounting irritation.

He looks up. "It's up to you."

Jesse sighs, feeling something in her deflate. "I guess I kinda wanted to celebrate."

"Let's go, then." He gets up, shuts his laptop.

Noah valets the car and they walk up to the small, crowded restaurant tucked into Laurel Canyon.

There are white tablecloths, white men in button-up shirts, white women with gold earrings. Noah and Jesse are seated in the corner, next to an all-white jazz band that begins to play.

The music is so loud they have to nearly shout to speak to each other.

"What's wrong?" Jesse asks Noah. She already knows that he doesn't want to be here, doesn't want to be with these people.

"Nothing, I'm fine," Noah shouts back. When she doesn't say anything, he shakes his head a little. "Don't look for problems, please."

Jesse orders wine. Noah orders soda water with lime. He toasts her. "Congratulations. I'm so proud of you."

Jesse wipes tears from her eyes. Everything is wrong. Everything feels wrong.

"Are you okay?"

Jesse shrugs. Neither of them speaks. She continues to dab at her eyes.

"Do you want to go?" Noah asks after a moment.

"Okay," Jesse says.

Noah asks the waiter to pack their pasta and hands him a card before Jesse can.

They exit in silence. Jesse feels lightheaded. She trips in her platform shoes on the uneven cobblestone. Maybe she shouldn't have had that wine before dinner; she wants more.

"Are you okay?" Noah asks again, as they wait for the car.

"Are you?"

"I'm fine. What's going on?"

"I just wanted to have a nice celebration night."

"Jess—"

The car arrives. Noah opens her door before the valet can, hands the man a ten-dollar tip.

He looks at her for a moment before pulling off. "You know I'm not into places like that, but I was down to go for you."

"I don't get why you couldn't just try to have a good time with me. Today is one of the biggest days of my life," Jesse says. And then, before he can reply, "Whatever. It doesn't really matter." It is a habit—protecting her anger, letting it out only a little bit, then drawing it back inside her.

Why couldn't he? Noah wants to say that he's not a celebration person, that he didn't grow up with that, but it's not really true, or it was true only after his mother passed. In the first years of Noah's life, they celebrated every good grade in school with donuts and dance parties. His mom would push the furniture to the edges of the room, put Marvin Gaye on the tape deck, and take Noah's hands as they spun across the floor together. Birthday parties were full-on affairs they spent weeks planning for. Noah helped with most of the preparations, but his mom always baked his cake on his birthday eve after he'd gone to bed, so it would be a surprise. She was bedridden by the time he turned seven, so her last cake came on his sixth birthday. It was Ninja Turtles themed. She was already starting to get sick then, and when Noah got up to pee that night, he saw her sitting to rest on the linoleum floor in the kitchen. But the cake was perfect. She had all the right color icings for the headbands. Donatello, Noah's favorite, was front and center.

"I guess it's just hard for me to be excited about spending a hundred dollars on pasta right now," Noah says as he stops at the light at Lookout Mountain. He knows it's the wrong thing to say.

It is code for: *Ritzy restaurants make me uncomfortable because when I was a kid, I watched my mom working her ass off to clean up after everyone in the cafeteria and we got by mostly eating leftovers from there. Because, later, when I ate what my uncle left for dinner, sometimes I was still hungry but there was nothing else there and no money.*

It is code for: *I'm broke right now and the idea of letting you pay for dinner makes me feel like a failure.*

It is code for: *Your success scares me, because I'm afraid you'll leave me.*

Jesse hears only his impassive tone. "I was going to pay," she answers.

"I can't be the Black dude in that white-ass restaurant who lets his girl pay for dinner."

Jesse stares out the window as Noah navigates the car up the canyon, wiping tears she tries to hide.

"The music was bad, anyway," she says, finally—an olive branch.

"Yep," Noah agrees. They ride in silence. He passes the turnoff for the house. She wonders where they are going but doesn't ask.

After a moment, he reaches out, puts his hand on her thigh.

"I'm sorry," he says. "I'm an asshole. You deserve better than that."

"Yep," Jesse answers, and they laugh a little bit. Noah puts on music—Marvin Gaye singing "Ain't No Mountain High Enough." Jesse lets her arm float out the window.

Twenty minutes later they arrive downtown to Grand Central Market. Jesse had forgotten about it, but they came here not long after moving to the city, when they were still exploring LA; she found it entirely romantic.

Noah leads her through the building, a collection of food stalls inside an open-air warehouse. He seems to be looking for something specific, and then they find it: an oyster bar that

Jesse doesn't remember. She loves oysters. Noah orders dozens of them, asks the bartender to select the best wine.

"How did you know this was here?"

"I was looking up the best spots for oysters in LA."

"You were?" It's hard for her to imagine Noah sitting around reading restaurant reviews.

"I was trying to think of where I might propose to you. When the time comes."

"Oh." Jesse feels a pang in her chest. Love always has the final say between them, it seems. Searching for the anger from earlier, she finds it faded.

The bartender pours Chablis. Noah raises his glass. "To your book. I'm so proud of you."

Jesse sips the flinty wine, leans her head on Noah's shoulder. All she wants in this moment is to crawl into him, to stay there.

# 14

"Yo," Noah says, as he approaches Katie, who is smoking her joint on Lenny's porch. "I gotta ask you something."

"Can you bring me a cap first?"

"All right."

Noah returns with her cappuccino, cinnamon sprinkled on top. He takes a hit of her joint when she offers it.

"You're looking buff," she says. "Are you taking steroids?"

"No."

"Good. Jeremy was taking them, apparently, and Lenny said he couldn't get it up."

"You think there's anything in this job for me, for real? To help me move forward? 'Cause y'all are cool, but I can't play errand-boy-slash-barista forever." It's been ten months, and the hours are eating into his time for writing. Jesse thinks he should quit.

"Maybe I can get Lenny to give you a little money. We've got a project we need help with."

"What's that?"

"Lobby cards." Lobby cards—small movie posters from the 1910s to 1940s, meant for the lobbies of theaters.

Lenny's friend, a famous writer/director, has a brother who just died. The brother was a hoarder who left behind a massive collection of lobby cards, potentially worth millions, which must now be excavated and organized. The writer/director is one of the writer/directors Noah hopes to emulate, an Academy Award winner. As Katie talks, he feels a thrill surge through his body.

He speaks to Lenny, and in exchange for Noah's help with the cards, he negotiates three hundred dollars a week and, more important, the promise that Lenny will share one of Noah's scripts with the writer/director. Noah agonizes for days over which script to send, begs Jesse to reread all five he's considering and help him decide.

When Noah knocks on the heavy wooden door of the home hidden in the Hollywood Hills, he's greeted by two greyhounds, followed by a fragile woman with long gray hair and a loosely belted robe.

"Hello—" Noah tries. The woman gestures to a narrow set of stairs inside the spacious but overcrowded home before she vanishes. The light filtering through stained-glass windows catches thousands of dust particles, making the air look alive.

As Noah steps inside, the sickly smell of the home overpowers him. It seems to travel all the way into his organs. He gags, runs outside, and vomits into the bougainvillea. How can white people begin with so much privilege and fuck it up so royally?

He throws up three more times before he has managed to load the entire collection—box after box of cards—into the rented U-Haul truck.

The smell of the home still clings to the boxes, vaguely, even after Noah has unloaded them into Lenny's guesthouse, and over the next weeks sometimes Noah has to take a break from his project of cataloging to breathe clean air on the deck. Nonetheless, there is something mesmerizing about the work—ancient Hollywood, painstakingly preserved under the layers of filth. Noah is a million miles from the place he imagined he was going when he drove Dev's Impala out of Chicago, across the country. But the dead brother who collected all these artifacts must have also believed in the magic dust of Los Angeles; Noah has an inkling that maybe he's finally been touched by a little bit of it. He rewatches the writer/director's movies, and he and Jesse finally settle on (what she considers) a smartly plotted, arty thriller to share.

"Money Trees" blasts from Noah's Impala as he makes his way through gridlocked traffic on Sunset Boulevard, trying to get out of Bel Air, refreshing his email. And then there is one from the writer/director: *Thank you, friend, for piecing together my brother's life's work. We grew up in a cave, of sorts—real darkness in our midwestern childhoods. Not everyone makes it out. Your writing is very good. Would you like me to share your work with an agent on my team? He's a dog, but Hollywood's a dog fight.*

Noah is euphoric. He has to slam on his brakes before he hits the car ahead of him.

Three weeks later, the director forwards the agent's reply: *Dude's a good writer. I like his voice. Shoot me his info?*

It is finally happening! Noah has a meeting with an agent. After all these years. He changes clothes five times, half his wardrobe draped over the bed, tries on six different pairs of sneakers, diligently scrubbing the smallest smudges from his soles. He puts his diamond studs in—a birthday gift from Jesse—and takes them out, then puts them back in again. He leaves an hour earlier than he needs to.

On the way out the door, Noah swears he smells his mother's perfume. He cannot help but feel that she is beside him. As he winds his way into Beverly Hills, he is remembering himself as a child in Chicago, walking beside her on the way to Ray Elementary. By the time he'd started kindergarten, his mom had saved enough to rent a third-floor walk-up on the very edge of Hyde Park. She was hell-bent on Hyde Park, because she wanted to make sure that Noah went to a good school. A school good enough for the children of professors, even.

After Noah's mom dropped him off every morning, she continued on to work. Noah's grandfather or uncle often picked him up, and he'd beg to go and visit her. They'd park outside the main campus dining hall, usually in a loading zone, and wait in the car as Noah would push through the heavy double doors and run up to his mom, her hair up in a net with a little white hat, cleaning the tables.

"Baby!" she'd say, breaking into her beautiful smile.

She'd get him a soft-serve ice cream from the machine and let him sit in one of the big chairs eating it while she went about her work sweeping floors, wiping down tables smeared in ketchup, stacking trays of half-eaten food. When she didn't know he was looking, she'd hold on to her back, or bend slightly to relieve the pressure. *Why can't they clean up their own trays?* he'd thought, watching as the students got up without a second glance. They passed by his mother as though they didn't even see she was there. From time to time, she'd sit beside Noah for a moment and tell him, "You're going to be one of these college kids one day."

She sent him home to do his homework, brought leftover

lasagna or slices of pizza or oily Chinese food from the hall back for dinner; she served it on the gold-rimmed plates she'd inherited from her grandmother. Wednesdays were her day off, the day that Noah got out of school early. She would pick him up herself those days, and they'd take the train downtown to the Museum of Science and Industry (Noah's favorite) or the Art Institute (hers). When they got home, there was chili on the stove, cookies ready to bake. She read to him before they ate; she stroked his head.

"Noah, you're going to build us an ark," she said.

Noah passes the hotel valet and parks five blocks away, checks his hair in the review mirror, pulls his curl brush out of his glovebox. He is nervous but buoyant. This could be it. He'll sign with the agent. His script will sell. He'll quit Hard Rock, he'll pay for Eric to go to The Lab School, he and Jesse will get married, he'll make a movie, he'll buy her a house, they'll have a baby—

He finds the agent, Josh, at the bar, wearing a baseball cap, designer sneakers, drinking a glass of white wine. He's close to Noah's age, a junior on the director's team. "Hey, bro. What's up," he says as Noah arrives. "Nice to meet you."

Noah smiles his too-big smile. He sits on the stool beside Josh and orders a beer he doesn't touch. Josh tells Noah he really liked his script, that he thinks Noah's a good writer— but. But the main character feels a little angry. Noah makes himself smile again, says no problem, he could work on that.

"I don't know if this is the one," Josh says. "I have to be honest; I found the concept a little generic. But you've got a great voice. People are really digging diverse voices right now. What else you got?" Noah ignores the seizing feeling in his chest, his heart squeezed out like the lemon the bartender is juicing for some craft cocktail. A waiter passes by—a Black man in a suit and tie—carrying a plate of meats and cheeses. Noah tells Josh about the romantic comedy, the action comedy, the family drama. Josh is only half listening.

"I'd definitely be down to read your next thing," he says. "Once you find your lane, you could be big." And then he tries to make small talk about basketball.

Josh is the same as the white boys Noah went to school with at U of C, in Lacoste polos and baseball caps, lightly wrinkled linen, and overpriced sneakers, always certain of their right to speak in class, of the importance of their own voices, the ones who used to leave their trays behind for his mother to pick up. They are the kinds of kids who become the men that run the world. Noah's always known that.

He leaves the meeting with a smoldering fury blanketing his whole body, suffocating, thick as the late-July heat that seems hotter every year. He has the desire to run, suddenly, but where could he go? What else could he be?

To his mother, Noah was the world, but after she died, to the outside world, he was hardly even a child—they already saw the man who would at best grow up and work behind the register at T-Mobile or Trader Joe's, clean bathrooms, drive a bus, if not become a danger. They didn't see that he was entirely vulnerable. He has spent most of his life trying to prove that he matters, despite every message to the contrary. It is exhausting.

He hears the news on the radio on the way home: acquitted. A fourteen-year-old kid coming home from a snack run, killed by a grown man, and his murderer is free. The rage in Noah's stomach turns dangerous, a wounded animal desperate to fight back.

# EXPOSURE

He stops at a gas station, buys Skittles and Arizona watermelon juice. If the clerk recognizes the significance, she doesn't acknowledge it. He places the snacks on the front seat of his car. Three blocks from his and Jesse's bungalow, he pulls over and cries.

# 15

2003

juliettemarker@uchicago.edu
(No Subject)
To: anniebobanny@nyu.edu

Annie, I don't know how I actually wake up and get out of bed, but I do. I put on whatever I pull off the floor and wait in line in the coffee shop in the student commons—they have our Einstein vanilla coffee, which of course I always get, and a bagel. I am basically living off bagels actually, and almonds. And tiny bottles of airplane whiskey? It's strange and lonely here, but at least, I guess, it is strange and lonely in a new place, where I can pretend everything is as it was back home. The fall here is beautiful and sad. I've been wearing my Chicago coat. I keep getting home to my dorm and thinking I'll call my mom to tell her about this madness. I keep thinking about going home for Thanksgiving, the leaves we'll collect for the table and the rosemary wreaths. It takes me too long sometimes to remember she is not there. She's not there. I feel like a circle with no center.

I miss you too much. Tell me everything about New York.

Your Juliette


anniebobanny@nyu.edu
Re:
To: juliettemarker@uchicago.edu

Julie, sorry I didn't pick up last night, I was at work. I think I like waitressing better than school? The owner lets me drink champagne through my shift as long as I don't fuck anything up. Makes it easier to smile. I am running to class, I'll call you later. Love you forever.


juliettemarker@uchicago.edu
Btw I'm still alive
To: anniebobanny@nyu.edu

Annie,

It's one of those days today, the kind when I wake up feeling frantic and lonely and go about my business trying to shed the pestering terror but to no avail. I'm always cold. Chicago is cold. An understatement, an obvious statement, but it's the most noticeable thing about it. When I come inside from class, I strip and run down the hall to the shower in my towel and I turn up the water as hot as it can go and let it turn my skin pink just to try to unfreeze my bones. The floor is co-ed and there is one bathroom for guys and girls, which I can't believe they actually allow. There is one dude, Max, who is in there like every time I go, he's so tall his head sticks over the dividers, and I worry he's always jacking off. Ughh.

Do you have friends yet? I don't.

The closest I've come is a group of girls from my math theory class that I study with—the nicest is Adele. She invited me to her dorm where we listened to music and made ramen in the communal kitchen. It kinda felt like a test and I think I failed it. She talked about her family, which led to my mom being dead, and then I was ugly-crying right there in her dorm room kitchen and she was just standing there awkwardly. I mean, what could she say? What can anyone say.

The only other person I really like is my poetry professor. He's a fan of Mom's work, so he's nice to me. It's all upperclassmen plus me in his seminar. Did I tell you I got in?

He gives extra credit, too, if we volunteer to teach creative writing in one of the local high schools. I signed up, I guess mostly 'cause I have a crush on him. (He's married and always talks about his wife, so don't worry I don't think an affair is on the table.)

Anyway, teaching was a little scary at first. I'm barely older than the students, but it has turned out to be the one thing I look forward to every week besides the seminar. The kids in my class are talented, and most of them write about some type of heartbreak in their lives, so it makes me feel like I'm not the only one with a stamp of sadness on me. I like the idea that maybe I can help them, insofar as poetry is helpful.

I guess I should go and try to write this paper. I don't want to be in the library anymore, but I don't want to be in my dorm either, or anywhere.

Love, me.

# EXPOSURE

anniebobanny@nyu.edu
**It's four in the morning...**
To: juliettemarker@uchicago.edu

---

Juliette, are you still beautiful and brilliant and my favorite human on earth? You are. I know I am the worst and owe you a call. I have time for nothing, I haven't done my laundry in a month . . . I am not wearing underwear and the socks on my feet have been worn three times. I am a pretty gross human being. We are reading this book called *Written on the Body*, in my English seminar, it's so pretty and reminds me of you so much. I love New York and want you to be here. When will I see you? I fucking miss you. I think of you, and Margot, at every moment.


juliettemarker@uchicago.edu
**Wheeerrrreeee arrrrrrrrre yyyyyyyooouu**
To: anniebobanny@nyu.edu

---

Annie,

I am hungover today—on the rare, only almost warm day, poking its head out of the fall weather. I need some fresh squeezed grapefruit juice and some Annie snuggles. I have not left my bed all day except once to pee. Believe it or not, after I cried in Adele's dorm room kitchen, she invited me to a party. I was sort of excited to have somewhere to go—I mean, the pit of dread/sadness in my stomach always looms over any other feeling but this was better than being alone and I even put on lipstick, and like, dressed up, kinda (I wore the "slutty sweater" I wore to Matt's that one night, the red lace-up one). There were two other girls with us—they were both nice, but you know, it's so much work to try to figure out how to be yourself—or even a self—around new people. Especially now. But the point is, Annie, I was trying. So we get there, and it's super fratty, and I'm just like, all right, whatever. I can for sure dance to Nelly or Ludacris, I just need some booze. Which, of course, there is plenty of. We pour drinks at a table stuffed with bottles of cheap vodka and cranberry juice and whatever the fuck. A long way from Mom's Riesling, Ha. God. I miss our life. Anyway, we started off dancing together, but the girls knew other people there I guess and sort of migrated away, and I was basically just alone so I found the cutest boy I could and started making eyes. He came over to me—I had definitely refilled my vodka Sprite a few times by then—and he's like, hey, what's up, I'm Jason, and I'm like, I'm Juliette. And he's like, you're hot Juliette. And I'm like, thanks. (I guess.) Honestly, I was relieved to have someone to talk to but then I could see it all unfold, sucking his dick in some random ass bedroom and I just couldn't. So I got out of there and somehow made it home by myself. I might be a virgin—technically speaking—forever because I do not think I will ever fall in love, except with you.

Annie! You haven't answered me, I have left maybe five voicemails on your phone and called a million other times, I know you're busy with your fancy waitressing job and your New York City shit but hello, I need you.

# EXPOSURE

juliettemarker@uchicago.edu
(no subject)
To: anniebobanny@nyu.edu

Annie,

I'm sorry I was awful on the phone. I'm not sure I'm fully human anymore — loneliness can result in insanity, I hear. I was mad at you for never picking up, for not being there when I need you when I love you when you are all I have, but I wish now I'd told you things, that I'd listened to things about your life, so I could see you better, imagine you where you are, light-years away from me. I've just been out wandering, looking for coffee so I can finish my Flaubert paper. I feel like Mom is watching somewhere and I think it might be the only reason I am even trying enough to fail at doing my work. Anyway. I got totally charmed by Hyde Park at 2 am, not like charming, but like a faery charm. The cold doesn't feel as cold in the middle of the night.

The green parrots are magic. These fairy-tale birds who escaped their boats when they were being imported as pets and formed wild colonies. You see them flying through the neighborhood, their bright bodies against the bare branches and gray skies. They somehow manage to survive even when it gets below freezing.

I hope one day you'll be mine again, and I'll be yours, and until then, Annie, I don't know what. Or where I am. Or how to tell you how hungry I am to make you love me. Almost enough, I think, to make you appear in front of me.

Annie is at the library, trying to finish a paper that was due last week. She closes the most recent email from Juliette, unsure how to respond, and promises herself she'll call later. But then she is late for work, rushing, so she doesn't call on the way, and then when she's off she goes out with her coworkers, and then it's almost 2:00 a.m.

When they last spoke, Juliette was impossible, as she often is, swinging between furious and tender, desperately morose, and finally ending the call in tears. The angrier Juliette gets at Annie, the more impossible it feels for Annie to find the energy she needs to reply to her, to return her calls. Still, the weight of Annie's love for Juliette has not lessened; she carries it everywhere, privately, even in her mad rush, even at the risk of exhausting herself.

When Annie tells Juliette that she's busy, that things have been crazy, it's true. Perhaps Annie has constructed an impossible life on purpose, trying to match the pace of the city, needing to be everywhere at once, always late for something. Searching out that old adrenaline rush, designed to drown out the twin losses of her own mother and Margot, the closest thing to a real mom she's ever had.

Her father is helping supplement Annie's financial aid, but he's not rich and the cost of living in New York is a struggle, so in addition to classes, Annie is also waitressing full-time. She takes pride in her job, and the French restaurant on Bleecker Street gives her access to a different dimension of the city. She is not just a student. She's nearly a New Yorker. She's started sleeping with Florian, a fellow waiter, a semi-adult at twenty-six. It makes her feel guilty, of course. She can't quite bear to tell Juliette, but her lust for Florian is ravenous. Grief is like this: savage. She knows it's selfish. She knows the desire to simply live—to feel alive—is selfish. But it seems like the only way to go on.

———

Late the following night, leaving work buzzed after a couple post-shift glasses of Chablis, Annie sees she has another missed call from Juliette and makes herself dial back.

"Hey," Juliette answers.

"Hi. How are you?"

"Okay," Juliette says. Annie can hear the tears slide into Juliette's voice. She turns on to Clinton Street, which makes her think of the Leonard Cohen song they love.

"What are you doing?" Juliette asks, after a long silence.

"Walking home. I worked a double today."

"Oh."

"Sorry it took me so long to call you back. I lost my charger, so my phone's been dead for days. The bartender plugged it in for me at work."

Juliette is silent.

"What are you doing?" Annie asks, eventually.

"Smoking a cigarette. You sound far away."

"I am," Annie says. And then, "But I'm on Clinton Street."

"You are?"

"Yeah. I miss you. I'll come visit soon, I promise."

"I'll come there. How about for Christmas."

"Christmas?"

"Unless you want to go to Mexico together, or something."

Annie laughs.

"I can't go home, Annie. I can't do it this year. It might kill me."

Annie hasn't missed a single Christmas on Candy Cane Lane since her dad bought the house when she was four. It's her favorite time of year in Southern California—she loves the combination of palms and fake snow, loves helping her dad string the lights, drinking hot chocolate together on the roof-top. No time makes her feel closer to him. But Juliette's right—how could her friend bear Christmas at Goldstone without her mom? And besides, Sandra moved in with Annie's father the month after Annie left for school, so the holiday would be weird anyway. Maybe Christmas in New York will be fun. Maybe if they are in the same city, Annie can make it all up to Juliette.

"Okay," Annie says. "I'll talk to my dad. Let's do our own holiday here. We'll go see the big tree in Rockefeller and go ice-skating."

They both have their last finals on the twenty-third, and Juliette arrives late that night. They do go ice-skating in Rockefeller Center, on Christmas Eve, and it is beautiful. They get just drunk enough on the little flask of whiskey Annie has brought along for the long walk, and they hold gloved hands and sing carols the whole way back. Juliette's voice is lovely as ever. They stay in an apartment in Chelsea that belongs to one of Margot's friends who is traveling for the holiday, a luxuri-ous break from Annie's dorm room. In the platform bed, Juliette's pale legs are pokey, her lips chapped and red, and she's breathlessly beautiful, raw. They spoon and let their feet brush each other's under the blankets, and, finally, make love.

They turn the kitchen into a disaster, making their own mini version of their parents' Christmas staples: Annie's dad's eggplant Parmesan, Margot's mashed parsnips, roasted ancho-vies with romesco. Moon-shaped cookies with powdered sugar. They drink mulled wine and Juliette buys them fancy bottles of Beaujolais.

Annie is hopeful: despite the distance, despite the tragedy, they are still Annie and Juliette. Juliette puts Annie's hair into a crown braid, and they have saltines dipped in Earl Grey. They go out for drunk brunch—cheap mimosas all day long—take long walks through the city bundled in scarves, visit the Whitney and the Met. Annie avoids taking Juliette to MoMA, which is home to a Margot Marker photo of naked six-year-old Julie doing a handstand beside the chicken coop at Goldstone, and another of her in a torn lace dress at twelve, asleep (or pretending to be) under the peach tree.

But as the week goes on, Annie begins to see signs of Juliette's fractures. Like a child, Juliette does not want to leave Annie's side. When they go out, Juliette makes eyes at boys in bars, in restaurants, on the street, apparently showing off to Annie the ease with which she commands attention. She wants to be looked at all the time, splaying herself naked across the bed as if she's waiting to be photographed.

Though she took as many days off from the restaurant as possible, before the end of Juliette's visit Annie has to return to work. Juliette refuses Annie's suggestions to see a movie or visit the Guggenheim and instead sits at the restaurant bar and gets drunk—too drunk. Florian is working that night; Annie still hasn't found a good way to mention him to Juliette. She tries to avoid flirting with him, but Juliette must pick up on something when Florian walks the girls home at the end of the night and helps Annie drag Juliette's fumbling weight up the four flights of stairs. The moment he's out the door Juliette opens her eyes, sits up on the bed, and asks, in a voice both slurry and accusatory: "He's your boyfriend or you're just fucking him?"

"I don't know. Somewhere in between," Annie hedges.

"And you didn't tell me?" The betrayal in her voice is bald.

"He doesn't matter. It's just sex. You know I like sex."

"We tell each other everything."

"I know. I'm sorry. I didn't want you to be upset."

"Why would I be upset?" Juliette hugs Annie's pillow against her chest.

"I don't know." Annie goes to sit beside her.

"You thought I'd be jealous."

"Maybe. I guess. Or I guess I felt bad for . . . I don't know. Trying to forget."

"If you have the luxury of forgetting, why wouldn't you?" There's an edge on Juliette's voice. She is surprisingly sharp for being so drunk. "You've been forgetting me all year."

"Not you," Annie says. "Never you. You're my soulmate, Julie. I love you more than any other human on this earth."

"If you are dating this guy, I want to actually meet him."

"Okay." And then Juliette begins to undress her.

The next day, in the light of morning, Juliette insists on meeting Annie's "fuck buddy," as she decides to call him. So that night, the three of them go out to dinner. At first, Juliette is at her most charming. She is the radiant Juliette that no one can help but fall in love with, and Annie feels proud to show her off.

"She's mine." Juliette smiles at Florian as they sit down to their Indian dinner. "Just as long as you know that." Florian smiles back. Annie feels flush, a little high from basking in their attention. They leave the restaurant with full bellies and a pleasant buzz, warmth in their cheeks to stave off the cold night air, and walk to an underground speakeasy. But as the night wears on, they have too much to drink, and when Juliette watches Florian brush his hands over Annie's legs, kiss her neck, tap her bottom, she gets sloppy. She sobs in the middle of the bar but refuses to let Annie take her home. Finally, she disappears, comes back holding hands with an older woman— she must be close to thirty—and tells Annie, "I'll see you in the morning."

Annie pulls at Juliette's arm. "Wait," she says. "Julie." But Juliette yanks her arm away. And then she is gone. The next day, Annie wakes early to the sound of Juliette's voice, and goes to the window to see her standing below, her dark hair tangled, barefoot, in last night's clothes, her scarf swaddled around her, shouting with desperation. "Annie! Fuck! Annie, Annie, Annie!"

Annie runs downstairs to let her in. Juliette walks past her, quickly, mumbles that she lost her phone. Annie can feel Juliette unraveling but doesn't know how to stop the pull of the thread that seems to be unwinding from the ball of her soul. Juliette takes a shower, and they go to the Sprint store and then to brunch, a sad, seasick haze surrounding them. A sick feeling nothing can soothe. They drink Bloody Marys. Juliette picks at her potatoes.

"What happened last night?" Annie asks her.

Juliette shrugs. "I hooked up with her."

"Did you like it?"

She shrugs again. "It was all right."

"You know Florian is just a for-now thing. You know I love you forever," Annie says, feeling helpless.

"When will we be together again?" Juliette asks. She is to fly back to Chicago that night. Annie asks Juliette if she'll come to her father's wedding to Sandra in the spring, makes promises about Paris that summer.

It is the last day that Annie will ever see her.

# 16

2013

"Isn't it beautiful?" Jesse asks, opening the door with the key the landlord left in the lockbox, eyebrows raised in hope. "There's even a little yard. Look." Dexter and the girls will be back home in a few weeks. Noah and Jesse have to find a new spot.

Noah doesn't share her excitement. "It's kinda small," he answers. "Especially for the price." The beach bungalow is twice the rent of their old Silver Lake spot.

Later, as they walk through the neighborhood, Noah adds, "Santa Monica is super-white, though."

Jesse scans the street and lands on a Black man with dreads and a baby strapped to his chest, coming out of Groundwork Coffee. "He's not white," she says.

The man wears a cheery grin, swim trunks, and Teva sandals. He sends a nod to Noah that Noah doesn't return.

"You sure?" Noah asks Jesse.

Jesse can't help but laugh. Noah smiles back.

"You can't make me love it, but if you want to move here,

we'll do it," he says, as a white girl with pink braids blows past them on her beach cruiser.

"We'll only be two blocks from the water," Jesse answers.

They sign the lease two days later.

After all the boxes are moved in, Noah calls Cal for help with his mandarin. The two of them haul the pot out of the back seat of his convertible, pouring sweat, and place it on the porch.

That night, Katie texts to tell Noah they've sold the collection of lobby cards for ten million dollars to royalty in India. Ten million, while Noah made three hundred fifty dollars per week to excavate and sort the entire dusty mass, plus the nothing he still gets to run Lenny's errands. The following morning, Noah quits his internship. He needs real work now, he says. Work that pays.

As Jesse unpacks dishes, Noah scours Craigslist for a second job and starts sending in applications to upscale hotels and restaurants. The kind he hates. Worms of guilt and worry begin to work their way through Jesse's body; when she dragged Noah here, she tricked herself into believing she'd talk him into letting her cover the rent, but Noah insists on paying half. She should have known better.

Jesse suggests that Noah ask their friends if anyone has a lead, but Noah's stomach for asking for favors has gone sour, so unbeknownst to him, Jesse asks them herself. Cal's mom reaches out to Noah the following week to tell him that one of her clients—a television executive, recently divorced—is looking for a part-time personal assistant.

When Noah arrives to the home in a gated community in Los Feliz, he finds the woman, Jodi, outside on the front lawn with her kids: a kindergarten-age girl is painting, and a two-year-old boy is absentmindedly scootering up and down the driveway. Jodi has limp blond hair, a fast smile, and the kind of body that comes only with a lot of hard work at her age (mid-forties, he imagines).

"Noah!" she exclaims. "Heya!"

"Hi. Nice to meet you."

"Jenna didn't tell me you were so handsome!"

Noah wonders if by *handsome* she means *Black*. He lingers at the edge of the bright lawn.

"Come on in. I'll show you around."

An hour later, Noah ends up in an old pair of Jodi's ex-husband's swim trunks, in the pool with the kids. The girl, Ivy, commands him, again and again, to toss her into the air. Her brother, Jax, who has not taken off his baby-sized sunglasses since Noah arrived, is on another planet. Noah likes the kids; there is something about the vulnerability of children, any of them, that he finds impossible to resist.

Jodi sits on a lounge chair, watching them. She has a glass of rosé, a couple days' worth of stubble on her tanned legs, a look of helpless exhaustion in her eyes.

When the two-year-old gets out of the pool, he runs to her, tugs down at her T-shirt. "Mama milk," he demands, and she removes her breast. Noah tries not to see as the little boy stands there and suckles.

"I know I should wean him," Jodi says, only mildly embarrassed, "but after the divorce . . . it just felt like the wrong time. He needs any extra comfort I can give him."

Noah nods.

"Ow!" she cries. He's bitten her. He runs away.

"So," Jodi says to Noah, tucking her breast back into her shirt, "Jenna says you're a writer?"

"Yeah, trying to be."

"Cool, well, once you're all done with us, I'll read you, see if I can help."

"Word," Noah says. "That would be great."

"Noah!" Ivy calls out. "Again! Throw me again!"

After several more throws, Noah helps Jodi towel off the kids and Jodi puts on the TV for them. As she and Noah talk, Ivy and Jax cry out demands sporadically, to which Jodi responds automatically, delivering water, reheating a quesadilla left on the counter, cutting a melon, delivering water again, but with colored plastic ice cubes this time.

"As you can see, I need a substitute husband." She laughs a flat laugh. "They're both in school every day, but I need someone to pick them up, do something fun afterward till I'm done at work. Take them to the playground or swim or whatever. Help me organize a little. There's just an endless mass of bullshit, field trip forms and soccer uniforms and playdates and whatever. I like that you're a guy—I want to teach them that this work is not just women's work."

"Sure, yeah."

"Since you're a writer, I'll ask you to do some reading for me sometimes. We get a constant influx of material, and my assistant can't always keep up."

"Word."

"Lemme run outside for a minute before you go," she says. "If that's okay. I'm dying for a cigarette."

"No problem." Noah sits down on the couch as another episode of *Fancy Nancy* begins.

Two months later, returning from a yoga class, Jesse peeks into the office to find Noah at his desk, staring intently into his laptop. She hasn't seen him since he left for Jodi's yesterday morning. He went straight to Hard Rock after that, and she was asleep by the time he got back.

"Hey, boo," she says. "I brought you a coffee."

"Thanks."

She walks over to Noah. He kisses her and returns to typing. She knows she's interrupting his train of thought, but she misses him.

"You wanna walk down to the beach with me today?"

"I wish," he replies. "I'm finishing a scene and I've gotta be at work in an hour."

"All right," Jesse says. Though she expected he'd say no, she still feels a little ache of disappointment in her chest. She wants to go over and sit on top of him, wants him to want to undress her. The only thing she can get him to do is go to the movies, which he considers work. On Saturday or Sunday mornings they sit together in the cool dark of a nearly empty theater. But even then, Noah is quiet and in his own head, or on edge.

Despite the fact he's working two jobs, most of Noah's money goes to rent and student loans, plus his gym membership, car insurance, cell phone, the little bit of money he sends to help his grandpa out. Jesse quietly buys the groceries, sometimes casually takes Noah's car out—the tank always hovering near empty—and brings it back full of gas. When Noah's not at Hard Rock or Jodi's or in front of his laptop, he takes his creatine supplement and a hit of last night's spliff and goes to the gym, spending hours there, his body turning to rock.

Jesse sees Suraya mostly on her own now. Last weekend when they had brunch (at the type of spot Noah would have hated), between bites of saffron-infused yellow tomato gazpacho Suraya showed off her rose gold diamond ring. Cal has cracked the seemingly impossible code of Hollywood and landed as a series regular on an ABC sitcom. Suraya has given up on acting but is still teaching yoga and hosts a wellness podcast that is becoming popular. They are aflutter with excitement, planning their wedding.

A dim unease lingers in Jesse's stomach; when she sits to write, her breath is hard to catch. She lights cigarette after cigarette. On certain days, she can't get any words on the page until she's had a glass of wine at five o'clock. She often ends up drinking the whole bottle.

The day Jesse finishes copyedits and turns in her last draft of *Grief Is Like This,* Noah comes home from work with tacos from her favorite spot and an absurdly expensive bottle of champagne that she feels guilty he bought. She takes a selfie of the two of them toasting, posts it on the social media accounts that she's created at her publishers' request. (Her presence on the internet makes Jesse vaguely anxious—becoming an author, she is realizing, will mean being seen, a suddenly terrifying prospect.)

Jesse and Noah drink their champagne. She nibbles at her food. There is too much silence; Jesse puts on music. When Noah looks at his phone, she is angry.

"Sorry, it's work," he says.

But when Noah looks at her, she doesn't know what to say. The tears rolling down her cheeks run away from her, turning into sobbing, shaking, messy cries.

"What's wrong?" asks Noah. "Why are you crying?"

"I don't know. Finishing the book . . ."

Noah looks back at her, waiting for her to finish the sentence. She doesn't say that finishing the book, which had been her way of grieving her father, is another goodbye. She doesn't say that she misses Noah, her twin.

# 17

2014

Ivy runs over to hug Noah as he comes in the door, calling, "Mom, mom, mom!"

"What?" Jodi's voice arrives from the kitchen.

"Mom, I'm hungry!"

Jodi delivers bacon and eggs and slumps onto the couch. The kids crawl onto her, curling in to her.

"Mom, mom, mom?"

"What, baby?"

"I love you."

"I love you too, Ivy girl."

The landscape of Jodi's life is foreign to Noah, Ivy and Jax's childhoods light-years from his own, but it's hard not to like a mother, especially a single one. It must only be desperation that would allow Jodi to open herself, her home, her children to the gaze of a stranger, making visible the messy details of their domestic life: used cotton rounds forgotten on the bathroom sink, child's nail clippings on the couch, easily lost tempers, threats to withhold television that never come to fruition, breasts pulled out at the breakfast table, lollipops handed out as bribery, wine bottles and chocolate milk cartons overflowing from a recycling bin. The hours turn from part-time to full. Noah can wait tables only on the weekends now.

When Jodi suggests he take her car for school pick-ups, Noah discovers she has a G-Wagen in the garage. It belongs to her ex-husband—his "kid car" (he drives a Porsche for daily use), already stocked with car seats. Her ex uses it only when he takes Ivy and Jax on the weekends. If he's gonna leave it sitting in her garage, Jodi says, Noah might as well make some use of it.

So now, throughout the week, Noah becomes the driver of one of the G-Wagens he's been so jealous of. He plays A$AP Rocky until he arrives at the kids' school and switches to NPR, and, when Ivy gets in, Disney tunes. He wants to enjoy it, tries to, but it's a ruse. The car does not belong to him but to some old white dude who abandoned his wife and children.

Jodi looks like a shark when she leaves the house, delicate gold jewelry grazing her collarbones, form-fitting dresses and defiant sneakers. For all the messiness of her life, she's a gatekeeper, a woman who makes decisions about what to put on television, a woman with access to the upper rungs of Hollywood, the agents, the filmmakers, the studio heads.

Perhaps it is the unguarded way she relies on him when she changes from Jodi to Mom, perhaps it is because she could help him, eventually, hypothetically. But when Jodi asks him to stay a little longer to help her get the kids to bed, Noah always does. He makes Jax laugh and then talks him into brushing his teeth; he drives Jodi's ex's G-Wagen home down Sunset Boulevard in the late-fall evening and answers her call when she dials to ask him to pick up some kitty litter on his way in tomorrow. He arrives by 7:00 a.m. and tells Jodi to sit down and drink her coffee, finishes packing the kids' lunches.

He wants to believe he is closer to achieving his dreams than he was six years ago when he arrived in LA, closer to the "somebody" he wants to become, but is he? He has an old laptop full of unproduced scripts and a job playing house with someone other than the woman he wants to marry.

Although Noah has become adept at dodging wedding invitations, there is no excuse not to show up for Cal and Suraya's, only an hour and a half away in Ojai. Especially now that Jesse's book deal makes it possible to pay for a room in the fancy hotel.

At first it seems that maybe the excursion won't be so bad. They have a pretty drive up, listening to nostalgic college music and letting their minds drift into the rolling landscape. But as soon as they arrive at the Ojai Valley Inn, where a well-coiffed crowd mingles on the sprawling, nearly neon-green lawn, Noah's whole body tenses. Between Cal's new Hollywood contacts and his well-connected parents, most of the guests look as if they've been dressed by personal stylists.

During the vows, Jesse gets teary. She glances at Noah as if searching for something. He takes her hand, tugs in discomfort at his cheap suit. He should have just worn clothes he actually likes. He wants Jesse to laugh with him, to joke all these absurd Hollywood people away, to cut out early and go see a movie, but his Jesse, his twin, is unreachable. She has receded into the role of wistful wedding guest.

Over cocktails and then assigned dinner tables, when people ask Noah what he does, he has three potential replies, which he cycles through over the course of the night: "I wait tables," "I'm a manny," or "I write." If he chooses the latter, a hipster music supervisor, or a creative executive from Amazon, or a just-promoted assistant now running an actor's company will inevitably ask, "Anything I've seen?"

"No," Noah answers, a blunt hammer of a word that shatters the conversation.

Noah wishes he could stand up at his friend's wedding and give a toast, joke about those early days when they were just kids drinking beers and dreaming, wondering if their cards would bounce, but Noah's still that kid. His girlfriend—girlfriend, after eight years—looks stunning in her red dress, red lipstick, that shiny brown hair. He sees people notice her. They notice him too; women always do, and he sometimes has to fight the urge to go home with someone and fuck her just to feel, for a moment, like he's significant.

It takes Noah a little while to realize that Jesse is getting drunk, not wedding buzzed but actually drunk, downing the passionfruit margaritas. By the end of the night, the tacos served, the toasts made, and the cake cut, she is on the dance floor with a group of girls, touching her hair and shaking her hips and throwing her head back. She comes over to where Noah sits on the sidelines, chatting about basketball with Cal's brother—mercifully neutral territory.

"When are *you* gonna ask me to marry you?" Jesse asks, a little slurry, falling onto Noah's lap.

His jaw clenches, but he forces himself to stay calm, not wanting the situation to become any more embarrassing than it already is. "Soon."

"When?"

"Soon as I can afford a ring," Noah says, his voice dropping to a taught whisper.

"Who cares about a fucking ring?" she asks.

"I do." Fortunately, Cal's brother has retreated to the bar.

"Well, maybe you could try acting like you're actually in love with me, in the meantime."

"Jess, please. Don't do this right now."

She raises her eyebrows, undeterred, her eyes lit up with hurt.

"I'm just trying to stay focused—" Noah says.

"And ignoring the fuck out of me—" she interjects.

"You've been drinking," Noah says, calling on his better self to avoid fighting with Jesse at their friends' wedding.

Noah's right: Jesse's too drunk, even, for a proper fight, so she lets him drive her back to the hotel, strips off her dress, and falls asleep with her makeup still on.

The next morning, she wakes alone to sharp sun in her face, a rolling nausea, and a sudden bottomless sadness. But then, a moment later, there is Noah, coming in with two coffees and a large bottle of Smartwater, which he hands to her.

"I am in love with you," Noah says as she sips the water. "You know that, right?"

"Yeah. I guess so."

"I'm nothing without you. I'm just trying to catch up, Jess. So you're not stuck with me at the starting line of life. So you don't decide to go ahead without me."

"Stop it. I'm not going anywhere without you."

"I hope not."

He lies down beside her. She puts her head on his chest, and they go back to sleep together.

# 18

2004

Annie opens her eyes and shuts them again, her head pounding. She can hear Florian in the kitchen, can smell coffee, butter sizzling. She is naked under his gingham sheets. Where is her phone? She has a moment of dread, thinking she left it at one of the bars they frequented last night, before she discovers it buried in a mess of clothing on the floor. It's almost one o'clock, and she has five missed calls from Juliette. Five. *Shit.* Annie feels her perpetual low-wattage guilt rev up. She opens a text message from last night. There is a grainy photo of Juliette, licking a boy's face in a bar. He's Black, handsome, smiling. *this is noah. if u think I'm trying to make u jealous i am*, her text says. Annie feels a pang, but not of jealousy, exactly. It's hard to place the emotion—sadness, maybe. Or worry.

She finds herself hoping that Juliette went home with Noah, that he's a real romantic prospect. It would be good for Juliette to have someone, Annie thinks. Not someone permanent. Not someone to replace Annie, but maybe someone to make her need Annie just a little less. Someone to ease her loneliness. Someone like Florian.

He comes in now, carrying a plate of eggs and hashbrowns along with a mug of coffee. Annie smiles and groans. "I'm so hungover," she says.

"You're so cute," he answers, and kisses her nose, sets down the food. Annie thinks she should call Juliette back, but she doesn't want her to hear Florian in the background and get upset. Annie promises herself she'll call on the way to work.

She does, a couple hours later. Her hangover has faded, the cherry trees are blossoming, and Annie feels almost buoyant. Juliette's phone goes straight to voicemail.

Juliette calls again during Annie's shift, but by the time Annie gets off, it's midnight.

She calls Juliette again the next afternoon, on her way to read in Washington Square Park. No response. Maybe she's in class, Annie thinks.

The following evening, when Annie is curled on her dorm bed, trying to finish her overdue humanities paper, the phone rings. She picks up.

"Annie?" The voice on the other end, a man's voice, sounds strained.

"Who is this?" Annie asks.

"It's Jack," he tells her. "Juliette's father."

It takes Annie a moment to orient herself. "Jack," she says.

"Honey, I'm sorry. I have to . . ." His voice drifts off and returns in a near whisper. "She drowned."

"What?" Annie lights a cigarette, her hands shaking. He starts talking about a service. "I have to go," she tells him. She tries to call Juliette again. Straight to voicemail. Juliette's voicemail that sounds as if it were recorded in a Chicago wind tunnel. *Hey, it's Juliette Marker, leave a message, thanks.*

Annie cannot move her body. She's been paralyzed, her

limbs suddenly stiff and heavy. She wants to light another cigarette but can't find the will to move her arm to reach for the pack. She thinks of calling Florian, but what would she say? She can't repeat what Jack just told her. She can't repeat it to her father, either. It cannot be true.

She looks up at the photo on her wall, her and Juliette at sixteen in the oak bed, tangled together like children. Margot gifted each of them one of the prints as graduation presents, and they promised each other to hang them in their respective rooms. Annie stares at the photo and keeps staring, until her and Juliette's bodies begin to blur into abstractions.

Finally, Annie manages to stand, to get her coat and cigarettes, but she has left some part of herself behind on the bed.

Annie floats along Manhattan sidewalks, chain-smoking. She goes by the apartment in Chelsea where she and Juliette stayed and slips into the building entrance behind a resident. Maybe Juliette is hiding out here. She bangs on the door of 3C until a woman answers in a silk robe.

"Can I help you?" she asks. Annie stares back at her but cannot find her voice.

That evening, Annie half expects Juliette to show up below her window, calling up to Annie to let her in, as she had that morning last December. To knock on Annie's door and crawl into bed beside her. When Annie's phone rings, she jumps, ready to pick up, thinking it might be Juliette.

It is her father. He arrives early the next morning to escort her back to Los Angeles for the funeral. He holds her, wondering, probably, why Annie doesn't break apart, cry on his shoulder.

Annie is sure that when she flies back home, she will find Juliette hiding out at Goldstone. She is so convinced of this, in some secret place inside her, that she still does not cry, even when they eulogize her best friend. She glares at the minister, chosen by Juliette's father, and thinks, *You don't even know her.* The ashes of Juliette's body are supposedly in an urn. Annie does not believe this, not really.

After the service, when Annie's dad offers to drive her to Goldstone, she tells him she has to go on her own. She takes the familiar path back to the house she has been told she now owns—prompted by Margot's estate planner after her death, Juliette said she'd want to leave everything to Annie. But it can't be real, it can't.

The air is stiff from being locked inside; the home, however, is alive—a rumpled cashmere throw on the back of the couch, dried herbs hanging over the sink. It seems as if Juliette and Margot have just run down to Canyon Gourmet to pick up some ingredient or another for dinner.

Annie wanders into the bedroom, finds a pile of clothes on the bed that must not have made it into Juliette's suitcase for Chicago. She pulls open a drawer and finds a stack of Margot's lace slips they all wore for nightgowns. Another drawer full of T-shirts. A stack of Juliette's old underwear, the rejected pairs that didn't get packed: Hanes Her Ways fraying or stained with blood. She shuts it quickly, as if in death the evidence of Juliette's living body is too intimate.

Too intimate, when Annie and Juliette once shared everything. The spring of eleventh grade, she ran with her best friend in a field of poppies, both of them high out of their minds, as Juliette dragged her away from the boys they came with, who were still smoking near the car. Once they were out of earshot, Juliette said to Annie, "Dude, my period came.

And I'm not wearing any fucking underwear!" They laughed so hard they cried. Annie took off her own and gave them to Juliette, who slipped them under her green linen dress.

*Where is Juliette?*

Annie opens the French doors to the gardens and imagines she might find her lying under the peach tree.

"Juliette!" Annie screams, as if her friend might be called out of a hiding spot. "Julie! Julie!"

"Julie!" A sob is breaking through Annie's body.

She has the sudden, adamant urge to flee.

The house has become quicksand—if she doesn't go now, it will sink her. She pulls a large woven tote off a hook in the bedroom—the bag that they used to fill with fruits and vegetables from the garden. She dumps in a candle from the night table, Juliette's gardenia bubble bath, a slip from the drawer, a few other artifacts of their lives together, and locks the door behind her.

When Annie returns to the city, she goes to class straight from her red-eye, and then to work that night, where she sips Aperol spritzes through her shift. Not quickly enough to get too drunk, just measured sips to make it possible to smile at her customers. Florian is not working tonight. She has not seen him since the morning she woke in his apartment to Juliette's missed calls. If only she'd just answered her phone. *Five missed calls.* They haunt Annie. What was Juliette going to tell her? Did it have to do with Noah, the boy she sent the photo of at the bar?

Annie hacks into Juliette's University of Chicago account, searching for clues. Her password is easy enough to guess. Goldstone0969, the date of Margot's birthday. She spends the weekend in bed reading Juliette's emails, but she doesn't find any from a Noah. There is no record of anything in the days before Juliette died other than class assignments. No clues as to where Juliette disappeared to. Annie combs the student rosters and sees there are five Noahs: Noah Hansen, a grad student studying trauma theory; Noah Zelden in the German department; Noah Friedmann; Noah Aarons; Noah Johnson—all of them white.

Annie goes out with coworkers to eat oysters at midnight on a Sunday, bottles of wine littered over the table. She goes home with someone that night, rushes to her dorm to shower the next morning, makes it to lit class on time. She's searching out her old adrenaline rush, but she can barely get a thrill out of the empty sex. She continues to cheat on Florian anyway, until he discovers it and ends things.

Annie's father suggests, again and again, that she take the rest of the semester off. Come home, let him take care of her. But Annie tells her dad she doesn't want to have to repeat her classes. She'll be okay. And then she tells him that she can't come home for the summer. She has work, and she signed up for a summer course on "Einstein's Universe" to get her last core requirement out of the way.

Her dad flies out to visit her instead, sleeps on an air mattress on her dorm room floor. She serves him at her restaurant, takes him to see *Wicked* on Broadway, to ride the boat to the Statue of Liberty. She fills their days to the brim, smiles for him, trying to prove she is keeping her head above water. She is. She is, but under the surface, it is so much work to stay afloat.

In a recurring dream, Juliette returns to Goldstone, where Annie has been waiting for her. Annie is overcome by a marriage of surging relief, tenderness, and rage at Juliette for leaving her in the first place. "I've been looking everywhere for you," Annie cries out. "I've been waiting." Death was not all that she'd hoped it would be, Juliette tells Annie. It did not make her happy, and so she has come back. Annie puts her arms around Juliette, holds her tightly. They take each other's clothes off in a fury, make love.

In the sea of subway cards, matchbooks, loose change on Annie's dresser sits the candle from Goldstone, forever half burned. The summer ends. The fall comes; the air aches with nostalgia. Annie becomes a sophomore.

In the city of eight million people, Juliette is everywhere. On her way to the Bistro, Annie spots a girl with dark hair and a swinging skirt ahead of her. She veers off her course to follow the girl for blocks, her heart in her throat, until whoever she is turns around, and her best friend vanishes. Annie shakes it off, crosses the street, walks to work, where she applies the same shade of CoverGirl lipstick Juliette gave her during their first party back in the ninth grade.

At the Met one afternoon, staring at a Vermeer painting Juliette loved, Annie bursts into tears, goes to the bathroom and wipes her eyes, then out for drinks with her friends, to a party, where she does a few lines and finds someone to take home with her. She is fine, she tells herself, knowing that she is not fine. Grief is like this: an ambush predator. She senses it stalking her.

Thanksgiving: no matter how she tries to drown it out, Annie can see the low winter light over the ocean, the sage stuffing, roasted squash with pomegranate seeds laid over the table in Topanga, Margot presiding, pouring Beaujolais Nouveau.

Annie promised her father she would go to a Friendsgiving hosted by one of her coworkers in a tiny apartment in the East Village. After searching several shops, Annie finds Margot's favorite Beaujolais and shows up to dinner with two bottles. She gets so drunk that night she throws up her meal. The next day, she gets the flu. It is the sickest she's been since she was a child with her father's Sunday macaroni pot beside her bed to catch the puke. Now, alone in her apartment eating only saltines, the fever does not break for days. The first snow of the year arrives; it is beautiful, then it turns to sludge that will last for months. Annie tries to get up, but she can't make it past the shower. She cannot run anymore, and the grief pounces on her, pulls her under.

It is a brutal winter that year—the kind of cold that grabs hold and won't let go.

Annie gets over the flu but keeps herself sick with alcohol and cigarettes. She often gets dressed only when she has to go to work, where she drinks through her shifts. On her days off, she neglects to shower, to eat, to brush her teeth. She wears the slip from Goldstone for days on end, sometimes skips her classes.

Annie has never known a desire so intense as the desire she has for the dead. She lies under her comforter, the heater clicking on and off, and she can feel Juliette's fingers tangled in her hair, can smell her.

Annie pretends to be okay for twenty minutes a day when she talks to her father. She is convincing enough to prevent him from staging an intervention, but he still asks if she wants to come home on every call.

"We'll be here when you're ready," Annie's dad tells her. "Your room is just the same. Sandra put her sewing machine in there, but otherwise, we haven't changed a thing." He sends her pictures of Candy Cane Lane all lit up. When even that fails to lure her, he lets it drop. He understands: it is too much.

In bed, Annie continues to stare at the boy in the photo, who stares back at her in his blue hoodie and leather jacket, Juliette's tongue on his cheek. Over and over, she googles "Noah, University of Chicago," and combs through pages of results, to no avail. She searches for him on Facebook again and again. If anyone would know what happened to Juliette, it would be Noah, right?

In the eyes of the medical examiner, Juliette was most likely a college girl who decided to go for a dip in the lake one of the first nice evenings of the year and met tragedy. The day was warm but windy. The waves were big. She had alcohol in her system, which would have impaired both her judgment and her swimming ability. She probably got caught in the undertow and couldn't get back to shore.

Annie tries to imagine her, the Juliette she knows, high off of meeting a boy she liked, maybe, warmed by the newborn sun, dazzled by the lingering warmth of a long spring evening, alive in her body, trying to find a streak of her old, wild, wonderful self by going for a spontaneous swim, shocked awake by the cold water of Lake Michigan, seduced by it, pulled out too far, unable to fight her way back.

Inevitably, Annie thinks of *The Awakening*, so beloved by both of them, and Edna deciding to drown herself, walking into the sea: *She did not look back now, but went on and on, thinking of the blue-grass meadow that she had traversed when a little child, believing that it had no beginning and no end . . .*

Beneath dorm sheets damp with sweat, Annie can hear Juliette reading the passage to her. She can see Juliette surrounded by bubbles in the tub, her long legs with matte white skin, the tiny stubbles of dark hair cropping up that she shaved away with one hand while she held the book in the other.

Annie does not want to think that Juliette gave up on this life. She does not want to think that it was a death born of despair, that if only she'd answered the phone when Juliette called, if only she'd been there for her last year, Juliette would be alive, with her still. But the feeling tugs at her like that undertow. It is unbearable. *Five missed calls.*

Annie pours another glass of wine, pulls the blanket over her.

For some reason, Annie thinks of Indigo, of sitting in the red vinyl booth across from her and sipping a Shirley Temple. She remembers clenching her heart so as not to fall in love with her mother, knowing those hours in the presence of her two parents would soon be over. Annie's old grief surfaces, entwining Indigo with Juliette in her mind. *Why couldn't they have saved her?*

There is so much Annie never knew about her mother. Although Annie used to wonder about her family sometimes, she'd never indulged her fleeting questions about her origins. Annie was a motherless child, her father's daughter. Italian like him and her grandparents—an identity that stemmed mostly from the food they made and ate. Annie's grandma Nicola rarely spoke about the Iowa farm where she grew up with her six brothers and sisters, helping care for their bedridden mother. Certainly not whatever it was that drove her family from the Old World. The traumas of her lineage went unaddressed, swept under the mink coat of the American Dream.

But one thing was certain: Nicola loved her son fiercely, would do anything for him. When Mikey called her at five in the morning from a gas station somewhere in Northern California, telling her he'd left Six Rivers, that he had a baby with him, his baby, he needed help, needed money, had nowhere to go, Nicola went straight to the Western Union and wired him the total of her savings account.

Annie's dad could easily have left Six Rivers on his own, but to get away with Annie he had to sneak out. He loved to recount the adventure of carrying her through the snow in the dark, tied tightly to his chest while she slept, hiking down the mountain as the sun rose.

As a kid, Annie wanted to hear the story over and over, and at the end, she always had the same question. "Why didn't my mom come with us?"

"She was brainwashed," he tried to explain.

Annie didn't understand.

"It's like being sick . . . You can't help it."

"Will she get better?"

"I don't know."

Annie senses now that maybe if she could find an answer to the unanswerable question—*Why did her mother let her go?*— going on with her life would feel more possible.

She begins by asking her dad during their nightly phone call. "Do you remember if my mom ever said anything about her family?" She tries to sound offhanded.

"She didn't like to talk much about her past, but I do remember her saying she grew up in Kansas."

"Right," Annie says. "Maybe I knew that. What was her last name again?"

"Sabel. She was Suzanne Sabel, before she was Indigo. She told me that when we heard the Leonard Cohen song together. The one, you know"—he hums a few bars.

"I know the one," Annie says. She and Juliette listened to that song more times than she could count during high school.

"Yes, right. When I heard it playing in your room, I sometimes thought of how your mother liked that song too."

"Why didn't you ever tell me?"

"I don't know," says her dad. "I was never sure how much you wanted to know about her. It seemed like it was maybe better . . . to let her go. She was a haunted woman, Annie."

"Then why did you keep taking me up there?"

"I promised her. Before I left with you. That we'd visit. She was your mom; she gave birth to you, and I felt compelled to keep that promise."

"She was never really my mom," Annie says. But she feels less sure of the statement than she once did. A twist of some shadowy, ancient ache forms in the center of her body.

Unlike the fruitless search for Noah, finding her mother's family is easier than it should be. Annie goes on Facebook and looks for people with the last name *Sabel* in Kansas. There are five. And one of them looks like her and her mother. Jonathan Sabel. He is freckle-faced, old, with a gut, playing golf in his profile photo. He has always been right there. How strange. Her uncle, maybe?

She plays "Suzanne" on her phone, again, and again. And then she opens her messenger and types a note to Jonathan: *I don't know if you will see this. It's a little strange to say, but I believe we're related. I grew up with my dad in LA, but I was born on Six Rivers Ranch, and I think my mom might have been related to you. I guess I am just curious to know more about her. If you are willing.*

Two days later, she gets a response: *You look just like her. You live in New York? My son is there. Your cousin. I've done my best to leave the past in the past, but you should give Con a call if you want. Connor Sabel. 212-948-3939.*

The last of the thin winter sun filters in from between buildings. Annie's heart is racing. But at least, for a moment, she has a pulse again.

# 19

2005

"Oh, shit!" Connor says, when Annie walks up to his table, covered head to toe in her down jacket, nose red from the cold, fingertips smelling of cigarettes. She is too thin, her skin pale enough to be transparent. He is halfway through his beer, with a ruddy glow and a big smile. He's in his midtwenties, beefy, square-jawed, and handsome-ish, freckled like her, wearing the uniform of the financial district, his button-up shirt and tie loosened at the neck. "What's up, cuz?"

Annie manages to smile back, both alarmed and relieved by his friendliness. "Hi. Thanks for meeting me." She feels unsteady, as if she's forgotten how to do this basic thing of speaking to another human.

"'Course. You wanna drink?" he asks as she pulls out the chair and sits, keeping her coat zipped.

"Sure. I'll take a Scotch." Margot loved Scotch, which always seemed so sophisticated to Annie. At the beginning of college, she'd adopted the drink in Margot's memory.

"Nice. I like it."

Connor disappears momentarily and returns with two drinks, proudly extending Annie's to her.

"Eighteen-year Macallan," he declares.

"Wow. Thanks." Annie sips, feels the easy burn glide down her throat and warm her empty stomach. She tried the expensive eighteen-year variety one other time, when Margot opened the bottle on graduation day.

"You look like your mom," Connor says.

"Yeah." Annie sips again and removes her jacket. She feels grateful for the dark wood of the upscale sports bar, the noise, the Scotch, all of which seem to lay themselves over her like a weighted blanket, providing muted comfort.

"It's weird. It's like I grew up looking at your face," Connor goes on, studying her.

Apparently, Connor's dad, Jonathan, kept a framed childhood photo of himself and Suzanne on the bookshelf in his office. When Connor was a kid, he used to stare at Suzi—as his dad called her—making up stories about their missing family member, inventing adventures, almost as if she was an imaginary friend of sorts.

Ironically, sitting across from her cousin, who could not be more different from Indigo, seems to confirm Annie's mother is real, that she once lived in the world, and not just in the liminal space of memory.

According to Connor, Suzi dropped out of high school and ran away from her family at sixteen. His and Annie's grandparents, Connor says, were drinkers and racists and assholes. Annie thinks Connor kinda seems like the grandson of assholes—not really an asshole himself, but the kind of person who's inherited a sort of easygoing confidence, an air of entitlement—the kind of person it might be nice to have on your side.

"Did her parents just let her go?" Annie asks.

"I told you. They were assholes. You know, uptight, religious WASPy types, and she was, like, a hippie kid. I think they caught her doing some wild shit, and her dad flipped out. He used to get them with the belt and all. My pops said he'd never hit us 'cause of that."

Connor goes on as Annie presses him for more, his hands moving for emphasis as he talks. She takes another sip of the Scotch and rolls it around in her mouth, trying to process the words coming out of his mouth.

"Dad was older than Suzi; he was in college when she left. He didn't even know till he got home for Christmas that year and asked where she was. Imagine, you come home and your sister's just gone. His father wouldn't talk about it. But his mom made it sound like she'd be back. The masks those people wore, it was crazy. When it became clear she wasn't coming home, my dad hired a private investigator to find her. He'd graduated by then, started making some money."

Despite the chatter in the bar, the screens playing sports, the bustling servers, Annie is so lost in Connor's tale it feels as if there's no one else here.

"When the dude figured out where she was," Connor continues, "my dad went out to the commune. I mean, you don't know my dad. He's WASPy too, not an asshole, but if you can imagine him walking onto this commune in the middle of fucking nowhere in his polo shirt, with all these naked people. When he found her, she told him she wasn't Suzi anymore, she was Indigo. She told him Suzi was gone. And he said it was true; the Suzi he knew wasn't there. He said she seemed like she was high, just super faded. She told him she loved him, but she couldn't go home. He told her she didn't have to go home, that he'd help her, she could go to college, or stay with him. She said, 'You don't understand. I can't, John.' My dad said he talked to her for all of five minutes before some older man—like in his forties—came over and put his hands on her. He said she was carrying his child, that he was taking care of her. My dad lost it on him—he was desperate—but the dude disappeared with Suzi. My dad came back the next morning, and the next, but Suzi wouldn't see him. She'd just turned eighteen, so what could he do?"

Annie's stomach drops. She leans forward, resting her elbows on the wood table to steady herself. "Carrying his child?"

"Right," Connor adds, as if it were an afterthought. "My dad said she was pregnant, like probably close to nine months."

"When was this? What year was it?" Annie asks, unable to hold the urgency back from her voice.

"Let's see. My dad's four years older than her and he was born in '59 . . . so she'd have been born around '63. If she was eighteen, it'd have been '81."

Annie lets go of the breath she'd been holding. Her dad came to the commune after college with a friend, in 1982. Annie was born in 1984, so the baby couldn't have been her. Maybe her mom had other kids at Six Rivers, maybe that's part of why she couldn't leave. Could Annie have half-siblings? If that were true, why wouldn't her father have mentioned it? Did he even know, if the children were supposed to belong to everyone? Or, maybe, if her mom was high like Connor's dad said, something happened to her baby? Annie feels a bit dizzy, her mind struggling to assimilate this new information into her memory of Indigo.

Connor leans back in his chair, studying Annie. She longs to pull her mom out of the restaurant and into the car with her and her father, to drive her back to civilization, to rescue her.

"That she answered your dad's letters and showed up to meet you every time seems like a miracle," Connor says, after a moment. "When my dad went up there, that was the last time she ever talked to him. He tried again a few months later, but she wouldn't even see him. And they were close, like super-close growing up. Honestly, I've seen the dude cry twice in my life, and telling me about his sister, after he found out she died, was one of them."

Perhaps Annie had mattered to her mother more than she'd thought. Indigo'd risked something for their fleeting contact—her sense of safety, the strange boundaries of the world she created for herself. The more real her mother becomes, the more devastating it feels to Annie to have lost the possibility of having her as a mom. Annie asked for this—she wanted to know, that's why she met Connor to begin with—but she feels her heart squeezing up in protest. No more anguish.

She finishes her drink in a single swallow.

"I'll be right back," she tells Connor.

At the Big Foot Steakhouse, when Annie and her father arrived early one evening, Annie went to use the bathroom and found Indigo there, rubbing dirt off her face with wet paper towels. A brand-new hairbrush sat on the sink, maybe bought (or, more likely, stolen) across the street at Ray's general store. Annie's and her mother's eyes met in the mirror, and for a moment, Indigo looked startled, as if she'd seen a ghost.

"When you were a baby," she said softly, "you looked like Mikey. But now, you look like me."

Annie nodded. She didn't know what to say, so she stepped into the stall, and by the time she came out Indigo was gone, waiting at the table with her father.

Annie turns on the sleek black faucet and splashes her face. Her reflection swims in the water of the mirror. It will not hold still. She half expects to find the ghost of her mother coming up for air.

When she gets back to the table, her cousin is taking the last swallow of his beer, his already-rosy cheeks a shade redder.

"You want another?" she asks.

"'Course."

She buys the next round (regular twelve-year Glenlivet for her), along with a pile of french fries. She hasn't eaten all day, and she's lost her center of gravity. But she lets the talk of her mother go and listens to Connor's tales of how he grew up, his life in the city. He tells Annie that he recently graduated from Columbia, is working at Merrill Lynch and "livin' the dream." For all of his father's lingering scars, at least on the surface Connor seems to have gotten out unscathed. He's friendly by default, one of those bro-y boys who treats everyone he's not going to sleep with like a sibling. It's strange to think that they have anything, let alone blood, in common. But Annie's been so lonely, and the human contact begins to melt her a bit, along with the warmth of her second Scotch. She nibbles her fries and starts to talk too, about school, about working as a waitress. She is afraid if she talks about Juliette, she will burst into sobs right there, but she tells Connor a little bit about growing up in Los Angeles with her father.

Connor asks if Annie has a boyfriend, and when she says no, he says, "I've got someone you have to meet."

"Okay. Maybe one day."

"Come on. You just told me you've been basically locked in

your two-hundred-square-foot apartment all winter. You gotta get out, kid."

"I guess you're right," Annie agrees, though she doesn't expect she'll ever see her cousin again when he flags her a cab, pays the driver up front, and sends her weaving through the night.

# 20

2014

As Noah and Jesse move through the bustle of the outdoor mall in the heat—still ninety degrees at six thirty—Noah is distracted, uneasy, looking into his phone. A Black man, father of six, has been choked to death by police. His crime? Selling cigarettes.

Jesse walks unsteadily in her heels; Noah puts away his phone, offers his arm. He feels queasy. *Please, just leave me alone,* the man begged, moments before they killed him.

Jesse stops in her tracks when she sees her face on a giant poster in the window of the Barnes & Noble. Today is her first book reading.

"Wow. You're big-time, boo," Noah says.

Jesse smiles her embarrassed-but-pleased smile. "Who thought it would really happen, when we used to come here and dream about this?"

"I did. I always knew you'd be a star," he says.

When they arrive inside the store, the events coordinator whisks Jesse away. As Noah approaches the gathering crowd, he takes a breath, trying to ward off the anxiety pressing on his lungs. He is trying to find some pocket of anonymity, some place where no one is likely to ask him what he "does." He's been writing extra coverage for Jodi, picking up Sunday brunch shifts—his least favorite—after working late on Saturdays to store up a little cash.

Sometimes Noah makes dinner for Jesse, stretching money he doesn't have to buy the nicest steak, which he sears in the pan with rosemary from the herb box on their porch. Or sometimes he stops at the store on the way home from work, so he can make breakfast the next day, splurging for boxes of strawberries and raspberries because Jesse loves them—the organic ones. But he sees her look longingly out the window when they drive by the crowds of hipsters and young professionals drinking their chilled reds and Aperol spritzes street-side, with their tiny, seasonally attuned appetizers.

So he saved the money to take her out, made a surprise dinner reservation. Nothing feels less appealing to Noah now than dropping hundreds of dollars on frisée and chanterelles and nettles—foods he once didn't even know existed. But Jesse's first book has just been published, and after her first reading, he doesn't want her to look at him like he's a disappointment because he didn't do the right thing to celebrate, on top of every other way in which he's a disappointment. He wants to make her happy; he wants her to be happy.

Noah wanders away from their friends and finds a seat in the second row, off to the side, next to a teenage girl holding a copy of *Grief Is Like This* neatly in her lap, *a novel by Jesse Baca*, written in pink letters across the cover. As the crowd waits, Noah scrolls images of protest on social media: *I can't breathe, I can't breathe, I can't breathe, I can't breathe, I can't breathe, I can't breathe, I can't breathe, I can't breathe, I can't breathe, I can't breathe, I can't breathe.*

He shuts off his phone as Jesse arrives, walking through the narrow aisle of chairs to step up to her podium. She's glowing, tugging on her new dress, still looking a little unsteady in her heels, all nervous laughter as she introduces herself. But once she begins to read, her voice grows steady, confident. She is captivating, he thinks, and keeps his eyes trained on her as a quiet terror creeps through him.

At the end of the reading, a long line forms of people waiting to get their books signed. Jesse takes her time, giving out hugs and taking photos with everyone. Noah silently wills her to hurry up as he stands on the sidelines, making conversation with Jesse's friend Morgan from high school and her fiancé. Somehow, Morgan landed a job in the writers' room for *New Girl* three months after moving to Los Angeles.

When, over an hour later, Jesse chats with the last girl in line, the remaining crowd has dwindled to Cal and Suraya, Morgan and the fiancé, Dexter with Maya and Sari. As Jesse wraps up, the group begins discussing the best restaurant in the vicinity, what might still be open. Ash, the girl who replaced Jesse as Dexter's assistant, and Ash's mother, who's visiting from out of town, emerge from the bathroom with matching Prada sunglasses still pushed atop their heads (though there is no trace of sun left in the sky) and join the conversation. Everyone is hanging around, wanting to be part of the after-party. Noah crumples. But when Jesse comes over, he smiles and puts his arm around her waist. When she agrees to the now nine-person date, he steps aside to cancel the reservation he made for the two of them.

They all end up at Jesse and Noah's old happy-hour spot—a French restaurant—per Jesse's request. Noah is seated at the end of the table, Jesse on one side of him, Ash's mother across. Noah can't eat. He can't stop thinking about the man dying, face pressed into the sidewalk.

Between bites of pâté, Ash's mother leans across the table. "What they did to that man in New York is terrible, I think." Noah nods. He feels sick.

Four bottles of wine later—half-finished plates of steak and fries, artichokes, cheese and quince paste strewn over the table—the check arrives. Dexter gives Noah a look, like "Should I?" Noah shakes his head and picks it up silently, slipping his credit card into the slot without looking at the number. It's a low-limit, emergencies-only card that he occasionally uses at the grocery store; he shuts his eyes, hoping it will go through. As the waiter walks off, nobody but Jesse seems to notice. She frowns.

"Noah, you don't have to pay," she says a little too loudly, her eyes grazing over the table as if to cue the others to jump in. Only Dexter and Ash's mother seemed to have heard her. Dexter sips his wine, watching casually, while Ash's mother pulls out her purse.

"I got it," Noah says.

Jesse swallows.

They say their goodbyes and walk off toward Jodi's G-Wagen.

"You were really great tonight," Noah says to Jesse as he opens the door for her.

"Thanks."

Noah starts the car.

"You didn't have to pay at dinner," Jesse says. "Everyone should have paid for themselves. Or you could have let Dexter do it, at least."

After everything, why doesn't she understand that it's impossible for him to sit by and allow another man—Jesse's former boss or anyone else—to pay for her dinner?

"It's fine," Noah says.

"But I'd rather you save your money. I didn't want you to have to do that."

Noah clenches his jaw. They ride in silence as he puts the parking ticket into the machine. He owes fourteen dollars, even with the validation. They've been here forever. Jesse pulls out her wallet. Noah waves her off.

As he turns onto Fairfax, Jesse rolls down the window and lights a cigarette.

"You're smoking right now?"

"Apparently."

They don't speak again until Noah unlocks the door to their bungalow. It's at least ten degrees cooler over here—the most significant benefit of their expensive, ocean-adjacent home.

He inhales the salty air, tries to let it calm him. "What are you tryna do right now?" he asks.

"I'm exhausted. I'll probably just read and go to bed."

"All right."

Noah walks into the living room and hears Jesse in the kitchen now, the sound of a wine cork coming out of the bottle, the long pour into a glass. He turns on the TV, plays *American Hustle*, falls asleep on it.

The movie is half over when he wakes to Jesse coming in, standing before him, her eyes narrow and watery.

"Good night," she says, her voice flat.

"Good night," he says.

AVA DELLAIRA

But as she turns, he grabs her hand and pulls her onto his lap. He kisses her deeply, thrusting his hand up her shirt. She moans loudly, the ropes of their desire pulling them together. In their ferocious lovemaking, they say everything they couldn't have said, rocking the scales of power, fear, surrender, until they find their balance and the message becomes clear: *I want you, I need you, I love you, don't leave me. Don't leave.*

# 21

Jodi likes to bake bread. She has a book called *The Bread Book* and a special scale and even asks Noah to drive to the health food store on the other side of town to pick up some type of fancy flour. It relaxes her, she says. Makes her feel like a "good mom" (she used air quotes when she said it). She hopes her kids will remember her this way—the mom who gave them the home that smelled like freshly baked bread, who served them that wholesome, buttered, melt-in-your-mouth goodness. She hopes they will remember the morning cuddle piles and her singing them to sleep. Not the frazzled woman late for work, fighting back tears as she puts on makeup, pinching herself to keep from yelling when she asks them for the fifth time to put on their shoes before school. She tells Noah this as he sits, hostage, at a stool at the kitchen counter. She's drinking wine while mixing the dough; she's always drinking wine, it seems, pouring small splashes into her glass, as if she wanted only a little, then repeating ten minutes later. She has on a nightshirt and no bra, short shorts through which he can see her underwear. The kids have been asleep for over an hour by now.

Noah has stayed tonight, sipping his "Sauv Blanc" and watching her bake, because he is trying to get up the nerve to ask her to read the new script he's just finished, despite her statement that she would read him once he was no longer working for her. The script is an edgy romantic comedy, and he thinks she might like it; he's hoping maybe she can pass it on to an agent or someone like that.

"I bought your girlfriend's book," Jodi says.

"Yeah?"

"Yeah, I read a few pages last night. She's good."

"She is." *Grief Is Like This* is a success, hit bestseller lists in its second week.

"Are you gonna marry her?"

"I hope so. I'm kinda trying to get my shit together first."

"You love her?

"Yeah."

"The sex is good?"

Noah side-eyes her, but Jodi doesn't seem to notice. "Uh. Yeah."

"Dave never really got me sexually, I feel like. You've got to have that connection from the beginning, otherwise the whole thing is fucked."

"How do you mean?" He ignores the quiet discomfort in his gut.

"Like, we had some enjoyable sex, of course—we were to-gether forever—but my fantasies never really played out with him. I don't know." She pulls her bread out of the oven. Her shorts ride up. "Not that all of our problems in marriage could be attributed to sex—I think so many women just get exhausted, you know. Like, how am I gonna be at work all day, get the kids fed, email the teacher back, remember I forgot to make their dentist appointment, get them ready for bed, load the dishwasher, slog through a reading pile, and then want to have sex when I've got to be up at 5:30 a.m. to work out if I want to have any chance at having any kind of remotely attractive body?"

"Right," Noah says, as if he knew what she meant.

"It's actually boring to talk about. I sound like a cliché."

Noah looks at his phone. It's 10:03. There's a text from Jesse: *Where are you?*

*Still at work*, he types back.

"You want some bread?"

"I'm not really trying to eat carbs right now," Noah says.

She laughs. "For what? You're young and hot."

"That's about all I have going for me. I better not fuck it up."

"Have a fucking piece of bread."

Noah laughs. "Okay."

She butters it, puts it on a plate in front of him, refills her wineglass and his.

"I'll be right back, I'm just gonna sneak outside for a cigarette," she says.

He glances again at his phone. "Okay."

While she is gone, Noah straightens up, sweeping flour from the counter, scrubbing dried strawberry jam off the table where Jax usually sits. Jodi said she would read Noah's writing when he was "done with them." But wasn't that a Catch-22? If Jodi helped him find work as a writer, maybe then he could be "done." Anyway, she said this seven months ago, before they knew each other. By now, perhaps she'll be willing to do him a favor. They seem to have broken nearly every other boundary; why not this one, too?

Noah finishes his bread, drinks his wine, checks his watch. 10:43. Jodi must be smoking the whole fucking pack out there.

He pulls his laptop out of his bag, looks over his new script.

He gets hung up on a flaw in the dialogue in the fourth scene and starts rewriting, his keyboard clacking through the quiet house when the door opens, startling him. Jodi's soaking wet, her white T-shirt clinging to her breasts.

"I jumped in the pool." She laughs. "Sometimes you got to live a little, right?"

Noah raises his eyebrows, does his best not to look at her chest.

"It's a beautiful night. Grab me a towel, will you?"

Noah goes to the bathroom, pulls one of the plush white towels off the rack. He hands it to her. She takes a step closer to him. He finds himself frozen. She kisses his lips. She tastes like warm white wine. Her cheeks turn bright red under her freckles, and she looks suddenly younger than she is, something girlish pushing its way through her aging skin.

He's a boy again, sixteen, seventeen, in the dorm rooms of college girls. His voice is thick, almost stuck in the back of his throat when he whispers to her, "You want it, don't you?"

She nods yes. And then she is on her knees. He pushes himself into her mouth; the rush of power is a drug. For a moment, it erases his feelings of failure. He sees Jodi looking up at him, guides her.

The instant he comes and the desire drains out of him, he feels sick.

Jodi gets up and goes into the bathroom. He hears the sink running.

"I'm, uh—I should go," he calls out.

He steps into the bathroom. Jodi glances over her shoulder, back at him. She is rinsing her mouth.

He's looking for something to say to her. "I—sorry."

"All good, kiddo," she says flatly.

Noah wants to take his own car home, but it's locked in Jodi's garage, and he does not want to go back into the house to get the opener, so he drives home in her ex-husbands G-Wagen and has to fight the urge to slam himself into the side of the 101 freeway, to go out Mulholland and veer off the edge of the cliff. He's a million miles away from the kid he used to be, with his puffy coat and hoodie up, riding the bus alone to the Art Institute, chasing his mother's ghost, and yet Noah can feel that boy in the car with him now: eight, nine, ten. He wants to get out and run.

On the radio, they are talking about the city burning in protest, after an unarmed black teenager was shot by a cop and left in the street for hours. Why don't they understand: anger has to go somewhere. Rage can't be swallowed forever.

Noah has no foundation on which to stake himself other than his ambition. To fail is to become nothing. He can't bear to see Jesse now, the only person who still believes in him; he cannot bear to tell her he betrayed her.

When Noah walks into the bungalow it's close to midnight and she's already in bed. There is dinner waiting for him under a clean dish towel—roasted chicken and rosemary potatoes, her greens he loves. There are white flowers on the table.

He does what he always does, pulls out his laptop, tries to

go back to his script. But it feels like bullshit. He's lost the thread.

He takes a hot shower. He can taste the loneliness of his boyhood, metallic, almost, like blood in the mouth. All that empty teenage sex, looking for a surge, searching for some power. A way to matter.

Noah tells himself he will tell Jesse, but seeing her in bed, her messy bun atop her head, her bony shoulder, half waking as he lies down beside her, rolling over to put her arms around him—how can he break this sweetness?

How can he hurt her? How can he lose her?

The next morning, when Jesse wakes, Noah is ready to make love to her. Afterward, when she wanders into the kitchen in her underwear to start the coffee, Noah follows. He tells her that it's not working out with Jodi. "I don't think I can do it anymore," he says. He takes two mugs out of the cabinet, the milk from the fridge. "She's looking for a husband, not an assistant."

"Well, so am I," says Jesse. "So tell her to back off."

Noah smiles. "I need to find something else."

"You have Hard Rock," Jesse says. "Just do that and focus on writing for a while."

"I've got bills, Jess. We have bills."

"I got us for a little while, okay?"

"I can't—"

"I got us, Noah. Just let me. Just write."

"I've been writing."

"I know." Jesse pauses. She pours the coffee, turns back to Noah. "Write something that's you. Forget about Hollywood and trying to be commercial for a second, and just write Noah."

"Like *The Red Balloon*," Noah says. And then, "But that went nowhere."

"Well, that was a long time ago. And you're an even better writer now. Maybe you should revisit it. See if there's something there."

Noah looks back at her. Without her faith in him, what else is there?

"All right," he says. Although he does not deserve her kindness, choosing to accept it is an act of surrender. He belongs to her.

# 22

Gray clouds glow behind sheer white curtains, the first hint of 6:00 a.m. sun drawing itself around their edges, the Chicago L train speeding out of Noah's dreams.

Last night was another book signing at a local festival, followed by drinks with Jesse's agent and the agent's wife. Noah would not mind it all if there were a way to avoid the awkward silences when they realize Jesse's an accomplished author with a boy who's been waiting tables and "trying to write" for his entire adult life.

Jesse rolls on top of him, shifting positions as if trying to find a way into his body. Noah puts an arm around her, stares out the window. He is hot; he wants to get up. He wants to run. He does not want to wake Jesse, but he can't muster the patience required to stay pinned to the bed.

He rolls out from under her. She stirs. Groans.

He finds running shoes, shorts.

———

Down at the beach, a dark-skinned boy skirts the waves in the dawn light, followed by his mother. He could have been Noah. Back at Lake Michigan.

Noah passes the mother and child, runs harder. His body goes faster and faster, tumbling past himself. If he could run fast enough, he would defy gravity.

He is a child on the beach with his mama, laughing, *Chase me, Mama.*

#Iftheygunnedmedown; Noah uses the hashtag and posts a picture of himself grinning with his mother and her Ninja Turtle cake on his sixth birthday, beside a grainy yearbook photo of himself in high school, his hood up, refusing to smile for the camera.

He could have been Noah, left for hours in the middle of the street in a pool of his own blood. His body that grew inside of his mother's womb: dark water, heartbeat, home.

Jesse changes the white flowers in the vase at his desk. Noah keeps his mother's gold chain around his neck.

In his dreams, he is drowning. Weights on his ankles, weights on his wrists. There is no way to swim up.

In his dreams, he hears his mom's voice: *Build me an ark, Noah.* He is searching for words, for the right words, he is going backward. He sits at his desk in the small room by the seaside.

Noah comes home from Hard Rock smelling like the vodka he's been pouring all night, Jesse's book in sixteen different languages on display on the living room shelf.

He tells her to get on her knees and she does. He pulls her up and onto the bed, flips her over, and pushes himself into her. There is a roar inside of him, a great buzz, and he comes on her back and pulls off his shirt and wipes it up. He says thank you. He kisses her head. She rolls away from him. He says sorry. He says I'll make it up to you. She gets up, turns on the shower.

She makes lentil soup for dinner. They smoke pot, and on TV, someone is saying the boy's mother never should have let him leave the house with a toy gun. Jesse switches the channel. They close the windows against the California winter, turn up the wall heater. They've already forgotten what Chicago cold feels like, but Noah's body knows it deep in his bones: under-the-skin cold is something you never forget. Turning on the oven for extra heat while the wind rattles the glass. Warming himself against his mother's body in bed, her skin soft, pressing himself into her as she holds him. It is still cold, but his mother is warm, and his chest is warm now and he closes his eyes. This is safety—he can remember the feeling at the very edges of himself.

And then the free fall when her body is gone, the way the winter sets its jaws into him.

Jesse is in Mexico City, Montevideo, São Paulo, gone. A twenty-three-day book tour in Latin America; this will be the longest they've ever been apart from each other. Noah is alone, staring at the same words on the page, swimming.

Jesse is in Buenos Aires, Guadalajara, gone. Noah feels lock-jawed, immobilized.

He scrambles eggs and spinach. He misses Jesse with an ache that makes his stomach hollow, no matter what he eats. She texts photos of the long lines of readers waiting for her to sign their books. They try to talk on the phone, but they are embarrassingly bad at it for a couple who has been together for so long.

He masturbates three times a day to increasingly violent pornography. He gets high in the middle of the afternoon and draws the shades and watches *Taxi Driver* for the fourth time.

He looks at the white gardenias on his desk, browning at the edges now. The flowers Jesse left. She is gone, has been gone for ten days. He will buy his woman a ring; he will marry her; he has to. He has to finish this. He cannot fail any longer.

The ocean is so close that on quiet nights, he can hear it.

He is a child on the beach with his mama, chasing, *Chase me, Mama,* he is saying. He is running along, skipping back, waiting to see if she will follow. It is their game. He is running ahead.

"Mama! Get me, Mama!"

"I can't, Noah."

She moves forward in slow motion. "I can't."

"Mama, please!" Why won't she run after him?

Something is wrong. When she gets to him, her breath is thin and wheezing. She touches his shoulder, trying to steady herself. "I got you, Noah," she says after a moment—it is a whisper, strangled. She used to pick him up, toss him up.

"Mama," he says. "I got you, Mama." It is a day in December, it's cold air off the lake, they're in their puffy coats, it's wind coming off the lake making tears in his eyes.

"Noah, it's so hot," she says.

"Mama, hold my hand."

In his old screenplay, Noah found the bones of his childhood grief. He found a boy trying to navigate the world alone. He found a prayer for some magic. There is more to say about all of it. Noah sits at his desk and types and fights against the tightness in his chest.

Noah is turning seven in the midst of winter: dark peaks of dirty snow out the windows, bright red balloons reaching for the ceiling. It is his birthday, and his mom can't breathe—the machine is pushing oxygen into her lungs, and Uncle Dev, Grandma, and Grandpa are singing. He wants to put his hands over his ears; he is curled like a puppy at her feet. They are trying to coax him to blow out the candles. He looks at his mom and doesn't know if she can see him.

He wishes, of course, for her to get better. He shuts his eyes and blows them out.

He could have been Noah, shot in the back sixteen times.

He could have been Noah, playing at the park. Twelve years old, the smell of winter in his nose, wet and cold and clean. The boy collects a snowball in his naked hands. He sits on a bench. A car pulls up and he stands. Before they even get out, he is shot dead at twelve.

Noah gets his shifts covered. He skips the gym; he stays sober.

He writes like his life depends on it.

# 23

2005–2011

Annie's nearing the end of her shift, the stragglers all drunk and ordering third bottles of wine, and she is finally able to go into the restroom to pee, reapply her lipstick, try to smooth the flyaway hairs that have been stuck to her sweaty forehead all night. When she comes out, she has a new table of two seated in the corner. She hopes the men aren't planning on a full dinner; she hates when people sit down to start a leisurely meal when the restaurant is clearly close to closing, still perusing the dessert menu as bussers stack chairs.

"How can I help you boys?" she says, doing her best to put energy into her worn-out smile.

"What's up, cuz?"

She focuses on Connor's face in the dim candlelit room. "Oh!" she exclaims. It has been several weeks since they met. "You came."

"I told you I was gonna! This is my boy Spencer I told you about."

"Hello," he says, with an air of assuredness. She examines

him: the just-thinning hairline, the high chiseled cheekbones, the narrow nose, the surprisingly full mouth. The clear blue eyes. He looks rich, a more aristocratic brand of Connor's bro-boy vibe.

"Hey," she says. "Welcome."

As he takes her in, she's suddenly aware of her slightly ill-fitting black sweater, the sweat around her bra line, the pilling leggings she has not bothered replacing, her black leather boots that have already had a glass of Malbec and a Negroni spilled on them by two separate customers tonight.

"What are you boys drinking?"

"Lady's choice," Connor says. "Surprise us."

Annie asks Jake the bartender to make her two black Manhattans and requests from the kitchen an off-menu appetizer they tried at last week's staff dinner—duck confit with black cherry bread pudding—as well as the parsnip agnolotti with sage and truffle. She delivers the drinks and snacks to the table, carefully chosen to communicate a sense of sophistication. It works; the boys are impressed with her offerings. As she walks away, she glances sideways and Spencer winks at her. She's turned on by the way he wields a careless sense of power. It makes her want to take it away, to make him beg her.

That small spark of desire he has ignited feels like a trail of bread crumbs, something to follow back to the land of the living.

A few weeks later, Annie stands under the shower letting the hot water rush over her for so long that it becomes tepid. She is going out tonight. A double date. A reason to pretend to be normal. She enters her room in her towel to the mountain of dirty laundry on the floor, the full ashtray, the unmade bed.

How is she possibly going to appear to be a functioning adult for these people?

She begins with her CoverGirl lipstick, some mascara. She tries to weave a crown braid like Juliette used to do, but she can't make it work. She gives up and finds a curling iron stashed in a drawer full of old lotion bottles in the bathroom. She smokes while she picks through her clothing choices—luckily, her few nice dresses are the only items that are still clean.

After a trip to the ballet with Connor and his girlfriend, Kelly, followed by martinis at an upscale bar, Annie goes back to Spencer's place in SoHo. He's the cliché of a rich bachelor, living in a building with security and marble floors, his apartment polished with just a few unkempt details—dry cleaning hung over the back of the chair, an unwashed whiskey glass on the counter. She half expects to find some other woman's lacy lingerie in his bedroom. After a whirlwind of sex in the wake of Juliette's death, Annie has not slept with anyone in months.

When he takes off her clothes, she unleashes herself on him. Normally, on a first time, she'd make herself demure, but one benefit of Spencer is that he appears impenetrable, so she believes he can stand up to the ravages of her desire. The sex is good, very good.

Afterward, she wants to go home, doesn't want to sleep in his six-hundred-thread-count sheets. But it's late, and he's already dozed off. Making an exit now would be dramatic, so she closes her eyes, and is surprised when she wakes past nine, the bed empty.

"You were out like a rock," Spencer says, coming in with a cappuccino that he hands to her. "Are you hungry?"

"Do you have any eggs?" she answers.

"Sure."

She pokes around his kitchen, gathering ingredients for her father's famous omelets. The simple act of making breakfast for another human seems to restore something inside her.

At twenty-five, a few years out of college, Spencer is already an adult, and he opens the door to a ready-made life Annie can simply walk into. The furniture is in place. He has already heard the story of Annie's dead, wayward mother from Connor, which probably lends her the air of a wounded bird, appealing in combination with her cooking and cocktail-making skills, her love of poetry (which she reads aloud to him in the coming months), her comparative literature degree-in-progress, her fluency in French, her ability to discuss the latest *New Yorker* front to back. And, especially, the Margot Marker photographs of her teenage self—Annie has the feeling that Margot and Juliette have reached across time and space, inadvertently helping her seduce Spencer as they once did Matt. Spencer's mother, Jacqueline, a highly intelligent, overbearing housewife, is an art lover—a donor at MoMA and the Whitney—and a fan of Margot's work. Charming her becomes effortless when Jacqueline recognizes Annie as the girl from the photographs.

For Spencer, Annie dresses elegantly, makes elaborate dinners, tells witty jokes. Then she returns to her dorm room and puts on the old, unwashed slip, eats two-day-old takeout if she eats at all, chain-smokes. She is always late on her schoolwork, but she ekes out passing grades. She shows up for her waitressing shifts. And as she spends more and more time in Spencer's world, there is less and less space for her to fall apart. Slowly, her performance turns into her life. She transforms into the woman Spencer believes her to be.

By her senior year at NYU, Annie moves into his SoHo apartment, entertaining on their rooftop, lingering through evenings at cultural events, at charity events, at endless fancy dinners, at exclusive clubs snorting expensive cocaine, while her undigested pain gets closed into a storage box located somewhere in her body.

Annie finds small release valves to let out just enough pressure—she begins to go to "Move," a thrice-weekly ritual of sweaty women in a loft studio on Park Place, performing "spiritual acrobatics." She runs miles a day up the east side highway. She has wild sex with Spencer, her ever-faster roller coaster. Nails into skin, teeth marks. Harder.

"You're feral," he says. "I love it."

Annie cannot go into a Starbucks that winter, because they put Joni Mitchell's "River" on the holiday mix CD they sell at all the registers and play endlessly. She cannot listen to Joni anymore, or Leonard Cohen, or Bob Dylan. Sometimes she'll have to walk out of a bar or boutique to escape the music.

But Joni Mitchell gets the better of Annie the following year, during her first post-college job interview, when "Woodstock" plays in the café where she is meeting a potential employer—a well-known author looking for an assistant. Grief is like this: trying to catch your breath on a Midtown sidewalk while your lungs collapse.

Spencer asks, later, how the interview went. Annie does not mention that she left in the middle of it. She continues working at the Bistro, though Spencer tries to convince her to quit.

They don't need the money, he insists. But Annie wants her own income, however meager it might be in comparison to his.

When Spencer learns that Annie owns a house, one that is just sitting there, empty, he is incredulous. He tells her she ought to rent it out. Annie just shrugs. She can't imagine taking apart the guts of Goldstone, sterilizing it, allowing strangers into the sacred universe that still belongs, in her mind, to the ghosts of Margot and Juliette.

But it must be a lot of work for her father, driving over every week to check on it, making sure the gardeners tend to the yard, that all the plumbing and everything else stays intact. He has done it without complaint, but still. What is she saving it for? When will she return?

She yearns for California in a palpable, physical way, for the open vistas of sea, for the smell of salt water, for the puncturing scent of fresh oranges, for the peel of eucalyptus bark, for the glittering light, for the smells coming from her father's kitchen, for Sundays in the canyon.

As long as she does not go back there, she can crave the California of her girlhood. She can make a myth of it. This, an alternative to the reality of the pain of standing in an empty room where Juliette should be and knowing that she failed her. Staying away is a matter of survival.

Eventually, Spencer convinces her to call a property management company. Annie asks her father to move some of Juliette and Margot's belongings—the record player and LP collection, a few other sacred items that she can picture when she closes her eyes—into the storage closet and lock it. She tells the company to keep the furnishings and yard as they are and gives them permission to do whatever else is needed to turn Goldstone into a vacation rental. When she imagines actors in town for pilot season sleeping in the oak bed, picking Meyer lemons or just-ripening peaches from the orchard, Annie wants to vomit. She tries not to think about it.

Jacqueline helps Annie get hired as an assistant to a famous literary agent who's an old friend, and Annie loses herself in the work. She enjoys the achievable tasks of securing plane tickets and floral arrangements. Most of all she loves the editorial part of the job, loves disappearing into stories, living there. She is good at making sentences cleaner, paragraphs lean, plots tighter. Her boss recognizes this and rewards her with more responsibility, a higher salary. Although Annie's ambition is tempered by what she believes, deep down, that she deserves, which is very little, she dedicates herself to her work because she needs it. It is both an anchor and a space where she feels confident, expansive. Helping authors share their stories allows her to engage with the telling of difficult truths, without having to tell her own. She can satisfy her need for art, for meaning, inside the safe boundaries of professional relationships.

Outside of work, Annie hangs out with the other assistants, along with the wives and girlfriends of Spencer's friends and colleagues—Connor's fiancé, Kelly, especially. Annie likes Kelly and the other girls she spends time with, but she can't shake the feeling that she is going through the motions of friendship rather than experiencing it. The shopping trips, the mani-pedis, the brunch dates feel like a part of the identity she has adopted. Her essential self lived in the fire of grief long enough to become liquid. She pours herself into the molds she is meant to fit.

Annie and Spencer move into a new spot so he can be closer to work, a flat in the Financial District with a marble wet bar, French oak floors, a fancy Italian espresso maker Annie picks out so they can "save money on lattes." The single vestige of her former self in the apartment is the photograph of her and Juliette in bed at Goldstone. She wants, at times, to take it down, but she keeps it up. Perhaps not only because she still feels beholden to the promise she and Juliette made to hang their matching prints, but because it is a way of acknowledging her past that is clean—framed, contained. The girl in the picture is an Annie from another dimension.

Her father is the sole human bridge between her former self and her current one, and she cherishes his trips to the city. Sometimes he comes with Sandra, but often he travels alone. His presence in her new home seems to make it real, providing continuity between the Annie who lives with Spencer and works in publishing, and the Annie from LA.

Between visits, Annie and her dad talk on the phone almost daily. She calls to report on the fall leaves in Central Park, to ask him how he makes his ceviche, to tell him about the book she's been reading, which he then begins reading so the two of them can discuss it. She asks him how to fix the garbage disposal, dismissing Spencer's suggestion to "call someone." She keeps him updated on Connor's wedding plans, which will culminate in Annie meeting her uncle Jonathan.

Tears spring to Jonathan's eyes when Connor introduces him to Annie at the reception—a lavish affair at the Rainbow Room. Annie thinks perhaps Connor's dad will hug her, but instead, he shakes her hand.

"Wow. Suzi's daughter. You came out beautiful."

"Thank you."

His grip is firm, his palms mildly sweaty. "It does me good to know that you've made such a nice life for yourself. Look at you." He gestures to Spencer beside her, as if he were proof of Annie's success as a human—*He's not wrong,* she thinks.

Two weeks later, a waiter serves frozen Negronis on the rooftop where Annie and Spencer enjoy the lingering light on an early summer night. Annie feels pretty in a new green silk dress, her freckles coming out, her skin dewy.

Spencer raises his glass. "To my brilliant girl."

Annie grins, toasts him. They are celebrating; she has been hired at a new job, a junior editor at a renowned publishing house. *Annie Ricci, associate editor.* She loves the sound of it.

"We should get married, don't you think?" Spencer says nonchalantly, eyeing her across the table.

A pulse of alarm echoes through Annie's chest. "I'm only twenty-six," she stammers.

Spencer laughs. "That's not exactly a child bride."

Annie doesn't fully understand why she feels panicked. Inside her life with Spencer is the only place she knows how to live. But can she live here *forever?* When she thinks about anything real, anything that matters, Juliette is still there, waiting for her. Reminding her. *You chose me.* And then the whisper, the fear, the guilt, the dreaded loop that haunts her, that stops her from believing she deserves this golden life with Spencer. *You abandoned me. You betrayed me. If you'd answered your phone, maybe I'd still be alive. If you'd been there for me that year, maybe I'd still be alive.*

Annie does not share these shadows with Spencer. She knows he can sense them in the dark when they make love, the rough shapes of them in the way she tears at him, the way she needs to be ravished. But for the most part, Annie leaves the mess there, in the bedroom. She picks herself up and makes the morning coffee, curls her hair for work. Keeps the hints of her sadness to manageable doses. She comes to Spencer as her best, her cleanest self. She likes that he allows her to be that version of Annie. He brings it out of her.

She has allowed herself to love Spencer almost precisely because it is so different from loving Juliette. Juliette is her chosen one, and Spencer is—what? He is her partner. If her friend hadn't died, she would not be sitting here with him tonight, discussing a possible marriage.

But she did. She is.

"Annie?" Spencer's voice brings her back. "You good?"

"Yeah—yes. Sorry."

"Did the idea of marrying me just send you into an existential crisis?"

"Maybe." She laughs a little, reaches for his hand. "Not because I don't wanna marry you. Of course I do." He must be a bit hurt, but he's not the type to dwell on it. Spencer projects a confidence that Annie finds deeply comforting. He is sturdy, privileged. He will never need her in the ways that Juliette did, and that fact is a relief. "It's just . . . I don't know if I feel like a grown-up, yet."

"Well, you are." He's right. And this is what growing up is, isn't it? You aren't *supposed* to stay the same person you were at eighteen.

"I think I should be thirty," she says after a moment. She is not ready for forever. But maybe she will be. Maybe she could be.

"I'll be thirty-five by then."

"That's okay. Not too late for babies." She smiles, a little flirtatiously.

"But will we want to get pregnant right away?"

"On the honeymoon," Annie says. "That's romantic." She's making this up as she goes but starting to believe it.

Spencer considers her. After a moment he says, "How many kids?"

"Two, I think. Being an only child is lonely."

"Okay. Two," Spencer says, his voice warming. "A boy and a girl."

Annie laughs. "I don't think you can order up the sex of the babies."

Spencer tips his drink back. "I'm counting on us getting lucky."

Annie feels an unexpected thrill, thinking about it. Children.

# 24

2014

"Your dad would be proud of me," Jesse's mom, Sara, asserts, sitting across from Jesse at the dining table where her family ate together almost every night of her childhood. They share a caprese salad with basil from her father's garden.

"He'd have lost his shit at the idea of you traveling alone." Jesse laughs, though her stomach feels queasy.

Sara laughs back. "Better than killing myself," she says lightly.

Jesse's mom has just broken the news: she's planning to volunteer abroad—there's a program in Fiji helping Indigenous communities, a teaching program in Nepal, another in Cambodia. She hasn't touched her part of the life insurance, plus she has her husband's pension, the rest of their savings. She was a stay-at-home mother. Now the kids are gone, her husband is gone, and there is nothing here for her. She will sell the house.

The next day, Jesse signs books at her favorite local store—a final stop that she arranged on the way home from her Latin American tour. When Jesse's mom drops her off at the airport, the Sandia Mountains glow their classic watermelon pink, a swan song. She wishes her mom would continue standing inside the space of Jesse's childhood, holding it open. But of course, she knows that is impossible.

As Jesse steps away, her mom reaches out, grabs her hand, pulls her back to hug her again.

What if she uses her father's life insurance money to buy the house, Jesse asks herself as she waits at the gate, staring out the huge window as the mountains slowly darken, sunset softening to dusk. She is living off her book earnings; the 100k that she's been saving all these years could be enough for a deposit on the home she grew up in. She could keep her anchor.

But then what? Would she want to rent it out? Would Noah ever move to New Mexico with her? He could write from anywhere, right? But he would lose his chance to get a foot in the door. It would feel like giving up. She knows that.

Maybe renting *could* work, if it would cover the mortgage. They could visit the house in between tenants. She could show the home to their children, one day . . . She and Noah and their babies could pick figs from her father's tree, could make tamales in the kitchen where Jesse learned to make them from her father.

Noah picks Jesse up from LAX at 10:00 p.m.; they hold each other in the midst of car horns and smog and chaos. He remembers the girl who stepped off the plane from Albuquerque all those years ago, how he'd felt about her then. The woman he would marry.

He feels yet another terrible flicker of hope: maybe soon he can. Maybe his just-finished script is good enough to become something.

"Come on," he says, taking her bag and putting it in the trunk.

Jesse smells like cheap wine.

"You drank on the plane?"

"Yeah."

"You good?"

"I'm exhausted. And starving."

"There's not much at the house."

Jesse sighs, as though she'd expected better. Noah had managed to clean up the place before he came for her. But he didn't go to the store.

"You wanna go through In-N-Out?"

"Not really," Jesse says. "I'm tired."

"Okay. Well, should we order something?"

"I guess. What's still open?"

"Vegan Thai?"

"Okay."

Jesse types their usual order into her phone. An uneasy silence settles over them, as if neither knows how to cross the chasm left by the three-week absence.

"I finished *The Red Balloon*," Noah says finally. "The new version."

"You did?"

"Yeah. I can't wait for you to read it."

The next morning, she does; the script is beautiful and devastating. Noah has rewritten his original take. This time, by the third act, the orphaned child has grown into a teenager, doing what he can to pay for a rented room, trying to finish school. Noah has fun with the conceit of it, the balloon bobbing impatiently outside a closed door where the teen boy is having sex.

When, in the end, the boy is chased by cops, the balloon finally fails in its many attempts to help him escape danger. Jesse is in tears as the boy is shot in the back and the balloon wilts to the concrete.

After years of reading and rereading every line of every draft of every script he's ever written, Jesse knows that this is it. This is the one that will change everything.

They talk about what to do next. Jesse suggests that Noah send *The Red Balloon* to Josh, the agent he'd met, who told Noah he'd be happy to read his next script.

Noah frowns. "Nah."

"But he said he wanted to read your next thing," Jesse insists.

"That was just something to say. It was a long time ago."

"He met with you. He obviously liked your writing, or why bother?"

In the end, Jesse talks Noah into it. He hates the idea of going back to a corny dude who rejected him, just to give him the chance to do the same thing again. But he doesn't have a lot of options on the table. He writes an email, has Jesse read it—they go back and forth on the two-line correspondence, until finally Noah hits send. *Yo, Josh, I know you said you wanted to read my next thing. It's been a minute, but I'm excited about this one. Let me know if you wanna check it out.*

Josh replies three days later once Noah's sure that he won't: *Sure bro. Send along.*

Noah does. And then, a stretch of silence.

On the nineteenth day of waiting, Josh calls to tell Noah he loves the script.

It takes Noah a moment to register what has just happened: it's Josh. He loves it. "You're fucking brilliant, bro," Josh says.

Three days later, over craft cider, Josh tells Noah again that he's fucking brilliant. "The script was like *Beasts of the Southern Wild* meets *Twelve Years a Slave*," Josh says.

Noah's stomach turns.

Josh taps his shoulder playfully. "I'm kidding."

Noah's stomach is still turning, but he laughs it off.

"But for real, I feel like people are asking for this kind of work right now," Josh goes on. "Real stuff. Especially after Oscars So White, you know, Hollywood is open to new voices." Still, he warns, the movie will be hard to get made; they'll have to package it.

Josh's agency sends the script to a couple of directors repped by the company. The first one passes, but the second loves it. He's made big movies—comedies with middling reviews and excellent box office results.

The director tells Noah he's been doing his thing for a long time now, and he's ready to try a lane change. He's been looking for something with real "teeth" and thinks *The Red Balloon* is it.

Noah and Jesse celebrate with takeout—mussels and fries—and share a bottle of cold red wine, start a movie. They make love before it's over, Jesse's legs spread open, Noah's fingers in her mouth as he cradles her from behind, his head pressed against her back.

"Let's make a baby," he says.

Jesse smiles. "After you marry me."

"I will," he says. "Soon, okay?"

He starts looking at Zillow—he can't help himself—sending Jesse homes for sale in Silver Lake, where they lived in their first years in LA. He tells her where he imagines they might put a Jacuzzi, what room would be the nursery.

The director is officially attached and the script is sent out to the handful of studios who make this kind of "arthouse" movie. Pitches are arranged.

Noah charges new jeans, new T-shirts, new sneakers to his emergencies-only credit card to wear to his meetings.

On his way to Fox, Noah takes a Xanax; he walks into the room with the director, and the studio executives smile at him.

"You are such a great writer," they say. "Seriously. Super brilliant."

Noah smiles and makes self-deprecating jokes and tries to hide his radiant hope. They ask the director about how he sees the movie and the director speaks, in platitudes, about the importance of social justice.

In the days that follow, Noah's gleam of hope is eclipsed by its shadow: anxiety. He cannot go anywhere without his phone, cannot stop checking his emails and missed calls for news. He's on his way to Hard Rock when the phone rings. It's Josh.

Both studios have passed.

"Okay," Noah says, ignoring the crushing pain in his chest. "What's next?"

"I know this isn't the news we wanted to hear," Josh says. "Major bummer. Let's just take a beat. You're a talent. We should talk about what else you wanna write."

Noah veers left and stops at Runyon Canyon. In his work Vans, he sprints up a hill and back, up and back, up and back in the afternoon sun, his lungs on fire, sweat dripping into his eyes, stinging, causing tears to well. He wipes it all away, goes again.

By the time he finally walks into the Hard Rock Cafe, he's fifty-four minutes late, covered in sweat, dirt on his shoes. It's only by the grace of all his infraction-free years there that he doesn't get fired on the spot. His manager looks him over, tells him to go home. He drives around the city aimlessly. He rolls a joint. He doesn't want to face Jesse.

At the sound of the door, she emerges from her office in slippers and a muumuu.

"Are you okay?" she asks.

"They passed," he says quickly, and walks by her. "I'm gonna go shower."

When he emerges, he finds Jesse in the kitchen, drinking wine, a plate of pasta and a bowl of salad on the table.

"Thanks," he says. "I'm gonna put on the game, if that's okay."

"No, wait," she says, her eyes flickering, her voice urgent. "We're going to make your movie, Noah."

"Maybe. You never know." Noah feels flattened, defeated. "If I get something else to pop off, maybe there will be a second chance." But he's been trying for so long to get something to "pop off," he doesn't know where else to go. He gave this one all he had, and it wasn't enough.

"Maybe we can still have a baby," he says. "I can be the stay-at-home dad." He tries to smile.

"Sure," she says. "After you direct *The Red Balloon*."

Noah laughs. "We couldn't get it made with an actual director. They'll never let me do it."

"It's yours," Jesse says. "It came from your heart and your brain. You were always supposed to do it. He was never gonna be right—they must have been able to tell. This is personal. You already see it."

"It's a pipe dream, babe. The only studios that might've made it already passed."

But Jesse made a contingency plan, in case of rejection. She promised herself not to let him fall again. She even has an email to Dexter sitting in her drafts folder:

*Dex, remember when I asked you to read one of Noah's scripts years ago, and you said you'd do it just once. Well, this script is genius, so you're welcome. We wanna do it as an indie so Noah can direct. We've got 100k on the table to get us started with a budget and investors. If you don't snatch it up, someone will, but I had to give you the first shot at coming on to produce. Xo*

"I'm going to invest my dad's life insurance in it," Jesse says to Noah now.

"What?" Noah shakes his head in disbelief. "Jess, that's crazy. I could never let you do that, and even if I could, it's not enough to make a movie."

"It will get us started—seed money."

He can't help his smile. "Nobody's ever had my back like you do, nobody but my mom . . ." He trails off. "But I can't take your dad's money—your money—"

"We're partners, Noah. It's an investment. We'll make the money back. It's a good bet. You are brilliant and so is the script." Jesse will let her childhood home go, the house that stored all that memory. She wants a future with Noah even more than she wants to hold on to her history.

"Jess . . ." He sounds unsure, but Jesse can see him beginning to inflate with the possibility.

"We're doing it now," she goes on. "We're not going to waste any time. We're going to get a budget done and raise the rest of the money. You're going to direct your movie. We're going to get married. We'll premiere *The Red Balloon* at a festival and sell it to one of these companies that just passed on it. Audiences are going to fall in love with it. We're going to have a baby."

Noah stares back at her. Eventually, he nods, as tears begin to stream from his eyes. He takes her hand. "Thank you," he says.

# 25

2014–2015

On Annie's twenty-ninth birthday, Spencer throws a surprise party, renting out the entirety of her favorite restaurant for a Tuesday-night dinner. Even her father is here with Sandra, in his corduroy cap, his favorite rayon shirt, his aftershave. Annie runs to embrace him.

She asks Spencer, jokingly, why he didn't save the big to-do for thirty, but when Spencer gives Annie her gift—a small box wrapped with a huge bow—she understands. Inside the package is an extravagant diamond ring.

He bends on his knee. "Will you marry me?"

"Yes," Annie says, her cheeks flush. The room erupts in cheers.

Annie looks over at her dad, sitting beside Sandra. He beams back at her.

"I know," Spencer says, "that you want to wait till you're thirty, but it's gonna take my mom at least a year to plan it."

Annie laughs with her friends and family as Jacqueline does little excited claps.

Admittedly, part of Annie wishes they could just skip over the wedding, but she's ready to be married now. She wants to become pregnant. She wants a baby—babies—to love. She wants to be a mother. It seems like the answer to the emptiness in her center that every so often she can't pretend isn't there.

It's so easy to see—she and Spencer pushing the stroller through Central Park, stopping at the turtle pond; making a mess of the kitchen as their kids help crack eggs for omelets on Sunday mornings; the four of them piled in bed together watching movies; hanging ornaments on the Christmas tree as Annie pulls freshly baked cookies out of the oven. Maybe she'll even take her kids back to Los Angeles, show them the lights on Candy Cane Lane.

Along with Jaqueline, Annie and Spencer decide on the New York Public Library for the venue. Fitting for a bookish bride. They reserve it eighteen months in advance, for the fall of 2015. Annie enjoys the role of bride-to-be more than she'd imagined: the engagement party, the dress shopping. She imagines what it would feel like to have a mother to stand beside her in the boutique, admiring her reflection in the mirror. She imagines what it would be like to have Juliette and Margot.

But she settles for Jacqueline, Kelly, and Deirdre, another editor she's made friends with at work. It is enough. Annie likes poring over the website of flower vendors in bed on a Sunday morning while Spencer delivers coffee. She likes sitting on the couch beside him after work in the evenings, discussing possible menu selections, debating which cocktails to serve.

She does her best to ignore the whisper that still lingers in the back of her mind: *You don't deserve this.* She has built this life, the kind of life she can point to with pride, as proof of her survival. She is not broken. She is a woman who goes out for cocktails with coworkers, who organizes a shared calendar with her fiancé, detailing opera tickets and weekend getaways, who is responsible for editing a book on the Indie Next list. Who has multiple sets of linen sheets, an impeccably decorated loft, a three-carat diamond on her finger, a bedroom full of lavender-scented candles. A list of possible baby names on her iPhone. She is lucky and privileged. She knows that.

And then, a few months after Annie turns thirty, as she sits curled on the couch sipping Chablis, on FaceTime with her father, he tells her carefully that his doctor has found a tumor in his abdomen. Annie's heart falls into her gut. *No. No, no, no.* But the prognosis is hopeful, her father is telling her. They'll do chemo first, and, depending on the results, possibly surgery.

"I'll come see you," Annie says. It's been so many years now.

"Stay put for a little longer. I want your homecoming to be happy."

"But, Daddy—"

"Your old man is gonna be okay."

"Okay . . ."

Annie and her dad continue to talk on the phone almost daily. He tells her about his treatments, about the latest meeting with his surgeon—he mostly tells her the hopeful things, glossing over his swollen joints that make it take over an hour to shower, glossing over his nausea and pain, focusing instead on the flavors of gelato he's trying out in order to gain weight (fig is his favorite) whenever he can manage to eat, or the rainbow he saw yesterday. He begins to reference death, but only in practical, never existential, terms: he's thinking of selling his record collection, he tells Annie on the phone, and asks if there's anything he should set aside for her.

"I want to start getting my things in order," he says lightly, "so I won't leave too big a mess for you and Sandra to clean up, just in case . . ."

"Stop, Daddy!" Annie says.

"It'll take more than a little cancer to knock me out."

He calls her sometimes from the lab where he gets his treatments, his voice growing softer, slower, more tired over the weeks. She plays his saved messages on her phone to remember his vibrancy.

"Let me come visit you," she says, again.

"Come when the treatments are over. Come when I can cook for you or, at least, when you can cook for me."

Annie and her dad have always talked about food. Now that he can't eat anymore and has to be fed liquid nutrients, Annie no longer brings it up, but he seems more eager than ever to know every detail of what she eats. "What's lunch?" he'll ask. She never wants to disappoint him by admitting she's dutifully stuffing down a salad from Sweetgreen at her desk—all that kale that feels like so much work—so sometimes she makes something up: pumpkin-filled bao, Singapore noodles. If it's later, the question will be "What are you doing for dinner?"

"I don't know, maybe I'll pick up some crab from the fish market and steam some corn. I still have some I need to use."

"Sounds delicious," he says, eager to advise. "And a good butter lemon sauce?"

"Of course." She smiles to him through the phone, her heart breaking.

"I think a little tarragon," he'll answer.

"Yes. That's genius."

Annie and Spencer's wedding date gets postponed, due to her father's inability to travel. They rebook the venue for December 2016. As her dad grows sicker and it becomes harder to hide from the truth of his illness, Annie begins to unravel. At first, it's little things: leaving the coffeepot on when she goes out, forgetting her credit card at the bar, forgetting to pick up the dry cleaning Spencer needs for a meeting, making their dinner reservations for the wrong day. Staring into space when they're out with friends, neglecting to laugh at a joke.

"I'm worried about you," Spencer says, in a tone that sounds tinged with irritation to Annie.

Still, she manages largely to contain her anxiety, to accustom herself to the heavy sadness that parks on her chest with her first morning breath, to cry only clean, containable tears onto Spencer's shoulder. To save her gut-wrenching howls for underwater, in the bathtub. They come from someplace deep in her gut, the storage box she made for all that pain. It feels ready to burst.

Three months into her father's last round of treatment, Annie tries to put her foot down. She calls him, tells him she's bought a ticket to visit.

"No, please." Her father sounds desperate. "I don't want you to see me like this. Come when I'm better. All of this is almost done with."

"Okay," Annie whispers, so she won't cry. "Okay, Daddy. I'll come when you're better."

The week after her father starts his final round of chemo, as Annie is sitting at her desk with her farmhouse Caesar, an

invitation arrives in her inbox. The Whitney is hosting a retrospective of Margot's work—*Margot Marker's Girlhood.* "As part of the artist's inner circle and Margot's last living subject . . ." the email begins. Annie's stomach tightens; her chest tightens; she can barely swallow her mouthful of kale. Her first instinct is to hit delete, but something stops her.

The longer Annie sits there, reading and rereading the invitation, the harder it is to hide her desire from herself: she wants to go. She is intrigued by the chance to be seen as the girl from Goldstone by all those museum donors and gallery-goers, intrigued by the idea of walking in with her fiancé on her arm. Somewhere in the back of her mind, she imagines that perhaps the event could be a way to connect her old identity to her present one.

On the night of the opening, Annie selects a silk slip dress, vaguely reminiscent of the nightgowns she, Juliette, and Margot used to wear to bed. She gets her hair braided into a crown at the salon, like Juliette used to do, but it's not the same. She takes it out when she gets home, leaving her hair full of waves and kinks.

As she and Spencer arrive to a sea of blazers and stilettos, Annie catches sight of Juliette's eyes on the wall in the famous pomegranate picture. There she and Annie are on the deck, eating strawberries.

"Look at you, baby," Spencer says. "You look the same as you did when you were seventeen." He brushes her hair back from her neck.

Annie tries to smile for him.

"You seem nervous," he says.

Annie's eyes dart around the gallery. "It's just, seeing all the photos together like this, it's . . . intense. It's been a long time since I've seen most of these . . ."

He squeezes her hand. "You want me to get you a drink?"

"Yeah. Thanks."

Spencer disappears. There is Juliette, in the torn-lace dress at twelve. There she is in the bath. There are she and Annie, sprawling across the grass. She and Annie, on the beach. There is Goldstone in its glory; Annie feels as if she could almost step into the pictures. There is Juliette, full of joy. Annie looks down at her Prada heels. Spencer returns with two martinis. Annie sips, trying not to let on that it is hard to catch her breath. The museum curator is talking to her, but Annie is barely following what he is saying. Her gaze tries to find a spot to land in the haunted gallery, as her body floods with memory: Julie, Julie, Julie. *What happened to Juliette?* She downs the rest of her drink. It does not stop the loop. *If you'd answered your phone when I called five times, maybe I'd still be alive. If you'd been there for me that year, maybe I'd still be alive.*

Did she drown herself on purpose? Did she want to die?

"Excuse me," Annie says, sucking air deliberately in and out of her collapsing chest as she rushes out, trailed by Spencer.

"Babe, are you okay?" he asks.

"Mmhmm." She is not breathing properly.

He hails a cab.

*What happened to Juliette?* The question has an undertow of its own; it would be too easy for Annie to drown in it. She knows that.

At home, still dizzy, Annie tries to convince Spencer she is fine. "It was just a lot," she tells him. "I still really miss her."

He rubs her shoulders. She fixes herself another martini and goes to bed in her silk dress.

———

Annie's father has in fact sold his records, and he mails the five albums that Annie requested before the collection got carted off. They now sit protruding on her and Spencer's bookshelf in the sleek apartment where there's no record player. Sometimes, as she drinks her coffee in the mornings, Annie sits, staring at them, hearing the music in her mind—Fleetwood Mac, Paul Simon—singing of the window in her heart. She thinks about returning to the Whitney exhibit alone, but she does not.

"Annie?" Spencer will say. "Where are you?"

"I'm here."

Her father will get better, she tells herself. He will walk her down the aisle.

# 26

2015

The air smells like salt and gold. Jesse is wearing the same white lace dress her mother wore to marry her father, and on this fall day in October, everything is possible.

Noah and Jesse have gathered twenty of their closest friends and family to watch them say their vows on the beach at dawn: there is Jesse's mother seated next to Noah's uncle and grandfather. Erica beside Lucy and Mei. Although he is already ten, Eric has been persuaded to play the part of the ring bearer. The sea is a rare and rich color of blue, the clouds high and painterly, crows riding the sky with the gulls. Noah wears a formal tux despite the casual setting. "I Only Have Eyes for You"—one of Jesse's dad's favorite songs—plays from a Bluetooth speaker as Jesse walks through the sand, barefoot in her gown, to meet her husband. She goes alone; there is no replacement for her father.

Though they feel the absences of their missing parents acutely, Noah and Jesse's wedding day is one of the rare moments when loss feels as if it is in service of something greater than itself—it has delivered them to each other. If Noah's mother hadn't died, maybe he wouldn't have fallen in love with Jesse at the University of Chicago. If Jesse hadn't lost her father, maybe she would not have taken the leap and followed Noah to Los Angeles. But here they are. Promising themselves to each other. Building a life.

After years of struggle, their dreams are coming true, together. The money for *The Red Balloon* was raised in record time—in part thanks to Dexter, in part thanks to Afreem's hedge-fund connections, and in part thanks to the strength of the script. In Dexter's words, it is "timely," and now, it is a movie. It's better than they could have hoped for, Jesse thinks, braver, more beautiful.

The messages continue to pour in from readers around the world, telling Jesse that *Grief Is Like This* made them feel seen, understood. She finished her second book in a whirlwind in the spring, as Noah began preproduction. After a year of struggle with it, the new book poured out of her in a matter of months. She thinks it might be better than her first. She dared to tell a coming-of-age story—barely fictionalized—that she's never told in real life: the quarter she spent in Paris, before she met Noah, that took a dark turn in an encounter with two French men. The character in the book falls apart afterward in a way that Jesse never allowed herself to, instead burying the memory. Though the writing process was painful, it was a catharsis Jesse hadn't known she needed.

After the ceremony, the wedding guests walk back to Noah and Jesse's bungalow for a reception, soliciting honks as Jesse crosses Main Street in her classic white gown. Fall bouquets adorn every corner of the home and yard, thanks to Elenore and Suraya. Noah and Jesse's favorite barbecue spot has catered the food, and a bartender—a friend of Noah's from his days at Hard Rock—mixes mint juleps. Jesse made the playlist herself.

The toasts go on and on. Afreem and John, Noah's friends from the University of Chicago, tell jokes about how Noah was the hardworking one back in college, passing up on all kinds of shenanigans. They talk about how they always knew that Noah would make it, how all those years when they seemed to get ahead, they knew he'd do something grand and leave them in the dust. As grand as his movie is, they say, marrying Jesse is his greatest achievement yet.

Noah has to start sound mixing and color correction on Monday, so after the celebrations Noah and Jesse drive out to a house they rented in Joshua Tree for a honeymoon. They stay up watching the stars in the hot tub, drinking champagne and listening to the desert night and reliving the day and making love until the sky is turning morning gray and they fall asleep in a heap, and then make love again when they wake, half hungover but happy, to the bright desert sun streaming through the window. Jesse feels incredulous. They have put the pieces of their lives together, built them up like a soaring skyscraper, and the air up here is clear.

By late afternoon, Noah and Jesse curl up in the living room in their plush bathrobes, a fire dancing in the fireplace, their pinot noir poured into crystal glasses and the perfect smell of desert fall air coming through the open windows, the cacti casting strange shadows with the white halos of their spines. Jesse loves those cacti, the violence and grace of their shapes, the magic of life that struggles up from the dirt.

They pass a joint and watch the night fall in that particular shade of pink, soft but wild, electrically alive. It is perfect. But at the sharpest edge of the sunset, Jesse feels a whisper of anxiety—their happiness feels almost gravity-defying. In the sky, each stage of beauty is as poignant as the last, muted purples, dim gold going down, the undertow of night pulling from below the surface. She sips her wine, rests her head on Noah's shoulder, whispers in his ear: "Make love to me again, I want a baby."

# 27

Cumulus clouds, a cinnamon candle that smells like her mother's holiday potpourri, a snatch of bird shadow darting across the floor, a half-eaten mandarin, heavy lids. Chamomile tea, comforter. Life accumulates in the corners. Winter is finally under way, the heat chased out of Los Angeles, replaced by restless clouds, sun as pure as snow, rain that refuses to fall. The baby is the size of a plum today. Brand-new to Jesse's body, it already feels as if their girl has been there forever, the fall of their wedding light-years away.

She's always ill, a vague, rolling nausea with her at all times of day, a strange heaviness gripping her body, dragging her underwater. She only wants to sleep. She does, and wakes both sick and ravenous. Pregnancy makes her crave the foods of her childhood: Eggo waffles, buttered flour tortillas, grilled cheese, apples.

Kate, the publicist Dexter has hired to see *The Red Balloon* through its upcoming film festival premiere, is six months along, due in March, her belly popping out under her business-chic blouses. She is bright and bubbly, taking Noah shopping, sending him schedules, coaching him on interviews, no signs of slowing down. Jesse marvels at it. Since the start of her pregnancy, she hasn't gone back to writing, abandoning a just-started third novel in a folder on her computer, spending her waking hours researching doulas, birthing centers, the best vitamins for her baby's brain health. She worries constantly, taking care to avoid pollution, and runny eggs, and plastic containers, and anything that could harm her growing child, desperate for each OB appointment where she can hear the little girl's heart beating inside her, confirming she is still alive.

Aside from morning walks, Jesse mostly stays hidden indoors. But today, she must face the world. She can hear Noah in the shower and pulls herself from beneath the blankets to get ready for her reading. She chooses a loose dress to hide her vaguely puffy belly. The early-December sky is restless: dark clouds, shifting sun. Her second book is out today.

As she and Noah navigate the holiday crowds through The Grove toward the Barnes & Noble, the giant Christmas tree lit, the fake snow blowing, carols blasting out of the stores with their extravagant window displays, a wave of melancholy moves through Jesse's body. There have been few reviews of the new book thus far, none in major outlets, and even the bloggers who'd loved her first offering seem to be ignoring her second. Perhaps it is not commercial enough, Jesse thinks now—too much poetry, not enough plot. Her publishers rushed it out, but perhaps the release is badly timed, the story too depressing for the holiday season. Or maybe it is just not that good.

Most of the time it's easy enough to pretend that she's not devastated by her impending failure, even to herself. There is the excitement of Noah's movie, about to have its world premiere at a major festival next month, and her new pregnancy, which has all but taken over her psyche. But deep inside her, Jesse feels the fear of losing the thing she worked for. Of trading her identity as an author for that of a wife and mother. What if the success of *Grief Is Like This* was an anomaly she will never be able to replicate?

When they get to the bookstore, Jesse hurries to the bathroom to throw up in the stall. She rinses her mouth with water, splashes her wan face, puts on a smile.

After the reading, Noah takes her out for a fancy steak dinner, but all she can stomach are mashed potatoes and ginger ale. Noah orders a martini, a glass of red wine, a ribeye, rubs her thigh under the table and tells her how proud he is of her, talks about the movie, the last person to rave over it, his upcoming trip to New York, where he has a few pitches and will do some early press. Suddenly, their lives have shot off on opposite trajectories: Noah is living his dream while she is on a boat, some mysterious tide carrying her farther out to sea.

December 24; Jesse is alone. It's three thirty in the afternoon, but the golden-hour sun is already low along the horizon. She feels sick with longing; no matter how many years pass, she cannot stop missing her father like this. It is her first Christmas away from her childhood home, away from her mom and Lucy. She pulls her tamales out of the pot—her daddy's recipe, of course, made from scratch—and goes back to the couch to close her eyes, imagines her baby turning inside her as she drifts off.

A bright light clicks on, startling her awake.

"Merry Christmas!" It is Noah, coming in the front door with his roller bag and a bouquet of red lilies.

"What are you doing in the dark?" he asks, and comes to her.

She forces herself off the couch and falls into him.

"I missed you," he says.

"I missed you, too. A lot."

"It smells good in here," he says, and hands her the bouquet of flowers.

"Did your new assistant pick those up?" Jesse asks. It is a mean question—she doesn't know why it comes out of her mouth. He's been away too long.

But Noah is happy. He doesn't take the bait. Instead, he puts his arms around her again. "I got them," he says. "And I got the Nike commercial. It'll pay 50k, just for a couple of days."

"That's so good." Jesse holds him, kisses him, and then, all at once, she is crying. She doesn't know why.

Noah puts his arms around her. "Baby."

Jesse's second book has indeed turned out to be a failure by all practical measures. She feels, three months into pregnancy, gripped by a strange dread as she palpates and cannot find herself anywhere.

Bewildered, Noah guides her to the couch, brings her water.

"Babe. Are you okay?" He holds her. "What's wrong?" he asks. "What's wrong?"

"Promise," she finally chokes out. "Promise you won't leave me."

Noah pulls her against him. "I'll never leave you, Jess. I got you. I can take care of you now. I can take care of us."

She leans her weight into him and feels something inside of her let go.

"I got you," he says again. "I got you, baby. I promise."

# 28

2016

Noah turns to Jesse and can't stop tears from springing to the surface. "We did it," he whispers into her ear. The audience stays on their feet, roaring, as Noah pulls Jesse up to the stage with him, calls the rest of the cast and crew. When he dreamed of succeeding, Noah thought of the money—the dignity it can buy in this country—and of the art most of all, his longing to be known. He never thought of what applause might feel like, the way the sound would lift him off his feet. He reaches up and runs his fingers over his mother's gold chain tucked beneath his shirt.

It's a long night, full of celebration. Jesse tires quickly, so Noah ducks out to walk her back to the hotel, where they are staying for the duration of the festival. He's had a couple drinks, and despite the biting air on his cheeks his body is warm and loose, anxiety now rushing out of his organs where it had built up.

At the hotel, Jesse gratefully pulls off her tights and shoes. At eighteen weeks pregnant, she is gorgeous: her breasts are

already swollen, her face round and shining with that glow—
it's a real thing! She chose the tightest dress possible tonight to
accentuate her tiny bump, in hopes, she said, that people will
think she's actually carrying a baby and not just that she ate
too many holiday cookies. She now pulls it over her head, collapses on the bed. Noah's heard other men complain about
complaining wives, already exhausted by their nausea, by trips
to the store to satisfy cravings, by foot rubs. Not Noah. He
relishes the feeling of being able to take care of Jesse.

He calls room service to order her grilled cheese and french
fries, tucks her in, kisses her good night, and goes back to his
after-party.

The Hollywood people who have transported themselves to
the film festival with their designer bags and designer jackets
fawn over Noah—the same people who were once assistants
writing coverage of Noah's work, calling it dark, sprawling,
angry, messy, the ones who told their bosses that he wouldn't
sell, who hit decline on his calls, the ones who passed on him,
who tossed him away—they are now smiling at him, gushing
about how "relevant" and "real" and "powerful" his work is.

A woman with brown hair and big teeth and a leopard-print
jacket approaches him.

"Noah," she says.

"Hi." She looks familiar, but he can't place her.

"I just wanted to tell you I loved your movie. I mean *lo*
loved it. I cried!"

"Thank you," he says. "It was a team effort, for sure."

"You are just so talented, like wow! I heard you were su
talented, but, I mean, this was just, wow. I've never seen a
thing like it."

And then it clicks. It's the girl who interviewed him for

position with the famous director, back in his first months in Hollywood, the one who wanted to know which "unproduced" scripts he'd read.

He smiles. "Thank you." He wonders if she remembers him, the hopeful, hungry twenty-three-year-old in his newly purchased sneakers, searching for someone to let him in the door.

She holds her phone out. "Can I be a nerdy fan and ask for a picture?"

"Sure." He grins for her camera.

And for the next camera, and the next one, letting the Hollywood people stock their Instagram accounts with Noah King, festival darling, as if that might prove that they are "good," that they are "allies."

Of course, Noah is aware of the irony. But he is becoming a "success story." It's hard to be mad at that. He can still see the look of pride on Jesse's face. Josh calls him all night with updates on which studios are making offers. For the first time, Noah believes that anything is possible. It is a feeling he knows that most of the people in these rooms grew up with, that was fed to them since they were children. Noah can't help but think that it is sweeter now that he and his wife have cooked it up themselves. He hopes they will pass it on to their own baby.

When Noah arrives back at the hotel, the sky is glowing blue before the break of dawn. Jesse's food is sitting outside the door, untouched. She must have fallen asleep by the time it arrived.

Jesse wakes to the first colors of the winter sunrise, Noah in bed beside her, his bare skin against her back. He wants to make love. She groans a sleepy groan and lets him rock himself into her, starts to purr. He can feel her body opening—hips expanding, belly, skin. She tastes clean, like water. He devours her. His woman and his child in one. Outside, the sun comes over the mountain, blades of light cutting across their bodies. Noah's phone rings. He silences it. Jesse comes, rests her hand on her stomach. Noah comes, rolls over, and picks up.

"What up," he says into the receiver. And then: "Ho-ly shit."

Jesse turns over. The baby is moving. She can feel it: the first tiny bubbles in her belly. Magic.

They've sold the film to one of the major studios that passed on it in the pitch, for a price higher than Noah had dared to hope. They are already writing the press release: *The Red Balloon deploys the lens of magical realism to portray racial injustice, in a timely film that is unlike anything we have seen. We are thrilled to partner with Noah King, a newcomer with an uncanny confidence behind the camera. Using the conceit of the beloved French classic,* Le Ballon Rouge, *King takes us on a journey that is both breathtaking and heartbreaking.* The studio committed to a significant marketing budget, a full press tour, and fall release. They have carried other indies to the Oscars.

Noah sucks in a breath. For a moment, he feels it: the whisper of fear, the feeling of vertigo looking out from such a height. But he will not allow it. He insists on happiness: for himself, and especially for Jesse. They have waited so long for this.

# 29

Annie dodges the editorial director and his wife on her way to the elevator. She has fled the book launch party, because after three Negronis, she saw the ghost of Juliette. The image was bright as life, arising out of nowhere: Annie glanced into the night from the window of the tenth floor, and there she was, barefoot, swaddled in her burgundy scarf, calling up to Annie, as she had outside the apartment in Chelsea.

Annie steps onto the street, heart still thudding. Of course, Juliette is not there. She takes a moment to catch her breath, muggy July air sticking in her chest.

Though she hasn't smoked in years, Annie buys a pack of cigarettes from the bodega near her apartment and lights one. After a few drags she tosses it reluctantly. Her father has fucking cancer.

She should go home and pack—her flight tomorrow leaves at an ungodly hour.

Spencer is on the leather chesterfield, opening his laptop, drinking from a glass bottle of Voss water. Annie hadn't expected him home yet, doesn't want him to smell the cigarette.

"Hey, baby!" She's too drunk for eight thirty on a Tuesday. "I gotta pee!"

She goes to the bathroom, washes out her mouth, splashes her face with water.

"You good?" Spencer calls out.

"Yeah," Annie says, emerging, and goes to give him a kiss, keeping her lips sealed. She feels as if it's not really her standing here. Is it really she who is going to marry this handsome, successful man?

Is it really she who is about to fly home to Los Angeles for the first time in twelve years for what is meant to be her father's life-saving surgery?

Annie goes to the fridge and pulls out a Voss water of her own. She eyes a half-finished bottle of Chenin Blanc but forces herself to leave it.

"Are you sure you don't want me to come with you tomorrow?" Spencer asks.

"I don't know," Annie says. "You don't have to." Then she adds, "I mean, I'll be fine. It's up to you."

"If you want me to come, just buy the plane ticket."

"You can come out and see him after," she says. "Maybe fly out for a weekend." It's legitimately hard for Spencer to get away from work for even, like, a day. Besides, it's probably better if she first faces Los Angeles alone.

"Okay," Spencer says. "You need me, just say the word and I'm there."

As her buzz begins to wear off, Annie's anxiety becomes palpable, a vine taking root in her stomach, snaking its way up to her chest, wrapping itself around her heart. In the bedroom she lays T-shirts on the duvet, trying to decide on which colors, and how many, and which leggings will go, if she ought to bring one nice outfit or not. As if having the right clothes is crucial to the outcome of the surgery.

"Hey," Spencer says, walking up behind Annie now, brushing her hair away from her neck with the back of his hand, in his usual way. His kiss brings her back to her body. "I love you; you know that?"

"I love you, too," she says, as she places the whole stack of shirts into the suitcase.

"You want a Xanax for the flight?" Spencer keeps a small stash for international travel.

"Yeah."

From the hallway, Annie catches sight of Juliette watching her, her limbs tangled up with the sheets. Annie has been inoculated, over time, to the power of the photograph that has lived with her since college. But now, Juliette's eyes seem to be calling to her. Annie blinks and looks away. She cannot let herself think about Goldstone. She is going back to Los Angeles tomorrow only for her father. She presses her weight onto the overstuffed suitcase, zips it shut.

Driving to Cedars-Sinai, Annie passes through two versions of LA, the current city overlaid on the blueprint of her memory—more buildings, more traffic, a density, on top of what in her mind's eye was an airy, languid sprawl. The pain in her stomach radiates into the gaps between her ribs, making her breaths shadowy. Thank God for Spencer's Xanax, or she'd probably have had a panic attack the second she set foot in LAX. She passes billboard after billboard on the 10 freeway, advertising some kid's YouTube channel, AG Jeans, a slew of shows and movies. She lingers on the image of a little Black kid holding a red balloon, floating over what appears to be Chicago. Juliette's Chicago. Annie misses her exit and has to double back.

Annie parks in a garage and pulls her shawl around her, despite the summer heat. She walks into the hospital and navigates the endless fluorescent maze until she finds the cancer ward. She pushes the button and tells the attendant her name. As she searches out room 1020, she tries not to look through the open doors exposing the body's many forms of betrayal.

She finds her dad awake—hooked up to tubes, skin and bones—sitting by the window, listening to "Harvest" by Neil Young. The diffuser she sent him as a gift sends out sputters of lavender mist. He turns to look at her and tears run down his face.

"Annie."

"Hi, Daddy."

"Annie," he says again, and takes her hand when she goes to his side.

Her father made it sound as if this upcoming surgery was a forgone success, and Annie wanted to believe him. It was Sandra who called her—a rarity—saying, "You really should come home, Annie. The truth is, we don't know how this is going to go."

As she sits down in the chair beside him, her dad reaches his hand out to Annie. "I was remembering," he says, "when you were a baby, and you used to nap on my chest." He puts his hand close to his heart. "Your little head, right here. You and I would sleep like that, together. In the apartment on Magnolia."

Annie smiles at him. She is afraid if she tries to speak, she will burst into sobs.

"Now I've hardly got any chest left," he says.

She brushes her hand against the skin over his heart and holds it there.

"You think they'll be able to put old Humpty together again, Annie?"

Annie swallows the fear balling in her throat, sends it down to her stomach. "When you get out of this surgery, I'm going to bring you home and make you roasted peppers and eggplant, and meatballs and angel hair with tomatoes and basil from the garden."

"I can hardly wait." He rubs his hand over his gaunt cheeks. "I got a shave this morning, in honor of your arrival. One of the nurses called this kid Jesus in from the ICU and he was just lovely. I mean, he really took his time. Last time I tried this, the guy nicked me, but Jesus was so careful."

"You look great, Daddy." She kisses his cheek. It doesn't smell the way it's supposed to, like his aftershave that comes in the candy-striped bottle. "Maybe we should take you out on the town."

He laughs a weak laugh. "Have you gone to the ocean yet?" he asks.

"No."

"Let's go, then," he says.

Annie had been kidding, but her dad is not.

"Are you allowed to do that?"

"It's not a prison."

"But, Dad . . ."

"I'll just tell the nurse I'm going on a drive with my daughter. I don't think there's any harm in that."

His surgery is tomorrow. The recovery could be weeks or months.

"Okay." She smiles. "Just a little drive."

"All right." He does a fist pump into the air. "I knew you'd break me out of here."

As Annie sails onto the PCH in her father's Volvo, she's overwhelmed by the vista of sky and water. She could almost turn and see Juliette beside her, back in the days when the music carried them on its wings over Highway 1.

When they arrive at Point Dume in Malibu, a low marine layer hanging over the crystalline ocean, Annie helps her dad out of the car, bends to remove his slippers, and walks slowly with him toward the shore. He sinks his feet into the sand and closes his eyes, the wind on his face blowing his remaining wisps of hair.

For the past twelve years, Annie has dreamed of this beach, where she used to come with her father, and then with Juliette. The smell of the salt water transports her, and she feels almost as if she has stepped back into another body, one that belongs to the girl she left behind when she fled.

"Are you going to get in?" her dad asks. As a child, she loved to swim.

"I don't think so. I want to stay with you," she says, and squeezes his hand.

"Go ahead," he urges. He's envisioning her younger self, she thinks, remembering her glee at plunging into the ocean.

"Okay."

Annie's father watches as she dives under a wave, still in her T-shirt and shorts. The water is nearly warm; she does her best to radiate the joy she knows he wants to witness.

In the car on the way back, he falls asleep. Out of pure habit, Annie makes the turn into Topanga Canyon—the way to Juliette's that she's driven countless times from the ocean. She looks out at the looming hills, mottled greens and browns. In another lifetime they were bright, lush, a dappled forest. Now they look ready to burn.

Defying the pull of her girlhood, she doesn't take the turn off Topanga that would lead to Goldstone, where she would only find guests enjoying their Airbnb.

Annie stays with her dad that night, sitting in the chair beside his bed, half dozing to the sound of machines beeping, until she is awoken in the early morning by Sandra's arrival, followed by a nurse who has come to take her father to surgery.

"Daddy," Annie says, and lays her head gently against his chest, the spot just above his heart, holding half its weight up with her neck so she won't hurt him. How has she allowed herself to be away for so long? He reaches out a swollen hand and brushes her hair from her face.

"Tulip. Wish me luck."

She squeezes his hand; she cannot speak. She watches as he is carted off.

# 30

The hospital is cold, oblivious to the deep summer heat outside its seemingly impenetrable walls. Annie tightens her shawl and nibbles on her vending-machine Lay's—she has used the greasy salt of potato chips to calm an anxious stomach since she was a child driving up north with her dad. Beside her, Sandra knits a blanket to keep Annie's father warm during his recovery. The buzz of her phone startles Annie—a text from Spencer: *Hey, you okay?* She's about to respond—*Still waiting*—when her father's doctor arrives. His normally jovial face looks grim. Sandra stands, goes to him. His eyes summon Annie, but she can't seem to move. She watches him and Sandra from across the room, hears Sandra cry out. "Oh, Mikey, no."

When the doctor comes over to speak to her, Annie can hardly hear him: they are so sorry, but the surgery has not gone as planned. There were just too many adhesions around his intestines. They did everything they could. He is on a ventilator that is keeping him alive; they have administered a cocktail of drugs to keep him sedated.

The next days blur into a single, endless moment in time; Annie sits by her father's bedside, reading to him, playing music, recounting stories from her childhood while the machines beep, and her father lies barely conscious, feet and hands swollen. When Sandra comes—they take turns staying with him—Annie drives around the city aimlessly in his Volvo, sleeps in her childhood bed at odd hours.

As Annie watches the machine moving air in and out of his lungs, she doesn't know when day turns to night or night to day. She is certain only of the fact that it is her father who tethers her to the world.

When Sandra, in the presence of the lead nurse, tells Annie that it is time they made a plan to take Mikey off the ventilator, it seems they have been gripping the secret of his inevitable death in closed fists.

The drugs are not working, the nurse explains. There's nothing else they can do.

"I have been watching him suffer for so long," Sandra says. "Annie, he's been suffering." It has been Sandra who has woken with him at all hours of the night when he's been sick, who has cleaned up the vomit, who has brewed him fresh chicken broth only to see him throw it up, who hooked up IVs to his arms at home. Sandra's eyes say all this and more.

"But," Annie says, turning her attention to the nurse. "But there's no chance he'll get better? If we keep him on the ventilator long enough, what if his lungs could recover, and even if they can't remove the tumor . . . at least he could see the ocean again, go home and—"

"Annie," Sandra says softly, her eyes welling up. Annie

wants to reach out to her, to hug her, but she doesn't know how.

Sandra wipes her tears. "I'm going to stay with him tonight," she says. Annie wants to be the one to stay, but she's lost that right. "Tomorrow we'll say goodbye."

Tomorrow, her father will die.

Annie takes Sandra's hand, holds it. For a long moment, they stand frozen like that.

In her dad's kitchen that evening, Annie makes her favorite meal from childhood: classic carbonara with fresh pasta. She sets a place for him, serves the food for two. She twirls her linguine and drops her fork, stares into the space where he should be.

Through the night, she lies awake in her childhood bedroom. Aside from Sandra's sewing machine tucked into the corner, it is still unchanged after all this time, down to the horoscopes cut from the *LA Weekly* and pasted to her headboard, the flower garden drawn in nail polish by Juliette. Sandra allowed Annie's father to keep her room completely intact for her as they awaited the day she would return. Why didn't she come sooner? Why didn't she pick up Juliette's call, stay in closer touch during those last months? Why does she abandon the people she loves most?

When Annie goes to the hospital in the early morning, the nurse comes in to turn down the dosage on the sedating drugs so that Annie's father will regain consciousness long enough for Annie and Sandra to say their final words.

As he wakes from his stupor, Annie can feel her father's swollen hand trying to squeeze hers. Her throat closes on itself; how do you account for an entire lifetime? In the end she

manages only to say that she loves him, that he is the best father she could have asked for. Tears spring to his eyes as the
ventilator fills his lungs with air and lets them collapse.

After Sandra has had her turn, the nurse asks them to step
out of the room, while a team comes in to take out her father's
tubes. They administer IV drugs that will "minimize his anxiety" as his body loses its breath forever.

Annie sits beside him, resting her head close to his chest,
imagining she is a baby sleeping there, riding the waves of his
breath. In and out. Each time there is a pause, she and Sandra
squeeze his hands, bracing, and then he sucks in the air all over
again. In this too-clean hospital room with a view of the Los
Angeles sprawl, he is hanging on.

Until he cannot, and his breath simply stops. The sound of
its absence fills the air.

Annie runs out of the room, unable to be near the body he
is no longer in.

# 31

Spencer opens the thick, heavy flowered curtains and glances back at Annie, gauging her reaction to the assault of sunlight. Annie's father had let her get those curtains at an estate sale when she was a girl, she tells Spencer. They seemed elegant to her, romantic, something that you'd find in a castle. Annie was always trying to add "feminine" touches to the house back then, an effort her father indulged.

Spencer opens the fridge in her father's kitchen, offers to make Annie some eggs.

"I'm not hungry," she says.

"Maybe we can go for a run," Spencer suggests.

"You can go."

Her father is dead, but there's not even a funeral to arrange. Sandra has said she is not ready. She left to drive up the coast and clear her head. A long-deferred vacation. She needs to breathe some ocean air, see something other than the walls of this house and the inside of a hospital room. To begin the process of healing.

Annie cannot even imagine what that phrase—*the process of healing*—might actually mean. She is in bed, tracing her finger over and over one of Juliette's nail-polish flowers on the headboard.

"You have to get out of the house, Annie." Spencer is standing in the doorway.

She looks over at him, says nothing.

"Please," he says. "Let's just go to dinner. Or let me take you to a movie." He looks desperate. Then he begins thumbing away at his phone. "There's got to be a comedy or something playing near here. It'd be good for you to have a few laughs."

She does not want to move, but she acquiesces, drags herself from the bed, puts on shorts and a T-shirt.

In the car, on the way, they pass the Baskin-Robbins that Annie's dad used to take her to as a kid. She bursts into sobs.

"What?" Spencer asks. "What is it?"

She can't stop crying. He has to pull over, and they miss the show.

After a few days that seem to be increasingly full of work calls, Spencer steps in from the porch and tells Annie he'll get them tickets home for Monday morning. He has to be back at work by Tuesday at the latest. But Annie says no. She can't go. She's promised Sandra that she'll be here to receive her father's ashes.

Spencer does not join her where she's sunken into the couch but stays on his feet, cell phone in hand. "Can't Sandra get them when she comes home?" he asks. "Certainly, the mortuary—"

"No," Annie says, emphatically. "I have to do it."

"Okay."

"I can't just leave," Annie adds. "I can't just run away this time."

Spencer sighs. She knows what he's not saying out loud: *What good does it do to stay now when there's nothing left?*

"But don't you have to be back at work?" he asks. "Eventually?"

Annie shrugs. The ergonomic pillow, covered in sheepskin fur, meant to pad her father's bony bottom after he could no longer eat, still lies on the couch. Annie brushes her hand over it. She picks at the tiny tears in the fabric. She knows this place, the home she grew up in, the house her father worked so hard to buy for them all those years ago, makes Spencer uncomfortable. He believes in this principle: you take on the characteristics of the space you are in. Their loft in New York is clean, sleek, aspirational, and so, too, they had been.

"Have you let Mark and Katy know that we won't make it tomorrow?" Spencer asks.

Annie looks at him blankly.

"The engagement party?"

His boss's son. She'd forgotten about it. She cannot imagine going to a party, or to dinner with their friends, or to a play or a book launch or a tennis game or to the grocery store, even. She cannot imagine going back to the life she loved, which, from the perspective of where she's sitting on her dead father's coach in Tarzana, seems hollow.

"I'll let them know," Spencer says. "Can you just forward me the evite?"

Has she paid the rent, he asks. She hasn't.

After a moment, he comes to sit beside her, puts a hand on her back. "I think," he says, "that you'll feel better when we get home."

"You don't understand," Annie replies. It comes out as an accusation.

"Understand what? Why you're so mad at me?"

Annie curls into herself, holding her knees to her chest. "I've lost everything."

She sees Spencer's face, which seems to say *What about me?* She tries to soften. "I mean," Annie says, "everyone from my past."

He's looking at her as if he doesn't quite recognize her. Spencer's Annie never asked him to hold the weight of her pain. Spencer's Annie made herself easy to love. His Annie, the Annie who was quick to laugh, the Annie who kept everything close to her vest, who kept it all together, who lived in the present and learned to think of the future, is nowhere to be found.

"Why can't you just hold me," she says quietly.

Spencer takes her in his arms.

Annie rolls over in bed with a little moan, still half asleep.

"Come home soon," Spencer says. "I love you." He kisses her cheek.

"Love you," she says. "Fly safe."

She imagines that as he closes the thick wooden door to the house, a flood of relief washes through him. She can picture him taking a moment to breathe in the humid predawn air, the palms lined up along the too-quiet suburban street. She can see him getting into his Uber Black, on his way back to the city, the noise.

But Annie, too, is relieved that he is gone for now, relieved that while she lies awake in the night, the sound of his breath will no longer interrupt the memory of her father's. She is relieved that he will stop trying to pull her from the quicksand she knows she must sink into.

Since losing her mother, in Annie's mind death had been abstract, intangible. Maybe all this time a tiny part of Annie had gone on believing that Juliette never really died at all, but only vanished. That one day Annie would return to Goldstone and find her out in the garden.

There is a difference between a death you see and a death you don't. Witnessing her father's last breaths made death real. Physical. And now Juliette's last moments haunt Annie anew.

What did her friend feel when she swam out in Lake Michigan, when she gulped water into her lungs where air should have been? Was the fear enough to knock her out? Did she struggle? Did she suffer? Of course. Was there terror? A moment of pure panic, before her body became one with the water? Did she surrender?

Did she drown herself on purpose?

When Edna drowned in *The Awakening*, she heard the hum of bees, smelled the musky odor of pinks.

What would it have been for Juliette? The jasmine? Mint leaves torn between her fingers? The rustle of oak leaves, the taste of fresh peach? The place where water meets sky, forever and ever after. . .

As the white light of the sun begins to leak in through the window, Annie texts the rental company running the Topanga Airbnb, tells them to cancel all upcoming reservations for the next month.

They reply: *There's someone arriving tonight. We can't do that on such short notice.*

*Tell them there's been an emergency*, Annie answers.

*You will lose your five-star rating.*

*That's ok.*

Annie starts her father's old Volvo in the driveway. His worn Ray-Bans are in one cup holder, his metal water bottle in the other. She puts on the sunglasses and pulls out.

*The Treatment* is playing on KCRW, which has been her father's default station ever since she was little. Elvis Mitchell is interviewing some director: *After my mom died, some days all I could do was lie on the couch and turn the TV on.* Annie turns up the radio as she turns onto Ventura, the sun beating down on the Petco and the Chick-fil-A, the corner liquor store and the Dollar Tree, the diner where she used to go with her dad. *The movies were like an IV,* the director says, *feeding me life when I didn't have the strength or ability to take it in myself. They made me believe that there was still a world out there somewhere, one that might be worth living for . . .*

Annie wonders what might bring her back to the living now, but she can't imagine it. What she knows for certain, all the way into the marrow of her bones, is that she's out of strength to run. Maybe it was always inevitable: she can do nothing but go back to Juliette.

She pulls onto the 101, the old route to Goldstone, her stomach churning, mouth going dry. She puts on "Woodstock," Joni Mitchell's voice blending into the memory of Juliette's, hovering in the air, tangible enough she can almost touch it. Annie can see Juliette pulling on her cigarette, tipping her head backward and exhaling, stretching her arm out the window like a single wing, as the song begins again.

They were too young for death then. It would never catch them.

Annie turns onto Topanga.

# 32

Jesse folds the new onesies, freshly washed with Dreft newborn detergent, beside Noah on the couch as he reads a script his agents have sent for his consideration to direct. Jesse lies back, shuts her eyes, and he reaches out to rub her feet.

For the first time in her life, the buzz of ambition seems to have been zapped out of Jesse's body. Her office is the nursery. Once the baby is out, Jesse tells herself, she'll get back to working, start a third book. Now she just wants to be with her girl in their last days like this. What scared her at first—the feeling that her body was not her own—is now something exquisite. She likes the sense of being possessed, life in service of life. She has surrendered herself to waiting, given herself over, spending her days cooking, gardening, nesting. It's okay. It's okay now. She'll let Noah take care of her. She has never been more in love with him, the father of her daughter.

Noah can feel Jesse's love, her satisfaction in him, and of all the summer's sweetness, that is what makes him happiest. She glows in her white linen dress, round and ready to burst.

He sets down his laptop, leans over and rests his cheek against her belly.

"Hello," he says, "how are you, little starburst? Are you getting ready to come see us?" He talks to the baby as much as possible, heeding the doula's advice so that when she is born, she will recognize her father's voice and be soothed by it. Jesse laughs, tickled by the baby's movements.

"Right here," she says, and points. Noah follows her lead and feels their girl press against his hand. He grins with delight. Noah can taste it on his tongue—the moments before the harvest.

As their daughter has grown bigger, readying for the world, Noah's career has taken off. *The Red Balloon* will be out in two months. His Nike commercial was a runaway success, a "piece of political art" that exploded on the internet, and he's about to do one for Apple. He is a "culturally relevant" person, according to public radio, an already sought-after director. He has been featured on the pages of *Forbes, Variety, The Hollywood Reporter*, wearing sneakers and daring the camera to look away from him. He photographs well, and now that he has shaken off some insecurity, he interviews well, too. Only five weeks after Jesse's due date, Noah will begin his press tour. He worries about leaving her, but Jesse doesn't give him any guilt. "Daddy will come home to us," she says.

Noah earned the guild minimums for his screenplay and to direct the movie. It is not "house money," at least not in LA, but it's a start. He is saving up. His agents forward him a constant flow of new scripts, and he's just been attached to direct a big action movie. He won't see more money from *The Red Balloon* until after it earns out at the box office, but in the meantime, between his writing and directing salaries and now the cash from the commercials, Noah's able to support himself and Jesse and send some money to his family. He took Jesse on a "babymoon" and bought all the expensive items left on the registry without worry. For Noah, who has spent his life struggling to have enough, the outward symbols of success are about more than just status. They lend him a feeling of safety.

Now that he's gotten rid of his Impala and is leasing the new Panamera, he feels less anxious when he drives by a police officer. Even the older white ladies who avoided him in grocery store parking lots look with interest. The Audis that used to cut him off now make space. He drives his pregnant wife around with the top down, watches her dancing her hands in the wind, leaning her face back into the sun. His pregnant wife—he loves that.

Noah wonders, sometimes, if he will know how to be a father. As a child, his own absent dad did not figure strongly into his consciousness. His mom was enough. Plus, there was Dev, his grandparents, the cousins. As he grew older, Noah became aware of the cliché of it—a Black boy without a father—and it bothered him, a little, but that feeling was eclipsed by the intensity of his grief for Gracey.

Dev has provided a good example of fatherhood with Eric. But Noah worries that there is something missing in him, something that did not get etched in on a cellular level. Until he looks at Jesse, carrying their baby in her belly. His love for her is so full, so total, he trusts that loving their child will be natural.

Jesse's so tired these last days—falling asleep beside him on the couch in that white linen every night—but somehow, she always wakes when the trailer for *The Red Balloon* comes on, as if she has a sixth sense. Her eyes peek open, dazed, and she looks at the screen as if watching a dream.

"You did it," she'll say, rubbing her belly.

"We did," he always replies. When the trailer ends, Noah lifts her from the couch and carries her up to bed, loving the huge, heavy weight of her in his arms. He can finally take care of her. That feeling has reorganized the world, has turned him from a man fighting to stay afloat, using every ounce of energy to avoid drowning, into a man navigating the waters, driving his boat.

# 33

Annie's hands shake as she punches in the code on the metal keypad, her heart beating in her throat. When she steps into Goldstone, she is staring back at herself, skinny and freckled in a black bikini, leaning in to Juliette. There is Juliette everywhere, frozen behind glass. Annie wonders, vaguely, about her decision to leave such valuable art hanging for any visiting stranger, but here it all is, looming even larger without the elegant jumble of Margot and Juliette's lives. On the long wood dining table where Margot used to host her winter dinner parties there is now a binder full of instructions, a vase of white flowers in the moonlight, a stark silence. The uncanny stillness of a body whose soul has left.

Like her father's, lying in that hospital bed.

Annie searches the home for whatever might remain of Margot and Juliette's possessions, the record player and whatever else her dad packed up for her before the rental company came in to clear it all away. She finds a padlocked closet in the hallway. She has no idea where the key might be, so she googles twenty-four-hour locksmiths and calls the first one to come up. She goes out to wait on the deck.

Unlike the home, the yard remains in full splendor, almost exactly as Annie remembers it, and it steals her breath. The stone fruits hang heavy on their branches, ripe and ready. She lights a cigarette, pulling the smoke into her aching chest, as the old loop repeats itself: *Five missed calls. Why didn't she answer the fucking phone? Fuck.* She can see Juliette, after Margot's death, sitting beneath the peach tree. *How could she have abandoned her best friend, her chosen one?*

An hour later, an old Russian man arrives in an ancient van. As he walks up the drive, Annie shoves a wine opener into her pocket in case she needs to defend herself. But he turns out not to be a threat; he struggles with confusion and bad vision. After what feels like an eternity, he finally finds the bolt cutters in the back of his van and frees the artifacts.

Annie returns the record player to its former credenza and picks up a jewelry box that belongs on the dresser in the bedroom. Inside are several pairs of earrings, a half-burned bundle of sage preserved in tinfoil, a wine cork that says *Annie + Juliette* in black Sharpie, from the last bottle of Riesling they drank. She drags a huge cardboard box from the University of Chicago into the hallway, stuff the school shipped back to Juliette's home address after her death—Annie vaguely remembers her dad mentioning it, saying he'd save it for her. She lights the sage, pulls out the LPs, plays *Songs of Leonard Cohen*, and sits in stillness—getting up only to turn the record over, and over—as the daylight drains from the living room, slowly and then suddenly. She is hungry, and lets the hunger gnaw anxiously at her belly.

Annie should purchase a plane ticket back to New York; she should go home to Spencer. But grief is like this: hypnotic.

She stays in place until the moonlight casts shadows shifting across the floor. Finally, she rises, opens the cupboards: a bag of dried mango from Trader Joe's, mostly gone. Salt and pepper, some Ralphs brand olive oil. In the freezer, there is Häagen-Dazs coated in ice crystals, Popsicles, a third of a bottle of Absolut Vodka. She considers the mangos, the aging ice cream, takes a swig of the cold alcohol, which absorbs almost immediately into her empty stomach.

She wanders out to the garden, picks a peach, rubs away the fuzz with her thumb. The savage heat feels softer now.

*How you holding up*, Spencer texts. She imagines him alone in their bed in his pinstripe pajama pants.

*Okay, how's work*

*Gonna be a busy week. When do you think you are coming back?*

*I don't know*

Spencer's dotted typing bubble lingers before he replies. *Annie, you should come home. We'll fly out when it's time to do a service.*

She puts down the phone. He expects her to clean herself up and turn back into the wife he wants, but she does not know how to fit back into her former shape.

*My dad just died*, she writes finally.

Another typing bubble.

Her grief has become a magnetic force, keeping her bound to the site of loss. And Spencer, the man who bent on his knee and put a ring on her finger, is 2,541 miles away, five hours by plane, on another planet.

She goes inside, opens the windows, lies back in the oak bed.

Her phone buzzes. *I'm sorry,* Spencer has written. And then: *You're right, your dad just died. It's hard for me seeing you so sad. I just want to fix it but I know I can't. You just need time.*

Annie sends back a heart.

*I love you,* Spencer texts.

*Love you, too,* Annie writes.

She looks out the window. The leaves in the orchard are beginning to come down too early; it's only just August. She shuts her eyes, drifts off.

When she wakes in the morning, Annie goes to the kitchen to find a knife and cuts open the box of Juliette's possessions sent by the University of Chicago—like a gift from her ghost. Annie pulls out the rose-patterned quilt that used to cover her, Juliette, and Margot in the big oak bed. The one they used to carry to the couch as they watched Turner Classics late into the night. She lifts it to her face, inhales; she wants to imagine Juliette's body still lingers in the fabric, but it smells mostly of cardboard. She pulls out the photograph of Margot breast-feeding Juliette as a toddler, a pair of pre-Raphaelite beauties in the garden, covered in bubble wrap. Annie and Juliette tangled together in bed.

There are sheets, clothes, Juliette's Chicago coat with bits of tobacco in the pocket. A box of matches from Jimmy's Woodlawn Tap, a tube of lipstick worn to a point. A dog-eared copy of *Arabian Nights,* of *The Communist Manifesto,* of Jorie Graham's poetry. And the journal—the one Annie had given Juliette for her nineteenth birthday, the night they first made love. Annie flips past the poems she copied for Juliette on the first pages in an inky gold pen. The rest of the book, handmade paper, pressed with flower petals—meant for Juliette to record her first year away, back when it felt like an adventure—is covered in Juliette's slanted scrawl, mostly poems in progress, lines crossed out and rewritten. Sometimes an entire poem in careful cursive—

*She goes through her boxes of shadows. Roots*
*breaking through the floor slats, she lays out*
*a shadow of her mother, a shadow*
*of a dahlia, a shadow of the afternoon*
*she spent floating out to sea. She hangs*
*a shadow of herself over the window. She finds*
*that she is full of blindfolds. Leaning into later on,*
*when it will matter that she is still young,*
*she glimpses the milk in her mouth.*
*See, there is no way out—*

The record comes to an end and all that is left is the sound of Annie's sobs. Grief is like this: endless.

Annie puts down the journal and goes into the kitchen, finds the leftover bottle of vodka from the freezer is nearly empty.

She gets in her car, hot wind whipping her fine hair, and drives down to the Topanga Creek General Store, sipping from her father's metal water bottle. When she walks into the store, Annie feels almost assaulted by the organized aisles, the fluorescent lights, the people simply going about their lives with such a sense of normalcy, the world rushing on, indifferently. *My father died,* she wants to tell the cashier. *I have no parents left. My best friend and her mother are also dead. I am an orphan.* She takes a basket but can't think of what she wants to buy. Finally, she arrives at the checkout line with a bottle of rosé, a bottle of chenin blanc, a bag of spinach, a box of Triscuits, a block of sharp Cheddar.

Annie drives back to Goldstone, too fast through the winding canyon. She walks through the front door, forgetting her groceries in the car.

She goes back for the bag, opens the box of Triscuits and slumps down on the floor, picks up Juliette's journal, continues reading. Finally, she lands on an entry dated the day before Juliette died.

*April 23, 2004*

*I was raped last night.*

*Noah was in my creative writing class at Hyde Park High. I liked him, I thought. He was smart, and talented, and quiet. His poetry was so good. I thought maybe he was someone who got it, whatever "it" is. I am so dumb.*

*I can't fit inside my body anymore. I keep staring at the bruise on my wrist and thinking it is not my wrist. It is not my wrist anymore, not my arm or my mouth or my face . . . If I were made of clay, I would smush myself flat, start over. Everything hurts.*

*Mommy, please come back. I need you. If you don't come back, I have to come find you because I can't do this.*

*All I want is to go home. All I want is my mom.*

*I called Annie this morning, but she didn't answer. She never does anymore.*

*I was waiting until I was in love. I was supposed to wait until I was in love. I got too drunk. I don't know why. I was nervous. I never go out. I think it was fun at*

*first, or something like fun. I remember the room
started spinning at the bar. I felt sick. He was walking
me home, I think—there was a big moon. And then
next thing I remember I'm on the bed, and he's pushing
inside me over and over again, like I'm just a doll. It
hurts. It still hurts. I wanted to go away somewhere, so
I left my body on the bed, and I flew back to
Goldstone, back to our garden. But now the fruit trees,
the pomegranates and the mint leaves and the plums,
they are all tangled up with his body, pushing inside of
me, vines choking me.*

*It's beautiful outside but the winter is in my skin and
I can't get my toes warm, no matter what I do, no
matter how hot the shower is. I can't get clean.*

*Mommy, please help me, I can't stop crying. I want
to come home to you.*

Here is Annie's answer to the question that has plagued her—
*What happened to Juliette?*—and it is awful. A violent wind
blows outside, green leaves glittering frantically in the afternoon sun. Annie wants to vomit.

*Who is Noah?* She asks herself the old question with new
urgency. *Who the fuck is Noah?* She walks in circles around
the kitchen, unable to complete the simple task of pouring a
glass of wine.

She forgets where she put the opener, takes out a glass and
misplaces it. Feeling dizzy and feverish, she finally lets herself
collapse onto the tile floor.

The memory arises like a stone that has learned to float: one
foggy evening in the summer—Annie was maybe ten or elev-
en—as they were saying goodbye in the parking lot, her

mother took her father's hand and squeezed it—a rare instance of physical contact—and said, quietly, "Thank you for getting her out of there."

Her mother, who was Annie's first home, the rhythm of her heartbeat, the swish of her organs, the flow of her blood the first sounds Annie had known. Her mother, who had just turned eighteen, nearly nine months pregnant with an older man's baby when her brother tried to bring her home. Her mother, who gave birth to Annie three years later and let her go. Who grew into an adult but still seemed to be a child.

You can't have consensual sex with a seventeen-year-old if you are forty. Her mother was also raped. It all seems so clear now. The umbrella on the deck blows over; oak branches come down. Annie finally manages to open the chenin blanc, drinks it straight from the bottle.

She cannot go back and rescue her mom. She may never be able to find the nameless leaders of a crumbled cult, some of whom must long be dead or departed. But she will find him. Noah. Now that she knows what he did, she will find him.

It is not so difficult: she goes back to the box from the University of Chicago and continues to dig through it, looking for clues. An old tube of lip gloss. A red scarf. A stack of papers: "Masks and Memories," "The Problem of Capital," "The Fourth Dimension" . . . and then, a book stapled together, with a cover titled "Fall Semester Creative Writing Chapbook." Annie flips through—a series of student poems. She scans the names until she sees "Noah King." Of course. He was in her class.

Annie googles *Noah King,* and there he is: his image from the cover of *The Hollywood Reporter,* "The Sudden Rise of an *It* Director." It is him. The same grainy kid with Juliette's tongue on his cheek, grown up into a star.

Noah King made that movie she's seen the billboard for all over town, the one with the kid with the red balloon. He graduated the University of Chicago the year after Juliette would have. "Hollywood Loves Noah King," says one headline. There he is on YouTube, talking about directing some Nike commercial. He was the one talking to Elvis Mitchell on the radio. Juliette is gone forever, and all the while, Noah's just gone on living, fulfilling his dreams.

She cannot bring back her best friend. But she will not let Juliette's rapist be plastered on magazine covers with his impassive face, anointed as the hottest name in the industry, here to save Hollywood from its racist self with his story of pulling himself up by the bootstraps, without a mention of the victim—or victims; could there be more?—he left in his wake. Annie is overcome by a desire to scream from deep in the pit of her belly and never stop.

She gets her computer and starts to type.

# PART
# THREE

# 34

Camille, three days old, sleeps in her newborn lounger pillow on the kitchen table. Jesse stares at her baby's eyelids. Her balled fists tucked close to her chin, as they were on the ultrasound. Jesse breathes her in. Camille seems made of the rich sun on the October day she and Noah promised themselves to each other, the laughter and song, salt smell of the sea.

Jesse's still wearing the disposable underwear and the huge pads they gave her in the hospital; she still feels raw, almost cut open by the fact of birth, the baby that was inside her now sleeping beside her. A feeling of recognition overwhelmed Jesse the moment Camille came out of her body, as if she'd always known her: *It's you,* she said aloud. *It's you. You're here.*

"It's you," she whispers now, stroking Camille's head lightly.

All night long, Jesse and Noah wake every couple hours, Jesse sitting up to feed Camille, eating macadamia nuts and guzzling water, Noah trying to keep his eyes open, getting up to change her when Jesse finishes. Even when Camille is not crying, Jesse wakes just to check that she is still breathing. It is a fever love, all-consuming.

There is Miles Davis's *Kind of Blue* on the record player, fresh orange juice in her cup that Noah has just poured. He is making breakfast. Jesse is ravenous. Her nipples hurt. She wears a threadbare T-shirt, stained with round circles where she's slathered on balm.

Noah will leave on his press tour next month. He will be gone for five weeks, flying home just in time for the premiere. Jesse had thought she could handle it all without him, but now she dreads his departure. She could not have predicted the reality of caring for their newborn, and she worries about doing it alone. Mostly, she worries about something happening to Noah while he is away. She suddenly fears for all of their lives; their happiness is so full it feels as if it could burst.

Noah's offered to hire someone to help, but Jesse does not want anybody else to touch their baby.

He sets down plates: fried eggs, steak sizzled in butter and garnished with rosemary.

"It's delicious, babe."

"Good." He smiles.

Jesse's phone dings; a text from her sister: *Are you okay?*

She types back with one hand, lifting food into her mouth with the other. *Just exhausted but yeah. I got three straight hours last night, which feels like a miracle.*

The dotted typing bubbles come and go, come and go again. Then: *You haven't seen.*

*Seen what?* Jesse's throat tightens as she types.

"You're up, pretty girl," Noah says to Camille, reaching out to let her wrap her hand around his finger as she stares back at him with her big dark eyes.

*I'm sorry Jess,* her sister replies. And then a link to a *Hollywood Reporter* article pops up in the thread.

"Noah King, *Red Balloon* Writer/Director, Accused of Rape."

For a moment, Jesse's vision goes to black. Camille starts to cry. Noah lifts her from her pillow.

"I think she's hungry," Noah says.

Jesse's breaths chase each other, faster and faster. Camille's cry escalates.

"Noah?" She reaches out the phone to him, displaying the article. "What is this? Is this real?"

Noah squints at it. Jesse takes their daughter from his arms, tries to bounce her. It doesn't work.

"What the fuck?" Noah says, in shock.

As Noah stares at the phone, Jesse carries Camille to the couch, pulls out her breast: it is huge, round, full, too full. Her milk has come in. Camille tries to latch, but she can't. She arches her back, screams out.

"Come on, baby," Jesse says, offering her nipple again. Why won't Camille take it? She glances back at Noah, who is searching frantically for his phone.

Jesse holds Camille to her chest. Her hands shake as she offers her breast again and again. Camille's mouth wraps around the nipple, but she won't latch on. She wails so hard her face turns red.

"Baby," Jesse says, "please."

Camille's desperate scream continues.

"Noah," Jesse calls, but Noah has left the room, doesn't seem to have even heard her.

Jesse carries Camille upstairs, lays out swaddle blankets on the bed while Camille wails. Jesse wraps her daughter's flailing arms inside. Camille fights to break free. Jesse layers another blanket atop the first. Wraps her tighter. Jesse holds Camille while she cries, jiggling her head from side to side like the *Happiest Baby on the Block* movie taught her. Her husband. Has been accused of rape. Camille continues to wail until finally, suddenly, she stops, closes her eyes. Jesse's breasts are burning.

When Noah finds his phone, he discovers six missed calls from Alyssa, the studio publicist, and a few voicemails he never bothered listening to from unknown numbers—one from when Jesse was in labor, another from around the time he would have first been holding his baby daughter: *The Hollywood Reporter*, calling to fact-check their story. And then Alyssa, frantic. *"I know you just had a baby, but pick up the fucking phone."* He sits down on the floor. He's swimming underwater now. He dials Alyssa back.

"This is not good," she says immediately. "Really not good."

"Right."

"You read the article, correct?"

"Just the headline. It's bullshit."

"We need a statement." There is chatter in the background, a yipping dog. He imagines Alyssa at Sunday brunch somewhere with all the other white girls with their big Michael Kors bags and iced lattes and sprouted pancakes.

"I've never raped anybody."

"Well, read the thing and call me back. We have to get ahead of this."

Noah walks in. A few minutes later? An hour? Jesse doesn't know. She's falling through time. He looks at Jesse: fear, shame, anger. Freezing over.

"She can't latch," Jesse tells Noah. "Give me my phone. I need to call the doula."

"It was a girl from U of C. I didn't rape her. We had sex. She was a Neighborhood Schools teacher who taught this creative writing class at my high school senior year."

"Why did she say you raped her?"

"It was a journal entry. Her friend published it. She's dead."

"Dead?"

"She drowned. A few days after we were together. I had no idea. I thought she just ghosted me. I didn't see her at school and she never answered my calls."

Jesse feels ill. "Give me my phone. Before she wakes up." Camille is starting to stir against her pounding heart.

Noah gives Jesse the phone.

There on Jesse's screen is the article, and a black-and-white photo of the girl—her name is Juliette Marker—at a fancy dinner table before a plate of floating oyster shells. She has pale skin, dark hair, a vague, half-open smile—the sort that says she has a secret, that makes you want to lean in closer to hear it. She is beautiful.

"You know I didn't rape her, right, Jess? I am not a rapist."

Juliette's best friend, Anais "Annie" Ricci, is accusing Noah of raping Juliette in college, the article says. Noah's senior year of high school, 2004.

And then there is a reprinted entry from her diary. Beside the text is an old, grainy photograph of Noah and Juliette in a bar together. If Jesse were not holding her sleeping newborn, she would go to the bathroom to puke. Instead, she swallows her queasiness as she reads Juliette Marker's words: *I was raped last night . . .*

Camille wakes up with a wail. Jesse takes out her breast to try again. Camille tries to latch and can't. And cries harder.

Noah is sitting at the edge of the bed, motionless. Jesse knows her husband. When he is terrified, he turns to stone, to ice, trying to wall off the panic—an echo of the seven-year-old freezing in the face of a loss big enough to swallow him whole, freezing in the face of a world turned suddenly monstrous without his protector, his mother. She knows her husband. He is not a rapist. He couldn't be a rapist.

"Noah," she says, trying to soften her voice. "Take her for a minute. I need to call Patrice." The doula. Jesse puts their screaming daughter in Noah's arms and steps out of the room to dial, but Patrice doesn't answer her phone.

*Can you talk? It's an emergency*, Jesse types and then deletes. Instead, she writes, *Please call as soon as you can. Having trouble breastfeeding. Camille is hungry but can't latch.*

Jesse abandons her phone, takes Camille back into the nursery and closes the door, rocks her while tears pour down Jesse's own face. She tries to sing to Camille, a song her dad used to sing to her. *Golden slumbers . . .*

Noah walks in. "It's Patrice," he says, almost too quietly to be heard over Camille's cries.

He hands Jesse her phone, lifts Camille from her arms.

"Your milk's come in," Patrice explains. "Sometimes the breasts get too full at first. For her, it's like trying to drink from a firehose! Forget the football hold they teach you at the hospital. Get her butt below her head. It will be easier for her to swallow. And you can try squeezing out a bit of the milk first, to soften the breasts."

Jesse does as told. Why didn't she know this? She took the breastfeeding class. As Camille latches and drinks, making small sounds of pleasure, the relief is so intense it brings Jesse to tears again. Camille passes out before Jesse can switch sides. As her daughter sleeps against her chest, mouth still making suckling motions, Jesse tries to use her free hand to squeeze some of the milk from her left breast, which is still on fire.

She looks down at the black-and-white photo on her phone, stares into Juliette's eyes. She tries to imagine Noah on top of her in a dorm bed and shudders. Did he put his fingers in her mouth, the way he does with Jesse?

Noah walks in as Jesse sits topless, milk spilling down her still-swollen belly.

"I talked to Alyssa again," he says.

"What did she say?

"We're putting out a statement. Denying the accusations."

Jesse just nods.

"Jess," he says. "I can't let this ruin the movie."

Jesse pulls a breath into her collapsing chest. "The movie will speak for itself. You saw how people reacted at the festival."

Noah is quiet for a moment, hovering in the doorway to the nursery.

"But, Noah, you can tell me the truth. You can tell me anything. About whatever happened."

His voice lights up with hurt, with anger. "I already told you. We had sex. I didn't rape her. I would never rape a woman. You know that. You have to know that."

Jesse looks down at Camille's face, her little mouth making suckling motions in her sleep, and feels a pain deep in her chest. How did they get here, having this conversation on the third day of their daughter's life? She takes a shaky breath. "It's just—that journal entry was intense. If she really wrote that, she must have actually felt . . . like something really bad happened. I mean, what actually happened?"

"It was one night twelve years ago. I had sex with a lot of women back then. I honestly don't remember it that well, but I know I'd never rape someone. I'd never force something."

"If she was blackout drunk, though—"

"How could I have known that? We'd both been drinking— we were at Jimmy's—what the fuck, Jess?" His voice is turning harder.

The doorbell rings.

Noah leaves the room. She can hear him accepting a delivery.

"It's from your publisher," he calls to her a moment later, from the kitchen. "A bunch of meat and cheese."

And then he appears again in the doorway. "I'm gonna go for a run, okay?"

"Okay."

He goes. She hears him getting his shoes on in the bedroom. Her hand has fallen asleep where Camille's head rests, but she's afraid to move and wake her. She feels as if she's sinking into quicksand.

"Noah?" she calls out to him.

"What?" He walks into the nursery.

"It's gonna be okay," she says, trying to make it true.

Noah nods.

"I love you," she says.

"I love you, too."

# 35

Noah and Juliette show up in forwarded articles, emerge in Twitter battles, are debated on podcasts playing on backed-up freeways from Los Angeles to New York. People take sides, cluster with their tribes. People post Margot Marker photos of Juliette, from toddler to eighteen—she is the distillation of childhood in its gory, lovely, transcendent glory—innocence and innocence lost. They repost Noah's five-month-old photo of his new Porsche, call him sick, disgusting, full of himself. They take photos of the run-down block in Chicago where Noah grew up. They post and repost the single photo of newborn Camille that Jesse took down from Instagram too late, Camille's one-day-old face all over the internet. They post photos of their own daughters: little girls in dresses alongside the hashtags #NoMoreToxicMasculinity, #StopRapeCulture.

Noah and Jesse step around each other, speaking only of necessities: what to have for dinner, on which credit card to put a diaper subscription. Jesse climbs upstairs to bed alone, carrying Camille and the empty weight of her swollen stomach. She lies inside the borders of the U-shaped pregnancy pillow, beside Camille, who sleeps in the bassinet until she wakes hungry and wants to stay in Jesse's arms.

Noah hardly comes to bed anymore.

He stares into the abyss of the internet, where Instagram sells lactation lattes and snap-on baby booties and the promise of happiness, where the football player takes a knee and the presidential nominee says he should leave the country, where the info wars rage on and fistfights are live-streamed from Walmart parking lots, and where his own face lurks. He looks out at the cloud-covered night, the sky an eerie shade of white, and finds nothing that might save him. Nothing, until an occasional smile: Camille's funny face when Noah burps her, her chipmunk cheeks all scrunched up. Camille's face is his face. She naps on his bare chest, her thin skin against his, her warmth hovering over his heart. She tears open a wound in him—a wound he cannot locate, shape-shifting by the moment. He recognizes himself in her as he's never recognized himself before. It is a strange, raw ache that his daughter at once exposes and salves.

Watching her husband and daughter falling to sleep together, Jesse wants to cry from longing. This is the family she wants, right there but out of reach.

She knows the warmth of Noah's chest, the sound of his heartbeat where her daughter lies. She craves it, craves his tenderness. But she doesn't know how to take down the armor her heart has erected—its hurried effort at protecting her from the onslaught in this tender postpartum moment.

When her father got sick, Jesse had a recurring dream: their home in flames. She would rush her mother out of the house, then her sister, and finally, she would run back to search for her dad, screaming for him.

In the weeks after the article, she has a version of the same dream: she's back in her childhood house, but it is Camille she's searching for, Camille she's desperate to carry to safety. She chokes on the smoke. Bricks are falling. She hears her baby crying. Camille. Camille.

She wakes to her daughter wailing in the bassinet beside her. Jesse switches on the lamp and lifts Camille into her arms. She feels the milk let down, a small release as Camille latches on.

Jesse knows there's space between did and didn't, between guilt and innocence, though her brain, fogged from exhaustion, from fear, consumed with the needs of her daughter, has trouble interpreting it.

It is pure masochism, maybe, but Jesse can't help it—she reaches for the glow of her phone in the dark room. As Camille nurses, Jesse scrolls Annie's Instagram, trying to discern something about the woman who shattered her world on the third day of her daughter's life. Annie's record of her existence in New York—brunches and ballets and books, artfully plated dinners, an engagement party in Cape Cod—looks like an advertisement for the perks of affluent white womanhood. Then come the Margot Marker images of Juliette's fairy-tale childhood, of teenage Annie and Juliette unabashed in their beauty.

When Jesse can't take them any longer, she turns to the moms—the "momfluencers" she started following during pregnancy. In her white linen dress with her giant belly, with the husband who carried her up to bed and the perfectly decorated nursery with the wooden rocking chair, maybe Jesse had imagined that she was not so far from their ideal. The nausea and heartburn and endless trips to the bathroom, the stalled career and aching feet were just part of it. She was living a miracle.

Now she scrolls through the cream-colored feeds, babies sleeping on perfectly made perfectly white beds, straw hats and picnic baskets and idyllic countryside, as her nipples ache and burn, as she listens to Noah's footsteps moving up and down the stairs, never close enough.

The loneliness that hangs in the air between them is so thick it almost has a flavor. There is no way to talk about all that lies ahead, about all that is at stake. The September heatwave has hit, bearing down on them, smashing the city under its weight.

Noah and Jesse's silence is not born of anger, not at each other, but it leaves a gaping hole that anger has begun to move into. They are in the same house, on separate planets: Noah is glued to his phone on the couch while Jesse nurses and nurses. She wants him to bring her water but doesn't ask. He seems unaware of the constant hum of the washer. Jesse folds the laundry while Noah goes to work out; he needs to get out of the house. Jesse's body feels as if it has betrayed her. The bleeding won't stop. Noah orders takeout. They eat in front of the television.

Noah can only imagine what the studio executives who bought *The Red Balloon* are saying about him. They are assuming his guilt, probably, and wondering if they can make their money

on his movie anyway. They are hedging their bets, certainly—
masters at self-protection.

The personal recusals are worded carefully, like the one
from Dexter: *You know I'm on your side, but I can't jump into the
fray. I've got the girls to think about.*

*I get it,* Noah replies.

*Be your best self out there. If you play this right, maybe we've
got a shot at saving the box office.*

*Right.*

The cavern of Jesse's absence threatens to swallow him. Noah
wants to climb over the wall of his shame to be with her, but it
is insurmountable. And so he is quiet, staying up late smoking
pot and watching old Tarantino movies, trying to stay off
Instagram, driving aimlessly around Los Angeles, trying to
keep his voice even as he speaks to the studio's publicists, and
now, to the "crisis manager," Beverly, to whom they've ceded
their ground.

Beverly pushes new headlines: "Noah King Was Still in
High School During Alleged Rape," "Juliette Marker Was
Noah King's Teacher," "Juliette Marker Was Too Drunk to
Remember Alleged Rape." There are only so many angles she
can take. Juliette is as close as it comes to a "perfect victim."

While Beverly is trying to lasso the narrative on the unruly
internet, Noah is trying to come up with some kind of contingency plan, trying to remember how to breathe. They taught
them in the birth class: *Put your hand on your belly and push
it out.*

Jesse steps into the hot shower, one of the few moments she
has to herself, and lets the water pound down on her. She

touches her arm, her hair, the nail of her finger, the curve of her enormous breast; her body is a new body, not her own. Lately, fragmented pieces from Paris have been jumping in front of her at strange moments.

When she turns off the water, she can hear Camille's cry and hurries to dry. Noah hands Camille over in the bedroom. As Jesse begins to nurse, still in her towel, she smells Camille's head, whispers to her daughter, a prayer. "Nothing bad will happen to you." A burst of birds send their shadows flitting out the window. The birds repeat themselves. The air is so quiet now she can hear her baby swallow.

When Jesse's mom and Lucy arrive to see Camille, they find the couple in shambles. Jesse's mother washes the stained sheets. Her sister throws out the old food stuffed in the back of the fridge, the platters and casseroles that arrived in the first days of Camille's life, and starts dinner. Jesse's body floods with relief; she did not realize just how intensely she has longed to be cared for.

As Jesse's mom makes up her bed, Jesse nurses Camille in a chair. Lucy's cooking drifts in from the kitchen—carne asada, fresh tortillas. It smells like home to Jesse, and she wants to cry.

"Honey," her mother says, placing new cases on the pillows, "I was thinking I might change my ticket. I can stay and help you. I can be with you and Camille when Noah goes on his tour."

"But what about your students? Can you be gone that long?" She wants her mom to stay, desperately, and at the same time, she doesn't want to draw her into this mess.

"Well," her mother says, only a slight hint of hesitation in her voice, "I can always stop the program, and find another, later on."

"No." Jesse says quickly. "I'm fine, Mama. Noah and I have to figure this out on our own." Jesse has seen how her mom lights up when talking about her students, her favorite Nepalese dishes, her little apartment with a view of the sunrise over the city—she seems happy for the first time since they lost Jesse's father. Jesse can't take that away from her.

"Are you sure?" her mom says. "I'd love to stay and be with you. And you know I'd love to spend more time with my beautiful granddaughter."

"No, Mom. Please don't. We'll see you again soon."

Camille finishes nursing and begins to drift off. Jesse's mom reaches out.

"Can I?" she asks, and Jesse nods, lets her mom take the baby.

Sara settles Camille on her shoulder against her worn T-shirt, her dirty-blond hair falling in soft waves, rocking her. Camille looks at home there, with Jesse's mother. Jesse shuts her eyes.

"Noah is a good man," her mother says, after a moment. "He always has been. He will be a great father."

Jesse nods.

"Why don't you lie down, sweetie," Sara says. "I've got her."

Jesse crawls into the clean bed, soft and scented with Downy, and feels her mom begin to stroke her hair, the body memory of being her mother's baby washing over her, soothing her into dreams that turn to nightmares.

And then, four days later, her mother flies back to Kathmandu, Lucy back to Costa Rica.

———

Noah goes to media training, practicing his smile; nobody smiles back at him. They say Noah has to apologize but without admitting wrongdoing. He must seem empathic toward Juliette—a lost soul—while insisting the sex was consensual.

"It was!" Noah tells them.

"You have to maintain composure," Beverly replies. Noah is normally good at seeing beneath a person's surface, but she is impenetrable.

"Okay," Noah says. "Don't worry. I've got this."

Apparently, Beverly doesn't believe him, because she tries to pull the plug on Noah's press commitments. She's decided they ought not test the "any publicity is good publicity" theory. Polanski went on to win an Oscar for the *Pianist*, but he stayed out of the spotlight, allowing people to separate the man from the movie, she argues.

But he's white. He's an established artist. He's also guilty. Noah is innocent, but it's different to try to rise above a scandal when you were nobody to begin with.

There's no way Noah can trust this fifty-year-old bottled-blond woman with his life. He insists on his deal-mandated press tour. He has to save his movie. He has to be able to support his family.

Noah walks into the living room, where Jesse sits, cutting Camille's nails. "You should get out of the house," he says. "I can watch her." Tomorrow, he leaves for five weeks.

Jesse puts down the clippers and gently bites at the nail on Camille's pinkie, peeling it away with her teeth. "I don't know," she answers.

"It'll be good for you."

Jesse does not want to be far, does not know when Camille will want to eat again, so she simply walks the three blocks to the ocean. The heat has been hanging on, but today, the twenty-second of September, the air is soft. She can feel the sea turning darker, the tiny crackle of cool under the warmth.

Jesse goes straight into the blue waves in her shorts and milk-stained T-shirt, dives past the break. She floats on her back under the cloudless sky, the summer half-moon, washing herself clean. It is a day so lovely it reaches its hands into her chest. She thinks of her daughter every minute of the twenty-six she is gone.

She comes home to Camille asleep on Noah.

"I'm going to give her a bath," Jesse says to him that evening. "Do you want to help?"

He nods, puts down his phone. They place the foam tub in the bathroom sink, measure the water temperature to a precise 100 degrees. Camille gasps with pleasure at the warmth, opens her eyes wide. They smile at each other. They made this perfect girl together, after all; maybe happiness is still possible. When she is done, Noah lifts Camille from the water, Jesse holding out the ducky towel to wrap her. They laugh when the bill covers her tiny head. As they go into the bedroom and lay on the bed, the tears begin to gather in the back of Jesse's throat. This is how it should be: the three of them together.

She wants to shut out the rest of the world that marched uninvited into her house in the tenderest, most sacred of moments.

Jesse nurses their daughter while lying on the bed, covered by a quilt, both of them naked. Noah does not get up and walk out, as he often does. He stays. He watches. She had not realized how deeply she has craved his simple gaze. The sun is falling low, a stream of gold light touching his cheek.

"I will always remember this image," Noah says. He leans down and kisses her forehead, as Camille drifts to sleep on her breast. "You are so beautiful. Both of you," he says. "I'm sorry. And I'm sorry I have to go. I'm going to try to make this right. I am going to try to save this."

"Okay," Jesse whispers as tears make their escape.

He brushes her hair from her face. "It's going to be all right."

# 36

*Oh, poor baby. The rapist @kingnoah is getting sent to movie jail. That man should be in ACTUAL jail. / @kingnoah saw Red Balloon this winter & it was the movie my fifteen-year-old self needed to see. Thank you. / I am Black and Christian and I will never see #RedBalloon / @anniebobanny it takes courage to call out the patriarchy. Bravo. Fuck #RapeCulture and #FuckNoahKing. / @anniebobanny is just a privileged white girl. / @annybobanny so she was drunk & her memory was in and out, what if she told him she wanted sex? / Accusing black men of raping white women is part of this country's foundation #NoahKing #WhitePrivilege, #IBelieveNoah / "He was seventeen" is a pathetic excuse. Rape is rape. #IBelieveJuliette. #StopCampusRape #BoycottRedBalloon / @kingnoah was literally a minor why is nobody talking about that fact??? / @kingnoah is the embodiment of toxic rape culture. / My sister is a rape victim. I will not see #RedBalloon for her. / @anniebobanny tryna get @kingnoah lynched or some shit? #Falseaccusation #bullshit #fuckwhiteprivilege / We discuss the quandary of Noah*

*King on today's podcast. / @kingnoah so full of himself with
his fancy car while Juliette is dead. Makes me sick.
#BoycottRedBalloon #Fuckrapeculture / #JulietteMarker's
mother was the first one who made her a victim who sells
naked pictures of their kid smh. / @kingnoah a girl is dead
because of you. You should be ashamed. #BoycottRedBalloon*

The tweets swim before Annie's eyes, drawing her into a vor-
tex where nothing else is quite real: not the box of her father's
ashes from the mortuary (surprisingly heavy) that Annie manages to carry into Goldstone on her own. Not the bathtub filling with bubbles, absent of Juliette. Not the life she has left
behind in New York City. The virtual world has become the
only one that feels inhabitable.

Annie tries to read a novel, and the words swim on the page,
so she opens her phone. She tries to sleep in the dark of the
room and is haunted by the ragged sounds of her father's last
breaths, so she opens her phone. Her pulse rises as she's greeted
by new followers, comments, likes, and she loses hours.

It is fire season. A film of smoke lingers on her skin. She
wants certainty that her Julie is finally being avenged.

She opens her phone and finds it.

Annie's Instagram follower count, formerly at 420, is now
267,000 and rising. Women contact her at all hours of the day
and night to tell her their stories: *Thank you for standing up
for Juliette. It happened to me, too . . .* Brands have approached
her to see if she wants to advertise period underwear, rosé
wine, online psychiatry services. Since the article came out and
Annie told the world the truth about what happened to
Juliette—since she "ruined Noah's life," according to certain
commenters—she is internet famous.

Annie posted her carefully crafted statement below Margot's photo of her and Juliette at the beach—she's good with words, thanks to all those years as an editor. It has gone viral, with almost half a million likes.

*. . . A different version of me would have kept this awful truth to myself. A different me would have tried to contain my rage at Noah, letting it eat away at me until I could no longer recognize myself. We, as women, are trained to let things go. To protect the men who harm us. To identify with our abusers. To pretend we are okay when we are not. To mistrust our own truths. To turn our anger on ourselves, instead of unleashing it on the world.*

*A different version of me would have kept silent, but I have lost too much. I have lost enough that I can no longer be quiet. Sexual assault has destroyed too many lives. Juliette was the brightest, the best of us. It is my duty to stand up for her.*

Over text message, Spencer asks proportions Annie uses for the coffee. When she replies, he asks where they keep the grinder (after three years in that apartment, he doesn't know?). He asks who is the backup dry cleaner they use if the one down the street can't have things ready in time (by *they*, he means Annie, who has always taken his dry cleaning). He asks for this or that login to pay this or that bill, hoping she will say she can do it, but she doesn't. She can't. She's angry at him but can't quite name why. Because he expects what she taught him to expect of her? To be the cook, shopper, social planner, bookkeeper? To be the soldier, carrying on at all costs?

He is asking her to come back, but she can't. Not now. Not yet.

———

She ignores her emails, the condolences from coworkers, the queries from her boss about manuscript deadlines. She joins an army of women all over the country who are angry. Their messages buoy her. "Thank you for standing up for women, everywhere." "It happened to me, too." She leans in to them, hearts their messages, replies with hearts, with broken hearts. She posts new pictures of her and Juliette as teenagers, sundrenched "Margot Marker photos" in which Juliette's beauty wraps itself around Annie. She posts links to feminist essays on the "Juliette Marker case." She posts Juliette's poems, and they are quoted in tweets, pasted over Juliette's face on Instagram.

She has started going to Move again, the same workout class she went to in New York—her only real-life human contact. *Push past the pain,* the instructor says, and Annie does. *You have to reimagine what pain is.* She screams until her throat hurts, and then goes back to Goldstone to drink. She buys bath salts and selenite sticks to put in front of her yoga mat, while sleepless nights she sits on the deck sucking down Nat Shermans by the packful—back to smoking for the first time in years—while she stares into the glare of her screen. Annie is stoking the flames, a new form of that old rush of adrenaline.

On the phone, Spencer sounds far away. Annie can hear the city in the background. "I'm on your side, obviously," he says, "but you've already said what needed to be said."

"What's that supposed to mean?"

Sharp car horns fill his pause. "You're online all the time. Your dad just died. I feel like you should let yourself clear your mind."

Annie stubs out her cigarette in the already-full ashtray, gazes out at the ocean on the horizon. "What I'm doing is important. It's about more than just me or Juliette; there are so many other women who've been through shit like this."

"Right. I know." Spencer pauses. "But the dude's got a wife, a new baby. He was a kid, too. I'm not saying—"

"What *are* you saying?" Annie can feel her pulse in her neck. She pulls out a new cigarette, twirls it between her fingers. "You think I should let him off the hook 'cause he went on to live a nice life after raping my best friend?"

Spencer exhales, his frustration obvious. "That's not what I meant. I just don't want you to lose yourself in this."

But Annie is already opening Instagram as they are speaking. She tells Spencer she has to go and looks back at herself with her arm around Juliette, seventeen, full of everything. She reads the messages, women applauding her bravery.

And what of the comments calling out white privilege, or referring to the history of false accusations against Black men? She didn't make anything up, she reminds herself. It was printed right there, in Juliette's journal. He raped her. Her privilege doesn't change the facts. His newborn baby doesn't change the facts. Twelve years doesn't change them, either. Juliette is dead and will be dead forever. There will never be justice, never jail time. Why shouldn't he at least have to face the consequences on the public stage?

Annie repeats these arguments to herself, again and again, moving through the empty house, and yet there is something stuck in the back of her throat. A seed of unease in her stomach. She ignores it. She does all that she can to avoid the gray area, for fear that she'd drown there.

She grabs for the anger, the fire of it. Anger feels clean. She tells herself were it not for Noah, she and her best friend would be here at the end of Goldstone Road together right now, making Margot's Sunday pancakes, singing at the top of their lungs. Juliette would have survived her grief. Annie would have grown up and helped Juliette get through it. They would have been together that summer, and the summer after. They would have hosted dinner parties in Margot's honor. Maybe they would still be making love. They would be family. They would be home, together.

If it weren't for Noah, Annie would not have been left behind with a lifetime of guilt. Five missed calls. Why didn't she answer her phone? Why wasn't she there for her best friend that year? How could she have let Juliette go? Without Noah, this torment would not exist.

As the sun sets over the orchard at Goldstone, Annie turns her eyes to her screen, disappearing into the only world that feels viable. Another actress has DM'd her, thanking her, and another singer has reposted her, and another woman, another and another, has told her that she is a savior. A warrior. A crusader.

That night, in her fitful dreams Annie sees fields of snow, vast, endless. She is cocooned against her father's chest. She is hungry, but it is too cold to cry. She hears his heartbeat, the loud crunch of his footsteps; they put her to sleep.

# 37

Portland, Seattle, Boise, St. Louis. Morning shows, NPR affiliates, local news. The breathing technique Noah learned in the birth class: in through the nose, out through the mouth. Shiny brown blowouts, shiny blond bobs, blue eyes behind wire-framed glasses, examining him. Smooth voices, accusing him. Noah remembers his media training. He smiles at them.

Roller bag through the airport, bourbon on the flight to numb himself out, Gucci Mane in his headphones.

Studio reps waiting at the baggage claim to escort him—studio reps with their breath mints and their tiny bottles of store-brand waters, their fake smiles and their granola bars. Their eyes dart at Noah; they put on the radio. They stare out the window. Or else they talk too much, nervous chatter, trying to paper over their unease.

"I guess you got yourself in a bit of a pickle," a balding white man says in the stale air of a Chevrolet Malibu. At Noah's silence, the man goes on. "You know, we're kinda famous for our pickles, actually—even got a baseball team named for them. The Portland Pickles . . ."

In the hotel room, Noah showers, swallows his daily ration of half a Xanax, rinses his mouth with Scope three times over, fixes his hair. When he's ready for his interview, he stares at photos of Jesse and Camille.

*I can take care of you now,* he'd promised her.

The video segment begins with images from the movie as they tell his success story: sweeping shots of Chicago, the child beside his mother's death bed, photographs of Noah on set behind the camera and with Jesse on the red carpet at the festival. *But then, controversy hit, when a journal entry was published, accusing Noah King of raping Juliette Marker when he was a high school senior.* Images of *The Hollywood Reporter* headline: "Noah King, *Red Balloon* Writer/Director, Accused of Rape." Big block letters cover the screen. Accused of Rape. The image of Juliette and her porcelain skin, smiling. The image of Juliette and Annie on the beach.

"Good morning, Noah. How are you?" asks the on-air host, a woman with an immovable helmet of blond hair.

"I'm great, thanks."

She starts out with a few softball questions about the movie; Noah's answers are elegant. He brings up his wife—part of his "media training," yes, but it is also genuine. He's married to an amazing woman, who's an incredible writer and has always been an inspiration to him. He learned from her, he says, what it looks like to pour yourself into your dream day in and day out. She believed in him while he was waiting tables for years. She stood by him. She believed in this movie. Without her, it never would have gotten made. She just gave birth to a beautiful girl. Their daughter is six weeks old, as of yesterday.

And then comes the next question, or statement, really: "So,

Noah, I know that many people watching this are wanting to hear from you on the issue of Juliette Marker. We have heard your statements denying the accusations, but a lot of people just don't feel your empathy."

If Jesse were there, she'd say she learned this about him when they first started dating: when he is anxious, upset, scared, Noah comes off aloof. Nobody can see the speed of his heart, how it crashes against his chest. It's also true that in this moment, it is difficult for Noah to really remember Juliette. In the midst of a survival response, he can't feel anything else. His life is on the line.

"Of course, I have empathy," he says. "I didn't rape Juliette—our encounter was consensual—but it is an awful thing to hear that she was in pain. I have learned a lot since those days, and I should never have been in a sexual situation where we'd both been drinking."

The reporter narrows her heavily mascaraed eyes. "Do you accept any responsibility for Juliette's death?"

Noah senses the cameras. His vision blurs. "I wish I hadn't allowed a sexual situation to happen when we'd both been drinking," he repeats. "I was shocked and really sad when I found out she'd passed away. I had no idea. My heart definitely goes out to her family and friends who grieve her. But as far as blaming me for her death," he says, "that's harder to swallow. The headlines are trying to sensationalize this, saying she killed herself, when she might've gone for a swim and got caught in the undertow. Just like all the headlines are saying I raped her. But you can't find someone guilty without a trial," he says, trying to remove the heat from his voice, "although that's been happening to Black men in this country for centuries."

The host widens her eyes slightly but nods to seem like she gets it. "I understand the temptation to insert race into the conversation, but is there not a level of right and wrong that goes beyond race or gender?"

As a child, in the face of trauma Noah froze. Curled at his dying mother's feet like a puppy dog. Laid up in front of the television for hours upon hours after she passed. As a grown man with a wife and a newborn, his response has to be different. He has to fight—not just for his life but for all of theirs.

"There is no 'beyond race' in America," Noah says, trying to keep his voice measured. "It's baked into our history. It's no coincidence, the fact that people see me a certain way. Juliette was older than I was. She was my teacher. Nobody brings that up. But I looked up to her. I had a big crush on her, and I wanted to date her. I honestly do not understand how or why she could have thought that I raped her . . ."

Noah sweats under the lights, as the hostess stares back at him.

*I've got this,* he tells himself, steadying his shaking hands against the leg of his pants. *I've got this.*

# 38

Jesse wakes, three, four, five times a night—it is impossible to encapsulate the breadth of those hours in the dark. She nurses Camille and checks her diaper. She rocks her until Jesse's muscles burn so badly she gives up and goes back to nursing. She ignores the tears that run down her own cheeks. They are two bodies, two souls searching for sleep.

When Jesse tries to go out in public, she still feels too raw, ripped open, an overexposed photograph of her former self. In the underwater world of new motherhood, there is only Camille. Jesse does not want to come up, does not want to see what the world looks like on land. She rises when she must, sucks in a breath of air, and dives back under. She refuses all prospective visitors; her only loose connection to her former social life is through her cell phone, and the string of tentative text messages from her friends leaves Jesse's nerves fraught: *How are you doing with everything?*

*We're good*, Jesse replies, and sends photos of her beautiful daughter in organic cotton rompers.

*Do you want a visitor?* Suraya asks.

*As soon as we start getting some sleep lol,* Jesse replies.

On their walks, Camille strapped to her chest, Jesse makes shushing sounds down the street to drown out the traffic while Camille drifts off. It feels as if they are in a different dimension than the men smoking on their stoops, the young women in short shorts walking their dogs.

When Noah calls, Jesse is attempting to make herself breakfast, Camille still in her jammies in the carrier.

"Hey," he says. "How are you?"

"Okay, I think. Tired. How are you?"

"I'm okay. Tired, too, but I think it's going all right."

"That's good."

Noah pauses. "The studio said a statement of support from you would be helpful," he says. "They want to emphasize me as a husband and father."

Jesse pushes the toaster down—warm bread is the most cooking she can manage—and steps onto the porch. The wildfires are everywhere, every year now, and the air smells burnt.

"Okay," Jesse says, although she can feel her stomach tighten. "Like what?"

"You know, that you know me, that we've been together for ten years, that I'm not the kind of man who would do something . . . like that. That we love each other, and we have a new daughter and . . . Beverly said she has a statement you could use. I'll send it."

Jesse can hear the falter in Noah's voice. She knows he had wanted to keep her out of it. She imagines this isn't the first time Beverly's asked. "Okay. Sure."

"She said it would be helpful if you could use your social

channels, since you have a large reach with a mostly female readership. She thinks it could make a real difference, to have a woman's voice in the conversation. She's a big fan of *Grief Is Like This*."

"Okay." Noah's trying to keep his tone even, but she can tell he's anxious—so much so that he's using the publicist's words, not his own.

It is not a small request; Jesse knows he wouldn't make it if he weren't desperate. She knows that, and it guts her. No other help that she's offered to Noah over all their years together has felt painful.

But Jesse senses—of course she does—that in defending her husband she will be handing over her own modest public identity, which she was once afraid to inhabit but has learned to cherish. It is a reflection of herself as an author—a person who has a place in the world. With motherhood, that identity has become all the more precious. It connects her to a self that seems, at times, to have vanished.

She looks over the statement, crafted by Noah's "crisis manager." It feels like bullshit.

At 2:43 in the morning, Jesse wakes at Camille's very first whimper, exactly two hours and seven minutes after she last put her down. She lifts her from the bassinet, unwrapping her swaddle and bringing Camille's perfect heart mouth to her nipple. She scrolls through photos on her phone of her and Noah. She doesn't know what happened that night with Juliette, but Jesse knows her husband.

They might be living in different worlds right now, but he is her husband. Who is Jesse if she can't defend him?

Jesse opens Annie's Instagram, lingers on the photo of her

and Juliette at the beach. They wear classic black bikinis, the glassy sheen of the ocean stretching toward the horizon like the endless possibility of their lives. Even Jesse is not immune to their images. Gazing at them brings the tender belly of her own girlhood from the banks of memory.

One of the press's favorite pictures of Noah is, ironically, the same one he'd used in an #iftheygunnedmedown post, from his high school yearbook. He is a Black boy soon to become a man, already wounded by the world, baby-faced but unsmiling, his hoodie up, his round, dark eyes guarded.

Jesse selects her own photographs: Noah and Jesse in Chicago at twenty-two, grinning in their graduation caps. A sleepy selfie of the two of them in her childhood bed in Albuquerque. Noah on the couch with his laptop in their Silver Lake apartment, Noah and Jesse beaming on their wedding day, Noah kissing her pregnant belly. She writes: *We have seen countless pictures of Juliette and her friend Annie in which the girls appear joyful, vulnerable, beautiful. Their teenage selves have been preserved by the immense talent of Margot Marker. Meanwhile, the media—social media and mainstream—keeps posting the one photo I have ever seen of my husband in which he could be called angry. Why is that?*

*When I look at that photo of Noah, I do not see a kid who is dangerous, as many people seem to. I see a scared teenager. On the night of his encounter with Juliette, Noah was still in high school, seventeen, a child, too, in need of protection, deserving of it. But the typecasting—Noah as a predator, Juliette as prey—is firmly planted under the surface of our collective conscious, making it that much harder for people to hear Noah's side of the story.*

*As his wife, I can tell you he is not a predator. He is not a rapist. He is a husband, a father. A striver. A man who worked tirelessly for the ten years I have known him to achieve his dreams against all odds. A man who made a home for me after the death of my father. A man who put his hand on my belly, night after night, waiting to feel his daughter moving. A man who whispered in my ear, after her first kick under his palm, "It feels like fireworks." A man who sang "You Make Me Feel Brand New" to our daughter in the hospital.*

*Of course, I support survivors. I support all women speaking their truths. But I don't support conviction without a trial. Only Noah and Juliette were there that night, but I know my husband would never intentionally hurt someone. He is a good man. A kind man. A tender man. He is the most beautiful man I have ever known. He is my daughter's father.*

Jesse adds a photo of Noah holding Camille in the hospital, gazing at her in wonder. As Camille falls to sleep at her breast, Jesse hits share.

And so begins the cycle: her words are reposted, picked up and republished by news outlets, as legions of her readers, angry, betrayed, turn against her, write scathing or heartbreaking comments, as strangers applaud her for calling out racism or deride her as an antifeminist. The world draws battle lines automatically. As if there aren't real humans on both sides. Jesse is cast as a character, and the life she made, the man she married, all of it is food now for the starved people sitting in front of their computer screens at desks in corporate offices, in coffee shops, in bed with the light of their phones.

Jesse diapers—all day she diapers—and makes sure to narrate to Camille each step of the process, no matter how much her exhausted brain craves silence. She spends hours on mommy boards trying to determine which is the best diaper rash cream. A hump grows in the back of her neck from breastfeeding so much, gazing down at her daughter. She doesn't even notice. When Camille falls asleep on her, Jesse stays in place, motionless, her arm tingling with pins and needles. Despite her exhaustion, Jesse will not allow herself to fall asleep with her daughter—it is not safe, the nurse had told her at the hospital.

Instead, Jesse scrolls with her free hand. She can't help it. Online, women write *"I believe Juliette"* and *"It happened to me too."* They write, *"You were my favorite author. I was raped five years ago. You broke my heart, defending Noah." "Jesse Baca, you should be ashamed. I will never buy one of your books again."*

On the news feed, the presidential nominee brags he can "grab 'em by the pussy." Violence breaks out at his rallies.

On Annie's feed, there are reposts of lines from Juliette's journal entry pasted over empty landscapes, more pictures of fruit trees, ocean, her and Juliette as dreamy teenagers. Jesse touches her own cheek, breast, empty belly. Where is she?

She needs to get out of the house. When Camille wakes, she spends an hour searching for her keys and becomes so frustrated that she punches the couch pillows, then sits on the floor, and cries, while Camille, in a rare moment of calm, lies on her mat and watches Jesse. Then Jesse finds the keys in the refrigerator. Pushing the stroller uphill to the park, Jesse tries to ignore the loose skin, the weight that won't come off, the fact that she can't feel at home in her body anymore.

"Isn't it a pretty day?" she says to Camille. "Can you smell the fall air?"

Despite Jesse's fastidious application of diaper cream, Camille has a rash. After a trip to the pediatrician, Jesse and Camille wait in line at CVS to pick up the prescription. Camille is wailing. Jesse tries shushing in her ear, but Camille only wails louder, drawing the eyes of the other customers. Jesse is being watched from all angles, scorned—in real life, online. She bends up and down, doing deep squats, because Camille likes wild motion. Jesse's thighs burn, but it doesn't work. Camille is inconsolable. If she were trying to buy anything else, Jesse would abandon the mission and take Camille home, but she needs the rash cream. The customer at the register is having an issue with his insurance. The line is not moving.

When they finally get back to the car, Camille continues to wail as Jesse straps her into her car seat, as she pulls out of the parking lot. Her nerves rattled, Jesse makes an illegal turn, trying to rush home, drawing honks. Her eyes burn. She is not sure she can do this. She tries turning up music on the radio. Camille's cry is almost intolerable.

And then she is suddenly silent. Jesse pulls over, worried that something has happened to her, but Camille has only fallen asleep, her heart mouth making small suckling motions. When they arrive home a few minutes later, Jesse lifts the car seat carefully so she won't wake Camille, awkwardly balancing the heavy weight of it on her forearm. (A mother with older children saw Jesse doing this in a parking lot and warned that she eventually got elbow tendonitis from it, but Jesse is worried only about the shortest-term solutions.)

As she approaches the house, Jesse finds a collection of bouquets on the stoop—roses and hydrangea. Her favorite flowers. There are ten in all. For 10/10, the date she and Noah were married. It is their one-year anniversary. She had forgotten. Jesse brings Camille inside and sets her car seat on the coffee table as she begins to cart the flowers in. But Camille wakes only a moment later and cries out. Jesse lifts her, carrying Camille in one arm, bending to lift bouquet after bouquet in the other.

With each trip to the dining room table, she feels more frustrated by Noah's gesture. She knows he was trying to be sweet, but it reminds her that he has no idea what it is like to be here, caring for a baby. Plus, without certainty of future income, they can't afford extravagance. When she has gotten all the vases inside, gathered on the dining table like awkward middle-schoolers clustered at a dance, Jesse falls onto the couch, exhausted. She is thirsty but doesn't have the energy to get water.

Night comes, like it always does, but Jesse's dreams of sleep are out of reach. Camille won't go down. Perhaps the rash cream is not working and she's uncomfortable. But Camille does not generally sleep well, anyway, as if she were infected with Jesse's anxiety.

Jesse sings "Dreaming of You" over and over—how long has it been? hours?—when, finally, mercifully, the lids of Camille's eyes drift shut. Jesse continues humming as Camille stops swallowing, her lips now making a soft rhythmic motion around Jesse's nipple, and Jesse can feel her small body growing almost imperceptibly heavier, letting go. It is a beautiful feeling, witnessing her baby's release. The sharp monotone of her phone startles through the silent house from where she'd plugged it in in the bedroom. Camille shifts, opens her eyes and cries out, and the moment has passed them by, the peaceful entrance into sleep now out of reach.

Desperate, Jesse pulls Camille closer as she cries, cradles her in her arms, presses her cheek against Camille's and shushes into her ear, *shhh* like a wave, loud as the ocean up close.

Camille tries to close her eyes, opens them again, tries to close them. She spits up and it runs against her cheek and Jesse's, but Jesse doesn't move her face, keeps the shushing rhythm steady and for a moment it seems as if Camille will fall back into sleep, but then she pulls away, cries out with open-mouthed abandon.

Jesse sways, she rocks, she walks, another hour passes, and she is defeated. What can she do? She sets Camille in her crib as Camille continues to scream in desperation. Jesse steps away, walks into the bathroom to pee, takes a sip of water, and begins sobbing herself. "I'm sorry, Camille," she whispers. "I'm sorry I can't make it better."

She goes back into the nursery and lifts her daughter. Ignoring her own tears, Jesse begins to sing the song that Noah sang to Camille in the hospital. "You Make Me Feel Brand New." Camille's cry softens, and then she is asleep all at once.

A surge of relief floods Jesse's body as she pulls the bundle of her baby against her chest, slowly lowers herself into the gray rocker. And then Jesse can't help it—she feels Camille's warm breath against her chest and begins to dive into heavy sleep. She wakes in her Hyde Park apartment with Noah, their baby girl between them. They are in love like they used to be, in love like kids. They have the daughter they always wanted. When Jesse opens her eyes it's dawn, and the stab of longing is so intense she struggles to breathe.

Sunlight twinkles in the leaves of green bamboo out the window, streaming in and falling across Camille's perfect face. She looks up at Jesse and smiles, reaches her tiny hand out to touch Jesse's face. Jesse wishes she could tell Noah what it feels like, to be fueled by the electricity of this love.

# 39

It's cold as fuck this weekend, snowing already in early October, twenty-eight degrees. Noah missed a call from Jesse and wants to get back to the hotel so he can talk to her. He thinks today's interview went well, all things considered.

The studio rep, Martha, is an Iowa native. She's unusually friendly, a middle-aged white woman with a surprisingly chic haircut. She chats about the ice on the road and how the city ran out of salt last year, then offers to take Noah out to supper somewhere downtown. She says with a nervous laugh that he could probably use a drink and tucks her hair behind her ear.

Noah tells her that he's pretty beat and better get some rest before his flight tomorrow. She hums along to "Dreams" by Fleetwood Mac on the car radio, steals a glance at him. She's attractive, in the way that an older woman can be when she's still trying. Part of him wants to give her what she wants—

Jesus. He thinks about sex all the time these days and then hates himself for it. As if he were in high school again, a lost boy roaming the streets of Hyde Park in his busted winter coat, searching for someone to make him feel like he mattered, even for a few moments.

He dropped the painful details of those years a lifetime ago, leaving only a blur of heat and cold, exhaustion, the taste of Stouffer's mac and cheese for dinner, the sweat from basketball practice and the thrum of hip-hop, the taste of lip gloss and vodka on the mouths of the college girls. The college girls. Looking back, someone could probably have said he was addicted to sex. But he would never have forced a woman, would never have hurt someone. He knows that for certain.

Why did Juliette think he raped her? She brought him back to her dorm, and they slept together. He never heard her say no. She never pushed him away. He searches his memory, wants to bring her into focus, but she eludes him, blurs around the edges. He pulls up a vague image of the outfit she wore to the bar, a large T-shirt, belted. It seemed sophisticated.

Her mother had just died, he remembers. Because of it, he'd felt they understood each other. A fatal error.

The Ramada, where they put him up, is the nicest hotel in the area. Noah turns the thermostat all the way up, but he can't melt the ice in his toes, in his bones. He tries to call Jesse but she doesn't pick up. They don't have room service at the hotel, not a bar, even, and part of him regrets dodging Martha's invitation.

He runs out of the hotel through the cold in his suit jacket to the Chili's across the parking lot. At the table, while he sips an old-fashioned and nibbles a blooming onion, his face comes on one of the overhead televisions, a teaser for the interview. Somehow, nobody seems to notice, but he still feels naked, as if they were all staring at him.

He asks for the check, puts on his coat, gets up. He thinks he hears a whisper: *rapist*. He's losing it.

He passes a booth where three girls in their twenties eat french fries, sip giant colorful cocktails. The one on the end, with pigtail braids, looks right at him. She lifts her chin. "Rapist," she says, as if she were launching an arrow from a bow, certain of hitting her target.

*Walk out*, he tells himself. *Just walk out.*

Back in the room, he tries Jesse a second time. When she doesn't pick up, he listens to her message again, thanking him for the flowers. She sounds so tired. He's tired, too. He pulls an airplane-sized bottle of Scotch from his suitcase and pours it into the glass cup from the bathroom, swallows in one gulp, turns on the shower to scalding, and steps in, almost burning his skin. But when he gets out and wraps himself in a towel, he is cold again. He should be home with his wife and their baby.

He calls Jesse a last time, but nothing. *What is she doing?* he wonders. Sleeping, hopefully. This time last year, they were conceiving their daughter.

There is such a thing as happiness; Noah tasted it. He'd made it. He made it! He's using every ounce of strength in his body, every reserve of energy, swallowing his rage and scrambling to keep his head above water—trying to get back to where he was.

He prays, after he opens another Scotch and sips, catches his reflection in the dark screen of the television. After he gets underneath the clean white sheets, he lays back on the too-puffy hotel pillow and shivers. He prays, though he does not generally pray. *Please, God, show me the way.*

He looks at the pictures from the hospital, little Camille

wrapped in the swaddle in his arms. This is what he wants to think about: Camille. Not a girl who accused him of doing an awful thing, a girl who saw him as a monster.

But he does not want to hate her, this girl who may or may not have drowned herself in Lake Michigan. She was nineteen, a freshman. He was still seventeen, in his last months of high school. They were kids, alone in the world, both of them.

He does not want to hate her. He hates her friend instead, then. The blond woman who dug up an old journal and published it as if it were facts. The white woman with unchecked privilege, declaring war all over the internet.

# 40

"Hey." Spencer answers on the first ring. He should be home from work by now; it's past nine o'clock in New York.

"Hi," Annie says.

"It's good to hear you."

Annie can imagine him on their chesterfield, feet up on the ottoman in his burgundy socks, a Manhattan on the side table, ESPN on mute.

She pauses. "Spence, I think we have to admit what's happening."

"What do you mean?"

She'd been certain of what she was about to say, but now her chest tightens. "I mean, we're not . . . I think we aren't getting married anymore. I think we aren't what we thought we were."

She can hear Spencer draw in a breath. "Slow down. You're still grieving your dad, I get it. But you have to come back to the city. Things will look different from here."

Annie hasn't told him that she already quit her job last week when her boss lost patience waiting for her to come back. It's been almost two months she's been gone, six weeks since she published her article. Annie had loved the book she was working on, loved her work. But she could not make herself back into the person she would need to be to return. All those years in New York, she did not realize how easily the identity she'd adopted could shatter. Grief is like this: a wrecking ball.

Now she feels her breath catch as snippets of her life flash before her at random: the Friday nights at Raoul's, her and Spencer's favorite restaurant since back when they lived in SoHo; the smiling man behind the counter at their bodega; the day they found that perfectly worn leather chesterfield at Mecox Gardens for their new flat; the easy orgasms. The wedding dress hanging in the back of the closet, in waiting. The summer vacations with his parents in Cape Cod. The babies they thought they'd have.

"I'm not who we thought I was," she says.

"You'll feel like yourself again, once you're home."

"But I am home, Spence, that's the thing," Annie says, running her hands over the wood of the deck where she sits at Goldstone. The horizon is clogged with fire smoke. The pomegranates are beginning to ripen.

"No, you're not. You're living on the fucking internet."

His anger makes it easier on Annie. She lets the silence last, takes nothing back.

"What about all your shit?" Spencer asks, finally.

"It doesn't matter. You can send it or throw it away. I just want the photograph."

Spencer hangs up.

It is not a secret suspicion anymore, but an undeniable fact: Annie is alone. There is no one and nowhere to escape to, no one to take care of her. She drives herself to the beach to walk in the witching hour, moonlight playing over the water. She slips the diamond off her finger.

*If you were about to get married to a Wall Street guy who you were living a perfectly good life with, and I were dead, who would you choose?*

You. I would always choose you.

Connor emails Annie three days later:

> Annie, WTF? You have not answered any of my calls. Spence is a wreck. I thought your Hollywood Reporter piece was brave. But don't poison yourself on the past.
>
> Ten years ago, I met a girl who had twinkling eyes and a will to survive and just needed someone to drag her back into the world. I offered up my best friend, and he offered up his whole life, and we've all been happy these past years, haven't we cousin?
>
> This move makes you feel like Suzanne's daughter.

Annie replies:

> I'm sorry, Con. I thought I could do it, thought I could be something close to happy, but it all caught up to me. I'll miss you. I guess running away runs in the blood.

The bathroom sink gets stopped up. Annie wants to call her father—in her years in New York, he walked her through how to fix a closet door, how to adjust the vents to force heat into a too-cold bedroom, how to get rid of the mold in the shower. Now she leaves the pipes backed up, brushes her teeth in the kitchen. Annie sleeps until midday, coerced from the bed only by her bladder. She lives off iced coffee, iced wine, saltines, the last of the peaches and plums from the tree.

If Annie were to go into the water after Juliette and never return, would there be anyone to mourn her?

Muscles burning, burning beyond their limits, painful until there is no more pain, and it feels good. Annie and the other spandex-clad women at Move stomp and jump and shake and let it out, unraveling the rage that has been locked into their muscles, their organs, that has been absorbed into their bones, that has kept them silent. Here it comes out in sounds and screams they share only with each other.

Back in her car driving home, Annie is alone again. There is no one tethering her anywhere anymore, no one to whom she belongs. She turns to the internet to ease the existential terror, finds 467,000 followers and counting. She is not alone after all, see?

Annie goes out to the garden and collects her fruit, lights a cigarette, scrolls her DMs. Halfway down the page, one of the messages stops her: *I am really sorry for what happened to your friend and applaud you for coming forward. I had an encounter with Noah a couple of years ago, before he got married . . . I don't know why I'm telling this to a stranger, but I guess I just had to say—I believe Juliette.*

Annie writes back: *Jodi, thank you for contacting me. You have to tell your story. Please. Juliette isn't here any longer. Do it for her.*

# 41

When Jesse picks Camille up from her crib after her late-afternoon nap, smoky orange sunlight spilling over the floor, she feels the heat radiating from her daughter's tiny palms. Jesse starts the terrible affair of taking a rectal temperature while Camille cries out, unsure of what has befallen her. 100.4. Jesse reaches the pediatrician on call in a panic; the woman says that Jesse should monitor her and, if the fever doesn't rise, bring her in the morning. Jesse stays awake all night, cradling her daughter's hot body against her own.

The next day, in the office, they tell Jesse Camille is okay; she only has a cold, but nonetheless Jesse is terrified. At home, Camille stays attached to Jesse's nipple, ensuring that her mother cannot move from her, and Jesse lets Camille sleep while suckling all afternoon, all night, the next day and the following, lifting her and waking her when Camille cries out in her sleep.

The fires continue to burn, ash falling from the sky.

By the third sleepless night, Jesse is beginning to unravel. She calls Noah.

"Camille's still sick. I'm so exhausted I don't know what to do." There is too much silence on the other end of the line. "Why aren't you here?" Jesse asks, sobbing. "I need help."

"I'm sorry. I wish I was there with you."

Jesse is still crying. Hearing his voice only makes her feel more alone.

"Do you want me to cancel the rest of this and come home? I will if you want me to."

Of course he can't do that. There is too much on the line. "No."

"Tell me if you change your mind," Noah says, and she can hear the feeling of helplessness.

"Do you want me to get a night nurse or something? Do you want me to ask one of our friends to come over?"

She can't imagine letting someone else into their home right now, or putting Camille in the arms of anyone who isn't Noah. "No, never mind. I'll be fine."

"I love you, Jess. It's gonna be okay. I promise."

When they hang up, Noah orders McDonald's french fries in the Atlanta airport, a childhood comfort, and puts his headphones in.

He has started keeping his headphones in 24/7 until he has to take them out to talk to someone, to answer more terrible questions, to pretend he is not an angry Black man. Imagine, someone pulls a knife on you, and you have to smile at them.

His daughter has a fever, his wife is losing it, and he's twenty-five hundred miles away. He wants to go home to them with an ache that permeates every part of him.

Jesse holds Camille in her arms, rocking her, cooing to her. "Nothing bad will happen to you," she whispers. A prayer. The fever breaks on the fifth day. Outside, the fires rage on.

In the many lonely, sleepless hours, Jesse's phone haunts her: *@jessebaca how could you write that book and then become a rape apologist?* / *@kingnoah is the poster boy for toxic masculinity.* / *This planet would be better if @kingnoah and his wife @jessebaca disappeared off it.*

She tells herself to ignore the cutting words, but she can't. She and Noah are real people, human beings. Why is it so easy for the internet to diminish that? In her anguish, she can't help wondering about the woman leading the opposing army, who is also human.

On Annie's feed, there is a selfie in a matching sports-bra-and-leggings set, leg warmers, her face dewy with sweat. She's geotagged herself at Move, a New Age exercise class in Santa Monica. Earlier today, Annie was working out less than a mile away.

On the moms' feeds, there are vases of wildflowers everywhere, shortbread cookies topped with edible pansies, lacy white laundry soaking in spotless farmhouse sinks, picture-perfect families in matching fall jammies, wooden rainbows and tiny snow boots and homemade doughnuts.

How many of the moms online have a story like Juliette's? Like hers. Like Paris. How many of them have learned to bury it—all that shame, that fear, that rage—beneath their linens and beautiful baked goods?

Jesse's back aches. Her stomach aches. The vases of pink roses bend at the heads, their petals coming loose. The hydrangeas go brown. The sink piles with dishes.

Jesse pumps milk to freeze and washes the parts of the pump, making sure they are cleaned with the gentlest soap, making sure there is no residue, that not a single drop of tap water lingers so that nothing can contaminate the milk, so that no impurity will enter Camille's body.

Online, they write *@jessebaca's books are trash anyway. / So tired of hearing #KingNoah and his defenders play the race card.*

In the lobby bar of the Four Seasons, Noah stares into the abyss of the internet, where people sell their asses and their workouts to lift their asses, where Jesse is an apologist and so is the first female presidential nominee, where the manosphere rushes to Noah's defense while confederate flags wave in the virtual wind and America can agree, at least, on the glory of Adele's Carpool Karaoke.

Beverly calls him. "Too much race talk, Noah," she says. "Stop bringing it up. It makes you sound self-righteous, not sorry. You're just fanning the flames."

*Have you ever been Black, Beverly?* Noah wants to ask. He ends the call as politely as possible, and presses play on his music, where Kendrick has a bone to pick.

People just have to see the movie. When they see the movie, they will see him. They will understand.

Why would Juliette have thought that he raped her? His brain cannot stop trying to answer the impossible question, as if in it, he might find his redemption.

He finishes his old-fashioned, goes upstairs to call Jesse.

*#BoycottJesseBaca / @jessebaca I thought u got it. / @jessebaca what a hypocrite. You write about sexual assault and then defend a rapist.* Jesse's eyes glaze over. When the phone rings,

waking Camille, her cry shakes Jesse into her core, a spike of adrenaline like a lightning rod up her center.

She could put it on vibrate. Instead, Jesse picks up her phone, goes into the bathroom, and drops it into the toilet, lets it drown. She cannot afford to look away from her daughter. She cannot fall apart.

She rocks Camille, ignoring the pain in her shoulders, her neck. She is so tired she feels unsteady. She puts Camille in her carrier, walking in circles in the living room, singing, shushing into her ear.

As Camille continues to wail, Jesse picks up a trash bag from under the sink and empties the vases of dead flowers into it, one by one, dumps the murky water with its rotting smell down the drain.

She retrieves her drowned phone and tosses it into the bag, too.

She lies down on the bed with Camille and begins the process, again, of trying to soothe her. As Camille starts nursing, in her mind's eye, Jesse forms a bubble around them, invisible but impenetrable.

# 42

Jesse paces, unsure what to do with her twenty to forty minutes alone while Camille naps in her swing. Each task seems too daunting for the small interval of time, the pile of laundry to fold too large, the time too short to nap herself. She glances at the novel on the table, picks it up, reads the same page twice. She fills the watering can and steps onto the porch, emptying it into the plants that are dying in the heat. It would have been better if she'd thought to water them in the morning instead of waiting until the midafternoon. Finally, she lies beside Camille on the couch, covers herself with a baby blanket. The weight of exhaustion pins her.

The doorbell rings, startling Jesse from where she'd been nearly dozing. She rises, weary, irritated, as Camille stirs, begins to cry. She picks her up, carries her to answer the door. Jesse is expecting to find an Amazon package, but instead there is Suraya, carrying a bottle of rosé and a wrapped gift.

"Hi!" she says brightly to Camille. "Oh my god! Aren't you a beauty."

*What are you doing here?* Jesse's face asks. "Hey," she says.

"I know," Suraya replies quickly, "that you said visit after you're getting sleep, but that might be a long wait. I'm worried about you." When that gets no response from Jesse, Suraya displays the contents of her hands. "I brought treats!" A gift bag and a bottle of rosé.

As Jesse takes in Suraya with her perfect blowout, her pointed crimson nails, and her crushed velvet dress, she realizes how she must look in her sweatpants and T-shirt stained with nipple balm. She's not even wearing a bra. It was not fair of Suraya to just show up like this, exposing her.

But admittedly, there is also a small part of Jesse that feels a little bit relieved to have some company. Aside from Camille's pediatricians, pharmacists, the baristas at the coffee shop, and cashiers at the market, Jesse has not spoken to a single adult in person since Noah left. Although it's been two and a half weeks, to Jesse it feels like a lifetime. After a moment, she steps aside to let Suraya in.

Suraya reaches out for Camille, who is sleepy-dazed in Jesse's arms.

"Can I?"

"Sure," Jesse says, tentatively. "Can you just wash your hands first?"

"Of course."

Suraya steps into the kitchen and washes her hands in the sink stacked with dishes. Self-conscious, Jesse shoves the pile of clean laundry aside on the couch to make space for them to sit.

"Sorry it's such a mess in here," Jesse says as Suraya returns.

"Oh, stop. You're alone with a newborn." She stretches her hands out to Camille. "Come here, cutie."

Jesse places Camille's fragile weight into her friend's arms.

"Oh my god, you are going to make me ovulate," Suraya says, brushing her cheek against Camille's head. "It's a hell of a ride, right?" Suraya and Cal's son is almost two. Jesse nods.

Camille stares back at Suraya for a moment and starts to cry.

"I think she's hungry," Jesse says, rushing to take back her baby.

"So," Suraya says, when Camille begins nursing. "Are you okay?"

"Yeah."

"You haven't been answering any of my texts! You left me no choice but to barge in on you."

"Yeah, my phone broke, actually. I haven't gotten around to replacing it."

Suraya looks at her for a moment. "I brought us some wine," she says eventually, and goes into the kitchen, returns with two glasses of rosé. "Do you drink while you're nursing? I didn't think to ask."

Jesse shrugs at the glass sitting on the coffee table. "Yeah. I mean, not a lot."

Suraya nods. "I didn't," she says, and then adds, "But I know lots of women do. I'm sure you could use a fucking drink."

"Thanks," Jesse says.

Suraya reaches for the gift bag next to her purse. "I'll open Camille's present for her," she declares, and pulls out a pair of baby booties and a stuffed flamingo. They look well made, the type of thing you'd buy at one of the expensive baby boutiques sprinkled across the city.

"Those are so cute. Thank you."

"Of course." Suraya takes a drink of her wine. "Tell me the truth. How are you? This is a lot of shit all at once."

Jesse forces a meager smile. "We're holding up."

"Jess, come on, it's me. You can talk about it."

Jesse looks at the stuffed flamingo, the tiny baby booties sitting on the table. She reaches over and picks one up, runs her fingers over it.

"I'm hoping it blows over soon," Jesse says after a moment. "Hopefully the tour helps . . ." She has not discussed Noah's accusation with any of her friends. She does not want this—the way Suraya is looking at her now, with pity. With the assumption of Noah's guilt. It's one thing for strangers to imagine her husband's a rapist, another for a woman she's known for nearly eight years.

"You should switch sides," Suraya says after a moment. "I got lazy about it, and my right boob was bigger than my left one for like a year. I tried to correct it, but Max always wanted the right because it had more milk." Suraya looks down at her chest. "I feel like it's still bigger, actually." She brings her eyes back to Jesse. "Sorry. You know I ramble when I have no idea what the fuck to actually say."

Jesse nods vaguely. She puts her pinkie into Camille's mouth to break the latch. Camille cries until Jesse manages to get her situated on her left nipple.

Suraya sips her wine again, the glass already half gone. "You don't sound mad."

"Mad at who? It feels like a waste of time."

Suraya frowns. "But he cheated on you!"

"What?" The dread in Jesse's stomach is an oil spill, uncontainable.

"Oh. Fuck." Suraya scrunches her eyes shut. "You haven't seen it?"

"Seen what? I've been off the internet."

"Jesus. Jess, I'm sorry."

"Seen what?" Jesse asks again.

Suraya takes a sharp breath. "An anonymous woman wrote a piece for *Vox* describing an encounter she had with Noah a couple years ago. She said that it began consensually—she was giving him a blow job, but then he got aggressive. She said that she was unable to stop the encounter because he was gagging her."

Darkness clouds Jesse's eyes; she goes black. When she comes to, she finds Camille still nursing, Suraya still staring at her. "I'm sorry, Jess."

Jesse looks down at Camille. She looks so much like Noah.

"This has to be impossibly hard," Suraya says. "I remember the newborn days. And then all this shit with Noah on top of that, it's too much. I don't know what to think . . . I just want you to know I'm here for you. I'm team Jesse, and honestly, so is Cal."

Jesse's anger at Noah is blinding.

The fucked-up thing is that she wants him to be here. To hold her. To tell her it's not real. She looks back at her friend and answers in a choked whisper, "I love him. He's my husband. He's the father of my daughter."

"I know you love him." Suraya pauses, seeing Jesse's tears. "I'm just saying, you've got to put you and Camille first right now."

Jesse wants to push Suraya out of her house, to never let anyone in again. She tells her she needs to lie down, says, "I'll see you later," as she gets up to let her out.

When Suraya's gone, Jesse shuts the door and locks it. Her heart races. Immediately, she gets her laptop, googles the article, and reads it, Camille on the mattress beside her, playing with a light-up rattle. Jesse's brain struggles to make sense of it; she feels dizzy. Noah can sometimes be dominant during sex—Jesse knows that, likes it. But it is an awful, sickening feeling to hear that trait described through someone else's negative lens. It forces Jesse to imagine Noah in a sex act with another person when he was supposed to be hers. The image warps every feeling she has about the rough, wild, tender lovemaking they have shared over all these years.

There is their daughter, beginning to whimper for her. Jesse thought she knew her husband. But everything she believed to be sacred is slipping away. All these years, she thought he was the one thing she could be certain of. She never questioned the idea that she could trust him, never considered that he would lie to her.

The house phone rings and keeps ringing. Jesse silences it.

She looks at Camille, lying in the spot in her bed where Noah had been, and sees the translucent bubble, enclosing them, alone together. She wills it to grow stronger; she wills herself to grow stronger.

# 43

Jesse won't answer Noah's calls, hasn't for days. Is this what it feels like to lose everything? Numbed out on Xanax just so he can breathe, stomach knotted with dread nonetheless, Noah paces the airport hallways as the phone rings and rings through his headphones. In the abyss of the internet, the first female presidential nominee runs a sex-trafficking ring out of a pizza parlor, and he, too, is a headline: "Noah King Has Apparent History of Sexual Aggression, Infidelity"; "Noah King Plays the 'Race Card,' Won't Apologize for Alleged Rape"; "Outlook for Highly Anticipated *Red Balloon* Uncertain After Second Noah King Accusation."

His flight is boarding. The phone has been ringing for so long it has become background sound.

He is startled when he hears her voice. "Hello?"

"Jess?"

"It was Jodi?"

"Yeah. I—"

"Fuck you, Noah. What the fuck?"

"It happened once. She started it. I didn't know how to tell her no. She was my boss; she was this super-lonely woman and I felt bad for her. I hated myself afterward. I promised myself I would never do it again." The airline attendant is making the final boarding call.

"All that time I was just there, loving you, all that time I thought it was just the two of us against the world and you were fucking someone else." He hears a fury in Jesse's voice he's never heard before.

"We weren't fucking." Noah feels nauseated. "She gave me a blow job one time. It was gross. I promised myself I'd never do anything like that again, never betray you again, and I haven't. That she framed it the way she did is fucking crazy."

"You're fucked now, Noah. We're fucked."

"Don't say that."

"It's true." If only he could be in the same room with her, if she could see his face, if he could hold her . . .

"Jesse—"

"I don't know what to say to you. I'm alone here. I have to take care of our daughter."

"Jesse, I'm sorry. It meant nothing. You are my everything. You and Camille are my whole world."

"I can't talk right now. I can't talk to you right now."

Noah can hear his daughter start to cry.

"I gotta go," Jesse says.

"Okay. I love you, Jess."

There is a beat of silence, a long beat, before she finally responds. "I love you, too, but fuck. I don't know if I can do this."

"Do what?" Noah asks. His breaths are shortening. "Jesse, what do you mean? Do you mean us?"

She has already hung up.

———

*Weights on his ankles, weights on his wrists. He is fighting to get to the surface, but he can't get up. The panic overtakes his chest. He cannot breathe, and then, there is Juliette's body on the floor of the lake, her dark hair spread in the dark water. He fights harder. He doesn't want to drown here with her, but he can't—he can't swim up.*

Noah wakes tangled in a sweat. He reaches for Jesse. Does he hear his baby crying? It is a phantom sound.

It was a dream; the drowning was a dream.

He does not know where he is, not right away. The hotel rooms with their white bedding are all the same.

He fumbles for a light; he tries to tell his body he is not underwater, tries to tell his body he can breathe. He tries to call Jesse, but there is no answer.

This is his city. The Ritz-Carlton in Chicago. He can see the lake from the window on the twenty-third floor, the black expanse of it. The lake that drowned her.

The lake where he swam with his mother, the lake where they walked together. He is in the Ritz-Carlton in downtown Chicago. It could have been a dream come true.

After Noah's *Windy City Live* interview, he visits the Art Institute to see his mom's favorite paintings, swept up by memories of her.

The very last time they came to the museum together she'd been sick already and was so much skinnier than she used to be. When Noah would crawl into her lap it wasn't soft and cozy anymore. Still, she'd had the same eyes, and she could hold him with those eyes.

In front of Picasso's *Mother and Child*, she stood staring for longer than usual. She began crying, her eyes swimming away from him.

When he asked her what was wrong, she wiped her tears, but they kept coming. She squeezed his hand, but she was still looking at the baby and the mom. They looked wrong to Noah; their bodies were the wrong sizes, heads too square.

"Mama, stop!" he'd shouted, unable to control himself. There was a goodbye in her eyes, and he wanted her to come back to him. He needed her. He thought he'd be in trouble for yelling in a museum—he never did things like that—but instead, she pulled him in to her, asked if he wanted to get ice cream.

It was less than a year later that he lost her.

If he loses Jesse, he will be lost forever.

Noah zips his coat, wind whipping against his cheeks—he's gone soft after so many years in LA. When he walks into Lem's Bar-B-Q, Dev is already at a booth. It's their old spot. Noah is suddenly eight, nine, ten, eating links, looking down at his ashy knees, no lotion on them since his mother passed. He was always missing his mom; when it was not a thought it was still a feeling, an empty pit in his stomach that could not be filled no matter what he ate. His uncle would try to make him laugh, or to make him mad, even, to make the frozen glass of his eyes go away. Dev brought him after school every Friday, let him get 7UP from the machine. He tried hard, he did.

Dev says now, to Noah, "You got yourself in some trouble, didn't you. You know I told you to stay away from white girls," he says, laughing like it's a joke. Eric and Erica are away, visiting her mom in Atlanta. "Don't look so dour," Dev says. "You were always so serious."

"Don't let him watch it, please," Noah says. He means Eric. "Don't let him see *Windy City Live*. I don't want him to hear them calling me a rapist."

"I'm not trying to let him see it but he's eleven, Noah, he has the internet."

Noah looks into the distance.

"Anyway, he's gonna have to know, sooner or later, how they do us," his uncle says.

"He doesn't have to know right now."

"Maybe he'll stay away from white girls like you never did."

"Does Erica believe them? What they're saying about me?"

His uncle is quiet for a split second.

"'Course she doesn't," he says. And then, "But you shouldn't have cheated on Jesse."

"I know," Noah says.

Dev takes a bite of his ribs. "You've got a beautiful wife and a beautiful baby. Beg for forgiveness. It'll pass. You made a movie. You're on TV. You made it, Noah, like your momma always said."

Noah is holding on by a thread.

# 44

Drowning in her maternity sweats and a giant T-shirt, Jesse drives down Main Street, rolls down the windows, tries to sing along to something as she dials the radio restlessly from rap to classic rock back to rap. She texts Kat, Dexter's oldest daughter, from the road, on her new phone: *Camille's okay?* She's been gone only ten minutes. Kat replies with a thumbs-up.

Jesse has hired a babysitter. Perhaps it has taken blinding anger to reawaken her sense of self, enough to acknowledge her own desires. The cascade of emotions in the wake of Noah's betrayal has led her to fantasize about sleeping with a stranger, getting high, packing a suitcase and taking Camille to another country, but the impulse that Jesse has decided to act on is, arguably, more reasonable. She is going to an exercise class. Not just any exercise class. She is going to Move, the class she saw on Annie's Instagram.

Maybe she's crazy. She drives to the studio with no clear sense of what she hopes will happen if she encounters Annie. Does she want Annie to have to face her, to see the cost of what she's done? Does she want to attack her, to yell at her? Does she want to uncover some hidden truth that would exonerate Noah? Or does she simply want to see who she is—this woman who has taken away everything—in real life?

Jesse arrives to Move frenzied, almost late after searching for parking, and texts Kat again as she rushes in. *Did she take the bottle?*

Kat replies, *not yet, but she's chill.*

Jesse takes a breath, puts away her phone, and finds a spot in the back corner. The air smells like sage and palo santo. Candles are burning, the shades drawn against the bright day. Jesse scans the room full of women in fancy workout clothes. Maybe Annie has not come today, Jesse thinks—but then she spots her in the front row, just left of center, with her pointless leg warmers, strands of white-blond hair escaping her bun. Jesse's heart is racing before she has even begun to move her body.

The music starts; the instructor tells the women to put their hands on their hearts and their bellies.

The women in the class begin to squat in unison. "Haaaaaaa!" they say, as the instructor instructs them to move the energy through their bodies, to let it out. They hop from side to side; they do jumping jacks. Annie stands out not because she looks much different from the army of skinny white women, but because she jumps with extra vigor, always on beat, and screams extra-loud.

"Haaaaaaa!" Jesse says from the back row, trying to release the swell of energy, of anger, inside her. Whatever this class is supposed to do, it might be starting to work on her. The body that birthed her daughter and then became unrecognizable to Jesse, the body that nurses and nourishes Camille and remains in a state of perpetual panic—for a moment, Jesse is inside it.

Jesse and Annie and these women, they are each the burning balls of energy at their center, says the instructor. They are full of power. They are telling themselves not to run from the pain. Jesse does burpee after burpee, calling on energy that has visited her out of nowhere. She is ravished, soaked in sweat, leaking milk—"Haaaaaaa!" It is unraveling, all of it, rushing through her: Jodi's *Vox* story. Pablo's apartment in Paris, the lock turning. Jesse's grip on her life slipping, the life she was going to lead falling away from her, Annie, the woman who took it all, standing feet away from her; her daughter at home, her daughter who needs her. She stomps her feet into the ground, throws punches at the air, possessed. "Haaaaaaaaa!"

"Haaaaaaaaa!" Annie lets the sound unravel from her belly. She imagines that the women filling this room are the same women she speaks to online, the women who share their stories, the women who mourn Juliette from afar.

"Allow your body to be felt, to be heard, to be seen," shouts the instructor. Annie is not alone here. "Haaaaaaaaa," she screams, along with the other women as they do jumping jacks in perfect unison, as they shake their arms and pound their feet. And then, through the swell of music, she hears a sound of ferocious agony from behind her, a primal scream turning into a primal sob. In the back corner, a woman with a curtain of sleek, dark hair folds into herself amid the stomping feet, bent into a ball on her mat. Annie has a sudden urge to go to her. As the song finishes with a final "Haaaaaaaaa!" from the class, something softer, musical and mournful begins. The woman rises and rushes out, still crying. Instinctively, Annie follows.

Annie stands in the lobby for a moment and watches her through the glass doors that lead to the parking lot. Her breath catches deep in her chest. She recognizes this woman. She is Noah King's wife. Jesse Baca, the author. She is thin-armed, with a long, graceful neck—a dancer's neck—wide brown eyes, clear skin. Unlike many of the other women in the class, she isn't dressed in matching workout clothes, but instead wears an oversized, worn-in T-shirt with a picture of Selena on the front, baggy sweatpants.

Annie remembers the spike of rage she felt, reading Jesse's defense of Noah. But now that Jesse's standing right there, so plainly vulnerable, that anger recedes to the background, over-shadowed by a strange ache. Annie watches her squinting into the sun, wiping her eyes, trying to catch her breath.

Annie steps outside, pulled as if by a magnet.

"Are you okay?" she asks.

Jesse turns to Annie and seems surprised to see her there. She doesn't answer the question. Annie can see that she is still trying to catch her ragged breath.

"I cried my first time, too," Annie says.

The woman—Jesse—nods.

"I'm Annie."

Another nod.

"Can I get you some tea or something? Or, I don't know, a drink," she says with a little laugh.

Jesse looks at her phone.

"I have a baby. I have to be home to feed her soon."

Now Annie nods.

Jesse studies her for a long beat. "But maybe we have time to walk next door," she says finally.

———

By the time they step into Starbucks Jesse has partially reassembled herself—her head is now held higher, but her eyes are still puffy, her outer layers still porous, thin from the outpouring of grief, or pain, or fear.

Watching her, Annie is strangely reminded of the first time she saw Juliette, of that feeling of being stunned by her beauty—a sort of lust that, though not sexual in nature, nevertheless provoked an unmistakable desire.

They order: a cold brew for Annie, a coconut milk matcha for Jesse. She pays before Annie can stop her. They sit at a table in the sun. It makes a halo around Jesse's head. Annie squints. There is electricity in the air, a charge between them. What will they say to each other? Does Jesse recognize her?

"The class is intense," Annie says, after a moment. "But after my dad died, and a bunch of other stuff that's happened, it's kinda been the only thing that's saved me."

"I'm sorry," Jesse answers. "My dad's dead, too."

"I'm sorry," Annie says. "It's the worst."

"It is. When did he pass?"

"It's been a little over two months now."

"Oh, that's so recent," she says. "I'm so sorry."

"What about you?" Annie asks.

"Around when I graduated college. Cancer."

"Same."

"I wanna tell you it gets better—I guess it does—but I feel like I've been grieving in slow motion ever since. Or maybe it's just having a baby—" Jesse interrupts herself. "I don't usually talk to strangers," she says with a nervous laugh. "Much less about dead fathers."

"What's your name?" Annie asks.

"Oh, sorry." She lets out more nervous laughter, her eyes glinting. "I'm Jesse."

Annie nods. "Nice to meet you, Jesse." They smile at each other, matching half-smiles that say they will leave it there.

# 45

Annie and Jesse get coffee after Move together a few times. And then Annie asks if Jesse wants to go out for a drink. Jesse tells her that she doesn't have anyone to watch her daughter. Her husband, she says, is traveling for work.

"Bring her!" Annie suggests.

"Maybe . . ." Jesse says. "It would have to be before bed-time. I'll let you know if she seems up for it." They exchange numbers.

Jesse tells herself she won't really call, but only one day later, faced with the blaring silence of the house, she does.

Why? She is still in her "fourth trimester," alone with her newborn daughter. The career Jesse fought so hard for might now be over. Her husband cheated on her—is it revenge that she's after? Perhaps. But Annie, the woman who ruined her life, is nice. She is funny. She fascinates Jesse.

Annie offers to drive to a wine bar in Jesse's neighborhood, and so Jesse dresses, puts on mascara for the first time since before Camille was born, packs a diaper bag. She puts Camille in a pretty cotton jumper, tells her they are going out. She worries that Camille will get tired or fussy, but she feels excited to have somewhere to go. She straps her baby to her chest in the carrier and they walk over to find Annie already at a table, waving enthusiastically. They order drinks, and Jesse breast-feeds Camille while sipping Chablis. Annie has no judgments on Jesse's mothering, no opinion on whether it is okay to drink and nurse, never asks if Camille's pacifier is organic. But she does ask Jesse about what it's like, being a mom, and she listens with rapt attention when Jesse tries to tell her the things she has not been able to tell anyone. About the mind-altering exhaustion, yes, but also about how she has never known a love this deep, this true. About how when Camille looks into her with a wide-open, unbroken gaze, it feels like the root of all that is human.

Jesse should be telling these things to Noah. She misses him with a pain that stabs clean through her. But he is gone, and Jesse is home, sleeping and waking and changing and feeding and bathing, with no one to share the miracle that is unfolding in front of her. They should be together. Instead, the whole world, or anyone with the internet who cares to read about it, can learn that another woman gave Noah a blow job seven years into their ten-year relationship.

Could Noah blame Jesse, really, for finding a friend?

A friend in their enemy.

Of course, he could. But he betrayed her first, didn't he.

As Jesse and Annie repeat their wine bar adventure—Annie always there waiting at five o'clock—they both say so much, more than you'd say to a near stranger. They talk about their dads, about what it is like to watch your father suffer, he who was a hero, a protector, in pain, relegated to bed. About the awful helplessness. About the time grief takes, its strange permutations, the way it leaks into every part of your life.

Annie is bare, raw, so Jesse can be, too. She has no energy for polite company anymore, but with Annie, she can be herself, worn thin with transparent skin.

Jesse fantasizes sometimes that her budding friendship with Annie could change it all, that she could salvage their lives, make Annie see the truth that Jesse still knows, underneath her anger—that Noah is no monster.

But Jesse doesn't know when she and Annie will come clean to each other. Annie talks to Jesse about everything, except Juliette. Sometimes, after their drink dates, Jesse can't help pulling up the photo, staring at Annie on the beach beside her friend. Annie is leaning against Juliette, looking at her, while Juliette stares straight at the camera. The joy on Annie's face is joy she borrowed from Juliette, Jesse sees now. Joy she has, maybe, never found for herself.

Annie has just ended an engagement, left a fiancé behind in New York. Annie laughs often, especially when talking about the life she has just "blown up." Jesse knows that Annie's laughter is a screen for her grief, that her loneliness is bone-deep. If Annie needs it, Jesse thinks, she's willing to loan some of the joy she herself has left—all of it gifted by her daughter.

Annie is looking for Juliette's replacement in the wife of her rapist—how fucked-up is that? And yet, in the flesh Jesse is so much more. With her easy laugh and messy style and well of tenderness, Jesse is the only one, it seems, who understands Annie's whirlpool of grief.

Annie's new friend is a mother, and this is, maybe most of all, what gets her: watching Jesse and Camille together. The way that Jesse takes care to tighten the little booties on Camille's feet that keep coming off anyway; the way that Jesse bends her neck to smell Camille's head almost unconsciously. The way that Jesse's own body hurtles itself into a state of alarm when Camille cries, the need to care for her daughter taking her over. The way that she traces the lines in Camille's palms; the way that they coo at each other in conversation.

Witnessing motherhood up close, in its earliest stages, triggers a deep longing in Annie. But she can't say what she is longing for, exactly. To be cared for by Jesse? To have her own baby?

Of all the pieces of her former life, it is the children she might have had with Spencer whom Annie mourns most. The children on whom she'd have bestowed painstaking care, feeding them milk from her body, bathing them, pointing out the flowers and the falling leaves, stroking their heads and singing them to sleep. Readying them for school, making pancakes and packing lunches and planting gardens and applying sunscreen. Becoming, perhaps, a different version of one of the mothers she'd yearned for as a girl, with the purses full of hair ties and snacks and various creams. Jesse is that kind of mother, and more. Jesse has the kind of magic that will make the world twinkle for her daughter. Magic equal to Margot's.

They are going to take the baby to the beach today. Annie packs a picnic basket, the kind you might see in a magazine, full of the last of the fall plums from Goldstone, the sweetest ones. Cold Riesling, metal cups. Cheese and bread and olives. The woven white blanket she used to use with Juliette. And then, she drives to Jesse's house in Santa Monica, where Jesse waits outside with Camille. They load into Jesse's car; Jesse asks Annie to DJ.

"What's the vibe?" Annie asks.

"Whatever you want. I'm just happy to be out of the house, going to do a real thing!"

Annie overthinks her selection—should she go classic? Leonard Cohen? Bob Dylan? But it doesn't feel quite right to repeat her and Juliette's music. Finally, she puts on *Lemonade*. Because Jesse is married to Noah and he cheated on her, Annie imagines Jesse will relate.

Jesse starts singing along with Beyoncé right away, as she turns up the Pacific Coast Highway.

When "Don't Hurt Yourself" comes on, Jesse loses herself in it, screaming along with abandon as Beyoncé asks her husband who the fuck he thinks she is. And Annie shouts along, too, bearing witness to Jesse's rage, which is not so different from her own. The ocean is in perfect fall form, deep blue and glittering. They fly their hands out the windows. Camille wiggles her toes.

In Jesse's presence, for the first time since Annie arrived in LA, maybe for the first time since she lost Juliette, she feels like herself—like a new self, like there is a kernel of a self that Jesse can see, like Annie is not just a ghost, not only empty. They have made an unspoken pact, her and her new friend: they will call another world into existence, however briefly. One where their friendship would be not only possible, but natural.

They park at Zuma; while Jesse gets her baby, Annie unloads everything else—the picnic basket and blanket, the rain-sized umbrella she brought to shade Camille. The tide is high, spreading out over the shining sand. Dolphins skirt the shore. While Jesse pulls down her bikini to nurse, Annie rubs sunscreen into her back—a surprisingly intimate act. Jesse came here on the fifth anniversary of her father's death, she says, and burnt to a crisp. But today she feels happy—as happy as possible as a currently single parent on four hours of sleep, she says, laughing. They picnic on the fruit that Annie brought from Goldstone, get buzzed on the wine. They show Camille the crabs in the tide pools and listen to the bells of her laughter ring over the sounds of the sea.

Camille falls asleep under the umbrella, and then Jesse falls asleep beside her. As Annie watches them, their bodies curling in to each other, she remembers a time she can't possibly remember: her babyhood in the pine-smelling mountains, Annie following behind her parents in the dirt, digging little holes for the seeds they were planting. A long walk in the finally cool part of a summer evening, the sound of her mother's breath. How high the trees reached, how fast the night fell, like a curtain dropped. Grief is like this: a sorceress.

When they wake, Jesse says she wishes she could swim.

"I'll take her," Annie says. She looks at Camille. "Is it okay if I hold you, while your mama goes in the ocean?"

Camille smiles, so Jesse reaches out and places her in Annie's arms.

Annie looks down at the tiny child, the feather weight of the body that holds a human soul; Camille looks back at her, into her eyes, and seems to know her. They both look out at the ocean, where Jesse dives under.

Time seems to slow; have they always been here? Can they stay?

They stay all day. The three of them watch the sunset, a regular miracle in rare form. Annie and Jesse drink the last of the Riesling.

———

"You have your daddy's smile," Jesse says to Camille impulsively. She glances over at Annie, looks away. She has conjured the specter of Noah, walked right up to the edge of their invisible line.

Annie lowers her eyes, down to where drops of salt water have dried onto the tops of Jesse's breasts. Jesse takes another sip of her wine.

"You remind me, a little bit, of my best friend," Annie says, sounding offhanded but responding in kind.

Jesse nods. Vines creep up from the bottom of her stomach, start to wrap around her heart.

"What's she like?" Jesse asks, after a moment.

Annie looks up. "She drowned."

Instinctively, Jesse averts her gaze. "I'm sorry," she says, as the vines tighten their grip. Will this be it? Should she just say it—*I know you miss Juliette, but there are other points of view to consider. What do you think your accusation did to my daughter?*

Annie stares into her wineglass, up at a gull circling. Camille starts to nurse, pulling on and off.

"She was like August," Annie says eventually. "In July, it feels like summer could last forever. In August, you get the sweetest fruit, the prettiest gold light, but you can tell, somewhere in your body, that it won't last. Fall will come. So it makes it all the more poignant. When I look back, I guess every day with Juliette was a little like that."

"I get that," Jesse says, meeting Annie's eyes now.

The sun has dropped, but the sky is still full of wild, pink light. Soon, it too will fade. Camille finishes eating, begins to whimper.

"Should we pack up?" Jesse asks.

"Okay." As Jesse calms Camille, Annie returns the empty wine bottle, the pits of fruit, the sandy remains of the cheese to the basket.

She takes hold of Jesse's hand and squeezes it. "Today was perfect," she says quietly.

"It was," Jesse answers. They hold on to each other.

# 46

Noah is cold in his bones, sleepless despite his Ambien, turning over and over again in the hotel bed with its clean white sheets.

He stares at the bottle of pills. It would be so easy to swallow them all.

He could pull the blanket over him, close his eyes, and wait to feel himself sinking.

He would see Jesse walking through the sand in her white dress, flowers in her hair, her bright eyes peering into him, promising to love him forever.

In his distress, Noah has begun to knot the two things together in his head: if he can save his movie, he will be able to save his marriage. If he can earn the forgiveness of the country, he will be able to earn his wife's. If *The Red Balloon* is a success after all, Jesse will stay. They could go back to their lives, their good lives, their happy lives . . .

Out there on the internet, puppies are adopted and shots

are fired and young professionals Instagram their *Hamilton* playbills, the pantsuit power flash mob goes viral, and he is a rapist. A philanderer. A no-good motherfucker.

He just has to convince people to go to the theaters. When they see the images that have been living inside him for as long as he can remember, they will understand he is not a monster. Then he can keep his promise to Jesse; he can take care of her, of their daughter.

He wakes in a cold sweat two hours later.

And then there she is, arriving at 4:00 a.m. in the last of his anonymous hotel rooms: Juliette, coming to him as a teacher, rather than a lover. Standing in the front of that classroom, her hands flitting like birds, her dark hair tangled in the back, her cheeks pink from the cold, lecturing. *You don't have to know exactly what you want to say before you start writing. Allow the poem to lead you to new places. Allow your unconscious mind to make associations . . .*

Why did Juliette think he raped her? Why did she write that in her journal? The question is maddening, as if she were living in an entirely separate reality from him.

He doesn't want to hate her, the girl who read them poetry with a lilting voice that lingered over every word, as if it were edible, as if she were tasting it. He remembers that he liked her. She was a good teacher. He remembers that much.

He rises in the dark, takes a hot shower, suits up.

In the dressing room, his face powdered, his coffee cup empty, Noah opens the photo of Camille that Jesse emailed when he was in Boise: his tiny daughter, smiling for the first time. He missed it, her first smile. He has been gone nearly five weeks now. *The Red Balloon* will be out nationwide in seventy-two hours.

"Three minutes." The PA peeks her head in—a pretty, dark-skinned girl, wearing all the right clothes. She does not meet Noah's eyes.

He shuts his, tries to focus on his breath, the way he learned in the birth class. Inhale to a count of three. Exhale twice as long. Relax. This interview is his last chance.

"Noah King, follow me—" It is the PA, returning.

He follows her through a series of hallways, and then he's on stage, in the blinding light. Inhale to a count of three. Exhale *twice as long.* Don't lose your grip. It's a long way down.

*Next, we turn to* The Red Balloon, *a film that created plenty of buzz and garnered early Oscar nods . . . but then the writer-director's past surfaced, leading to an allegation that has become the topic of extensive conversation . . .*

Jesse feels a burst of adrenaline in her chest. Part of her wants to turn the television off, but she cannot. She abandons the toast she was about to butter, goes to sit on the couch, and brings Camille to her breast.

Noah's heart is beating out of sync. His palms feel sweaty. But he answers the questions, keeps his voice even. It would have been better if he could have slept last night. He does not feel well; something is wrong in his body.

"A lot of survivors are still waiting for you to take responsibility. Why haven't you been able to say that you are sorry?" asks the anchor.

Noah takes a breath. He sips from the mug on the table and imagines mothers and fathers across the country looking over at his face on TV while they make breakfast for their sons and daughters.

"I'm trying to tell the truth as best as I know how," he says. "I liked Juliette. She was my creative writing teacher and she helped me love writing. After I'd stopped taking her class, we ran into each other at a museum, where I was visiting the paintings I used to see with my mother, and then we hooked up, and then we went out on a date together. We had too much to drink and had sex. We were both underage and our judgment was impaired, and that was a mistake I truly wish I could take back. But I did not force her into anything, and I have no idea why she felt that I did, except that perhaps she was drunk enough that her memory was impaired, and she imagined something that didn't happen."

The host frowns. "With all due respect, that feels like another way of avoiding a true apology."

Noah strains to hold the tension back from his voice. "Please. I don't know how else to explain it to you. I'm sorry that Juliette was in pain, but I can't apologize for a crime I didn't commit . . ."

The host raises her eyebrows. Noah's desperation is becoming apparent.

"I would love to keep this on the movie, which is a story that I think is so important, about what is happening to Black men, Black boys in this country—"

"Yes, I hear that, but what happened can't be ignored."

"I'm not ignoring it. I've been speaking to it, but I feel like nothing I can say changes what you think of me." He exhales. How many times has he been through this? He feels something inside of him inching close to a breaking point. "If people make me into a monster, it's a reason not to have to really take in the message I'm trying to put out there with this movie, which is a human message about the lives of Black people in this country, the racial, economic injustice—"

"And you do a beautiful job of speaking to that, but before we get into the film, there's one other issue I'd like to address."

The wedding photograph of him and Jesse appears on the screen before him.

"You have talked a lot about your wife and your love for her. But there is also an anonymous accuser who describes a sexual encounter you had with her, only a couple of years ago, while you and Jesse were together. The accuser describes your behavior as aggressive, inappropriate. Is sexual misconduct a pattern for you?"

He can't take his eyes off his Jesse: her smile radiating, her happiness tangible even through the photo. He is powerless to protect it, powerless to protect her. An echo of the feeling of powerlessness that has haunted him most of his life. It triggers his shame, the most tender of wounds, the most dangerous. That shame touches everything sacred—his role as a husband, a father. It threatens to erase him. Noah takes a breath, steeling himself.

"Obviously I'm not proud of what happened, but the woman who wrote that piece was my boss, and she was the one who came on to me. That she's calling me aggressive is insane. It's really an impossible position I'm in, being forced to defend myself like this again and again. I'm a filmmaker, and I think if people just get out to the theater—"

"You and your wife recently had a child, is that correct?"

On the screen there is Noah and newborn Camille—the closest he's ever been to God, he thought in that hospital room, was holding his baby girl. Now his daughter has been pulled off Instagram and placed on national television in a segment about his rape accusation.

"As a father, if you imagined something like this happening to Cam—"

"Keep my daughter's name out of your mouth," Noah says, his voice low and icy. "Leave my family out of this bullshit."

The hush that descends over the room is chilling.

Camille pulls away from Jesse's breast, asleep now in her arms. Jesse's panic is not just in her chest, but all the way down into her guts, the deepest part of her belly, the place where she carried their baby, where her body clenches itself like a fist in fear.

She shuts off the TV and places Camille in her bassinet. She goes to the liquor cabinet, pours a glass of the expensive whiskey that Dexter bought for Noah when they sold the movie. It is seven in the morning. The day ahead of her feels impossible, the weeks, the months, the years, even more so.

Camille wakes moments later, crying for her.

All day Jesse stays in Camille's room, rocking her daughter, allowing the weight of Camille's body to tether her to the world. *Nothing bad will happen to you. Nothing bad will happen . . .* But where will they go? What will they do? She'd wanted for Camille a life of chasing waves with screeches of laughter, blown dandelions, melting Popsicles, stained party dresses, dance recitals and Halloween carnivals, splashing in puddles . . . Is such innocence still possible?

*Nothing bad will happen to you,* she says to her daughter,

over and over, but Noah is her father. How will it affect her to know that he was accused of rape? That he cheated on her mother?

Annie texts her: *You need to get drunk, I'm sure of it. Come out with me tonight. I'll pay for a babysitter!*

Jesse stares down at her phone. *I can't*, she finally replies. Noah will be home this evening. The premiere is tomorrow. Jesse smells Camille's head to assuage the dread.

*Noah is drowning. Weights on his ankles, weights on his wrists. He cannot swim up. The panic overtakes his chest. He cannot breathe, and then, there is Juliette on the floor of the lake, her dark hair spread in the dark water. He fights harder. He fights harder, until he just wants to drown with her. Darkness.*

He wakes with a start as the airplane touches down in Los Angeles.

# 47

The black car sent by the studio smells like too much cologne, like decades of cologne. "Hotel California" plays on the radio. Jesse rolls down her window. All evidence of the sun has already drained from the November sky. She opens her phone and uses the camera as a mirror to wipe the mascara from under her eyes, left behind in trails when she locked the door behind her and Noah. Hearing Camille crying on the other side, she could not stop her own tears.

Jesse and Noah have not spoken about Jodi in the twenty-four hours he's been home, nor about Noah's last disastrous interview. They haven't spoken about anything other than Camille. Jesse let Noah hug her when he walked in the door of their bungalow, but as soon as she felt the tears beginning to rise, her body wanting to melt into her husband's, she pulled away.

"You look beautiful," Noah says now, breaking the silence. She feels anything but. She's wearing the diamond earrings he bought her for Valentine's Day right after the festival sale, her hair in a twisted bun, her body clad in the cascading red gown she rented on the internet, just too-tight enough to make her feel ridiculous.

Jesse left Kat with two typed pages of instructions, pumped her breasts empty of milk before she got dressed, but she can already feel them starting to fill again and worries she'll leak through the pads. The driver changes the radio station, and now the voice is talking about the white working-class voter. All the polls say the first Black president will be followed by the first woman.

Jesse unsticks her shoulder from the leather seat and texts Kat for word on how Camille is doing, wanting to know if she's calmed, if she's eaten, if Kat found the pajamas Jesse left out. She's never been away from Camille at night before, never not nursed her to sleep, and rather than the premiere or the abysmal box office predictions, rather than her country on the brink of a historic election, rather than the gash between her and her husband—the feeling that they are unrecognizable as the Noah and Jesse who married each other a year ago—it is the anxiety of being away from her baby that Jesse feels seizing her chest. Kat texts back that she put on the pajamas, but Camille won't take the bottle. The Spanx Jesse crammed her still-loose belly into make it even harder to breathe.

The car is arriving, and it is worse than Jesse thought: there are maybe a thousand protesters lining Hollywood Boulevard, holding candles. They are silent, wearing white T-shirts where they have written in red letters: I BELIEVE JULIETTE.

The driver pulls up as far as he can, and then there is no way in but past them. Jesse glances at her husband. Noah's looking straight ahead, expressionless.

One of them has to open the door; they have to get out of the car.

And then there is the driver, on Jesse's side, escorting her out. Noah opens his door, walks around, and reaches for her hand. His palms are sweating. She holds on to him. One foot in front of the other; she feels lightheaded, out of her body. The protesters stare. Jesse looks away from the women whose eyes call her a traitor.

As they reach the front of the line and turn toward the red carpet, Jesse sees Annie in her handmade T-shirt: I BELIEVE JULIETTE. With her blond hair pulled back tightly, her freckled forehead, her face free of makeup, she looks almost like a child. She meets Jesse's eyes, and they both freeze.

Noah pulls at Jesse, but she can't move. For a moment, Jesse thinks that Annie will shout, or cry. Or reach out to hug her, maybe. Maybe Jesse wishes she would. But Annie only stares, never breaking her gaze, from her side of the battle line.

Finally, Jesse turns, sees Noah watching her.

Inside the lobby, there are neat rows of popcorn and soda lined up for the taking, people mill about, doing a mediocre job of pretending the protests don't exist, clapping Noah on the back but avoiding his eyes, congratulating him on the movie, asking about his baby. This is the first time Jesse has been forced to socialize since Noah's "scandal," and making conversation with all those people, she feels shaky, barely able to pretend at normalcy, her chest burning, her head swimming from exhaustion and anxiety.

Sitting beside Noah in the dark of the theater is almost worse. The last time Jesse saw *The Red Balloon*, they were together in the festival audience. As it plays, she feels her stomach drop out of her body with sadness. The part of her that wants to protect Noah, that wants to protect what he's made, rises up. They worked so hard for this movie, and it is beautiful. Whatever his sins, it is a terrible thing to see the world trample her husband's creation.

Noah and Jesse ride home in silence. When they arrive, Camille is asleep. Jesse thanks Kat, hands her the money they owe, says good night. Her breasts are too full, painful. Perhaps a part of Jesse had hoped that Camille would be up, crying for her. That Jesse could feed her, soothe her, bypass any interaction with Noah. But as soon as Kat walks out the door, Noah follows Jesse to the couch, where she sits to remove her heels. She glances at him.

"I'm sorry, Jesse."

She nods. There is a heavy silence. Just as Jesse is about to stand to get some water, Noah asks, "Why were you and Annie Ricci staring at each other like that?"

"Like what?"

"Like she wanted something from you."

"What do you mean?"

"When we were outside. You were staring at each other."

Jesse swallows. "I met her," she says after a moment. "At an exercise class."

"What?" Noah looks at her in confusion.

"We had coffee a few times," Jesse says, half-admitting her transgression. She feels dizzy. "She asked me. She didn't realize who I was."

"What?" Noah says again, the hurt in his voice sharpening.

"She's not . . . as bad as she seems." Meaning: she's human. She laughs and bleeds and aches and grieves, just like us. What would Noah think if he knew she'd held his daughter? Jesse feels a wave of nausea.

"You befriended the woman who told the world I'm a rapist?"

Jesse feels her guilt swell and tries to push it aside. "I didn't mean for it to happen. I wanted to see who she was. I thought maybe if—if she got to know us, she'd see it's not what she thought."

"And how'd that work out?"

Jesse looks away.

"This woman destroyed us, Jesse! How could you do that?" The anger in Noah's voice has given her permission to unleash her own. "Did she destroy us? Or did you?" she asks pointedly.

Noah shakes his head in hurt.

"You don't know what it's been like," Jesse says. "Being here alone with Camille. We were supposed to be a family. You've been gone. I've been doing it alone. I needed someone to talk to."

"Someone to talk to?" Noah's voice rises. "You could have called me. You could have talked to me. You threw away your fucking phone. You never answered when I called the house. Instead, you chose the person who took away everything we've worked for?"

"You cheated on me, Noah, you cheated on me and I found out through our friend who found out through the fucking internet when I was home alone with our newborn!"

Jesse can imagine it from Noah's perspective, she thinks: Which is worse, a onetime blow job? Or a friendship with the woman who accused Noah of rape, tanked the movie he fought eight years for, and foreclosed upon the promise of a dream come true, an entire career?

But Noah does not know the violence his dishonesty has done to Jesse, to her love for him, to the very foundation upon which she has built her adult life.

He is silent for a moment. His voice drops. "I'm sorry," he says.

A part of Jesse that wants to fall into him, but she can't.

"Are people allowed to make mistakes? Aren't I allowed to fuck up without being punished for it forever?" Noah asks.

Jesse feels the fight drain from her body, replaced by a totalizing exhaustion. "I guess not," she answers quietly, and walks out of the room.

# 48

#RedBalloon is an epic box office fail / @kingnoah maybe you'll never work in Hollywood again, but if they didn't lynch you, you're winning. #RacisminAmerica / Don't Blame racism. Blame @kingnoah and his heinous actions for his movie's failure. / The poor daughter of @kingnoah is gonna be raised by a rapist unless @jessebaca grows some balls and leaves his ass. / @anniebobanny so u succeeded in taking down a black man. r u proud of yourself? / #RedBalloon is an example of the #BlackExcellence they don't want us to see. / @anniebobanny got hella famous off of this / Wow I cried. So good. So real. #RedBalloon / @anniebobanny maybe think twice before you ruin people's lives based on a ten-year-old journal entry. We don't know what happened that night. / @jessebaca should be canceled along with her husband. / #RedBalloon is a beautiful movie. / Don't let the Noah King controversy stop you from seeing Red Balloon. It is an EXCELLENT film! / @jessebaca I know he's your man but @kingnoah is a rapist. #Believewomen / Standing ovation for #RedBalloon in Chicago theater!! /

*@anniebobanny u are literally my hero. / @jessebaca wake up
he cheated on you darling why are you defending him. /
#FuckRape / #FuckWhitePrivilege*

Annie sets down her phone. The movie is starting.

Though *The Red Balloon* opened in 2,130 theaters, a week
later there are only a smattering of showtimes. She is at the
Laemmle in Santa Monica at two o'clock on a Tuesday. She
thought it would be empty, but there is one other person in the
theater, an old Black man who comes in with a walker, sits in
the third row from the front.

It is true; the movie is beautiful. What else can Annie say
about it? The man who raped Juliette made a beautiful movie,
painfully beautiful, as the best art is. If Annie learns one thing
from it, it is not that he is talented—she'd assumed that. It is
that he is wounded. She does not want to get close to his pain.
She does not want to know that he is also an abandoned child.
She wants to hold on to her anger. For her, for Juliette, for her
mother. What does she have without it?

A bottomless sadness.

That afternoon, Annie DMs Matt Brody. He'd found her on
Instagram after she became internet famous, sent her a series
of messages:

*I'm so sorry about Juliette. I know how much you guys loved
each other.*

*I was always jealous of what you two had.*

*What happened to her was fucked. Good for you for having the
balls to call it out.*

*Thanks, Matt,* she'd replied.

Two days later, he'd written: *I feel like it was yesterday we
were sixteen.*

*I know,* she said. *Me too.*

And that's where their conversation ended. Since then, she's been quietly liking his photos of buddies in bars, horses, mediocre views of Dodgers games.

*What are you doing tonight,* she writes now, as she walks out of Noah's movie onto the crowded Promenade, already decorated for the holidays. She wants him to fuck her. She wants to get so drunk she doesn't know where she is anymore.

He replies an hour later and they agree to meet at Sagebrush Cantina in Calabasas, the sprawling, wealthy, half-rural suburb where Matt still lives. Annie has overdressed for the place, in her New Yorker boots and a tight black dress. They sit at a dirty wood table and Annie orders margaritas. Matt is sober now and runs a start-up—something to do with digital marketing. He drives a Corvette. His once perfectly smooth skin has aged beyond his thirty-five years. Annie tongues away the salt from her glass, nibbles at the chips. They are sitting close enough to the band playing country songs that they have to raise their voices to be heard, but Annie talks anyway. It is easy to talk to Matt, who now has a soft belly, a brain softened by too many years of Ecstasy, the same impassive eyes she remembers.

They drive back to his condo in the Corvette. Annie closes her eyes and feels the hot wind in her hair and tries to excavate her old adrenaline rush. Several drinks in, it is easier to see the boy Matt was, hovering just under the surface of the man.

She ought to take up skydiving. She ought to go to Australia. She ought to find another way out of herself. Instead, she takes him back to his oversized, frigidly air-conditioned bedroom, pulls up her dress. She sleeps with him to try to feel sixteen again, to try to remember what it was like to walk out of his house into the afternoon sunlight, still wet and warm, to find Juliette in the stables, whispering to his horse Dancer. What it was like to drive back down the canyon with her best friend, freshly sexed, lighting cigarettes, hair blowing in the wind. She knows she will never be that beautiful again.

Back in Juliette's bed, Annie hardly sleeps, and when she does, she dreams of Jesse. She longs for Jesse in spite of herself, for the girl with the too-big T-shirts, with the big breasts she pulls out while drinking wine, with the pretty baby who makes the softest *mmhumm*s. Annie gets up at six, drinks coffee in the garden in a daze. She changes her workout clothes five times. She picks the first of the persimmons, thinks of bringing them along to give to Jesse, in case she comes to Move, and then decides it is silly, leaves them in a basket on the counter and drives out of Topanga at nine. She is early, the first one in the studio. She chooses a mat in the back, in the corner where Jesse always goes, and saves the one next to her with her sweater. In case she comes.

The instructor begins the first song, tells the class to stand at the top of their mats, to put their hands on their bodies, to tap their heels. No Jesse. Annie glances toward the door as the music picks up and a roomful of legs begins to bend and straighten.

And then suddenly, miraculously, there she is in her Selena T-shirt, late as always.

They look at each other only once as Jesse steps onto the mat beside her. For sixty minutes, they squat, they jump, they shout, they plank and bridge and sweat. They push their bodies harder than ever—too hard, maybe—but what else can they do with all this? They shout again. At the end, they sit beside each other and swing their arms back and forth in an effort to open their hearts.

As the song finishes, Annie turns to Jesse, feeling a sudden, desperate urge to grab ahold of her. They are both soaked in sweat.

"I should get home," Jesse says, before Annie can speak, hurrying to gather her things. "Camille's probably hungry. She was sleeping when I left."

"Wait."

Jesse turns to her.

"Come over tomorrow," Annie blurts out. "I'm having a dinner party."

Jesse hesitates. "A dinner party?"

Annie nods.

"I can't end up on the internet at your house."

"You won't, I promise."

"Who's going to be there?"

"Nobody."

Jesse looks back at her, eyebrows raised.

Annie smiles a small smile.

And then Jesse laughs. "Literally nobody?"

"Well, not nobody. You, and me. And Camille if you want to bring her."

Jesse is quiet for a beat. And then she says, "Text me your address."

It will be beautiful, just like it used to be. Annie spends all day preparing, making the tarts with the basket of persimmons, slow-cooking the lentils, roasting the squashes, extracting the seeds from the pomegranates, chilling the wine, stringing the lights, collecting wood for the bonfire. She goes out shopping, buys a white linen tablecloth like the one Margot used to have, brass candle holders. Goldstone fills with the warm smells she remembers.

She waits outside, fall air on her cheeks, oaks rustling. And then there is Jesse's car pulling up the long drive to Goldstone, and there she is—Jesse—in black boots, lipstick, a black flowered dress, carrying Camille.

Jesse steps inside and is greeted by photographs of Juliette, overwhelming the living room. They are gorgeous and oppressive, almost, in their scale. Annie takes her hand and pulls her out through the double French doors and into the yard. There is a grove of fruit trees, a rambling garden, a long wooden table set decadently. Twinkling string lights, firelight.

"Wow. This is so pretty."

Annie hands her a glass of wine.

"Thanks," Jesse says. Her stomach feels uneasy. She told Noah she was taking Camille out to dinner with Suraya.

"I hope you're hungry," Annie says. Her familiar laugh cuts the awkwardness. "I know I seem crazy, but I really like to cook."

Jesse sits. "I'm always hungry."

While Jesse nurses, Annie serves her a plate, her blond hair catching the candlelight. She looks beautiful; the food is incredible. Jesse keeps asking herself if this is real, if she is really here.

And why is she here?

She wanted to come. She wanted to escape the heavy silence in her and Noah's house, their mutual desperation thick between them. She loves him. Of course she loves him, all the way into her marrow she loves him, but she does not know yet what it means to love him without trusting him.

Jesse did not want her and Annie's last moment together to be at Noah's premiere, on opposite sides of a battle line. There is something unfinished between them.

As if she had entered a strange fairy tale, Camille falls into a peaceful sleep almost instantly and stays that way as Jesse wraps her in a blanket and lays her in her car seat. The smoke from the fires has cleared and it is a perfect fall night. Annie and Jesse luxuriate in the food and the Riesling. They go back to pretending.

Annie pours out the rest of the bottle of wine and scoots closer, rests her head on Jesse's shoulder. She feels Jesse's body tense and then soften. Annie loves the smell of her, rose and milk and salt.

*I want to kiss you,* she almost whispers.

And then, as if on cue, Camille cries out from her car seat. Annie had almost forgotten the baby was right there.

"I should get home," Jesse says. "It's past her bedtime."

"But you didn't have dessert! The tarts are the best part." Annie feels frantic. Camille's ongoing cry echoes the feeling in Annie's own heart.

"I have to get her back. It's almost ten o'clock."

Jesse's face is clearer than ever, in sharp focus. Annie wants to reach out and pull her close, to keep her close. She stands, feeling shaky. She can't let Jesse leave; she will be alone again.

"You knew who I was all along, didn't you?" Annie asks as Jesse collects their things, reaching for anything to stop Jesse in her tracks.

"Yeah." Jesse takes Camille out of her seat, and she stops crying for the moment. "Did you?"

"Yes," she says. And then, "I guess I liked the idea that we could exist in a different dimension, apart from all this."

"Me, too." Jesse shifts Camille. The fruit trees are eerily beautiful in the moonlight. "I wanted to hate you, but I couldn't. I liked you. I saw myself in you. And in Juliette . . ." Jesse pauses. "I'm a survivor, too, I guess . . . I was eighteen. In Paris."

"I'm so sorry," Annie says. She takes a step toward Jesse. "You wrote about it." And then, "I loved your books, both of them."

"You read them?"

"Yeah. You're brilliant."

"Thank you. My career is over now."

"Not forever, probably."

"If I do ever write again," Jesse says, after a moment, "it'll be about this. How more than one thing can be true in the same breath." Camille begins to push against Jesse's chest, reaching for her breasts. "It can be true that Juliette's a survivor, and that Noah's not a rapist."

Annie looks back at her with a small flicker of defensiveness.

"I'm not saying Noah's innocent," Jesse goes on. "None of us are. But he's not a monster. He wouldn't hurt somebody on purpose." She checks her own heart for the truth of this, the part of her that has been hurt by Noah, and still believes it. "You wanna be able to say she's good and he's bad," Jesse says, "and it would be easier if it worked that way. We all want to be one of the good guys. But we have to live inside of the same story, and it gets messy."

Annie nods. Her racing heart slows, and time seems to slow, too. She feels stuck here, like one of the oak trees rooted into the ground.

Camille continues to squirm. "I should go," Jesse says, moving toward the door.

"At least take it with you," Annie says, picking up a tart.

"Okay."

They go into the house, where Annie wraps the plate in foil. Jesse bends her knees and bounces Camille. Juliette watches them from the walls, as Annie walks Jesse to the front door that she first walked into seventeen years ago.

"I'm really sorry," Jesse says, as she steps outside. "About Juliette. That you lost her."

Annie's chest aches. Camille whimpers. Jesse goes to her car. Annie lingers on the porch, gazing down the dark driveway as Jesse buckles Camille in.

Annie wants to stay, wants to stare. She wants to get in Jesse's car, to tell her she's sorry, to tell her she's hungry, to tell her she needs a mom, that she never had one. She and Jesse and her baby, they could just drive away, somewhere far from this city. Somewhere quiet, somewhere back to the promises of girlhood.

As Jesse looks out at her, Annie waves goodbye. She knows that it's likely the last time they'll ever see each other.

Camille sleeps in her car seat as Jesse drives down the dark canyon, a knot of immovable dread in the center of her belly. She wants to be beside Noah, wants to breathe him in. She wants to go back to before all this happened. She doesn't know what to do with the tart. Where will she say she got it? She can't bear to throw it away—the patterned persimmons on the top are too perfectly placed. Annie looked too lost, too young, too full of yearning when she said goodbye.

Jesse parks a block from the bungalow and eats the whole thing with her hands; it is both light and rich, sweet, complex, luscious.

# 49

Noah pulls a pair of sneakers from the neat line of shoes in his closet. He sets them on the table, photographs them from several angles, uploads the images to GOAT, a resale site. He thinks he can get maybe one hundred fifty. He pulls out the next, a pair of rare Jordans that should be worth five or six hundred, he hopes.

He uploads them and stares into the same abyss of the internet, where all anyone can talk about is the new president. His name is no longer a trending topic. Neither is Annie's, Juliette's, or Jesse's. Endless postmortems hypothesize about where we went wrong. Is racism to blame? Sexism? The FBI director? The female candidate's lack of "likability"? Foreign interference? Fake news? The fact that we do not understand each other?

Noah and Jesse do not know how to begin sifting through their own rubble; they do not know how to look at each other, let alone face their terror or make plans for the future.

Instead, they are slowly draining what is left of their bank accounts. They have the remainders of Noah's checks from directing, and Jesse's royalties, which are slowing down. She will not get her investment back. In addition to the sneakers, Noah sells his jewelry on eBay, the earrings, the chains, the watch he'd been so proud to wear to the festival premiere. All but his mother's gold necklace that he is saving for his daughter.

Despite the sick feeling in his stomach, Noah smiles big smiles at Camille. She touches his face with her hands as they lie side by side on the play mat.

His daughter is beautiful, like he was once beautiful, and he is desperate to protect her. She calls for her mama, cries for her mama. Her mama—his wife. He has failed them both.

He was a fool to let himself be seduced by hope. A fool to become so attached to the idea that he could live a life of ever-expanding possibility. He knew better. Cruel optimism, as his favorite professor at the University of Chicago called it.

Before he breaks his lease and returns the Porsche early, he drives it across the city and back again, as if he could decipher something about what went wrong, about where to go next: there is his and Jesse's first apartment in Silver Lake, the young and hungry crowding outside coffee shops; he inches into Hollywood through throngs of tourists, and there is his Hard Rock. He parks in the garage where he used to park. He thinks about going in and asking for his old job back, but he cannot make himself get out of the car. He is frozen in place. After sitting there for over an hour, he pulls out, drives his old path from work into Laurel Canyon, alongside the bougainvillea and jasmine, out Mulholland Drive to the 405. He crests a hill in Santa Monica to see ocean sparkling on the horizon.

———

He is a ghost in his house.

Night after night, Noah lies alone downstairs on the couch, trying to sleep. He wishes for Jesse to come to him, hears her footsteps, thinks for a moment maybe she is walking toward him.

But she goes the other way, into their daughter's nursery.

He stares at his bottle of Ambien, picks it up to test the weight of the remaining pills. There'd be enough, he thinks. Camille has Jesse, an amazing mother. Maybe his daughter's life would be easier without her father.

He could close his eyes and feel himself sinking.

He would see his own mother, rest his head on her chest and feel her fingers with their long nails tickle his back, his lids drifting open and closed as the snow falls and falls out the window, rare slow-motion snow, falling fat and white over the earth.

As a child, he used to pull himself away from dreams and lurch toward her, look into her face. It was electric, her love for him; he could feel it burning pathways into his brain, pathways where now nothing travels.

It would be empty, quiet, like a blanket of snow that has covered over everything, muting the world . . .

It is his daughter's cry that startles him out of his thoughts. His daughter is crying like he wants to cry. And then her mother comes. And she calms. From where Noah lies, he listens to Jesse whisper to Camille, drawn to their baby with the magnetic force of a planet.

He wakes tangled in his blanket on the couch in the dawn light. On the clock radio, NPR is talking about the deeply divided country. A crow flies past the house, cawing. He feels an almost ghostly sensation of Juliette's presence.

His mind wanders back to the day he saw her at the Art Institute. He remembers it more vividly now—her sitting in front of his mom's favorite painting, wiping tears from her eyes. How she followed him around the museum, smelling of cigarettes, sadness, jasmine, orange blossom.

The memory leaves him threadbare.

They were just kids back then, weren't they? That's how he remembers it, anyway. Two lonely kids in Hyde Park, a boy and a girl both looking for a way out of themselves, both longing to be seen. Hoping for connection. Two motherless children.

•

# PART
# FOUR

# 50

1992

When Gracey thinks back on her life, it's the beginning of Noah's that she remembers. As if she were born when he was. It was a stupid high school party. Well, not exactly, and that was the problem. It was Sheena's brother's party. He'd graduated the year before and worked at the plant now, and a few other guys from the plant were there, guys who looked vaguely familiar, guys who Gracey might have seen when they were boys, before their faces turned sharper and bonier and already tired.

Gracey had gone with girlfriends; they'd gotten dressed together, changed outfits, walked to the drugstore to buy lipstick and body spray. At the party, the boys—or men, rather—were making piña coladas, bright yellow. Gracey didn't normally drink, but they were so pretty, and they were passing them out in big glasses with little paper umbrellas, which made them seem harmless. She took one and liked how it started to make her head feel as if it were floating—a balloon on a string attached to her body. There was a man from the plant, and he was cute. He looked younger than the rest, shorter, slimmer, his face still round. He was watching her. It made Gracey nervous and excited all at once, the way their eyes latched on to each other like heavy magnets, then released, and then reattached. When she was halfway through her second drink, breathless from dancing to "Let's Go Crazy" and "P.Y.T." with Sheena, he approached, stuck out his hand in an oddly formal way.

"Joel," he asserted, and his nervousness made her feel more confident.

"Gracey," she replied, and he said, "Gracey."

When Joel asked Gracey to go for a drive, she agreed. Why? Because she was half-drunk, or, really, all the way drunk, off the piña coladas. Because he was fine.

Rolling down the street in his old Cutlass Supreme, the windows down, she felt as if her life were beginning. An older man, telling her she was beautiful—it flattered her so much, the way his gravelly voice said it, that she let him run his hand over her thighs, along the small of her back, brushing her ass, as he kept the other hand on the wheel. It felt so different from when the boys at school did it. This was for real. Adult. Romantic. As he parked the car up against the lake, he talked to her about the phases of the moon, about the history of the city. It was early summer, and the air was warm in a soft way, in a promising way. He put on the Shirelles—her mother's music—and tapped his hand against the steering wheel. When they started making out, she reached her hand out and placed it against his chest the way she'd seen in the movies, the way she'd rehearsed with her girlfriends, but what she felt was the too-fast throbbing of her own heart. He tasted like tobacco and work and the sticky sweet of fruit that was no longer fresh.

Still, she let him reach out and fill his big hands with her breasts. It wasn't until he put her hand on his crotch that she pulled away.

"You want it," he said, and forced her back. Her body reacted—aroused—as if she did.

"No," she said. "Not that."

"I can't do this," she kept saying. "Please, no, don't. I can't." She was too scared to sink her teeth into his skin to draw blood, like she imagined doing, too scared, even, to scream. On the stereo the Shirelles were singing "Baby It's You." The feeling of him inside her was a lightning bolt splitting her apart. Before she could figure out what to do, she felt him shudder, moaning a moan that she would remember when she couldn't remember much else about him, a sound that wrapped pleasure and pain into one. He clutched her shoulders and laid his head against her chest and cried. He tilted her chin up, looked into her eyes.

"You're a good girl," he said. "I'm sorry."

He took her, then, for a burger and fries, and though she felt sick she ate every last bite, and when it was gone, she pressed the salt from the bottom of the container onto her finger and licked it off. He talked, and she did not. She was sore, and the string that had attached her balloon-head to her body had been severed. She felt herself floating away, looking down on the world from the deep black Chicago sky.

She didn't have her period the next month, or the month after that, and she'd begun to suspect the reason, though she could not say it out loud, even in her own mind. She never puked, though she felt nauseated all the time. She started back at school at the end of August, pretending as if nothing had happened until her mother came into her room early one morning, the gray light of dawn warming the yellow curtain, and sat down on her bed. She brushed her hand softly along Gracey's forehead like she'd done when Gracey was a child.

"I had a dream," her mom said. "Are you pregnant?"

Gracey started to cry like she'd needed to cry since the night with Joel, the world opening up beneath her, swallowing the girl she used to be.

"I don't know," she said, although she did.

That day, her mom took her to the doctor and confirmed it. She was three months along; the baby's heart was galloping like a herd of wild horses. She felt that it meant that he'd be strong, that he'd survive. Her mother told her, before the blood test would, that he was a boy.

She found a crumpled brown paper where Joel had written his number, but she didn't call. The baby was hers; he didn't have anything to do with it.

Once, it was reported to Gracey, Joel came by the high school, making circles in his Cutlass, asking any passing students for her. Her brother threatened to kill him if he ever came back. By then she was eight months along and could no longer hide her belly, not even close, so her parents had started letting her stay home and sleep until she woke late in the morning and flipped on the TV.

From the outside, someone may have said Gracey was depressed, but Gracey wouldn't have put it that way. She felt as if she were going blank, shrinking, like the more room the baby took up inside her, the less of her there was. She took comfort in her parents; all she wanted was to be their little girl again. When Gracey's mom got home from work she rubbed her daughter's feet, and her dad brought her crates of California oranges—she craved them all winter, little orbs of sun under the cold, white sky.

Noah was born in April, during a blizzard. When labor started—eight days late—it was fast and furious. She was a wild animal, writhing on the hospital bed, bucking and screaming until a man came in and held her down and shot something into her so that her legs became paralyzed, and then her mind, and time, seemed to freeze, too. They told her to push, and she pushed, though it seemed impossible that she could ever push out that which lived inside her. Who knows how many minutes, or hours, later, there was a baby—her baby—crying, and she was empty. The home where he had lived, the home her body had made for him, was still there—her stomach now a soft, round hill—but he was gone. He wanted to go back inside, she thought at first, as she heard his cries.

"Noah," she said, when the doctor brought him back to her, clean and wrapped up like a little package. He would not drown like the other boys who came from where he came from. He would not work at the dying steel plant or at a fast-food restaurant. He wouldn't become a hustler. He would be nothing like his father. He would build a ship and sail them out of there.

That summer came on as fast and furious as he had, hot as the winter was cold, and suddenly, Noah was a little person who would spend eternity staring into Gracey's eyes. She fell in love with him, three months after he was born, smack-dab in the sweaty middle of July. All she wanted to do was lie in her bed with her son, the two of them gazing at each other atop her pink satin covers, Prince staring down at them from the poster on the wall. She fed him from a bottle when he was hungry,

and when he still cried out, she lifted him against her chest and
stroked his head until he fell asleep on top of her. Sometimes
she fell asleep, too, and their two bodies nearly became one
again with the rise and fall of breath, their edges blurry with
sleep, melting together.

By the time Noah was approaching his second birthday, Gracey
was starting to feel like herself—not her old self, not herself
before Noah, but a person who was becoming visible again,
awake to the world. In her dreams, she ran through ancient
forests—the likes of which she'd never seen before in her life,
but she could smell the rich earth on the air, feel the pine needles slipping and cracking beneath her feet. She was running
from something; the feeling was a mix of terror and elation.
She was running from something awful, but she'd broken
away. She would scream at the top of her lungs, from the depth
of her being, letting it all go free.

In real life, there was nowhere to scream like this. But she
could run. On the first real morning of spring, she went out to
the lake with Noah and her brother, Dev. Noah was toddling
along the edge of the shore, pointing at the lake and saying,
"Wawa! Big wawa! Wow!"

"Mama's going to run," she told Noah—she'd worn her exercise clothes; Dev would stay with Noah while she did her
sprints. Gracey took off, fast, faster, faster; she could feel the
ragged air in her lungs, the power in her legs, the forward pro-
pulsion as though she'd break through a wall, make her own
door. *Push harder,* she told herself, as she cleared a tree in the
distance and circled back, and that's when she saw Noah, running after her, his little arms flailing, legs kicking at the
ground.

"Too far, Mama!" he called. "Too far!" he said as she sprinted up alongside him, panting. He took her hand and looked up at her, a hint of betrayal beneath the relief in his eyes. He held on to her.

"Noah, I'll never leave you," she said. "Mama was just running."

"Too far, Mama," he said again. And then, as they walked on, hand in hand, "Mama," he said simply, a note of deep satisfaction in his voice, security, a singular love.

He stopped to pick up a yellow dandelion. He examined it and handed it to her.

"See?" he said. "Lello flower."

"Yes, baby," she said. "I see."

"For you, Mama," he said, and pointed at a dog running on the grass, and laughed with delight. She wished the whole world for him.

Her Noah will build his ship yet, Gracey thinks, from where she lies in her bed, cold despite the pile of quilts. It's snowing again. Her thoughts are slow but swimmy, slithering out of her reach. Sometimes she can't find the word she wants. Her mother says it's because she doesn't have enough blood. All she does is wait for Noah; he is all that matters. When he gets home from school every day, he gets in the bed with her, and she holds his body against her own, stroking his head as he rests it on her chest. The pain in her never lets go, but big as it is, it is smaller than her love for him. They lie together like that until her mother comes in and says it's time for homework, and Noah unloads his backpack and tells her about his day, and Gracey smiles when he smiles, and laughs when he laughs, and tries to follow the words out of her son's mouth, tries to see him in the sea of kids at the school. She tells Noah that he'll discover treasure, will build his own ark.

Gracey can no longer run. She can no longer chase him along the edge of the lake. She does not want to die, but she knows she is dying. She does not want to leave her baby. She does not want Noah to grow up without her, without the harbor of her body, his home, without her love in real time. Gracey would give anything on this earth to stay with her son. But she can feel the slow-motion arrival at the end of her life, a train rocking its way into a station. She wishes she could give him something, something that would last forever, but all she can do is whisper his name under her breath, "Noah, Noah, I love you," as he falls asleep against her breast.

Grief is like this: inheritance.

# 51

2004

Juliette is late for their date. Noah doesn't like late; waiting makes him anxious, and then bereft. It recalls for him the months after his mom died, waiting on his uncle or his grandpa to show up at the school. Wednesdays were early dismissal days. When Gracey was alive she'd always been on time, ready to wrap Noah up in her arms as soon as he came out of the building. But once she was gone, Dev had to rush over from work, or his grandpa did during lunch break (his grandma didn't drive), and they often arrived after the last bell, leaving Noah standing at the edge of the schoolyard, longing for his mama.

Packs of college kids brush past Noah and stream into the bar. Noah walks down the block and back. Though the evening temperatures have started to rise, the damp spring air gets into his skin and chills him. The bald face of the moon watches him. He stands a little way from the entrance, not wanting Jason, the bouncer, to spot him waiting on a girl who may never show. Maybe he should just get out of here.

Then there she is, coming down the street. She smiles at him—a smile that is at once confident and apologetic. A smile that knows she's kept him waiting, and also that once he lays eyes on her, it won't matter. A smile that is hard to argue with. He smiles back.

"Sorry I'm late," she says.

"No worries. You good?"

"Yeah."

Noah daps Jason, who lets them in, giving Noah a little nod like "nice" in regard to Juliette. Noah's more nervous than he'd like Juliette to know and hopes a beer will help.

"P.I.M.P." plays on the jukebox—the drunk white kids singing along to rap irritate Noah, and he doesn't like 50 Cent. While he's waiting on the bartender to make Juliette's drink and warm his burgers, he puts in quarters and selects a few Prince songs, favorites of his mom's. The queue is often long, so he doesn't know if the songs will play in time. Worth a shot, he figures.

Noah returns with a Jameson and ginger ale for Juliette, her request, a beer for him, and three cheeseburgers in paper trays.

"You want one?" he asks as he slides a tray across the table.

"No, thanks. I don't eat meat."

Noah shrugs, takes it back. He hasn't eaten since the morning. He can't stand the free cafeteria lunch.

"A rat died in my wall," Juliette blurts out. "In the closet."

"Happens a lot in old buildings," Noah says. His uncle's included. The landlord never showed up, so they had to cut it out themselves, drywall over it.

"It does?"

He nods. "Yup."

She's drinking faster than him, already up before he's

finished his beer to get another, but soon enough, he more or less catches up with her. He opens up a little bit—more so than usual. He's not generally a talker, but something about Juliette having read his writing, having dotted it with little exclamations of approval, makes him feel safer with her.

Still, he prefers listening. He loves the college girls partly because he loves to collect stories, loves the windows they paint into worlds so different from his own. The land of Juliette's childhood she describes as a fairy tale. Enchanted.

As far as her mother's death goes, she only alludes to her grief, picking up a handful of sand from what he imagines must be the whole ocean of it. She tells him that without her mother's camera to record her, sometimes she can't tell if she's really here.

*I see you,* Noah wants to tell her. *You're right there.* He wants to reach out and touch her.

When she gets up to go to the bathroom, she is gone for too long. Noah orders a vodka cranberry with his last four dollars and drinks it quickly. They are playing his song.

When Juliette gets up to pee, the room spins. Maybe she should have eaten something for dinner. The sea of bodies seems to hold her aloft as she drifts in the direction of the bathroom. Prince is singing. Juliette mouths along as he reminds her we're all gonna die. Better live in the moment then, let yourself go crazy. Another whiskey, maybe. She shakes her hair out a little. Stares at her face in the mirror. The pieces don't make sense to her. She tries to see the girl in the car with Annie, the girl in her mother's arms, the girl in front of her mother's camera, but she can't find her. The person she sees here looks tired, too old, a sad stranger. She wishes she hadn't had so much to drink, yet she wants more. She splashes water on her face, takes out a tube of red lipstick once stolen from Annie and reapplies it.

She wants him to see her.

"Let's take a picture," she tells Noah when she returns, pulling out the Nokia phone that used to belong to her mom and holding it at arm's length. "Come on." He leans in close to her. She sticks out her tongue and licks his cheek—a trick she used to play with Annie—and snaps the photo. He laughs and wipes off her slobber. She sends the picture to Annie, types a message: *this is noah. if u think im trying to make u jealous i am.*

"I brought a poem," she tells Noah, intending to make good on her promise to share one with him. She took her time selecting it, and now, however many drinks in, she has the courage to offer it up. She wants him to know her; she wants to be known.

Later, she won't remember this part of the conversation— the alcohol is seeping in, sending dark clouds over sections of her mind.

She reaches into her miniature backpack, pulls out her journal, the one that Annie gave her for her birthday. The paper is hand-pressed, with rose petals. She flips it open and stops on a page near the end. She reaches it out to him.

"Here," she says. "You wanna read it?"

"I want you to read it to me."

"Right now? It's loud in here."

"In your room, then."

Juliette feels her cheeks getting warmer. "Okay."

They walk out together.

# 52

The moon tonight is absurdly bright, mystical and unsettling at once. The trees are still barren, save for sudden bursts of fragile pink blossom. Juliette leans her weight against Noah as they walk down Woodlawn, past the brick homes of the professors. He senses that she wants someone to hold her up—both literally and figuratively. He can do that, he thinks. He can hold her. She is asking him with her eyes to undress her. The air is cold enough that they can see their breath. She is smoking a cigarette, stumbling. He has to guide her. He feels a little unsteady himself, fuzzy in a pleasant way. Drinking takes the weight out of his anxiety, makes him feel as if he can fill himself out to his edges.

When they get to Juliette's room, she kisses him, sloppy and searching. The act of trying to reconcile this girl he's about to undress with the girl who stood lecturing in front of his creative writing class is a turn-on. She'd seemed to be an authority on art, a young woman with so much privilege she believed all you had to do was show up and the poetry would arrive, like magic. And it did, didn't it?

Her warm, boozy breath grazes his neck. She reaches for his belt, starts tugging. She has trouble unfastening it; he helps. She stumbles. *She's messy,* he thinks, *maybe I—shouldn't.* But before the thought can complete itself, her hand is on his dick. It's too late; his desire has already taken over. His mind is on her legs, her ass that's been playing peekaboo out from under her T-shirt-turned-dress all night. He pushes her back onto the bed. She closes her eyes as he runs his hands up her tights.

Juliette closes her eyes, trying to make the room stop spinning. Her body is suddenly so heavy. Noah is kissing her neck, but it's almost like he's kissing someone else's neck. She makes a soft moan, almost reflexively, as he runs his hands up her Edie tights, under the T-shirt. She is spinning as if she were on one of those spinning cylinder rides at the fair, the kind that makes the floor fall out.

She should stop him, should tell him to stop.

She tries to sit up and he pushes her back, kisses her mouth. She feels like she might throw up. He wraps his hands around her wrists.

As he thrusts himself inside her, a pleasure-pain cry comes out of her, pure as a bell. He fucks her so hard he doesn't know where he is anymore. And that's the truth of how he fucks, as a sixteen, seventeen-year-old: to lose himself. To escape the confines of his body and mind.

Later, he will let himself forget his fleeting understanding: just seconds before he is about to come, her little animal sounds go quiet, her body becomes ever so slightly heavier, dead weight. He is about to finish; he doesn't stop. There is so much that can change everything, so much that takes only an instant.

When he falls off her, her eyes are still closed. He brushes his hand over her cheek, but she doesn't react.

"Juliette?" he asks. If she were awake to hear him, she would think that his voice sounds childlike in its uncertainty, its need for reassurance. But she's not. He lays his head beside her, her hot breath on his neck, and falls into a heavy sleep.

# 53

Grief is like this: ancient.

It is earlier than Juliette thought: the campus quiet, the sun only just now filtering between stone buildings. The air holds its chill, but the first breaking rays of light touch her with a warmth she has not felt in months; it seems spring has chosen today of all days to begin its glory.

She steps into the laundry room to restart the wash, only to find the quarters from Jimmy's are missing. Maybe they fell out when her coat tumbled to the floor last night. She opens the washing machine full of her moldy clothes. The smell makes her ill. She is already ill. Her body feels as if it is glued shut, bruised somewhere deep under the skin, so tender she would cower from her own touch. There is throbbing in her head, waves of nausea in her chest.

Resting her head against the cold metal of the machine, Juliette sits on the cement floor and sobs.

The clothes were left in a clean tumble on the bed, waiting to be folded, smelling of Tide and spring-rain dryer sheets, the day her mother never came home. She can't remember what she did with the clean laundry her mom had meant to fold when she got back from her walk at the ocean. *What happened to them?* Juliette wonders now.

After a moment, she pulls the whole heavy mess of shirts and pants and sweaters out of the wash, throws the damp, moldy mass of them into the trash bin.

She starts to walk without knowing where she is going, away from campus, her head throbbing. There are the branches, bare. There is a crow, landing. *I am here,* Juliette tells herself, as she walks down the street. *I am here,* she repeats. *I am here, I am here, I am here,* she says again and again. The man who was sleeping in the shelter of a fire escape leans into the light. She touches her face, tries to move it around. It does not feel like a face.

She tries to call Annie, but Annie doesn't answer. She doesn't leave a message; she can't think of what to say.

She tries again, and again. No response.

She keeps walking until she reaches the end of the neighborhood, where the park butts up against the lake, the sun now risen high enough to graze the treetops. She sits on a swing, watching the people start to come out: a bearded man with his black dog, a young mother pushing her stroller covered by a rose-printed blanket. The mom talks to the baby who's presumably hidden beneath. Juliette watches these people who are alive in a separate universe. She tries to call Annie again. No answer.

A runner passes by in color-coordinated Nike gear, and then a couple jogging together. Another mother with a stroller.

In childhood, Juliette used to bury herself beneath her

covers and practice leaving herself. The body would be dead weight, and she would be floating—at first hovering just above, but then she learned to slip out the window, to float into the night, moving through the garden. She could go anywhere.

Last night, as she lay motionless while Noah pushed himself into her, she saw the icy streets of Hyde Park in the dark, the still, leafless trees, the struggling buds, the mass of the dark lake. It still hurt. She flew further, flew faster, and found herself back in her secret garden at Goldstone, a riot of blossom: the jacaranda, the plums and peaches and jasmine. Her mother was on the deck, waiting for her.

She takes out her journal, the one from Annie with the flower paper: *I was raped last night,* she writes, her hands shaking as they trace out the words that stare back at her with insistence, with indifference. A confirmation of what only her body knows. She cannot call her mom. Annie won't pick up the phone, but these pages can hold the awful truth.

*Noah was in my creative writing class at Hyde Park High . . .*

The first mother with the stroller circles back around and peels off the blanket. Juliette peeps her tiny daughter, whose newness seems to match the tentative gold of the early day.

Her own mother talked about taking Juliette to the park in the first months of her life, how she'd pull her out of the stroller, wanting to show her the magic of the world, the green grass, the patterns of the old pine trees, the flight of the birds. She never wanted to sleep when she was a baby, her mom said, never wanted to stop seeing everything. Now she only wants to close her eyes.

The mother circling the park no longer seems to inhabit another universe, but just another time. Thinking about her young mom, Juliette feels a craving deep in her stomach for something she can't possibly find. She does not get up from her swing.

The following day she comes back, sitting with the sprouting daffodils. She brings the flask she and Annie used to carry, filled with whiskey. As the warm sun begins to set, she walks to the edge of the lake, the air soft on her cheeks, a weight pressing into her chest. A pair of green parrots sit in the nearby tree, watching.

She wants to get in the water. At the beach with her mom, as a little girl, Juliette would sprint up and down the shore, running in and out of the waves, her mother running after her, beaming with laughter. Her mother would never let her drown—Juliette knew that implicitly. She was free to abandon herself to her joy.

She's taking off her shoes now; she's dipping her toes into the freezing lake; she's talking to her mother, calling for her mother. Tears are falling down her face. She is here, in her body; she is here, breathing this spring air; she is here, feeling this sun on her skin; he did not take her body from her. She is here, wading in, feeling the shock of the cold on her skin. She is here; she dives under, into the wild water.

# 54

After Juliette rushes out of the room, Noah pulls her too-soft rose-printed quilt over his head and lingers, for a moment, in her bed, which smells of her: that strange intoxicating smell. He wants to shut his eyes and drop back into sleep. Instead, he pulls himself up, finds his clothes piled at the foot of her bed. It is suddenly a bit haunting, being alone in her empty room. He looks up at the photograph of Juliette and her mother looming over him, insistent in their beauty. And the other, of Juliette and a blond girl tangled in this same rose quilt. He takes in the glass candles on Juliette's desk burned all the way down, the open bag of almonds, the scattered bobby pins as he dresses and walks out. Although he has to pee, badly, he hurries out of the dorm and across the quad, as if he were a student himself. He feels like a stranger, on this campus where he hopes to belong.

It is the following afternoon that his letter comes in a big envelope, welcoming him to the University of Chicago's class of 2008. "Mom," he says aloud. He feels dizzy. Uncertain.

He walks into the next room, where his uncle is watching basketball.

"I got in," he says.

Dev jumps to his feet, slaps Noah on the back. "Yeah, you did."

They call his grandparents to give them the good news—they tell Noah his mother would be proud—then Dev and Noah and Erica go out to dinner to celebrate.

He wants to tell Juliette. Sex did not, as he'd hoped, erase her hold on him. Maybe it loosened it, just a bit, but he wants to see her again. He wants to fuck with the lights on. He wants her to read him her poem. Three days later, he calls. His palms sweat. He paces around his tiny makeshift bedroom as it goes to voicemail. "Hey. It's Noah. Just, uh, saying hey, maybe we can get some food sometime." She never calls back. He does not know she is dead.

In his first year on campus, Noah thinks of her, sometimes: when he passes Snell, where she lived; when his humanities class reads "The Love Song of J. Alfred Prufrock," a poem that he first read in Juliette's neighborhood schools class; when he goes to visit his mom's paintings at the Art Institute and remembers the day that she followed him around. He can't help it. But he brushes off the thoughts as quickly as he can. He feels a fuzzy hurt when he thinks of her, paired with a sense of unease deep in his gut that he can't quite place as guilt. Part of him wonders if he'll see Juliette on campus, on the third floor of the Reg, in the Classics Cafe, in the student commons. Not in the dining hall. No, he can't bear to eat there. Instead, he uses his dining points at Maroon Marketplace, the overpriced convenience store, where he buys ramen he microwaves in his dorm kitchen, oversalted nuts, bottles of Sunny Delight.

He is lonely that first year. He strove so long to achieve acceptance to the school, he must have imagined that it would be enough. Enough for what? To prove his worth? It is not. Instead, he discovers that is an endless, exhausting task.

At the U of C, where he is one of the only kids he knows who is both Black and poor, he uses his intelligence like a weapon—guard up, ready to fight. He will never be the one to struggle like they expect him to, he tells himself. As he wades through seas of pages, spends countless all-nighters poring over essays in fluorescently lit reading nooks, the work is often overwhelming, but not uninteresting: it is like taking apart a clock, seeing what makes us tick. Economics, sociology, psychoanalytic theory, anthropology, and film theory. He is earnest in his efforts to decode the world with his books. His university education constitutes a "paradigm shift," as they'd say in his classes.

He even adopts some of the pretentious language of his fellow college students. Some might call it pretension, anyway, and it is, but it is also creativity—language as play. He's always had an ear for dialogue and can replicate it without effort. He uses their words—some of their words, and some of his own—so that he speaks in a hybrid language that is enough to make him a rare and often sought-after bird.

He has friends, or friendly acquaintances, at least, as much of a social life as he cares to indulge in, but still, he does not feel at home anywhere. He goes back to the dorm he shares with a white boy from Greenwich, puts on headphones and blasts his music to soothe himself, sometimes taking hours to fall into dreams.

———

Noah gets the news of his grandmother's death in the fall of his sophomore year. She's passed away at home, of a stroke. He's seen her only sporadically since she and Noah's grandfather moved to St. Louis when Noah was in the fifth grade, but he'd always imagined that one day he'd be able to take care of his grandma, that he'd do the things for her he once dreamed of doing for his mother.

He hits a low point that semester, starts to struggle in his classes, to wonder if it's all worth it. Then he meets Jesse, the bright-eyed girl in his creative writing seminar. His need for connection has begun to tip the scale against his fear of abandonment, and there is something about her that touches a deep longing in him—her empathy, maybe. He reads it in her own writing and in the way she reads his. She does not overuse her smile, but when she shines it on him, he feels burst open.

At Doc Films, the student-run film society where he volunteers, he organizes a Wong Kar-wai series mostly so he can invite Jesse to *In the Mood for Love*. She has no idea how nervous he is when he asks. She says yes.

It is when Jesse invites Noah to her dorm room on their second date that he sees a home in her. Her bed is made with matching bedding; there is sage burning, real curtains, and vanilla-smelling candles lit along her windowsill. She has a mini-fridge with sensible food in it; she offers him cheese and crackers, apples, grapes. The thought strikes him like a lightning bolt: he wants to marry this girl. He loves the piano touch of her fingers on his chest, the way she strokes his head with her long nails, like his mother once did, soothing the demons that have never stopped clamoring inside him. He loves her long pauses and careful speech, the intensity with which she looks at him as if he were all that she sees.

They make out and he begs for more. She refuses him; he asks to sleep beside her instead. Two months later, the two of them are sandwiched together on her single mattress, waking up to winter sunlight streaming in through the frosted windowpane, when she whispers into his ear: "Let's have sex." It catches him by surprise. He had gotten used to the morning erections, to tucking them up and kissing the baby hairs at the back of her neck, the way she'd refuse to face him, hiding her morning breath. Now he pulls her into him, buries his face in her thick hair, sweeps his lips over her skin.

Jesse is different from anyone he's been with before; she forces him to stay in the room. If Noah starts to check out, as he's always tended to do during sex, she reaches out and pulls him back into himself. In some moments it's difficult, even painful. Still, when it's over, he feels filled up.

Noah knows he loves her much before he'll say it.

# 55

2016

*In his dreams, he is drowning. Weights on his ankles, weights on his wrists. He is fighting to get to the surface, but he can't get up. The panic overtakes his chest. He cannot breathe and then, there is her tiny body—his daughter's—on the floor of the lake, her dark hair spread in the dark water. He tries to pick her up, to lift her up. He carries her back to the top, trying to breathe life into her lungs.*

He wakes up.

It takes Noah a moment to register where he is, although he's been sleeping tangled in his blanket on the couch for almost two weeks. Moonlight pours through the window. A shawl of crows covers the eucalyptus. He feels, again, the ghost of Juliette—the strange scent of her, her long, swishing hair.

They were just kids back then, weren't they?

But he hadn't really looked at her, had he, once their bodies crashed into each other. Once he was inside her, he was just hungry, he was eating with his eyes closed, maybe; he was trying to feed the gaping hole in his center that was so empty.

The weight of remorse smothers him. He struggles to stand. The full moon watches him.

All that's left is to try to do right by his wife and daughter.

Noah tiptoes into the bedroom where Jesse and Camille sleep together. He lies as gently as he can in the bed and puts Camille on his chest, like he did when she was a newborn. And then there she is, his mom: Camille's dark almond eyes blink open and they are Gracey's, their shape just the same. His daughter looks into him with boundless presence as he takes in the smell of her, milk and starlight, her fingers closing over his finger. They fall back asleep together.

When Jesse opens her eyes hours later, she finds them beside her.

"Hi," he says.

"Hi," she answers. He lets his fingers move forward, brushes her hair.

Finally, she reaches out a hand, lays it on his shoulder, and says, "Let's get out of here."

Noah packs the last of the boxes. Jesse walks along the ocean with Camille, where they've walked so many miles together. At five months she still drifts to sleep curled against her mother, the soft animal of her body growing ever so slightly heavier.

Jesse remembers that first winter in LA with Noah when they fell in love with California. They came to each other as everyone they'd ever been, as everyone they wanted to become. Everything, back then, was possible.

It is the end of an era.

She feels Camille's heart beating against her own; the days when she can carry her daughter against her breast like this will soon be over. She breathes in Camille's head, a tie binding her to this earth. "You are safe," she whispers. "Nothing bad will happen to you." A prayer.

The water washes at Jesse's feet, evening sky staining the sand. She is almost surprised, every time, by how quickly the sun slips away.

Noah and Jesse stuff their twelve-year-old, new-to-them Highlander with as many of their belongings as it can carry. Noah picks a mandarin from his tree, peels it for Camille, and watches her face scrunch up with surprised pleasure. He leaves the rest of the fruit behind for whoever else comes to live here.

They drive east on the 10, past palm trees and strip malls, through Ontario, Riverside, Redlands. Past a wind farm near Joshua Tree where they had their honeymoon, into the Mohave. Noah can't stop the feeling of dread that creeps in, the sense that something is about to go wrong.

But it has, it already did.

As they cross the California border, Camille asleep in the back seat, Jesse asleep in the front, Noah finally gives up the fight and allows tears to stream from his eyes. It is a new grief: What will it mean to live without a dream? What might add up to a life?

In the abyss of desert, he can feel the history, bodies deep, calling to him; they have been here all along, haven't they. His ancestors, who built the country's wealth and got none of it. Whose stories went untold, names unknown—all those men and women who left behind only their fingerprints, the fruits of their labor. Who brought him here.

He made a movie, he reminds himself: not a success, but it is his story, and it exists.

The future is a vacuum; the only thing Noah can see in it is a vast, empty stretch of land. The figure of his and Jesse's daughter on the horizon.

They stop for the night at a Motel 6 somewhere in Arizona. With Camille asleep in the bassinet, moonlight leaking through the curtain, Noah and Jesse make love for the first time since she was born. Jesse whispers, "Please," as he runs his hand over her, the other wrapping gently around her throat. She scratches his back as he pushes himself inside her: two selves speaking a secret language to each other.

It's easy with Noah, even now; it's like water. Her breasts full of milk, her stomach still soft—her body is a new body, but it is hers, and their bodies know each other. They fuck hard. When they are done, Jesse wants to cry. Noah kisses her eyelids, her neck, her nipples. "I missed you," he says.

They come back to each other in pieces; for years it feels as if they will come apart.

# 56

A few miles up the narrow dirt road, Annie begins to feel a dull anxiety clutch at her chest as her father's old Volvo bumps along. The speedometer hovers around fifteen miles an hour. The fir trees tower on either side of her. Twenty minutes later, squinting out the windshield, she spots an old, weathered sign—SIX RIVERS RANCH—and pulls off.

Annie steps out of the car. She does not think she has ever breathed in clearer air. She can imagine why her mother might have fallen in love with this place when she arrived, still a child, a runaway from Kansas.

The internet has offered Annie zero clues on what she might find here. She'd imagined this might be the next step in her confrontation with injustice—could there still be girls here, like her mother, in need of rescue? But there is nothing left of the commune or its residents, save for a few abandoned structures.

Lying on the forest floor and looking up at the ancient trees that tower into the sky, she feels her smallness with a surprising sense of relief. This world, this radically beautiful world, with its dirt, its pure air, its generous rivers, is always right here.

This, the place of her birth. Annie imagines Indigo kneeling on the bed of pine needles, howling in pain. Maybe it felt impossible until it wasn't.

She lets herself imagine Indigo taking a breath and growing quiet, just long enough to feel the texture of the moonlight. The next time Indigo pushes, she is able to touch her baby's head, and then, new life. Indigo pulls Annie up and onto her chest. The cord goes uncut, Indigo's blood still pulsing into Annie's tiny body. Annie still bound to her mother before everything that will sever them rushes forth.

That night, Annie eats at the Big Foot Steakhouse, savors her strawberry mousse, allows herself to feel the pain that threatens to swallow her but doesn't.

She steps out to find the sky ablaze with color. Her mother loved sunsets. It was the only time that Annie remembers Indigo holding her—when they exited to the parking lot outside the Big Foot one night after their tri-annual supper, to discover the sky painted in a miraculous shade of pink. She put her arm around Annie, suddenly, pulling her close to her body.

"Look, Annie," she said. "Isn't it beautiful?"

Annie stood beside her, frozen, uncertain, wanting to be sure she would not shake away her mother's embrace. Indigo was right; it was beautiful; it was so beautiful.

Grief is like this: impossible.

Impossible, and yet, Annie goes on. Back at Goldstone, the sprawling plum offers up the last of its dusky fruit, and the persimmons begin to ripen once again. The chorus of Me Toos rings across the country. Annie finds a job a few minutes down

Topanga Canyon, at Canyon Bistro. She is going by Anais now—it has felt good to slip into the name her mother gave her, to claim herself as Indigo's daughter.

Even pushed up against the limits of loss, even scattered by trauma, most people continue to lead their lives—they self-medicate, maybe; they work too hard; they dissolve into tears in their cars; they drink after work; they scrape by, but they show up in the world. Annie recognizes them—the grievers like her. She sees the look in the old woman's eye, the one who sits at the same table every day and orders mussels at five; Annie does not charge her for her pinot gris. She sees the father who comes in alone with his two young daughters and asks the kitchen to add extra cherries to their sundaes.

Come Christmas, Annie goes to Candy Cane Lane to put up the lights for the last time, greeted by a Compass real estate sign. Sandra is selling, moving back to her own childhood home in Michigan.

The house has been painted beige, stocked with new furniture, wiped clean of her father. In the kitchen, Annie makes hot chocolate for two in the remaining Father's Day mugs that Sandra has left behind for her. As they sit at the table and sip their Swiss Miss, the older woman reaches out and takes her hand, squeezes it. Annie squeezes back.

"I'm sorry," Annie says. "I'm sorry that you lost him. I'm sorry I wasn't here, all these years."

"I know you are," Sandra answers. She looks at Annie and says, after a moment, "I think it's time to forgive yourself."

Sandra gets in her Prius and drives away as Annie climbs the ladder to the rooftop. She spends all day stringing up the display, as her father would have.

She goes home to Goldstone to cook: fingers stained yellow

with turmeric, coconut lentil soup in the Crock-Pot. The sound of the dryer, of a distant electric saw, of a wind chime. Languid gulls. Fogging glass with cold Chablis. Maybe one day, Annie will go to culinary school. Maybe she will write a book. Maybe she will write a cookbook, in honor of Margot and of her father. Maybe she'll travel. She hopes she will become a mother.

For now, she signs up with WriteGirl to become a volunteer mentor to teen girls, coaching them in creative writing. She is staying put, waiting tables—at least she's not running anymore.

There is an entry in Juliette's journal, written the week before her death, that Annie reads over and over. Proof of the girl she knew.

*Things I miss: Bob Dylan on vinyl, the mint patch under the sycamore tree, Sunday pancakes with raspberries, collecting sand dollars on foggy beach mornings, driving the windy canyon street in the green Subaru (Buba-su! As I called it when I was little) and singing with mom to Fleetwood Mac, the Topanga shopping mall and its Dippin' Dots, the smell of horses, the smell of pine, mom's laughter with the grown-ups faint through the window while I fall asleep, rubbing the soft fuzz of peaches from the tree against my cheeks, making crown braids in Annie's golden hair, singing to Joni Mitchell on the PCH, the sound of wind chimes during a storm, Mom in her pink robe, rocking me to sleep—how everything was safe.*

Grief is like this: a thief.

# ACKNOWLEDGMENTS

To my editor, Bridie Clark Loverro, I cannot thank you enough for believing in this book and helping it become the best version of itself. I have so much admiration and gratitude for your keen intelligence, your open heart, and your unwavering dedication and focus.

Richard Florest, my wonderful agent and partner, thank you for being on this journey with me, for seeing this book and meeting it, for your astute early edits, and for leaving space for my roller coaster of emotion along the way.

To Zibby Owens, Kathleen Harris, Jordan Blumetti, Leigh Haber, Graca Tito, Diana Tramontano, Sherri Puzey, Gabriela Capasso, Sierra Grazia, Anne Messitte, and the entire team at Zibby Books—you all are building something extraordinary in the literary world, and I am so grateful to be part of it. Thank you for your unparalleled dedication and passion, your expertise and generosity, and for taking a chance on this novel.

To my early readers and dear friends, thank you for the invaluable insight and encouragement that helped shape this story: Willa Dorn, who waded through the first, messiest draft and believed it could be a book; Lila Shapiro, for pushing me to be bolder and braver; and Mayana Geathers, for seeing both sides with sensitivity and grace. Trace Albrect, for helping me to stay intact and writing through the hardest parts of grief, pregnancy, and postpartum. Kate Trefry and Marina Dabel, for giving me a space to write and my kids a space to play, especially in that tender first year when we were new moms of two. Hannah Davey, for expert editorial advice and a golden, lifelong friendship that began back in ninth grade, like Annie and Juliette's. Katie Tabb, for the college years and the grown-up ones, too. Stephen Chbosky and Liz Maccie, who told me I could become an author in the very beginning. Heather Quinn, for helping me summon courage and faith along the way, for seeing the waterfall and believing. My radiant sister, Laura, who reminds me of who I am.

Small pieces of Annie and Juliette's emails were taken from emails written to and from Hannah Davey and Anat Benzvi during our college years; thank you for the faery charms, unwashed socks, and promises of eternal love.

To my loving stepmother, Jamie Welles, thank you for the happiness you brought to our father and for caring for him during those difficult years as he battled cancer.

Thank you to my amazing mother-in-law, Tammi Hall, for your unwavering love and support, for taking such tender care of our children while I was writing, for being there for all of us. It would not have been possible to write this book without you.

Gia and Dominic, I began *Exposure* during my pregnancy with Gia, and as I am finishing, you are five and nearly two. My early experiences of motherhood have informed parts of this novel in obvious and not-so-obvious ways. Thank you for the joy and awe of each day with you. Thank you for a love deeper than I ever knew possible that infuses everything I think and do and am.

To my parents, Mary and Tom, who paved the way for my

# ACKNOWLEDGMENTS

dreams. My love for and grief for you have permeated this story. I carry you with me.

Gloria, who welcomed me into your family with open arms, you continue to be a guiding light.

To my husband, Doug, my love, my twin, who's been in it with me since the beginning, when we were writing our first screenplay and first novel in your apartment on Cloverdale and sharing the table in the shoebox kitchen in Venice. Thank you for dreaming with me, for the wonder of building this life together. Thank you for teaching me to look more deeply, for reminding me there's always more than one side to a story. Thank you for supporting me while I've been writing this book these past years, full with children born and parents lost and so much else. You are my inspiration and my home. Thank you for everything, for always.

# ABOUT THE AUTHOR

Ava Dellaira is the author of the young-adult novels *In Search of Us* and *Love Letters to the Dead*, which was named a Best Book of the Year by Apple, Google, *BuzzFeed*, and the New York Public Library, and was also featured in *Vanity Fair*, *Entertainment Weekly*, *USA Today*, and *The New York Times Book Review*. Her fiction has been translated into twenty-four languages. She is a graduate of the Iowa Writers' Workshop, where she was a Truman Capote Fellow. She grew up in Albuquerque, New Mexico, and received her undergraduate degree from the University of Chicago. She lives in Altadena, California, with her husband and their two young children.

@ava.dellaira
www.avadellaira.com